D0501361

THE AIRMEN
WHO WOULD
NOT DIE

Books by John G. Fuller

THE AIRMEN WHO WOULD NOT DIE

THE POISON THAT FELL FROM THE SKY

THE GHOST OF FLIGHT 401

WE ALMOST LOST DETROIT

ARIGO: SURGEON OF THE RUSTY KNIFE

FEVER: THE HUNT FOR A NEW KILLER VIRUS

200,000,000 GUINEA PIGS

GAMES FOR INSOMNIACS

THE GREAT SOUL TRIAL

THE DAY OF SAINT ANTHONY'S FIRE

THE INTERRUPTED JOURNEY

INCIDENT AT EXETER

THE MONEY CHANGERS

THE GENTLEMEN CONSPIRATORS

THE AIRMEN WHO WOULD NOT DIE

by
John G. Fuller

G.P. PUTNAM'S SONS, NEW YORK

Copyright ©1979 by John G. Fuller.
All rights reserved. No part of this publication may be reproduced, stored in a retrieval system, or transmitted, in any form or by any means, electronic, mechanical, photocopying, recording or otherwise, without the prior permission of the publishers.

Library of Congress Cataloging in Publication Data

Fuller, John Grant
  The airmen who would not die.

  Bibliography
  Includes Index
    1.   R101 (Airship)   2.   Psychical research.
I.   Title.
TL659.R28F84   133.9'3   78–13728
ISBN 0–399–12264–8

Printed in the United States of America

Contents

AUTHOR'S NOTE

All the events in this story are true. They have been verified through extensive interviews, records, and documents of the British Air Ministry, the British Museum Archives, the University of London Library, the British Public Records Office, the files of the British Society of Psychical Research, the Royal Aeronautical Society, the Royal Air Force Museum at Hendon, the Parapsychology Foundation, the British College of Psychic Studies, personal dossiers, tape and shorthand transcripts, correspondence, news clips and other sources as listed in the bibliography. No material in the book has been fictionalized.

Particular care has been given to the transcripts of the psychic sessions with mediums. These are reproduced verbatim from either expert shorthand transcriptions or from copious notes of the transcripts of the purported messages. Because they carried so much information and so many clues to the possible validity of the process, such details had a strong influence on the lives of many people. The author has attempted to show these apparent communications with the minimum of editing. They have been taken from the original transcripts still preserved from 1928 to the present.

NOTE TO THE READER

This book had to be written; and I, for one, am profoundly grateful that it appears just at the end of my generation. It will become a prime source for evidence of human survival after death. To deny the basic evidence of Mr. Fuller's excellent and dedicated work would be as foolish and childish as to deny the existence of the Battle of Waterloo, all of which can be classified as so-called anecdotal material. But only superficial and ill-trained scientists and their followers now deny the great cases of impeccable evidence for survival, of which this triple study constitutes one of the finest. For Mr. Fuller has set down the Hinchliffe, Lowenstein and R.101 cases, in sequence, as they are now seen to be interlocked.

And not only do these cases constitute a prime source of survival evidence; but aeronautical historians, too, must indeed be grateful for the solution, particularly, of the Hinchliffe and R.101 mysteries. The latter is now revealed to include the incredible removal of certain essential documents from the formal evidence in the enquiry, for reasons of either loyalty or self-protection. As a long-time government servant myself, I pray that these documents were not physically destroyed; and that they may one day be recovered from the dark recesses of Whitehall, where some guilty civil servant of the past thought fit to hide them

CHARLES H. GIBBS-SMITH
formerly Lindbergh Professor
of Aerospace History,
National Air and Space Museum
(Smithsonian Institution)

THE AIRMEN
WHO WOULD
NOT DIE

FOREWORD ·

We drove toward Hythe, on the English Channel, in a rented Morris Marina, through the hedgerows of the twisting Kentish back road identified on the map as B 2067. It was a scowling October day, windy, gray and inhospitable. The curves in the road left no margin for error. I felt strange and uncomfortable driving in the driver's seat on the right-hand side, and shifting with my left. Elizabeth, my wife, seated on my left, felt we were brushing too close to the bushes and hedges. I was feeling that we were too close to the middle of the road.

The countryside and the villages we passed through were of surpassing beauty, in spite of the rather angry clouds. The trim, white, half-timbered pubs, with their colorful signs exhorting the traveler to quaff some Courage lager, were inviting. But we had no time to linger. We were just setting off on a new story that was to take us from the English Midlands to the Channel coast—and we were a little shaky and uncertain as to how to go about it.

It was to be another ghost story. With Elizabeth as researcher, I had just finished one, called *The Ghost of Flight 401*. At that time, we had started out to explore how a jet-age myth or legend could possibly evolve in this day and age. Instead, the story bent back on us to show palpable evidence of the continuation of life after death.

11

Researching and writing that story had, in fact, changed both our lives. Neither Elizabeth nor I had believed in an afterlife before. We had been forced by the flight 401 story to accept it as a distinct probability. We were further led to believe that verifiable, documented facts could be transmitted from those who have died. Although this has been claimed for years by students of parapsychology, it was entirely new to us, and extremely hard to accept.

Faced with this likelihood for the first time, it became almost impossible to drop the subject, controversial as it is. We wanted to explore other evidence, provided it was well-documented and involved people who were unlikely to be prone to fantasy and exaggeration, and whose experiences interlocked with others in a story that would be difficult to fabricate.

We had with us in the car the raw background material for such a story. It consisted of an enormous dossier of letters, memos, transcripts, news clips and other material preserved over the years since 1928. The material had been made available to us from the files of the Parapsychology Foundation in New York and those of the British Society for Psychical Research. It had been written about before in bits and pieces, but never assembled in a coherent and orchestrated way.

Beyond the material itself, we knew that some of the principal people involved with it were still alive, and willing to talk at length. One of them was Major Oliver G. Villiers, D.S.O., who had assembled a great mass of material involving the story that is to follow, and whom we were driving down to Hythe to visit. His was to be the first of many interviews during our three-month sojourn in England.

The Major was now in his ninety-first year. He had been blind for many years. I had called him from London the evening before. His voice was robust and yeasty, with the rich cadences of the Royal Empire Society, of which he was an honorary life member. He would be delighted to talk with us, he said, and looked forward to having us as guests for lunch the next day.

In the car, we passed by a village pub near Lympne, where a scarlet-coated group of horsemen were preparing to go on the hunt in full regalia. The scene could have stepped out from a Christmas card.

"It's all so delightfully British," Elizabeth said. It was the first word that either of us had spoken for several miles.

"I was wondering when I was going to hear from you," I said. "I thought you were asleep."

"Just a little drowsy," she said. "And thinking."

"About what?"

"About this whole story. How complicated it is."

"You're right," I said. "And we haven't even started."

"Do you ever blow hot and cold on this whole business of life after death?" she asked.

"Of course I do," I said. "Half the time I believe it's possible, and the other half, I don't."

"It's just about the most important question there is, isn't it?"

"I think it is," I said.

"Why?" she asked.

Elizabeth was like this. She would set up a question, and then start to pin you down on it.

"Tell me why you think so, and then I'll tell you," I said.

"Well," she said, "if everybody were convinced of it, it would be a helluva lot better world."

"That answers the question. Just as they've been saying for the last two thousand years or more."

"What I'm getting at," Elizabeth said, "is that most of us today have a hard time taking this on faith. We can't do it, even if we try. We talk a different language today. We've been brought up on physics and chemistry and electronics and computers. What we've been learning in our research is that the old truths become stronger today if they're translated into computer language. Does that make sense?"

"Sort of," I said. "But what are you ultimately driving at?"

"I guess what I'm trying to say is that it's important to work on this story, even though the research will be tough."

I agreed with her. We would have to be digging up dusty information from buried files scattered all through England. If we didn't believe the story was important, we'd probably give up too easily. Piecing together the background for any story is always difficult. When it goes back nearly fifty years, and deals with such an elusive and ephemeral story as the possible reality of life after death, it can become exhausting and overwhelming. At the start it looks like climbing Everest. When it's over, it seems as if that's what it was. Elizabeth and I found that we had to constantly jack ourselves up to keep going. It was something that never got easier.

By now, we were moving down a steep hill into Hythe. Not far off to the east were Folkestone and the white cliffs of Dover. After circling back up another hill to the Saltwood section of Hythe, we could catch a glimpse of the Channel, which for years had been England's moat, from the days of the Romans. Major Villiers' white stucco, blue-trimmed house sat along a quiet suburban street, high on the Saltwood hill, not far from the ancient castle there. By now, it was cold and rainy.

From what we had seen of the research material, however, the story looked promising. From letters and diaries and memos, it would be possible to reconstruct the thoughts of many of the people involved. They would provide a stream of consciousness and a flow of reaction without fictionalizing. This to me was important. A book of this nature must be accurate. But it should also be as readable as a novel, if the mood and atmosphere were to be preserved. A sense of immediacy can enhance a nonfiction book, if it precisely reflects what the character involved was thinking and feeling at the time. Already, much of the research showed such support. Further interviews would reconstruct many missing links, all of which would add to the readability without distorting facts in any way. We were encouraged by this. We hustled from the car to the doorway, trying to keep our files of materials and tape recorder dry.

Mrs. Hayes, a cheery housekeeper from London, admitted us. We walked through a darkish hall to the door of the drawing room. The hallway was English: it was cold.

"The Major is expecting you," she said. "There will be lunch in half an hour."

She tapped lightly on the door and opened it for us. The Major was sitting in his chair by the electric fireplace. It was rather dark in the room, and a little hard to see him. He rose without effort, for all his ninety-one years, and his hand went out to the corner of the mantle. This must have been a key buoy marker for navigating without sight. The paint on the corner was worn off.

"So nice to have you visit," the Major said. "Please sit down close to the fire. It's a bit raw today."

After an exchange of pleasantries, we did so. The Major cautiously backed to his chair, using his right hand as a guide, sliding it down the smooth surface of the Queen Anne chair, then easing himself down in it. The Major was tall. His smooth face showed almost no wrinkles. Although sightless, he seemed to look directly at us with closed eyelids. He was dressed in a Harris tweed jacket over a Shetland sweater, out of which peeked a regimental striped tie. He wore gray flannels and slippers.

"You have the duplicate file with you?" he asked.

We had. It almost filled a large cardboard carton. We had spent days having the material photocopied from the archives where the Major and others had deposited it for safekeeping. It was only part of the story, for there were still other files and archives we would need. The Major, however, was a focal point. The rest of the story would be woven from a variegated background that involved almost the entire pioneer history of aviation.

"I think it is best," the Major said, "that we begin at the beginning, and read straight through to the end. Of course, with my blindness, that puts an enormous burden on your vocal cords. Are you up to it?"

"Elizabeth and I will trade off," I said.

"I imagine it will take many days," the Major said. "We shall probably get to know each other quite well by the time we're finished, old boy."

"We're prepared for it, Major," I said.

"Good," said the Major, as the chime on the clock announced the time: quarter of one. "And now it's time for our sherry. And then lunch if you're ready for it."

I assured him we were. Within moments, Mrs. Hayes entered with a sterling silver tray carrying three delicate sherry glasses and a cut-glass decanter. She poured the Major's glass carefully. Then she put it down on the table beside him, reaching for his hand and locking his fingers carefully around the stem. Then she served us.

"Cheers," said the Major.

We returned the salutation.

"I'm glad you have come," he said. "I am convinced that the time has arrived when the story should be told in full."

THE PRINCIPAL AIRMEN

This book could be called a case history of a phenomenon that began in 1928 and continues to the present. There are many people involved. They are all real. No names below have been changed.

Lt. Commander N. G. Atherstone
First Officer of the British Airship
R-101

Lord Beaverbrook
British newspaper magnate

Sir Sefton Brancker
Director of Civil Aviation British Air
Ministry

Edward Carpenter
British social commentator

W. Charlton
Supply Officer, R-101

Wing Commander R. B. E. Colmore
Director of Airship Development
(Technical)

Ian Coster
Australian journalist

Air Chief Marshal Lord Dowding
Chief Air Marshal, credited with
winning Battle of Britain

Sir Arthur Conan Doyle
Creator of Sherlock Holmes

Eileen Garrett
Leading clairvoyant, psychic
researcher, and publisher

Sir Victor Goddard
British Air Marshal

Col. G. L. P. Henderson
RAF pilot

Capt. W. G. R. Hinchliffe
Pioneer trans-Atlantic flyer

Emilie Hinchliffe
His wife

Lord Inchcape
Chairman, P. & O. Lines

Flt. Ltd. H. C. Irwin
Captain of the R-101

Sq. Ldr. E. L. Johnston
Navigator of the R-101

James Joyce
Novelist

Charles Levine
American backer of trans-Atlantic
attempts

Alfred Lowenstein
Belgian financier

Hon. Elsie Mackay
Prominent British heiress

Hewat McKenzie
British College of Psychic Science

Sq. Ldr. Rivers Oldmeadow
RAF Staff College, Hants.

Harry Price
Prominent psychic investigator

Lt. Commander V. C. Richmond
Designer of the R-101

Major G. H. Scott
Director of Airship Devlopment

Nevil Shute
Aeronautical engineer, novelist

Sir John Simon
British statesman and jurist

Capt. Gordon Sinclair
close friend of the Hinchliffes'

Lord Thomson of Cardington
British Secretary of State for Air

Maj. Oliver G. Villiers
Air Ministry Intelligence

Flt. Lt. W. H. Wood
RAF pilot and commentator

CHAPTER I

On the evening of March 12, 1928, there was set in motion a long chain of events that has brought many discerning, and even skeptical, people to the una_erable conclusion that there is life after death.

It all began in the most unlikely way, in the Lincolnshire village of Grantham, not far from Boston, England. It was from this English port that the founders of Massachusetts Bay Colony had set sail, nearly three hundred years before. But it was now 1928, and on this damp and chilled March night, a decision was made for a venture that held even greater risks than those faced by the Bay Colonists. Yet the target was the same: a safe voyage to the New World.

This time it was a Stinson Detroiter monoplane, instead of the fragile sailing ship that carried John Cotton and his Puritans in 1633. But the monoplane was fragile, too. It was only 32 feet long, with disc wheels and a tail skid. Its single engine was a 200 horsepower Wright Whirlwind. Its speed, at sea level, was 128 miles an hour. Unloaded, it weighed about 2,000 pounds. It was appropriately named the Endeavor. It had gold-tipped wings and a black fuselage. Its pilot would be Captain W. G. R. Hinchliffe.

Hinchliffe was one of the most seasoned pilots of his time. In the First World War, he had shot down seven German planes, and for

17

this he received the Distinguished Flying Cross. In one of these flights, a German bullet had shattered the bridge of his nose and left him blind in the left eye. He wore a patch over it, but he bore it as a mark of modest heroic distinction. Despite this loss, he was reported to have more flying time than any pilot in Britain. He had collected 9,000 hours of flying time as a pilot for both KLM, in its early days in the Netherlands, and Imperial Airways, the first major British airline. Because of his eye patch, he liked to fly in the co-pilot's seat on the right-hand side of the cockpit. This, he felt, gave him better visibility.

At dinner at the Hotel George in Grantham that night, Hinchliffe was tense, but confident. The atmosphere in the dining room of the ancient hotel was relaxing; the food was steaming; the service was excellent. Dickens stayed there once, writing part of *Nicholas Nickleby.* He had pronounced it "one of the best Inns in England." Isaac Newton lived in one part of it for a while.

There were two people at the table with Hinchliffe. One was Captain Gordon Sinclair, a fellow pilot. Like Hinchliffe, he was in his early thirties, and full of the obsessional passion for flying that marked the early history of aviation. There was also Elsie Mackay—the Honourable Elsie Mackay—striking, vivacious, persuasive. Now at the age of thirty-four, she had conquered the London stage and British cinema as an actress. She was also an accomplished horsewoman, a marine engineer and a pilot in her own right. She was considered one of the best-dressed women in England.

She was the daughter of James Lyle Mackay, Lord Inchcape, who ruled over the profitable P.&O. shipping empire. It was noised about that she was probably the richest heiress in England. And she was certainly the reason that these three were meeting at dinner that night. The final decision was about to be made to fly the Stinson Detroiter against the winter headwinds across the Atlantic. It could become the first east-to-west trans-Atlantic airplane flight. The Hon. Elsie Mackay could be the first woman to make the crossing in either direction.

What none of the diners could know was that this event would launch a complex and incredible ghost story that would carry down to the present time, through a labyrinth of circumstances involving leading airmen, air ministry officials, air marshals, ships, planes, lords, ladies and notables.

These were the days of hope and glory. The bitter memories of the First World War had faded; the clouds of the Second had not yet gathered. The Twenties was the decade of record breakers and "firsts": the first television demonstration, the first woman to swim the English Channel, the first talking picture, the first Oscar Awards, the first Mickey Mouse cartoon, the first New York–to–London telephone call.

Jelly Roll Morton and his Red Hot Peppers were breaking records in Chicago, while Babe Ruth cracked his record-breaking sixtieth home run in Yankee Stadium. Everyone was singing *Making Whoopee* and *Crazy Rhythm*, while they were sweating under the heavy gyroscopic demands of the Charleston and the Black Bottom. Gene Tunney was taking the heavyweight championship away from Jack Dempsey.

Everything that happened in aviation seemed to grab headlines. Lindbergh, of course, had grabbed the biggest the previous year. In the balmy May days of 1927, he flew alone from New York to Paris. He set up a mad scramble of followers to conquer the Atlantic, either because it was *there*, or because there was lavish prize money ready to be plucked from the carrot stick.

On any route, the hop across the Atlantic involved some 2,000 miles of open water with no place to land. Several precarious flights had been made. One of them saw twenty-one U.S. destroyers stretched in a line across the interminable ocean, as if to catch a faltering plane in a net. They did. They safely picked up the American plane NC-4, as if it were a drenched, faltering water spaniel. The outlook for practical commercial or even military flights in heavier-than-air machines was considered a myth, a daydream.

There was one hope, though: the dirigible, the rigid airship. These cumbersome giants pointed the way with optimism. Copied from the German Zeppelins that had brought bombing terror to London during the First World War, the big airborne cigars could, with proper development, create the only way to conquer the Atlantic with a reasonable payload of freight or passengers.

It was only natural that the dirigible held the greatest hope for mass travel. Back in the 1780's, they were designing elongated, sausage-shaped balloons. They were to be propelled by enormously wide paddles. Some of them had a mainsail, a jib and a rudder. Some of the paddles had webbed feet, like those of a swan. One of these balloons actually sailed in Paris in 1783. For lift, they used "inflammable air," as they called hydrogen.

In 1852, a French engineer named Henri Giffard tried a steam engine in spite of the danger of hydrogen, and managed to reach the speed of 7 miles an hour. When the twentieth century began, Germany began taking the lead from France, after Count Ferdinand von Zeppelin designed the first rigid dirigible. Count von Zeppelin was a visionary. He looked forward to the time when his rigid-frame ships, holding individual cells filled with hydrogen, would carry mail, passengers and freight.

He wasn't wrong. Powered by Daimler gasoline engines and fitted with cabins equipped with upholstered seats, they flew well. By 1914, they had made 1,588 flights for a total of over 100,000 miles and over 3,000 hours. They carried nearly 35,000 passengers without a fatality. Some were wood-framed, but Count von Zeppelin liked metal. He also held many basic patents, and his lead over other countries enabled Germany to put nearly 80 of these ships into war service, some of them over 600 feet in length. The British ended the war with only four airships in service, while Germany's foresight and expertise made the country a pace setter in this hope for the future.

Although the winged gnats were breeding faster than these huge silver whales, the British airship R-34 had softly and neatly slipped across the Atlantic from Scotland to Long Island all the way back in 1919. The same airship also returned safely under the command of Major George Herbert Scott at an average speed of 45 miles an hour, a complete round trip that would take years to duplicate in any aircraft.

In 1928, a David-and-Goliath battle was shaping up between the airship and the aeroplane, as it was spelled then in England. No one took these heavier-than-air midgets seriously for long-distance travel. Britain, vying with the United States and Germany, already had two enormous airships on the drawing boards. The ships were plunged halfway into reality, in sheds large enough to hold the biggest ocean liner. The R-100 and the R-101 would be the largest airships in the world, each over 700 feet long. They would carry the hopes of the air-age empire with them. In 1928, they were not far from completion.

Captain Hinchliffe, at the dinner table with his two confederates in Grantham, was not likely to be thinking about the airship competition. He had had his mind set on conquering the Atlantic since 1919, when two other British airmen, John Alcock and Arthur Brown, had flown their clumsy Vickers Vimy biplane from Newfoundland to Northern Ireland. It was just a short time ahead of the R-34's quiet triumph. The Vickers Vimy ended nose down in a watery Irish bog, its canvas wings and fuselage crumpled and its struts buckled. But the feat inspired Hinchliffe relentlessly over the years.

All through his days as a commercial pilot with KLM and Imperial Airways, the trans-Atlantic fever burned in Hinchliffe. Once, in Amsterdam, he demonstrated a tiny craft called the Avro Baby, and let it be known that he wouldn't mind trying the Atlantic in it. There he also met Emilie, a tall, appealing Dutch brunette who was soon to become his wife. For a while the trans-Atlantic fever subsided. They had a daughter. Another child was on the way. They were devoted to their daughter and to each other.

Then 1927 arrived. Just days after Lindbergh, a pilot named Chamberlin, with his flamboyant fiscal sponsor named Charles Levine, flew the single-engine Bellanca *Miss Columbia* from New York to Germany, nearly 4,000 miles nonstop for a record. On that run, of course, they had the wind with them. For Levine, hardly a pilot, the trip was a lark. He wanted to turn around immediately and fly back to New York. But Chamberlin knew the risks of the west-to-east headwinds. He refused to accommodate him.

With the mood of the Twenties and the status of aviation, anything could happen. Levine managed to fly his own plane back from Germany as far as the Croydon aerodrome in London. But he couldn't land it. After bounding high off the runway, a local plane went up and guided him down. Undaunted, Levine looked for a pilot and more financing. He got both. Hinchliffe, promised a leave of absence from Imperial Airways, volunteered and began making meticulous plans.

It would not be easy. The fuel required would take up every inch of space. As the petrol tanks became depleted, they would have to be thrown overboard to lighten the load and make some space for resting in the cramped fuselage. The actual cruising speed was only 84 miles an hour. The flight against the headwinds could last up to forty hours, if not more.

Behind Hinchliffe's drive was not only the glory. He needed money and more security. He had a wife he loved and a family to support. He figured his needs carefully. His price was £10,000— about $50,000 in those days, at a time when the distinguished author Aldous Huxley was living comfortably in the South of France on £300 a year. In the Twenties, $50,000 was a considerable fortune, worth roughly a quarter of a million today. It would take care of his family, if the worst happened. If the best happened, his fame would automatically bring him security.

But the flamboyant Levine's next move brought Hinchliffe up short. The hopes of being the first woman to fly the Atlantic smouldered in the breasts of several women—notably heiresses. Levine got a last-minute offer he couldn't resist. Mabel Boll offered £10,000 if she could tag along with him and Hinchliffe. She had just succeeded in lifting the eyebrows of Paris by stepping out of her bright green Rolls Royce wearing a £25,000 jumper put together with gold and platinum threads. It was framed by a 62-carat diamond on one hand, and a 42-carat diamond on the other.

Hinchliffe, cautious and painstaking in spite of his burning ambition, flatly refused to fly with her as a passenger. The flight was canceled, and Hinchliffe went on to explore other possibilities.

Hinchliffe's caution was well-founded. He had watched two of his friends take off from Salisbury Plain for Montreal in a Fokker monoplane in 1927. Pilots Minchin and Hamilton were hired by the sixty-year-old Princess Lowenstein-Wertheim to ferry her across as the first woman contender. They set off into rugged headwinds, crossed Ireland, went out over the Atlantic, and were never heard from again.

Meanwhile Elsie Mackay, the British heiress, was pursuing her own dream. She was placating her father, Lord Inchcape, by designing the interiors of the P.&O. luxury liners that steamed regularly to the Orient in those glorious days of the Empire.

Elsie Mackay was both posh and popular. She knew people, people who counted. She also knew that her ambition to be the first woman to fly the Atlantic must never reach the ears of her father.

She worked quietly, pulling strings everywhere. She persuaded
high officials at the British Air Ministry to put her in touch with
Captain Hinchliffe. She also swore them to secrecy. If Lord Inchcape found out, he would do everything in his power to stop the
venture.

Aware of her father's predilections, Elsie Mackay approached
Captain Hinchliffe cautiously. She took him to lunch at the Ritz.
While the traffic rattled by on Piccadilly, she made offers. They
were not sexual. She offered him £80 a month and all expenses.
She offered to send him to America to buy a plane. He was to have
carte-blanche in choosing it. She guaranteed him all prize money,
and she would insure his life for £10,000. He, in turn, must keep
everything secret about her involvement. One slip would bring the
wrath of Lord Inchcape down on them. She, of course, was to be
co-pilot and passenger. They would share the fame, and he, since
she didn't need it, would receive the fortune.

At home, Hinchliffe discussed the project with his wife, Emilie.
There was a lot to think about. Hinchliffe was no amateur. He
knew the risks. But he also knew how to cope with them. They
both agreed that it was now or never. His dependence on only one
remaining eye was bound to affect his future as a commercial pilot.
He could no longer consider medicine, a subject he had once studied. With their second daughter now born, Hinchliffe's career and
security were vital. As an east-to-west prototype of Lindbergh, he
could bring honor to England and security to himself and family.

The key to the matter was the insurance. If the worst did happen
it would be there, and Emilie and the children would not suffer.
The thought of a possible tragedy of course occurred to them both.
Except for the baptism of their daughters, religion played little, if
any, part in their lives. Hinchliffe preferred to rely on himself, his
initiative, his skill.

One of the few times the subject of religion was mentioned was
when both of them happened to read an article by a prominent British journalist in London's *Sunday Express*. It was on the subject of
spiritualism, of the possibility of life after death.

These were the days when Sir Arthur Conan Doyle had forsaken
Sherlock Holmes to explore the psychic world, with all the agility
and acumen of the fictional detective he had created. Sir Oliver
Lodge, the distinguished physicist, had become convinced of the

survival of life after death, and had written eloquently in his book *Raymond* of his spirit communications, through mediums, with his son, killed in battle in the First World War. The Earl of Balfour, the former Prime Minister of England, was assembling communications from mediums that convinced him he was in touch with the deceased woman he loved. Henri Bergson, the major French philosopher and Nobel Prize winner, had become convinced of survival after death. Camille Flammarion, the prominent French astronomer, announced his conviction that there was palpable evidence of an afterlife.

Carl Jung, after intensive study of psychic phenomena, became impressed with their reality, and urged that they be studied scientifically. A medium named Eileen Garrett had recently emerged, startling scientific and psychic researchers in London with her capacity to uncover massive, confirmable details in apparent communication with those who had died. Dr. Nandor Fodor, a prominent psychoanalyst, was working on his studies about the relationship of the paranormal to psychoanalysis. Even Sigmund Freud had written a letter stating: "I am not one of those who, from the outset, disapprove of the study of so-called occult psychological phenomena as unscientific, unworthy, or even dangerous. If I were at the beginning of a scientific career, instead of as now, at its end, I would perhaps choose no other field of work, in spite of its difficulties."

Hinchliffe and his wife discussed the article briefly and dismissed it. Their consensus was that it was all ridiculous, absurd and impossible. Captain Hinchliffe punctuated his feelings by telling Emilie at the time: "It's all total nonsense." Hinchliffe would have to depend on more than religion or spiritualism to get a 32-foot-long airplane over the Atlantic. Within the previous ten months, seven men and one woman had lost their lives trying to cross against the west-to-east headwinds.

The tempo of the Roaring Twenties was unique, and it was frenetic. It seemed that nothing could be done in moderation. Millionaires were in the headlines every day. They were worshiped as well as hated. They made good copy, whatever their exploits.

Captain Hinchliffe had a friend who typified these millionaires. He was Captain Alfred Lowenstein, a Belgian financier who turned

bankruptcy into millions through this uncanny genius. And he lived
up to the tradition. He had palaces in Belgium and England, but he
would often take an entire floor at Claridge's when he stayed in
London. He liked airplanes. He owned a Fokker Tri-Motor, fitted
with luxurious carpeting and furnishings, which ferried him back
and forth between London and Brussels in two hours. He was a
skilled horseman, with an obsession for physical fitness, even
though he suffered from the gout. He had professional boxers and
a physical trainer among his numerous attendants.

Lowenstein often talked with Hinchliffe about planes, but never
offered to back his projected flight across the Atlantic. But
Hinchliffe was fond of him, often referring to him as Old Lowenstein. Neither knew that they might be meeting each other in the
future, under the strangest of unearthly circumstances.

For nearly two weeks, from the beginning of March 1928,
Hinchliffe had been checking and rechecking his plane at the Cranwell aerodrome of the Royal Air Force College, near Grantham.
Elsie Mackay, using her charm and persuasion, had seen to it they
could use the mile-long RAF runway, because no other in England
could handle the takeoff of the high-wing, black-and-gold Stinson,
with its full load of gasoline to handle the 3,000-to-4,000-mile trip.

The field was isolated, on the edge of the East Anglia fens, swept
by the winds that have been said to drive the local citizens mad at
times. There was snow and ice everywhere, and unending, uninviting leaden skies. It was a good place for the needed secrecy. About
the only intruders near the aerodrome were the fox hunters in their
scarlet tunics. The hunters were sometimes forced to clear the
RAF runway of the fox and fox hounds.

While Hinchliffe went about his business, life continued as usual
in the Grantham area, especially the hunt. One local squire had
sufficiently recovered from a sprained hip to join the Prince of
Wales, the Duke of York and the Duke of Marlborough for several
rousing hunts over the snow-covered heaths during the week before the Hinchliffe flight. For the most part, the scent was lost and
the fox got away unscathed.

In the first days of March, Hinchliffe had arrived at the Hotel
George in Grantham with his wife and friend Gordon Sinclair, trying to shroud everything in secrecy. In this town of 25,000, where

Richard III had condemned the Duke of Buckingham to death at the Angel and Royal Inn, secrecy was hard to come by. Elsie Mackay arrived later with two maids, two cars and two chauffeurs. One maid, Sophie Ries, signed in for the party.

By dinnertime on Tuesday, March 12, Hinchliffe was confident he was ready. In fact, he had to be. The Royal Air Force had made it known that they could no longer continue to make the aerodrome available to him. Further, Lord Inchcape was now sure his daughter was going to attempt the trans-Atlantic flight, and had dispatched her brother to Grantham to plead with her. Her explanation that she was only an interested bystander, with a minor financial interest in the project, did not ring exactly true. Gordon Sinclair, who wistfully wanted to make the flight as co-pilot, knew that he was only acting as a shill to divert attention away from Elsie Mackay. Further pressure on Hinchliffe was the announcement that a German crew would shortly be ready to attempt the east-west crossing, nullifying all of Hinchliffe's efforts to be first.

The main subject at dinner was weather maps and charts. There was no turning back now, and in spite of the pressure there was no desire to. After dinner, there was only one minor job to do. Someone had taken some motion pictures of the *Endeavor*, showing how she handled on takeoff from the snow-covered runway at the Cranwell aerodrome. It would be helpful for Hinchliffe to study the results.

At the Grantham Picture House, a double feature was playing. Laura La Plante was starring in *The Cat and The Canary*, followed by Charlie Chaplin in *The Pilgrim*. When both pictures had been run for the general audience, Hinchliffe and his confederates slipped into the theatre to screen the film of the *Endeavor*'s takeoffs. London reporters, now on the trail, caught them at the empty theatre. They demanded to know if Elsie Mackay was going to try to be the first woman to fly the Atlantic. They denied it. Gordon Sinclair continued the ruse by announcing he was to be the co-pilot, and that they still didn't know whether the *Endeavor* was going to fly east or west. Hinchliffe, in a skillful maneuver to give the slip to the reporters, invited them to the theatre the following night to view the flight pictures with him. By that time, Hinchliffe hoped to be nearing Newfoundland.

The party returned to the George Hotel, past the gas lamppost on

High Street, and left a call with the night porter for 4:00 A.M. Before she went to bed, Elsie Mackay ordered enough sandwiches to feed two people for a period of three days. They were made of *paté de fois gras,* chicken, beef and ham. She supervised the packaging of them, along with Thermos flasks of chicken soup, turtle soup, tea and coffee. She assembled her flying kit. leather suit, helmet, gloves and goggles.

The call left with the night porter was unnecessary. All awoke before dawn. In the darkness, Elsie Mackay slipped out of the hotel and made her way to the Rectory of the Grantham Catholic Church. Here she took Holy Communion from a sleepy priest and received his blessing.

On the way to the airport in two cars, there was evidence that Hinchliffe was having second thoughts about having Elsie Mackay as his co-pilot. There was no room for three, yet Gordon Sinclair was a veteran pilot. Hinchliffe could use his experience and muscle. Sinclair didn't like being a shill, but he also recognized that without the young heiress, the flight would have been impossible. From a distance, Sinclair saw Elsie Mackay crying and apparently pleading with Hinchliffe not to change his mind. He didn't.

The winds blowing into town from the snow-covered heath were biting. Even the local hunt for the day was cancelled; the snow was too deep. At the Cranwell aerodrome, the *Endeavor* was waiting, a clumsy, flimsy, hump-back silhouette on the bleak grass runway, trembling in the stiff winds. Gordon Sinclair got in the plane first, pantomiming the ruse to the bitter end. An RAF officer handed Hinchliffe a weather report. A rare easterly wind was forecast; a good omen.

Someone took a picture of Elsie Mackay and Hinchliffe, standing in their leather flying suits near the flimsy tail of the plane. Elsie Mackay was smiling, but the smile looked forced. Hinchliffe, with the patch over his left eye, looked grim. After the picture-taking, he scrawled a final sentence in his diary, and handed it to Sinclair. It read: "My confidence in the success of the venture is now 100 per cent."

At 8:35 A.M., Elsie Mackay replaced Gordon Sinclair in the crammed cockpit. Hinchliffe climbed into the co-pilot's seat, not because he wouldn't be flying the plane, but because of his useless left eye. The plane lumbered down the runway.

The aircraft stumbled along the grass and snow, swaying under its brutally heavy load. Just as it seemed to be running out of runway, the plane lifted. It appeared to be struggling to climb, but it climbed, shrinking into a black dot in the sky. Only Gordon Sinclair, two chauffeurs and some RAF staff men saw it fade in the distance. The next communication to be heard from Captain Hinchliffe would be so strange that only a rigid examination of the facts revealed would make it even remotely believable.

The crew of designers, engineers, airmen and laborers at the elephantine hangar of the government's Royal Airship Works in Bedford-Cardington, in the Midlands, were little concerned with flights like those of Hinchliffe. Most of them knew "Hinch," liked him and wished him well. But they could afford to wait. What future trans-Atlantic passenger would be interested in jamming between gasoline cans on a hard seat in a moth-sized airplane, when he could be riding in comfort in the new R-101 airship? Within months, perhaps before 1928 was over, this mammoth 732-foot-long skyliner would slip out of its shed to be tested in its role as an air link for most of the British empire. Its sister ship, the R-100, would be ready soon, too. It was just a few feet shorter and it was being built by Vickers, a private company. The Air Ministry, therefore, looked on it more as an adopted child.

The R-101 would be the largest dirigible ever constructed. Britannia would not only rule the waves; she would become the Mistress of the Air. Passengers would literally be able to fox trot all the way to India on the floating *palais de danse* gracing the passenger deck. They would be able to promenade along the slanted windows of the ship, or relax in deck chairs to look down on the sea or land below them. Fifty dinners could be served at one time in a separate salon, with freshly cooked, seven-course dinners supplied from an all-electric kitchen. After dinner, there would be a cigar or two in the safely sealed, lavishly furnished smoking room. Then to bed in a comfortable stateroom that could almost match those on an ocean liner.

All this was not a dream. The 732-foot frame of the R-101 was already two-thirds completed. The bones of stainless steel and duraluminium hung from the ceiling of the hangar like the skeleton of a giant dinosaur. It would rank in size and comfort with the largest Cunard and White Star ocean liners.

At the time of Hinchliffe's precarious takeoff, Major Oliver G. Villiers, Senior Assistant Intelligence Officer in the British Air Ministry, had his hands full. All phases of civil aviation were burgeoning, including the blossoming of the R-101. As editor-in-chief of both the official journal and the annual report of the Air Ministry, Villiers had to keep on top of every aviation development scattered throughout the empire. As it neared completion, the R-101 was demanding more and more attention, because the prestige of the empire was considered to depend on it.

At the age of forty-four, Villiers still carried with him vivid recollections of the First World War, when he rode in the nose of a Vickers "Gun Bus," a propeller whirring behind his head, eager to chop it off if he was thrown backward by a steep nose dive. Using the Morse Code and an Aldis signal lamp, he would flash back the German positions to the British artillery posts. From the plane, he would take occasional pot shots at the enemy with a conventional infantry rifle. He had many narrow escapes. For his work, he received the Croix de Guerre, the Legion of Honour and the Distinguished Service Order awards.

In 1928, he was pressed to the limit in keeping up with his boss, Air Vice Marshal Sir Sefton Brancker, Director of Civil Aviation. Villiers both loved and hated Brancker. The pace Brancker set in his drive to make British aviation the world leader was barely short of breathtaking. Brancker was short, jaunty, dapper and relentless. He was an evangelist, a missionary for air development. He had an RAF-type mustache, and he constantly wore a rimless monocle. As a born prankster, he would at times shock his fellow airmen by literally chewing up and swallowing the eyepiece.

Few of his staff could keep up his work pace. Impatient, he would often startle Villiers by bursting into his office, shaking his monocle at him, and yelling, "For God's sake, man, use your damned intelligence!"

Villiers, in fact, was using his intelligence, and using it well. He was just a little slower than the hyperthyroid demands put upon him by Brancker, who was otherwise a delightful character. Both men were preoccupied with the R-101, which was facing the scrutiny of taxpayers, critics and members of Parliament.

The critics felt the big silver fish could easily turn into a white elephant. In spite of the 1919 Atlantic roundtrip of the R-34, the track record of these behemoths was not good. The French dirigible *Dixmude* had smashed into the Mediterranean in 1920, killing all fifty-one hands. In 1922, the U.S. Navy bought the Italian-designed *Roma*, and watched the huge airship nose down into high-tension cables near Langley Field in Virginia, killing most of its crew. Undiscouraged, the Navy then ordered the British R-38 and watched it break in half over the Humber River, with all but a handful of crew killed. The American-built *Shenandoah* shared the same fate, snapping into three parts over Ohio in a violent updraft. Thanks to helium gas instead of inflammable hydrogen, twenty out of thirty-four crew members lived to tell about it. Even the successful R-34 was smashed to death at its mooring mast during a violent storm.

There was still optimism, even though the British public had to be sold on airships. Brancker and Villiers saw to it that the press was supplied with every chunk of data they could assemble. There were many good things to talk about.

Both the R-100 and the R-101 were to be the safest airships ever built. Both would supply an impossible dream for the Empire: India in 5 or 6 days; Egypt in 2 or 3 days; Canada in 3; Australia in 10 days. The ships would carry scores of passengers and tons of mail to the scattered imperial countries. Already, there were requests for reservations on file. Mr. Samuel Jacobs, of Paterson, New Jersey, had sent a $5 deposit to book a single-berth cabin at the projected trans-Atlantic price of £120; he could have ordered space in a four-berth cabin for only £80. Giant mooring masts, nearly 200 feet high, were being erected in Karachi; in Ismailia, Egypt; and in Montreal to handle the craft. They would be taller than Lord Nelson's column in Trafalgar Square. Large elevators would carry passengers and cargo to the top of the mast, where they would enter the nose of the ship through a covered gangway. Jules Verne and H. G. Wells could not have had such a dream. The luxury hotel of the air had arrived. The future had come to pass.

The R-101 was the brainchild of Lord Thomson of Cardington, Secretary of State for Air for Ramsay MacDonald in 1924 and again in 1929, when MacDonald returned to his post as prime minister. When he had received his peerage, he picked the "Cardington" designation because of his love for the R-101, born in the RAF works there. Like Brancker and Villiers, who worked under him, he was driven in his desire to bring these aerial liners into fruition. He made little secret that the R-101 was his pet. As a member of the Labour government, he leaned heavily toward the state-built R-101 over private enterprise's model, the R-100. The competition between the two groups was fierce; each wanted to be first off the line.

Lord Thomson, tall, aloof, classically handsome, was fifty-five years old and a bachelor. He spoke with the lyricism and timbre of the Old Vic theatre. For years, he had been having a frustrated love affair with Princess Bibesca of Romania. She was married to Prince Carol, and therefore unavailable in conventional terms. A man with a massive ego, Lord Thomson had an additional reason to favor the R-101. The ship was being groomed for the run to India, and he had his eye on the post of viceroy there in the not too distant future.

From the start, reaction to the flamboyant Lord Thomson on the part of the operations officers and men was sullen, but not quite mutinous. According to Villiers, he was arrogant. To Brancker, he was a puzzlement. To a young chief engineer on the R-100 staff named Nevil Shute, he was a pompous ass. Shute, a skilled aeronautical engineer who was just beginning to learn he could write good novels, saw in Thomson the vainglory of a political opportunist who was pushing the R-101 as his own personal air yacht.

However, Nevil Shute considered his engineering job on the R-100 a religious experience. He was annoyed by the male and female laborers frequently found copulating in the dark corners of the huge Vickers shed but he willingly climbed the icy, naked girders of the airship, slung over a hundred feet above the ground, because he believed and agreed with Lord Thomson on one point: the importance of practical air communication throughout the British Empire. Britain had to take the lead in this, or it would cease to be the Empire.

Brancker and Villiers, the personification of Empire men, felt the same. This tenuous thread kept the in-fighting to an almost acceptable level. They were all in this semireligious enterprise together, which in turn made the extensive love-hate syndromes sufferable. As with Hinchliffe and his fragile Stinson, nothing could stop them from plunging ahead.

Although there were no giant airships in the English skies at this time, there soon would be—if not by the end of 1928, at least in

1929. Meanwhile, the British public waited with mixed emotions. In general, it was intrigued by the idea of the floating hotels and the potential British dominion over the skies, even if it was not enchanted with the million pounds sterling the ships were costing the taxpayer.

During this period of watchful waiting, Eileen Garrett, the medium who was drawing so much attention with her uncanny perception and insights, had other thoughts on her mind. She had startled psychic researchers at several institutions with her apparent gift for clairvoyance and precognition. She was in her thirties, dark-haired, striking in appearance, vivacious, and not at all in the cliché image of a medium. Her only connection with airships was that in her youth she had seen the German Zeppelins moving over London and dropping bombs during the First World War. The scenes didn't leave her with happy thoughts. But right now she was mainly concerned to discover just what this mediumship business was all about.

She found her slowly developing ability to foresee future events and to experience dramatic episodes of clairvoyance and telepathy considerably disturbing. She could not explain the incidents to herself, and was having trouble finding anyone who could explain them for her.

As a child, she had had some alarming experiences involving precognition—the ability to sense the future—but she thought little about them. She had also had experiences indicating that she had communicated directly with her deceased uncle and others. In fact, she had assumed that anyone could do the same thing, since she had no basis for comparison. The perceptions that she received, she told a friend, were clearcut and distinct, like the unrolling of a film. Gradually, such incidents were becoming everyday occurrences.

She was a woman who plunged into life with zest. She was a realist, a pragmatist, and a thinker. In London, her friends and associates read like a list from *Who's Who*—George Bernard Shaw, D. H. Lawrence, James Joyce, H. G. Wells, Robert Graves, Carl Jung, Lord Dunsany, Katherine Mansfield, Aldous Huxley, William Butler Yeats, Conan Doyle and a host of others. Although only informally educated, she could match them tidily with wit and perception and she was liked and respected by the literary giants. Most of them flocked to her own London tearoom that she had established and operated as a latter-day version of Ben Jonson's favorite coffeehouse.

But there were still these strange, surging powers that set her apart. They continued to nag and worry her. They were anything but cerebral; they came from her guts, her solar plexus, through her fingertips or the nape of her neck. She would see scenes in the lives of people she knew, as if they were projected on an inner screen in living color. Later, the scenes would take place just as she had seen them. In a crowded dining room at the Savoy, she saw a terrifying scene of her husband as he was shattered by a shell during the First World War. Two days later, the news from the War Ministry confirmed it.

Her intense desire to find out what this was all about had led her to Hewat McKenzie, a fiery Scot who had founded the British College of Psychic Science. As an enormously successful businessman and skeptic, he had gradually become convinced of the reality of psychic phenomena and of life after death, to say nothing of communication with those who had died. He appreciated the skepticism of those who had not studied the psychic evidence in depth and was a stickler about any fraudulent mediums who tried to use trickery or deception.

Of the many mediums he developed and trained, Eileen Garrett interested him the most. She had a no-nonsense attitude. She was interested in analyzing herself. She had a fearless desire to get at the truth, and so did McKenzie. Something rare and unusual was going on in this woman, but the ultimate answer still eluded him.

In 1928, McKenzie was preparing to retire from both business and the college, with his wife taking over the active work. In spite of working with many talented mediums, he found himself continually asking the question: Would there ever be another Eileen Garrett?

One day during these times of Britain's struggle to establish air supremacy, Eileen Garrett was walking past London's Holland Park on her way to the British College of Psychic Science, at about two in the afternoon. She was immersed in her thoughts about how to understand the mechanism of her constant psychic experiences.

She was becoming convinced that man's consciousness floated away from and above the mind or brain, into vast unknown regions.

For a moment, she paused in her thoughts to look up at the sky. There were thick but fleecy clouds up there, with the wind blowing them across the horizon. Suddenly, she saw a giant airship emerge from one of the clouds. It was brilliant silver, with a long and graceful streamlined shape. It was a beautiful sight, and she watched it intently, as it moved slowly westward.

Then it faltered. She saw it begin to wobble. Then it dipped down toward the ground. She was frozen with fear. Suddenly, puffs of smoke began pouring out of the envelope. The smoke swallowed up the control cabin and the engine pods. Then the clouds obscured it, and it was lost from sight.

The experience was vivid and real to her. At the college, she was hesitant to speak about it. The shock of the incident almost made her numb. He reaction was amplified by another reason. Just two years before in 1926, she had gone through an almost identical experience, seeing a similar scene in the sky as she walked her dog near Hyde Park.

After she left the building, she rushed to a newsstand for the late newspaper editions. There was no news at all about any accident to any airship or airplane. All through the week, she checked the papers. There was still no news. She was deeply disturbed—was this another incident of precognition, a misplacement of time that had no rational explanation?

There were, of course, no airships flying in Britain at the time. Major Villiers and Sir Sefton Brancker were still busy preparing Parliament and the public for their eventual arrival, but that was the extent. The vision seen by Eileen Garrett was nothing at all like Captain Hinchliffe's skimpy Stinson that had taken off so bravely on its intrepid journey. But all three of these airmen would be linked eventually through the single channel of Eileen Garrett's paranormal capacities, in a way that none could know at the time.

As soon as he saw Hinchliffe's plane fade into a black dot, Gordon Sinclair's one thought was to slip away from the aerodrome. He had promised Elsie Mackay that he'd do everything possible to keep her role as co-pilot secret. He partially succeeded. Even *The*

Times of London was to report the next morning that Sinclair himself was flying with Hinchliffe.

Sinclair's escape into anonymity was short-lived. He tried to lie low in London briefly. When his scent became warm to reporters, he drove down to Surrey to join his wife and Emilie Hinchliffe to wait for news of her husband. Like Lindbergh's *Spirit of St. Louis*, the *Endeavor* carried no wireless radio. They could only wait anxiously for whatever word would come in from Ireland or the ships at sea over which the fragile airplane might fly. Emilie knew that the plane had been poised and ready to take off, but she did not know exactly when. Gordon Sinclair confirmed it for her when he arrived. That Elsie Mackay was the passenger was, of course, no secret to Emilie. She knew the reasons, and there was nothing surreptitious about it.

She knew that her husband had taken every kind of precaution for safety—a special drift indicator, an advanced aircraft compass, the coating of the wings and fuselage with paraffin to discourage the forming of ice. Even though they both knew of the heavy risk involved, they had seldom spoken of it. When Emilie got the news of the departure she was thrilled and excited. She was filled with confidence, but she was also frightened.

At her home, she waited for news with Sinclair and his wife. The easterly winds across the British Isles were not altogether favorable. They extended for almost 1,000 miles out over the winter Atlantic, if Hinchliffe kept his ship on the northerly route. But there were snow and sleet showers that hung over the western coast of Ireland. A depression was centered about 800 miles west of the Scilly Islands, with the air moving east-southeast. More ominous news came that for some 500 miles of the route, there would be extremely thick clouds, with freezing rain and sleet. In the middle of the Atlantic, there would be stronger and more powerful northerly winds. They would be carrying snow and more sleet, with heavy squall showers. If the *Endeavor* could fight its way through this, there were lighter winds to the westward with clear, cold skies.

Sinclair, an expert, was not cheered by the weather news. Emilie Hinchliffe didn't need to be an expert to agree with him. Her mind was sharp and precise; she had shared even her husband's technical preparations. Although she was not religious, she found herself praying. In spite of her objections to orthodox theology, she recognized that she did believe in a Supreme Being of some kind, whatever it was. After stern, obligatory church and Sunday school in Holland, she had found no intellectual or emotional comfort in the conventional Protestant doctrines. She could never understand why anyone was supposed to worship in a crowded church. The more she had explored the world's religions, the more she realized that she found no satisfactory answer at all in any of them.

Gordon Sinclair was in touch with the RAF station and the press by phone. It was now well past noon, and there was nothing but silence. A vague Irish report had come in to the papers that a plane had been sighted over County Waterford, 280 miles west of Cranwell aerodrome, at 11:30 A.M. Greenwich mean time. All vessels on the North Atlantic shipping routes were warned by wireless to keep a special watch for the plane.

Then suddenly, at 1:30 P.M., the chief lighthouse keeper of the Mizenhead lighthouse, in County Cork, looked up at the skies and saw a monoplane. It fitted the description of the *Endeavor*. It was passing over the village of Crookhaven, and it was heading westward toward the Atlantic, toward the steamship routes. Mizenhead and Crookhaven were some 400 miles west of the takeoff runway. The plane was averaging only 80 miles an hour.

The news—skimpy as it was—seized Emilie with joy. Shortly after, a radio message was intercepted from the French steamer *Roussillon*. The steamer was four days out of Bordeaux, heading toward America. The message was brief. It said that a plane passed low overhead, headed in the same direction. Commandant Fitzmaurice of the Irish Free State Air Force surmised that the craft was on a direct course toward Newfoundland.

Then there was total silence. At 3:45 A.M., the Sinclairs and Emilie were still up, finding sleep impossible. They had exhausted every source of news. Questioned by the press later, some forty hours after takeoff, when the last of the fuel would be certain to have run out, Emilie refused to give up hope.

If the plane had come down in the open sea, survival would be almost impossible. Two British airmen had been saved in 1919 by a small ship without wireless radio. For seven days no word had come of their safety. But that was a freak encounter. In spite of vague rumors of planes over the Newfoundland and New England coasts, there was little hope for optimism. By the time two weeks had gone by, it appeared certain that the North Atlantic had claimed two more victims.

At two o'clock in the morning of March 14, some 18 hours after Captain Hinchliffe's monoplane had lifted from the runway at the Cranwell aerodrome, Squadron Leader Rivers Oldmeadow and Colonel G.L.P. Henderson, both of the RAF, were steaming northward toward England on the P.&O. ship *Barrabool*. Each was in his own stateroom asleep. They had been spending the winter of 1928 in South Africa, on a pleasant tour of duty, introducing Avro planes to that country.

The ship was well out at sea, somewhere south of the Canary Islands. Away from any newspapers for a considerable time, they knew nothing about Hinchliffe's projected flight, even though they were old friends of his. In these days of pioneer aviation, practically every airman knew every other who flew for the Royal Air Force, or in a civil capacity. The bond was strong. There was great camaraderie among them. At the Royal Aero Club on Piccadilly or the Royal Aeronautical Society near Hyde Park Corner, discussions, dinners and cocktails created scenes of reminiscences of the past and projections into the future. The old school tie and the silver wing emblems blended together without effort.

Colonel Henderson had a rather strange capacity. It was one he was not very fond of. Several times in the past, he had discovered that he could look at a group photograph of an air squadron or family group or school activity and immediately point out those in the picture who were still living, and those who were dead. He had demonstrated this penchant only to his close friends. Squadron Leader Oldmeadow was one of them. Telling Oldmeadow about it, and demonstrating the ability to discern the living from the dead, gave Henderson a certain sense of relief by sharing this uncomfortable talent. It was a catharsis for him, if nothing else.

Outside the P.&O. ocean liner, the sea was untroubled in the South Atlantic waters. There were none of the squalls, the sleet and the snow that Hinchliffe—they called him "Hinch"—was facing in the North at that exact time, unknown to his two RAF friends. Squadron Leader Oldmeadow was comfortably asleep in his cabin. Very suddenly, his cabin door burst open. Oldmeadow sat up in shock and turned on the cabin light. Standing in the doorway was Colonel Henderson. He was in his pajamas. They were soaked in sweat. His face showed panic. He struggled to get words out. Then he said:

"God, Rivers, something ghastly has happened."

He still had trouble with his words, but he went on.

"Hinch has just been in my cabin. Eye patch and all. He woke me up. It was ghastly. He kept repeating over and over again: 'Hendy—what am I going to do? What am I going to do? I've got this woman with me, and I'm lost. I'm lost!' Then he disappeared in front of my eyes! Just disappeared."

Rivers Oldmeadow tried to calm his friend down. Nothing seemed to work. He poured three fingers of straight Scotch and it helped. Henderson calmed down. He finally went back to his cabin, and tried to sleep.

Three days later, a ship's news sheet was posted on the bulletin board. It read: CAPTAIN RAYMOND HINCHLIFFE MISSING AFTER TRANS-ATLANTIC ATTEMPT.

CHAPTER II

Colonel Henderson and Squadron Leader Oldmeadow did the only thing they could do. They kept quiet. It would not be politic to talk about the ghost of a fellow airman. Such things could only be discussed in hushed whispers if at all. Serious interest in psychic matters was extant, but it was confined to a few. The collective mind could never seem to pinpoint exactly what it wanted to believe.

Deep as she was in the subject, Eileen Garrett could only search. With the writers that had flocked to her tearoom, she had a high-level sounding board to bounce her uncertainties from. She was not just interested in her psychic capacities. She devoured the works of Emerson and Walt Whitman. She jousted often at the Café Royale and other gathering spots in London with H. G. Wells and George Bernard Shaw on politics, and nursed D. H. Lawrence through his moods of bitterness and self-contempt. She viewed the contemporary scene through these eyes, and others equally perceptive, constantly weighing both the inner and outer world with a sense of wonderment.

There was a lot to wonder about. Through the decade there were violent changes under way, some of them not yet clearly defined. No sooner had the 1920's begun than Einstein dropped his thoughts with the impact of the bomb that was later to follow from them.

The shock was so great that it left people numb. They were barely aware of the impact, yet they sensed it: the old-fashioned classical physics was done with. Suddenly there was no hitching post in the universe. Atoms were no longer solid. They were microsolar systems, composed mainly of empty space. A nucleus the size of a pinhead would require half a football field to bridge the distance to its nearest electron, which would be barely visible. But more than that, Niels Bohr, Pauli, Heisenberg and others were revealing the mysterious world of subatomic particles. To Eileen Garrett, the new physics was begining to appear as mystical as the paranormal.

To step inside the nucleus of an atom was to find yourself in a Fermi sea. But it was a sea made up of a swarm of excited, infinitely small gnats. They, in turn, were in a globular cluster, sort of a deformed sphere. They were rotating and vibrating. But the big cluster of the nucleus was probably made up of smaller clusters— forming a structure like a rasberry. Far in the distance were even smaller gnats, the electrons, with practically no mass. This new picture of the atom presented a new question: Was the material world *material* after all?

Physics was on the way to discover that these elementary particles might not even be particles. They might be just packets of energy that appeared and disappeared. They had no individual existence of their own. Discrepancies were everywhere, as they continue to be. So were uncertainties. If an observer poked his nose into this fuzzy ball of gnats, he'd upset the applecart. What he was trying to observe was no longer there. He might be able to find the speed of a gnat, but if he did that, he couldn't tell where the individual gnat was. If he found its position, he couldn't measure the speed. He had to work in probabilities.

It would boil down to the realization that matter was nothing more than regions of space where the field was very intense. The field was the only reality. Einstein said it. Others began to back him up.

This was the stuff that captured Eileen Garrett's attention. She wanted to blend the strange psychic experiences she was encountering with a rational, scientific explanation. She disliked the ambience of the occult, yet she wanted to explore the startling phenomena that were bursting within her. Her intellectual spectrum was broad; she did not want it confined. She was in the spotlight as a medium. Yet she was more interested in finding out what makes a medium tick, a question she felt she could not answer without the aid of science.

She blended her work with Hewat McKenzie and the London Spiritualist Alliance, with London's most chic literary salons, and the boiling sociopolitical controversies of the Fabian Society, as she continued to look for answers in the new trails science was blazing.

The absolute silence that followed the disappearance of Captain Hinchliffe and Elsie Mackay fractured all hope and replaced it with the certainty that death had come somewhere over the Atlantic, out of sight of both ships and shore. Emilie Hinchliffe hoped and prayed for days and weeks, even after it became obvious that no news would ever come again. Intellectually she accepted his fate; emotionally she did not. But Hinchliffe's bright confidence in the venture before he left had dissolved to mourning and sorrow. His parents in Liverpool refused for days to give up hope, until the utter silence made it obvious there was none. Lord Inchcape, taciturn always, made only one statement to the press: "I know nothing about the reports of the flight."

At the R-101 base in Bedford-Cardington, the flight crew and the builders of the R-101 scanned the papers and the aviation news for days in the hope that their fellow airman Hinchliffe might possibly be saved.

Every hazardous flight made at the time was followed with interest and a certain amount of apprehension. The R-101 airship crewmen were eventually going to face their own ultimate great adventure: the long air passage to India. Instead of the icy North Atlantic that Hinchliffe faced, they would be having problems with the blistering heat they would encounter. The critics were already assaulting the builders with the charge that the girder construction was too rigid. It would not permit the giant airship to flex. Its weight and balance, they claimed, would force the airship to fly most of the time either nose-up or nose-down, making the elegant dance floor a travesty. Lt. Colonel Richmond, the designer, was claiming that the new, plump design of the R-101 would offer less head resistance and less bending effect. The slimmer more tubular airships of the past were supposed to have 2 percent more drag. He was confident that the R-101 could take all the stresses it faced, either under way or at the mooring tower. What's more, he was sure that the angle at which the ship would have to fly wouldn't spill even a cup of tea.

Squadron Leader E. L. Johnston, who was to be navigator of the impending historic flight to India, was more interested in the navigating equipment he would have at his disposal than the tilt of the dance floor. Johnston had been a close friend of Captain Hinchliffe, and he viewed his loss over the Atlantic with painful intimacy. He had been loaned by the Air Ministry to Imperial Airways, and had flown as navigator with Hinchliffe many times just a year before, Johnston had navigated on the first Imperial Airways flight to India with him and they had struck up a close friendship. Johnston found it hard to understand what went wrong with the Stinson over the Atlantic.

Sir Sefton Brancker, whose faith in both the airship and the airplane was monumental, also found it difficult to understand what had happened to his friend Hinchliffe. Aside from the personal loss, he considered the tragedy as a severe setback to his passionate aims for the future of practical commercial aviation. At a time when it looked like a pipe dream he was convinced that planes and airships would actually carry tons of mail in the near future. He was also brash enough to say that planes might someday be flying at 30,000 feet—at over 300 miles an hour. They would even be able to navigate through any clouds or storms.

Of course, he was laughed at. He bustled about his business as Director of Civil Aviation, intent on opening up an aerodrome in every town in Britain for light "aeroplane clubs," to build up a reserve of civil-trained pilots. Brancker always worked hard. But he rarely failed to show up at a first night on Piccadilly. Noel Coward and John Van Druten were his special friends, along with Gertrude Lawrence and Peggy Wood. He would dance half the night, and would persistently wilt half a dozen of the spare starched collars he carried with him.

Major Villiers was still trying hard to keep up with Brancker, sometimes despairingly. Brancker was crisp, abrupt, and always drove to the point at hand. He rarely permitted any diversionary chatter. Villiers looked up from his desk one day, when Brancker had just returned from giving a sermon on air progress in Spain.

Brancker had shaved his mustache, and to Villiers he seemed completely demilitarized.

"Good God, sir," Villiers greeted him.

"He won't help you," Branckers said, adjusting his monocle. "What's on your mind, Villiers?"

"Your mustache is gone, sir," Villiers said.

"Forget it," said Brancker. "How is the R-101 doing?"

Since the airship was the key to the future, it took up more and more of Villiers' and Brancker's time. Neither had any direct technical connection with it, but the delays in production made it urgent that the public continue to be informed, if not placated. Of special attention were the possible routes to India. Brancker had mapped them out himself. The hot days and cold nights that would be encountered could spell disaster if not fully prepared for. The R-101 could stay afloat only through the hydrogen gas in its bags. The heat would cause them to expand. The ship would then rise. The gas would automatically escape. When the cold of night struck, the reverse would happen. The gas would contract. Ballast would have to be thrown out to keep the ship from sinking. But there was just so much gas and so much water ballast to play with. It was a clumsy system. Secretly, Brancker worried about the R-101. He was not alone.

Captain Hinchliffe had had all the attributes of an old-fashioned hero. Aside from the war escapades that brought him the Distinguished Flying Cross, he was a well-rounded man. He spoke four languages. He was an avid reader. He won trophies in every sport he turned his hand to. He could paint. He had nerves of steel. Shortly after he had lost his eye, he was back in a plane, flying again.

He was a dedicated husband. Whenever he had been away on a trip, he would either call or cable his wife. He was never out of touch with her, in spite of his travels. Just a few days before the ill-starred flight, Emilie Hinchliffe talked with both her husband and Elsie Mackay. The subject was the insurance policy, which none of them wanted to talk about but all knew was of critical importance. Elsie Mackay assured the Hinchliffes that there was nothing to worry about. The policy would be sent directly to her bank, along with the six-week salary check that was slightly overdue.

There was no concern, and the excitement of the preparations took over the thoughts of all three. The Hinchliffes had a small but adequate savings account that could handle the bridge of time before the policy would be paid off, if the unthinkable did happen.

Just before she had left Grantham, Hinchliffe said to Emilie: "If the worst happens, you will be able to keep our home intact. Miss Mackay has assured me that you and the children have been fully provided for."

When it became obvious that her husband would no longer return, Emilie Hinchliffe, sleepless and exhausted, reluctantly made her way to the law firm of Edridges, Martin & Drummonds, on High Street in Croydon. They had been the family solicitors for some time and greeted her with sympathy and understanding. The time had come to face reality for herself and her two young daughters. The unthinkable *had* happened, and finances were becoming a matter of urgency. Edridges, Martin & Drummonds would contact Elsie Mackay's bankers immediately, and would handle the matter with dispatch.

The news came a few days later. Yes, Elsie Mackay had arranged for the policy, at a stiff premium because of the risk involved. Yes, she had drawn a check for £2,605 to pay for it, and an additional check for the money due Captain Hinchliffe for his last six weeks as her employee, and for expenses involved with his preparations for the flight. There was no concern there. But Miss Mackay did not have the funds in the bank to cover her checks. Her estate was frozen, and in the hands of Lord Inchcape as trustee.

There would be no insurance whatever; the transaction had simply not gone through. The payment for the final six weeks was in a very ambiguous state, and might not be available at all.

The shock to Emilie Hinchliffe was stunning. On top of her sorrow and bereavement, there was now the prospect of unvarnished poverty. She was assured that there was some possible comfort. There was little question that Elsie Mackay's estate was one of the largest in England. There was no question that she had intended to provide for Emilie and her children. But the waiting and the wondering might be long.

Emilie Hinchliffe went home. She was desolate. She was also nearly penniless. There was a heavy mortgage on the home. Joan,

her oldest daughter, was only four; Pam, her younger one, only a
few months. Although she was expert at shorthand and typing, the
care of the children and the home came first. Unemployment was
everywhere. Economic uncertainties made jobs almost impossible
to find. She did the only thing she could think of doing: she sat
down and wrote to Lord Inchcape.

Eileen Garrett was continuing her probe of the psychic world she
unwillingly found herself in. It was full of contradictions, uncertainties, probabilities and immaterial events—but so was the world
of science. The psychic world dealt with absurdities and paradoxes—but so did the new science. Time and Space and Matter
seemed to mean nothing in terms of the psychic world—but now
they were becoming that way in science. The past and future,
cause and effect, were all turned upside down in the psychic
world—just as they were in the world of Einstein, Max Planck and
the other physicists. She continued to ask herself: Could these two
worlds come together?

Through her experience, she was convinced of one certainty: human consciousness and perception were far wider than our five
senses were capable of reaching. She was persuaded to believe that
the human soul was a psychic factor wedged between the Univer-
sal spirit and the human ego. Egotism was a fragment of the whole.
The Universe was the eternal Unity. "In death we surrender substance," she later wrote, "but just as we daily abandon the world
in sleep, and so renew and revitalize all of our capacities for further living, it is probable that in death we fuse the diverse impressions of our earthy experience into a new and unified capacity for
more abundant living."

One incident that disturbed Eileen Garrett deeply happened at a
woman's study group at the London Spiritualist Alliance. The
women in the group were interested in studying psychic development in themselves and others. Eileen Garrett was the center of interest in this particular group, because of the sharp, factual information that would come through her, apparently from friends and
relatives of the group who were no longer alive. The information
was so clear and detailed, with names, dates and places that it was
hard to ascribe the source to any other than the deceased.

The study group would meet in one of the conference rooms at the Alliance, sitting in a circle, and meditating quietly, as in a séance. Eileen Garrett would often begin to speak when she reached an altered state of consciousness, although she would retain her consciousness as she did so. In this particular incident, Eileen found herself dozing off in a full sleep-like condition. She remembered nothing after that point. When she awoke, she was told by the others that a strange, masculine voice had spoken to them through her vocal chords. The message contained identifiable facts in the most explicit detail, purported to be from people known to those in the study group who had died. Eileen was alarmed by this new turn of events. She did not like to lose consciousness, and the experience left her feeling unwell.

She sought advice from a Swiss expert in parapsychology and behaviorism. The same thing happened. She fell into a deep trance state almost automatically. At this time, she was informed that a distinct personality came through her altered voice. It purported to be a man reflecting ancient wisdom and intelligence, who identified himself as an Oriental. He gave the name "Uvani," she was told. During the trance, he stated that his purpose was to prove beyond doubt that the human personality continued after death as a free and conscious entity. There were other things that had emerged through this strange voice she learned. He spoke with apparent profundity in measured and mystical Oriental cadence.

This was almost too much for Eileen Garrett. Was she possessed by some strange entity? She began to doubt her own sanity. Why had this so-called Oriental sage invaded her physical body and taken her psyche over? With a name like Uvani, of all things. It was terrifying. She wanted to get away, to forget about the whole dismal business.

Yet she raked her mind for an explanation. Since it was a fact that this strange thing had happened, there had to be a logical explanation. She recalled Occam's razor: When in doubt, pick the simplest theory. Obviously, this voice, this entity would have to be a split-off of her unconscious. Freud, she was sure, would see it that way. The unconscious was there; it was only barely explored. Its depths could really never be reached. She had probed the theory of the unconscious with James Joyce during informal gatherings at the Café Royale. Joyce would not talk much about it, but Eileen knew he had shown great knowledge of the unconscious in

Ulysses. If she could get a clue from him, she might be able to answer this perplexing question.

But Joyce was not the answer. He talked only about being a heretic. He would not reveal his own analytical processes, or perhaps he could not. She turned back to her sessions with Hewat McKenzie, at the British College of Psychic Science. Here, the dour Scotsman explained that a voice that came through in a trance like this was called a "control." It was nothing to worry about. There was much to be learned from it. The trance state and Uvani would enhance her talent, and bring wisdom as well as communication from those who had died. McKenzie was convinced of the spiritual hypothesis. He was sure that Uvani was an actual Oriental sage from past history who would use Eileen to prove to a skeptical world that we did continue as conscious personalities after death.

In spite of their respect for each other, they clashed about this. Eileen Garrett wanted scientific reasons as much as she wanted to continue with these experiments to probe the matter. She was giving three or four "readings" a day to people who sought news of loved ones who had died. Her success was extraordinary, but she was annoyed because those who came to her for readings sought trivia rather than substance. They used the sessions with her as an opiate, rather than a guide to their spiritual development.

She found a great deal of solace with a well-established British author of the time, Edward Carpenter. Now in his eighties, he had written brilliant social commentary in his books *Towards Democracy* and *Civilization, Its Cause and Cure.* Ordained as a minister from Cambridge, he had renounced religion to become a rationalist. Carpenter assured Eileen that her strange new expansion had to be part of an inner cosmic consciousness, that her perceptions were not pathological, but simply beyond the accepted norm. He felt she should continue to follow her instincts, and not suppress them. He urged her to read the Oriental mystics and Spinoza. He convinced her that her startling perceptions were not hallucinations, but were an expanded comprehension of the Universe. In this, she found comfort and stability. With what was to follow, she would need them.

Probably the last shred of hope for Captain Hinchliffe faded by the end of March 1928. Nearly three weeks had gone by since his takeoff from Cranwell. If there had been any conceivable hope that a small ship without a wireless radio had picked up Hinchliffe and Elsie Mackay, there would have been word of some sort by this time. It would have been impossible to survive in the trackless wilderness of Newfoundland in winter, if the plane had crash-landed there. If the plane had done the same near a remote village, word would have reached the world within days, at least. Although no one but Squadron Leader Oldmeadow and Colonel Henderson knew it, their encounter with the apparition of Hinchliffe was the only feeble sign that indicated he had crashed. Of course, ghosts and apparitions were hardly an acceptable form of communication. But there was one thing of interest: Neither of the two airmen knew at that time that Hinchliffe had been attempting the flight the same night when Colonel Henderson believed he saw Hinchliffe's apparition clearly and was given a message of distress.

Such a phenomenon was not so unusual as it might seem, according to several studies by the British Society of Psychical Research. Its researchers had catalogued thousands of cases of a similar sort. They were labeled spontaneous apparitions. An absent friend or a loved one would be reported as an apparition at a specific hour. Later, the death would be confirmed at exactly that time. A patient might die in a hospital, for instance, miles away from his home. At the exact moment he died, a close relative might wake up from sleep, and see the patient standing in front of the bed. It would be, perhaps, three in the morning. The apparition would disappear. Then on the next day, the relative would learn that death had occurred at the exact time he had seen the apparition.

A classic case among many had been carefully recorded and verified by the Psychical Research Society. Lt. J. J. Larkin of the RAF was reading in front of the fire in his barracks. It was 3:30 in the afternoon. The door of the barracks opened, and his friend Lt. David McConnel walked in. He gave a cheery, vocal greeting. Larkin turned in his chair and returned the greeting. He noticed that McConnel was wearing full flying clothes, but a naval cap.

"Back already?" Larkin asked.

"Yes," McConnel replied. "Got there all right. Had a good trip."

At that, Lt. McConnel said another hasty cheerio, and left the barracks.

Then the news came in: Lt. McConnel had been killed in a flying crash at exactly 3:25 that same afternoon. He was wearing his naval cap.

But Hinchliffe's appearance before Colonel Henderson could not be checked against the exact moment of death. No one knew when Hinchliffe had been killed; it was only known that he was missing. What remained in the minds of Henderson and Oldmeadow was a phenomenon they could not understand or explain. Yet Henderson, at least, *knew* it had happened, and Oldmeadow believed him. Were the ties among the airmen of the day so strong that a fellow pilot could defy the natural laws of physics to achieve communication. It all seemed nonsense, and yet they couldn't erase it from their minds.

At the end of March 1928, another curious event took place. A pleasant, elderly lady from Surrey by the name of Mrs. Beatrice Earl* returned to her home from an experimental session with Eileen Garrett at the London Spiritualist Alliance. For some time, she had been both puzzled and startled by Mrs. Garrett and the strange voice of Uvani that came out of her during the sessions.

What startled her most was not the quality of Uvani's voice. It was the precision and accuracy of the facts that emerged during the sessions. Mrs. Earl had lost her son in the First World War, and had found comfort in a series of detailed messages she had received through her visits to the Alliance. But none of the messages had been so vivid and clearly verifiable as those she had received through Eileen Garrett.

Mrs. Earl had found a modicum of psychic ability in herself. She sometimes experimented with the Ouija board, writing down brief messages that were spelled out by the indicator as it roamed across the alphabet on the board. She was aware that such a device was a very primitive tool in psychic research, but occasionally she would get direct messages from her son, which brought her comfort. She was a rank amateur, and she never considered herself a medium of any kind.

*Pseudonym used in Mrs. Hinchliffe's notes and records.

On the evening of Saturday, March 31, she was filled with loneliness and decided to see if it might be possible to communicate with her son. She sat down at a table, placed the board in front of her, and rested her fingers lightly on the indicator. She had a tablet and a pencil beside her in the chance that her son might possibly "come through," as she called it.

After several moments of random circles on the board, she felt the force of whatever energy it was that moved the indicator take over.

There was no conscious movement on her part. The indicator swept to a consecutive series of letters, which she jotted down at intervals, without breaking up the letters into words. Instead of a message from her son, the first series of letters baffled her completely:

CAN YOU HELP A MAN WHO WAS DROWNED

This was strange. She had never received a message like this before. She asked out loud: "Who are you?"

The indicator moved again, more swiftly this time. A new series of letters were spelled out. In her hurried transcribing, they appeared not to make sense:

IWASDROWNEDWITHELSIEMACKAY

It took only a moment to separate the letters:

I WAS DROWNED WITH ELSIE MACKAY

She knew of the Hinchliffe matter only through the newspapers. Could it possibly be that the airman was trying to communicate with her? She went back to the board.

"How did it happen?" she asked.

The letters came faster. She had to stop several times to mark them down in the middle of the next sequence:

FOGSTORMWINDSWENTDOWNFROMGREATHEIGHT

Did they make sense? She studied them for several moments, marking the separation of the words. It was obvious they did:

FOG STORMS WINDS WENT DOWN FROM GREAT HEIGHT

Mrs. Earl was excited now. The information was coherent, if nothing else.

"Where did it happen?" she asked.

Again, the cryptic, unseparated letters came through. It was difficult for her to keep up with them. As in the previous sentences, they looked scrambled and unreadable at first:

OFFLEEWARDISLANDSTELLMYWIFEIWANTTOSPEAKTOHERAM
INGREATDISTRESS

But again, it took only a moment to separate them:

OFF LEEWARD ISLANDS TELL MY WIFE I WANT TO SPEAK TO HER
AM IN GREAT DISTRESS

The message was as clear as if a cable or telegram had been sent. The note of urgency was obvious. But what was she to do about it? She could understand the communications she had from her son, because she could confirm intimate details from him. But here was a perfect stranger, apparently the downed Atlantic flyer, about whom she knew nothing.

There were no further messages that day. The indicator failed to move at all after the last tragic sentence. It would be very awkward to try to contact the widow of the flyer with such skimpy evidence. Besides, she didn't have the faintest idea where Mrs. Hinchliffe lived. For all she knew, the thought of such a communication might be distasteful to the distraught widow. She put the board away, and tried to put the messages out of her mind.

She held on to her resolve for some ten days. But on Wednesday, April 11, she felt compelled to try the board again.

It wasn't long before another stream of messages came out:

HINCHLIFFE TELL MY WIFE I WANT TO SPEAK TO HER

Mrs. Earl hesitated, then asked: "Where did you say you went down?"

OFF LEEWARD ISLANDS STRAIGHT DOWN I MUST SPEAK TO MY
WIFE

Mrs. Earl continued to be hesitant. But she couldn't resist going on.

"Where shall I find her?"

The letters on the board came fast again:

PURLEYIFLETTERDOESNOTREACHAPPLYDRUMMONDSHIGHSTR
CROYDONPLEASEFINDOUTWHATISAYISQUITECORRECT

When she finished splitting up the letters into words, Mrs. Earl read them carefully. For the first time, she had received clear, confirmable information. Information that could be checked and verified. If it was wrong, it was wrong. If it was right—she still didn't quite know what to do. The new sentences were there, directly in front of her eyes:

PURLEY IF LETTER DOES NOT REACH APPLY DRUMMONDS HIGH

STR CROYDON PLEASE FIND OUT WHAT I SAY IS QUITE CORRECT

The information hung together. Purley was the next town to Croydon; both were suburbs of London. Many pilots and their families lived in Purley. It was next to the Croydon aerodrome, the hub of air activity then. Even Lindbergh had landed there in the *Spirit of St. Louis*, just after his Paris flight.

But most important was the name of a possible contact, including a possible address. Mrs. Earl had no idea who or what "Drummonds" was. Somehow, she would find out. Then she would make her decision whether or not to take the chance and notify the widow.

But before she took another step, she hesitated again. Doubts began to come back. She asked herself how she would feel if her position were reversed with that of Mrs. Hinchliffe. A perfect stranger writing her, with news purporting to come from her own dead husband, mysteriously missing over the Atlantic. She decided to wait another day.

The next day was April 12. She took the board out with considerable anxiety. She knew now that if further clear information came through, she would be obligated to take the next step. Within moments, the story repeated itself:

HINCHLIFFE PLEASE LET MY WIFE KNOW MRS E I IMPLORE YOU

There was the agony of indecision again. Then she said: "It is such a risk. Such a terrible risk. She won't believe, perhaps."

The indicator spelled the answer out on the board firmly:

TAKE THE RISK MY LIFE WAS ALL RISKS I MUST SPEAK TO HER I WISH I HAD NOT BEEN OVERPERSUADED TO COME

The last sentence was somewhat ambiguous. It seemed to mean that he regretted attempting the flight at the time he took off. But whatever the ambiguity, Mrs. Earl knew now that she would have to take action. She still had trouble in finding the courage to face the widow. She thought long about how to do it indirectly. Perhaps it would not come as such a shock if she did it through a third party. But she knew of no one who had even a slight acquaintance with Mrs. Hinchliffe.

As a first tentative step, she went to the alphabetical listing of phone numbers in Croydon. She looked under the name "Drummond"—and found the name, at Number Four High Street, in Croydon. It was cross-referenced to the law firm of Edridges,

Martin & Drummonds at the same address. She was half-frightened and half-delighted. She had never heard of the firm before, and had no familiarity with any of the three names. How could it be possible that a correct name and almost an exact address could be received through an inanimate board from a personality purporting to be the missing trans-Atlantic flyer?

She still shrank from the idea of writing the widow directly. Then a thought struck her. Sir Arthur Conan Doyle was an active Spiritualist. The creator of Sherlock Holmes was dedicating his life to this cause. He was prominently associated with both the British College of Psychic Science and the London Spiritualist Alliance, where she attended Eileen Garrett's study group. She knew Doyle slightly, and knew that his literary stature would help to remove the heavy doubts that anyone unfamiliar with the psychic process would have.

She hastily made copies of the somewhat cryptic messages purporting to be from Captain Hinchliffe. She took out a piece of paper, dated it April 12, 1928, and wrote Doyle a letter explaining the material she was enclosing, and the circumstances in which it was brought about. Perhaps he could tell better than she if it was of possible value. She felt above all that she needed support.

In addition she decided to take a plunge. She wrote to Mrs. Hinchliffe, in care of Edridges, Martin & Drummonds, the solicitors.

April 12, 1928

Dear Mrs. Hinchliffe:

Will you excuse a perfect stranger writing to you? I am supposing you are the wife of Mr. Hinchliffe, the airman, lost the other day. I get writing, and I had a communication from him the other day that they came down into the sea off the Leeward Islands, at night, etc.

His great anxiety is to communicate with you. Of course you may not believe in the possibility of communication, but he has been so urgent, three times, that I must write direct to you and risk it.

Yours sincerely,
Beatrice Earl

It was not a literary tour de force, but it was sincere. The phrase "get writing" was awkward and ambiguous, but she hoped it would get across the story. She enclosed the transcript of those brief messages. Then she posted both letters and waited. She could only hope that neither Conan Doyle nor Mrs. Hinchliffe would think that she had taken leave of her senses.

CHAPTER III

Sir Arthur Conan Doyle was having his own problems. He was still suffering from the curses and condemnations, and the slings and arrows of outrageous readers all over the world for giving up the greatest detective in literary history, Sherlock Holmes. Not only that, he had forsaken Holmes for the sake of Spiritualism, of all things—a name, incidentally, that Conan Doyle himself hated. Literary critics throughout the world were incensed. Some pretended he had never existed. Others pretended that Doyle's own creation, Dr. Watson, was really the author of the Sherlock Holmes escapades. Conan Doyle was merely his literary agent, they hinted. Elaborate biographies of the nonexistent Sherlock and Watson were created, as if these characters were or had been living flesh. Doyle himself was ignored in them. No comparable phenomenon had ever existed in literary history.

But Conan Doyle had created Sherlock Holmes from his own loins and brain. As the great detective's creator, Doyle obviously had to embody all the talents, the perspicacity, the shrewdness, the analytical power, the rationality that Holmes possessed. In fact, Doyle had to be bigger than Holmes, because he had to create Dr. Watson, too, along with the fiendish plots and byways encountered in the adventures.

A dominant characteristic of Sherlock Holmes was that he consistently looked beyond the obvious. He could be considered the first modern criminologist. Scotland Yard would scurry off in one direction; Holmes in another. Holmes never went for the top cookie. He never ran with the crowd. Invariably, Holmes would come up with the answer found deep beneath the obvious clues. But he would never reach his breathless conclusions until he had examined every shred of evidence, however absurd it appeared.

In the spring of 1928, Conan Doyle was looking at the clues for the greatest mystery of all: What happened to our conscious self after death? No greater detective story could be conceived beyond that, he was sure. Doyle believed in God, admired the character of Christ, but flatly refused to buy conventional theology. He found it narrow, inflexible and mystical. He wanted evidence, if not proof, of the survival of human consciousness after death. This, to him, was the key.

He had to have a scientific approach to the matter, an approach instilled in him since his days at medical school. His favorite professor at the University of Edinburgh had been Dr. Joseph Bell, who later became the rough model for Sherlock Holmes. Bell had hammered at Conan Doyle never to accept first impressions or surface symptoms.

Dr. Bell frequently berated his students about overlooking apparent trivia. "If you know your *trifles* well, you can make your diagnosis with ease," he told his class. "There are myriads of signs, eloquent and instructive, but which need the educated eye to discover. *The importance of the infinitely little is incalculable!*"

As Conan Doyle listened to Professor Bell, the roots of Sherlock Holmes were unconsciously forming. Bell liked to dramatize, to startle his students. He once brought an ailing derelict into class one day, who limped over to a chair in front of the class. Bell demanded of a student to diagnose the man without touching him. "Use your powers of deduction!" he said.

The student was baffled. "Hip joint disease, sir?" he asked.

"Hip, *nothing!*" Bell told him. Bell always spoke in italics. "One problem comes from his feet. Study the shoes. There are slits cut in them to relieve pressure. The man has *corns*. But we don't treat corns here. We are not chiropodists. His trouble is far more serious: Chronic alcoholism. Notice the red nose, the puffed face, the bloodshot eyes, the pulsating temporal arteries. But we need *concrete* evidence. What *confirms* the diagnosis?"

The student had no answer. Dr. Bell went over to the patient and pointed.

"The diagnosis is confirmed without question by the neck of a whiskey bottle protruding from the patient's right-hand pocket!"

Doyle carried these lessons with him on his search for a rational God. He looked at the big evidence, and he looked at the trifles. At his study in Sussex, where his manor house and gardens brought him peace and quiet, or on his lecture tours around the world, Doyle was pondering and searching. He had raked the Bible, and thrown away large parts of it that he found mummified. He often reviewed his notes, which said: "I have no desire at all to be baptized, confirmed, receive the Eucharist or any such form. I do not wish extreme unction and I desire to die as I have lived, without clerical interference, and with that peace that comes from acting honestly up to one's own mental convictions."

His convictions had not come suddenly. They had grown over the years. He was a convinced materialist from the start. But he asked the same question Napoleon did when he looked at the desert skies in Egypt "Who was it, gentlemen, who made these stars?" With his cold sense of logic, he had never believed in an anthropomorphic God. He did, however, believe in an Intelligent Force.

Doyle took on the bulk of this biggest detective story of his life in his later years. But his initial interest began not long after he graduated from medical school in 1886. He had determined to look at all the evidence. Right away, he regarded Spiritualism "as the greatest nonsense on earth." He amused himself at one or two séances some of his friends attended, and his mind didn't change. They chiefly made him regard his friends with suspicion.

But one thing bothered him, at a ridiculous table-tipping session. Doyle and his friends actually got connected messages. The messages could not have come by chance. The obvious answer was that his friends were cheating. Yet this bothered him, too. They were not the kind to cheat.

He put all this out of his mind to concentrate on his first Holmes story, *A Study in Scarlet*. He would reserve his logic and deduction for his prize detective. However, he stumbled across a book called *The Reminiscences of Judge Edmunds*. Edmunds was a judge of a high U.S. court, who frankly admitted that he had kept in touch with his wife through a medium, after she had died. Doyle read the book with fascination, but with total skepticism. All his medical training told him that this sort of thing was impossible. A fractured skull, and a man's whole character could change. Drugs or alcohol could completely change a man's spirit. The spirit depended purely on the material brain. It was ridiculous to think otherwise. Or was it?

Several hundred books and forty-four years later, Conan Doyle had made a complete turnabout. He had not followed a lone, single chain of thought. He took Sherlock Holmes' own advice: "When you follow two separate chains of thought, Watson, you will find some point of intersection which will approximate the truth." Doyle had followed the line of reason and the line of deductive intuition, and had proved to himself where they met.

Doyle answered his own first objection through a leading physicist he admired greatly: Sir Oliver Lodge. Lodge's research on radio waves and electrons had brought him fame and a knighthood. Lodge probed at the point where Conan Doyle had at first dismissed the subject: the dependence of the spirit on the material brain. Lodge challenged the conventional theory that consciousness and memory are solely located in a man's brain. The brain, he felt, was merely a notebook where the memory was recorded. There had to be a kind of race memory somewhere, which worked through a mind separate from the brain. A newly hatched chicken instantly began pecking with accuracy. "No experience or memory can be lodged in the *brain* of the newly hatched," Lodge noted.

There was a physical, stored facility in the adult brain, Lodge acknowledged. But this did not prove that any kind of consciousness was located there. If the brain was damaged, it simply meant to Lodge that consciousness was latent and inaccessible, not necessarily destroyed. It was there, but we couldn't get at it. What was missing in brain damage was the *display* of consciousness, not consciousness itself. We didn't have the right to say it was nonexistent.

Lodge gave an example that impressed Doyle's Holmesian instincts. It could be said, correctly: "It is known that a continuous supply of oxygen is essential for consciousness."

This is clear. But if you analyze it deeply we don't really *know* that oxygen or any form of matter is necessary for consciousness. A more accurate way to state the premise would be: "Without a supply of oxygen, consciousness *gives no physical sign.*"

It was this quality of digging into underlying statements that Doyle and Lodge applied to their gradual acceptance of a rational life-after-death, with a confirmable channel of communication with those who had died through legitimate mediums.

Sir Oliver Lodge found his most convincing evidence in a long series of messages that came through several different mediums, about his own son, killed in the First World War. He found massive, incontrovertible hard evidence in the material including the most intimate details of his son's life and family history. Doyle answered his own questions by studying case histories and screening psychic mediums for over thirty years. Both men put their reputations on the line. They paid for it, but they stuck to their guns. Both men had the same lament: the bulk of the scientific world was not even peeking at the evidence. Scientists, for the most part, were breaking the first law of science, Doyle thought, "by pronouncing upon a thing without examination."

Pushing Doyle was one major impulse: The most important thing on earth was to *prove* immortality. Doyle was convinced that anyone with intelligence who took the time and effort to study the entire evidence of psychic research, and to separate the chaff from the wheat, would have to be convinced of the reality of life-after-death. Those who knew Doyle as the rugged athlete, the sane and sober logician, took his conclusions in two ways. One was that he had to be right because of these qualities of logic and reason. The other was that he had been taken in by the psychic frauds who practiced on the outskirts of the phenomena.

There were a lot of frauds around. And many of Doyle's admirers who agreed with his ultimate conclusions felt that Doyle had let the chaff filter in with the wheat. Over the previous decade, Doyle had been locked in a brutal battle with Harry Houdini, the unexcelled magician. Most observers of the day agreed that in spite of the fraudulent mediums, there were many cases of psychic manifestations that simply could not be accounted for by fraud. Not so Houdini. He was drawing huge crowds by demonstrating how mediums could pull massive deceptions on the unsuspecting public. Houdini would not admit a single case. According to Doyle, if Houdini were to admit the legitimacy of a single case, Houdini's own credibility would be ruined.

In spite of their differences, the two men formed a deep friendship and conducted a long correspondence over many years. Misleading newspaper reports eventually brought a wide breach in their friendship. Devotees of both Houdini and Conan Doyle eventually leaned toward thinking that Doyle and Houdini were both right in their views of the psychic—and at the same time they were both wrong. Doyle was correct in accepting many valid psychic communications, Houdini was right in exposing the fakes. Doyle was wrong in buying almost the entire field; Houdini was wrong in condemning the whole field.

In between two opposing points of view was a dogged psychic investigator of the time named Harry Price. A brilliant, successful business entrepreneur, a student of magic and an accomplished photographer, he was devoting nearly all his time trying to find out what this strange business was all about. He was a maverick, and he was merciless.

As a magician, he knew how much faking could be done. As a photographer, he knew how to catch fraudulence at the moment it happened.

He had little interest in Spiritualism. He simply wanted to know clinically how and why a psychic medium could possibly get through factual information that purported to be from the dead. He wanted to find out whether ghosts or poltergeists really existed and—if they did—could the facts be established? There was one thing he was sure of: No one was going to get away with anything so far as his investigations were concerned.

In 1926, he began by renting space on the top floor of the London Spiritualist Alliance, on Queensberry Place, though he had little traffic with the group. He set up a lab and a séance room that could be hermetically sealed and locked against any outside trickery. He had a chemical laboratory, darkroom, workshop, and an enormous library that later was to become the Harry Price Collection at the University of London.

His equipment list was staggering. It included ultraviolet, infrared and x-ray equipment. All the lighting was controlled by rheostats. There was thermostatic heat control, a 35-mm Zeiss and 16-mm Bell Howell cameras, electroscopes, galvanometers, thermographs, lathes, tools, gauges, Bunsen burners, photographic enlargers and other equipment designed to trap any medium who was foolish enough to try any trickery. It was all part of his National Laboratory for Psychical Research. Price had gathered around him as co-workers and consultants an internationally respected board of scientists, ranging from Sir William Barrett, the physicist of the University of Dublin, to Dr. Julian Huxley, the noted Oxford biologist.

Conan Doyle's feelings toward Harry Price were ambivalent, with wide swings between approval and disapproval. Price believed that there was no question of the validity of some psychic phenomena, such as clairvoyance, telepathy, precognition and psychokinesis. But his testing was so rigid and harsh that only a precious few were able to squeeze by. Doyle felt that the very severeness of the tests were destroying the phenomena that Price was trying to examine. The tests were like attempting to examine the shape of an egg by hitting it with a sledgehammer.

Price neither believed nor disbelieved in the theories of the Spiritualists. He thought the phenomena might be explained on natural grounds, but admitted that the spirit theory covered many of the facts. Writing about a meeting he had with Doyle in Paris in 1925, Price revealed:

For more than half an hour we discussed the various differences between us. Doyle accused me of medium-baiting. I suggested that his great big heart was running away with him and that he was no match for the charlatans who, like giant parasites, battened on his good nature.

I pointed out that the history of Spiritualism was one long trail of fraud, folly and credulity, and that he, as High Priest, should do something to make his religion a little more respectable in the eyes of the public, and especially orthodox science.

Doyle laid emphasis on the fact that every religion has its black sheep.

We parted good friends once more.

* * *

In the spring of 1928, their friendship was on precarious grounds. Price was getting weary of the long line of mediums who failed to pass his rigid testing program, whether they were fraudulent or simply inept. Doyle was admiring Price's objectivity, though not his lack of sensitivity. But on one point, they both agreed: The skeptical scientist was not looking at the facts. He was dismissing them before looking. As Price put it: "It is as unfair as it is futile for a person to scoff at psychical research if he has had no practical experience, and has made no attempt to investigate the subject for himself. The greatest skeptic concerning paranormal phenomena is invariably the man who knows the least about them. . . . It is now the duty of science officially to cultivate the field."

There was a further area of agreement the two men shared: Eileen Garrett was unquestionably the most valid, honest, competent and credible medium of them all. Price liked her especially because she was *not* a Spiritualist, and never became emotional in her testing. Her quality of wanting to probe into the phenomena with scientific interest also appealed to Price. At his tests at the National Laboratory, she never made conditions. She was as puzzled about her powers as he was.

But neither of them foresaw at the time how she and Price and Conan Doyle would soon be linked in what would eventually be called the most remarkable case in psychic history.

At her modest home in Purley, Emilie Hinchliffe listened to the planes as they landed and took off at the nearby Croydon aerodrome, punctuating her feelings of sorrow, bereavement and insecurity. Joan, her four-year-old, kept waiting for her father to return. Emilie could not summon the courage to tell her. Although Emilie knew intellectually there was no hope left now, in mid-April, a month after the flight began, she could not accept the fact emotionally.

She had had no reply from her letter to Lord Inchcape. Her only news of him was that he was reported to have come back from Egypt with Lady Inchcape, who was suffering from a heart condition. The press was offering a lot of conflicting speculation about the apparently invalid insurance, in one case attributing the problem to the policy being effective only for test flights, and not for an Atlantic crossing.

Emilie Hinchliffe faced the harsh reality that her savings were running out, with no word from Inchcape. Whether he would assume any responsibility for his daughter's commitment to her husband's insurance was a moot question. It was being bruited about that Lord Inchcape had not condoned any of his daughter's escapades, and that there had been an irreconcilable rift between them.

When Emilie read the letter from Beatrice Earl on April 13, she was seized with an overwhelming feeling of distress. If what the message said was true, they seemed to signal that all her hidden hopes for her husband to be found alive had gone. She neither believed in nor knew anything about the possibility of an afterlife. She had already covered that subject in her brief discussion with Hinchliffe—she had called him either Ray or Walter—and the idea had fallen on barren ground.

She put the letter aside, and tried to go on planning how she could stretch the little that was left of her savings. But something about the letter haunted her. She couldn't get it out of her mind. She didn't really resent the intrusion, yet it made her uncomfortable. She thought of tales she had read about mediums in novels, how they often exploited the bereaved with their fraudulence. As a sensible and intelligent woman, she wanted none of that. She was content with her silent prayers to the ambiguous nontheological God she turned to at times.

Finally, she reluctantly showed Mrs. Earl's letter to some of her friends. She asked them if they knew anything about Spiritualism, and they did not. In fact, they scolded her for ever considering the idea that the letter had any value. They seized on one obvious point that proved to them the information was useless. The letter had mentioned "the leeward islands." The only islands known by this name were far to the south of Ray Hinchliffe's course, in the West Indies, an impossible distance away. With his experience he would never have even considered turning toward them, nor could he have gone down near them, as the message read. This apparent absurdity alone was enough to rule out the information. She should not waste her time in replying.

In spite of these warnings, Emilie still flirted with the idea of contacting the woman. She would think it over carefully again, and not tell anybody about it. She would make up her own mind.

As Emilie Hinchliffe puzzled it out, Beatrice Earl was having further thoughts in her home in Sussex. She wondered and she worried. Had she done the right thing? She was a gentle woman. She recoiled from the idea of bringing distress to anyone. She knew the agony of bereavement from the loss of her own son in the First World War. The comfort she got from the messages that she believed came from him was all that she wanted, except to help others who faced the same sort of loss.

On the day after Mrs. Earl mailed her letters to Conan Doyle and Mrs. Hinchliffe, she decided once again to try to communicate with Captain Hinchliffe. She felt she needed some kind of confirmation, that she hadn't just set off a set of fruitless messages that could wound anyone. She had by now looked up in the papers the details of Hinchliffe's flight, in an attempt to ask more intelligent questions.

Before long, the words began spelling themselves out again on the board:

THANK YOU FOR WHAT YOU HAVE DONE MY WIFE STILL HOPES I
AM ALIVE GLAD YOU HAVE TOLD DOYLE

As she divided the stream of letters into separate words, she took comfort that the words "glad you have told Doyle" might confirm her confidence in sending the material on.

Conan Doyle had received Mr. Earl's letter, but he did not answer it right away. He was still jousting in the hustings with Harry Price, conducting a long correspondence with Houdini's widow in an attempt to blend the two opposing points of view, and planning a series of lectures in South Africa, Rhodesia, Kenya, the Netherlands and Scandinavia. Now at the age of sixty-seven, Doyle found travel grueling and arduous. But he and Lady Doyle were intent on getting the message across: We live after death. There is hard, *logical* evidence of it. We *can* communicate with our loved ones. The facts were *there* for anyone who took the time to study them seriously, in spite of many frauds that clouded, but didn't destroy, the facts. He felt, as a doctor, that a case of false angina did not rule out another case of someone who had real angina. Like his mentor

Dr. Bell, the job was to differentiate between the two. He was still very much the father of Sherlock Holmes.

In spite of his preoccupations, Doyle was impressed by the seriousness of Mrs. Earl's letter and the material sent with it. Immediately, he looked for the hard evidence. The mention of the "leeward islands" bothered him, too. It was obviously a serious error, and one that could damage the possible authenticity of the evidence. He checked the map. The West Indies would be impossible to reach on such a flight. But, like Holmes, he thought again. Could the reference be to *other* islands, south of Hinchliffe's course, *to the leeward side of the winds that were blowing at the time? In other words, islands to the leeward of Hinchliffe's plane as opposed to the windward of it.*

There *were* such islands, which Hinchliffe could well consider if he were in trouble. They were the Azores. They were reachable. They were to the leeward of his course. They could have been as close as Ireland, and could possibly get him out of the bad weather. They would fit the logic of a pilot in distress, if the winds were sweeping down from the north. But *were* they sweeping from the north? Doyle would have to check this.

What startled Doyle the most was that the name and street of a firm of solicitors had come through the message, clearly and unambiguously. Doyle lost no time in checking the telephone directory. This was a strong piece of evidence, in fact an almost incredible one. The address checked out.

Before raising false hopes for the airman's widow, whom he had never met and knew nothing about, he decided to take another step. Mrs. Earl's messages should be verified by another medium. Doyle immediately got in touch with Mrs. Earl and arranged for her to have a session with Eileen Garrett.

Mrs. Earl felt comfortable about the idea because she knew Eileen Garrett, and could relate to her. Further, if additional information did come through the strange voice of Uvani, she would be corroborated. Her letter to Mrs. Hinchliffe would not have been a silly, frivolous impulse.

The session was set up for April 18, just six days after Mrs. Earl had sent her as-yet-unanswered letter to the widow. She met Eileen at the London Spiritualist Alliance. She sat in a chair opposite Eileen, next to a flickering gas heater in the fireplace.

It was only a matter of seconds before Eileen, breathing deeply, was in a trance. Her eyes closed. She slumped slightly in her chair. All this was routine now, a prelude to the voice of Uvani, which would come through, heavy and masculine, as if an entirely new being were speaking. Mrs. Earl waited. She was still hoping that she had not misled the flyer's widow.

In a moment, the voice of Uvani—whatever kind of entity he was—spoke through Eileen Garrett: "Greetings, my friend. I hope I may be of some help."

Mrs. Earl had a pad and pencil ready. She could not take short-hand, but she could scribble fast. She went straight to the point:

"Can you tell me anything about Captain Hinchliffe?"

Eileen breathed deeply a few more moments, then Uvani's voice spoke through her again.

"Yes," the voice said. "He has been about you a good deal. He has been trying to get messages through, but thinks he has succeeded well with you."

Mrs. Earl scribbled down the information, then asked: "Can you tell me what happened?"

There was a pause, then the voice went on: "He went far out of his course. South. Five hundred miles or so south. Warned by the Air Ministry that there were winds in the Atlantic."

Trying to keep her notes up with the words, Mrs. Earl asked: "What happened? Was it at night?"

"He is not sure," Uvani's voice answered. "It must have been twilight or dawn, as he talks about the grey light, and did not know whether it was fog or water."

"Was the machine injured?"

"No."

"Was he short of petrol?"

The voice from the medium stopped a moment, then continued: "Had not enough to get to land anywhere. Buffeted about by wind, rain and storm."

The voice coming from Eileen had suddenly changed in tone. This was a common phenomenon with her. Some times Uvani would speak as an outside observer. At other moments, the actual person concerned would seem to be ushered into the conversation. Often the voice of Uvani would alternate with the other person purporting to speak, and it would be difficult to follow which was which. But the information coming through seemed to be clear enough. It seemed to be Hinchliffe talking.

"Did you suffer?" Mrs. Earl asked, as if she were now talking directly to Raymond Hinchliffe.

"No. It happened too quickly."

Then, after a brief pause, the voice changed back to the measured tones of Uvani: "His great anxiety is his wife," it said. "He wants to speak to her. I don't think his wife is English. There is a small baby, I believe, and I am not sure if there is another child. He is very confused."

The theory of the psychic researchers, growing out of their many studies of alleged messages through mediums from the dead, was that many who died suddenly found themselves extremely confused and found it hard to believe they were dead. Later studies by two medical scientists, Dr. Raymond Moody, in his book *Life After Life,* and Dr. Elizabeth Kubler-Ross, the internationally known neuro-psychiatrist, suggested this in the 1970's. Frequently, there was a desperate sense of urgency in this sort of message, especially if the purported communicator wanted to clarify situations that had surrounded their sudden demise. But the sense of urgency often seemed to cause garbled messages, as if they were trying, in panic, to get too much information jammed into a long-distance phone call.

In analyzing the messages, researchers in parapsychology tried to take this sort of thing into account. What counted most was straight, factual data. The accuracy of these was the only thing that could possibly confirm that there had been communication. Even trivial bits of information, if correct, could lend greater credibility to other material that flowed through the channel of the medium. Without certain basic root facts, it was impossible to tell whether there was any validity to the more general information that might follow.

Another factor weighed by psychic researchers was the apparent personality characteristics revealed by the purported communication. Did the material reflect the defined personality that the person communicating possessed when he was alive? And if obviously incorrect information came through, was this the result of a faulty channel in the medium, or did it rule out everything else? In other words, could garbled messages be acceptable if there was other accurate material in the same lot? There was no pat answer for these questions. They had to be weighed in the light of logic.

Conan Doyle was immediately furnished with a copy of Mrs. Earl's session with Eileen Garrett. Although it took him some time before he was able to study it, he compared the results from the Uvani material with that of Mrs. Earl's original communications.

The first things Doyle went for again were the evidential information bits. He had already noted that the name and address of the law firm, with Drummonds' as one of the partners, was a startling piece of evidence. Now he noticed that the Uvani material clearly stated that Hinchliffe's wife was not English, and that she had one, perhaps two young daughters, one of them a baby.

This was interesting, but it could not be counted as unassailable evidence, because there was a possibility that this might have been unconsciously noted by Eileen Garrett in the papers, although nothing extensive would be written about that subject until July. It would have to be rated as provisional evidence. If the case was to hold up, many more details would have to come through to be assessed. It would be only through the collection of strong, cumulative, even repetitive evidence of this factual sort that the case could be assessed properly.

On May 14, Doyle sat down in his study in Sussex and wrote a letter to Mrs. Hinchliffe. Regardless of how she might feel about such a delicate situation, he was convinced by his long years of study of similar cases that she might find comfort in her bereavement.

In spite of her precarious financial situation, Emilie Hinchliffe felt that she had to get away for a short holiday. Her close friends, the Sinclairs, arranged it for her at the beginning of May. It gave her a chance to think and reflect, and to ponder whether she should reply to the strange letter from Mrs. Earl. She knew nothing of what had been going on at the London Spiritualist Alliance, or of Mrs. Earl's follow-up session with Eileen Garrett.

She was in such despair that she was even losing her faith in the existence of a Supreme Being. Perhaps if she followed up this stranger's letter, she was thinking, there might be some shred of hope to help her find some remote consolation. But suppose she should fall into a trap?

Emilie returned home the day after Conan Doyle had written his letter to her, still in grief and uncertainty. The letter was waiting for her when she arrived. Nervously, she opened the envelope and read:

Crowborough, Sussex
May 14, 1928

Dear Mrs. Hinchliffe:

May I express deep sympathy in your grief.

I wonder if you received a letter from a Mrs. Beatrice Earl. She has had what looks like a true message from your husband, sending his love and assurance that all was well with him.

I have every reason to believe Mrs. Earl to be trustworthy and the fact that the message contained the correct address of a solicitor, known to your husband and not to Mrs. Earl, is surely notable.

A second medium has corroborated the message. The medium remarked that you were not English, and had a baby and, she thought, another child. I should be interested to know if this is correct. If not, it does not affect the message of the first medium.

I am acting on what appears to be your husband's request in bringing the matter before you. According to the message the plane was driven far south. I allude to it in a guarded way in my notes in the *Sunday Express* next week.

Please let me have a line.

Yours faithfully,
A. Conan Doyle

The entrance of Sir Arthur into the case removed any hesitation on the part of Emilie Hinchliffe. Whatever anyone thought about Doyle's interest in the psychic, he was still a hero to the world. The creator of Sherlock Holmes would be welcome in almost any household. People who had read few books in their lives had devoured the *Adventures of Sherlock Holmes,* reread the stories, revered them. Holmes was the great leveler, cutting across age, intelligence and income groups. Doyle's search for a rational religion centered on one factor alone: verifiable evidence. He had first looked on Spiritualism as "a vulgar delusion of the uneducated." It was only when he had studied the observations of scientists like Sir

Oliver Lodge, Sir William Crookes, Flammarion, Richet and others like them that he had shifted his view. He was aware that he and some of these men had, at times, been taken in by false claims. But he was also aware of the preponderance of evidence that was verified.

Even Conan Doyle's severest critics would grant his overwhelming sense of love for the human race, his moral fiber, his gentle bearing of ingrained courtesy and fairness. A true Edwardian gentleman, he had been a top bowler in cricket, an unerring billiard player and an avid sportsman serving on boxing commissions and Olympic committees. He never looked at the psychic in terms of the occult—another word he hated. He looked at it as the only way to combat the irrational aspects of conventional religion, and bolster blind faith with cold reason.

If the Hinchliffe case could show reasoned evidence to indicate that there was communication with the missing pilot, more strong material would be added to the enormous bank of other evidence being compiled and analyzed. Further, there was a technical aspect to the case. Mediums were notoriously weak in anything mechanical or technical. Harry Price was claiming that the mediums he had examined had never brought any information through that was beyond the boundaries of their own intelligence and knowledge. Doyle knew there were scores of cases that showed this wasn't true. If the Hinchliffe case developed the way Doyle thought it would, bringing in data that went beyond the capacities of Mrs. Earl or Eileen Garrett, it would help to answer Price's objections.

Emilie Hinchliffe wrote to Mrs. Earl the same day she received Doyle's letter. Four days later, Emilie called on her, on the Saturday afternoon of May 19. Emilie was still hesitant and wary. If it weren't for the confidence expressed in Conan Doyle's letter, Emilie felt she might be falling into a trap.

Emilie was immediately relieved to find that Mrs. Earl was not a professional medium, and had no intention of charging any fee at all. Emilie had expected a request for a fee as soon as she walked in. Instead, she found Mrs. Earl kind and gentle and anxious to help, because of the loss of her son in the war.

They talked for several hours, over several cups of tea. Mrs. Earl revealed how much comfort she received from messages from her son, and from those received from W. T. Stead, a prominent Spiritualist leader who had died and apparently communicated with many mediums in an attempt to convince people of the reality of an afterlife.

Together, they went over the messages from the Ouija board in detail, along with the transcript of the Eileen Garrett session. The information that Emilie was not English was correct, as well as her having two small children, one a baby. Emilie was puzzled as to why the message showed "Drummonds" instead of "Edridges and Martin," which is the name her husband usually referred to. It was a minor point, but she was analyzing every scrap of information in order to make up her mind whether all this could possibly be true.

She still had her reservations. Her instinctual skepticism was strong. The reference to "the leeward islands" still bothered her along with the others who had pointed this out to her. While she no longer mistrusted Mrs. Earl, she was weighing what part imagination or telepathy or other factors might be involved. She was impressed by the intensity of the expressions that purportedly were coming from her husband. The words seemed to leap off the page: "I must speak to my wife . . . please let my wife know . . . I implore you . . . take the risk . . . my life was all risks. . . ." But was it an unconscious dramatization of Mrs. Earl's unconscious?

If all this were true, Emilie could not let her husband down. She wanted to go on, to explore more, to weigh the evidence. She would not lose her sense of perspective. She would check and double-check any further information she received.

They talked about the best way for Emilie to continue her tentative and provisional search. Mrs. Earl was certain that the Ouija board was too clumsy, too slow. It was a primitive tool and could bring in confusing and erroneous material. She was convinced that it could also be dangerous, because what she called "low-grade spirits" could intrude. Since she was not a trained medium, however, she did use the board occasionally, but would not recommend it for extended use.

Further, Emilie Hinchliffe needed involved and lengthy details if she was to confirm the reality of the possible communication with her husband. Her hesitation about the whole field could only be overcome in this way. Mrs. Earl suggested Eileen Garrett, because as a trance medium she could probe deeply and extensively into evidence that could either be discarded or verified.

Emilie agreed. But she had great fears about going to a trance medium. She shrank from being alone with someone in a trance. It was a terrifying thought. She would only attempt the experiment if Mrs. Earl would come with her and remain with her during the session. Mrs. Earl agreed.

When Emilie arrived back at her home late that Saturday afternoon, she was greeted by Gordon Sinclair and his wife, who were staying with her during these days of stress and strain. She explained her position to them: She didn't believe or disbelieve anything. It could or could not be true. What she had learned from Mrs. Earl seemed quite possible, she said, "but I shall not believe in the possibility of communication with the dead, until I get something that will absolutely convince me. And I shall only be convinced if my husband tells me something that only he knows, or communicates something which is now unknown to myself."

Mrs. Earl lost no time in arranging for a session with Eileen Garrett. She would be glad to accompany Emilie and stay with her during the entire time. She was as anxious as Emilie to find out if these apparent messages could be confirmed. She was looking forward to Emilie's ultimate appraisal of what might be revealed.

The conviction was growing in Beatrice Earl that if the case of Captain Raymond Hinchliffe continued to develop as she thought it would, it would eventually represent one of the strongest cases yet disclosed to prove that life was continuous, that dying was merely going through another door, that it was a transition rather than a final curtain.

The fact that Hinchliffe had apparently "come through" Eileen Garrett, as well as through her own amateurish efforts, convinced her of the strength of the case. The links were coming together. Independent links were important. They tended to confirm each other. The backup provided by the voice of Uvani gave her more confidence.

She went to a Spiritualist meeting that Saturday evening, after Emilie Hinchliffe had returned to her home. It was an informal group, some of whom had psychic ability, some of whom didn't. They would meet at frequent intervals to hear an address on the subject and discuss it afterward. Speaking that evening was a fairly well-known medium of the time, named Vout Peters. He was a serious researcher in parapsychology, and his talks were usually informative.

Mrs. Earl sat listening to him, taking notes, as she usually did. Then he suddenly stopped in the middle of his speech, and said:

"I must interrupt my talk to say there is an airman in the room who is such a strong personality that he insists on being noticed."

Mr. Peters' eyes had closed, and he spoke as if he were receiving a clear image of the scene. "He stands with his face averted. He had terrible difficulty in speaking for a bit, as he said he was cold and suffocating. After a while he said there was a little dog he thought a lot of." Mrs. Earl paused in her notetaking. Impulsively, she spoke up:

"I think I know who he is," she said.

Vout Peters nodded, his eyes still closed. "He is pleased to be recognized, and says he will come again and again."

The unusual incident punctuated her deep interest in the case. She looked forward to the Eileen Garrett–Emilie Hinchliffe session she had arranged. She would be interested to find if Hinchliffe had a small dog he was fond of.

When she got home, she went to the phone and called Emilie. There was no question about it, Captain Hinchliffe had a small dog, Bonzo, who had rarely left his side while he was at home.

Four days later, on May 22, 1928, Beatrice Earl and Emilie Hinchliffe arrived at the white-columned townhouse of the London Spiritualist Alliance. They went upstairs, past the library overflowing with books on psychic research, and into a pleasant room on the second floor. It was cheerful and cozy. Emilie felt immediately at ease.

They were greeted by Eileen Garrett. Emilie was impressed by her warmth and cordiality, and her infectious smile. She hadn't expected such a striking, cultured, fashionably dressed woman. The cliché of the shrouded gypsy fortuneteller was still with her, and she was glad this didn't apply. Her fears subsided.

The three sat down by the fireplace. Emilie was not introduced by name, but merely as a friend of Mrs. Earl. The attempt to shield the identity of a subject seeking information was a usual custom.

There was no guarantee, of course, that information about the subject might have leaked out through conscious or unconscious channels. In this case, the anonymity was not essential. What Emilie Hinchliffe wanted to know were those pieces of evidence that might convince her of the reality of the communication. There would have to be a considerable number of these bits of information, for she was a practical, analytical woman who would screen and weigh the evidence objectively.

Before the session started, Eileen Garrett explained that, like all trance mediums, she had what was called a "guide" or a "control." The voice of the control would usually come through after she had put herself into the trance state. At that point, the entity that apparently was the guide would temporarily take over the sleeping medium, including the voice organs. The medium then became only a channel, with little or no consciousness of what was being said.

No communication could be perfect. The conscious mind of the medium could intrude at times, or the communication channel might suffer static or interference in its purported frequencies. Errors could creep in this way, but it was not necessary to throw out the total evidence because of this. Eileen emphasized that the trance voice could switch back and forth from her guide, Uvani, to the entity that was apparently communicating. This would create certain shifts in diction and in point of view that would have to be analyzed and separated to make sense. This was very important, because the shift might come in the middle of a sentence.

Emilie Hinchliffe was ready. She placed her shorthand notebook on her knee, and poised her pencil above it. She was glad she had developed her stenographic skills, because now she would be able to transcribe and analyze the material later, verbatim.

Emilie had met Captain Walter Raymond Hinchliffe when he was Chief Pilot of the Royal Dutch Airlines and she was the executive secretary to the company's general manager. The job demanded accuracy and precision, qualities for which she was noted. She knew the airline business and jargon well. Any information of the sort that came over she would be able to check and judge against reality. All this would come to good use now, she was sure.

Emilie watched as Eileen Garrett began breathing deeply. In moments, it appeared that she was falling asleep. Within a minute or so, Eileen shifted in her chair. Slowly, she sat upright. Her arms crossed in an Oriental manner, and she bowed to her somewhat startled guest.

Emilie was glad that the sunlight was streaming in through the window and that the room itself was cheerful. It gave her a sense of security. Then Uvani's voice came through—a voice and a personality that even Eileen herself was unable to explain. The refined British accent changed to the cadences of Oriental speech, definitely in the lower range of a man's voice.

Emilie gripped her pencil tighter, and waited.

CHAPTER IV

The talk in the soft leather chairs of the Royal Aero Club on Piccadilly still centered on the Hinchliffe tragedy and the state of trans-Atlantic flying that May. Sir Sefton Brancker, the champion of civil aviation, was concerned about Emilie Hinchliffe and the problem of her economic survival. He knew of Lord Inchcape's stern disapproval of his daughter Elsie's attempt to be the first woman across the Atlantic, and despaired that any support for Emilie would be forthcoming from the irascible shipping magnate. Brancker was trying to organize a fund for the widow through both the RAF and the loosely bound civil air associations, but it was difficult to get so many widely spread groups together in the face of a demanding schedule that might take him to Turkey or France at the sudden spin of a prop.

Brancker put pressure wherever he could, especially pushing for support of the newspapers through his friends at the Northcliffe papers, the *Daily Mail* and *Mirror*, and Lord Beaverbrook's, the *Daily Express* and *Evening Standard*. Both of these men had built journalistic empires of great power, although only Beaverbrook was still alive. Brancker himself had power and influence, and he wasn't afraid to use it in a good cause.

Emilie Hinchliffe was a good cause in his eyes, because her husband had given his life for the cause of the infant aviation industry, and because he had been an outstanding World War hero. Branck-er, like other airmen, wasn't sure "Hinch" had done the right thing in taking off when he did. But the deed was done and the man had died a hero's death.

Brancker had been in touch with Emilie Hinchliffe several times, keeping her advised as to his progress in assembling some kind of funds, or at least in putting heavy pressure on Lord Inchcape, through the press, if nowhere else. So far, the results were not good. He encouraged Emilie to come and see him at the Air Minis-try any time, and in the meanwhile he would do everything he could to help. He also tried to help her face the fact that her hus-band would not return. Brancker was like this. Friends said he overstretched himself trying to help people.

The question of whether Hinchliffe was a man of great courage, or simply foolhardy to have made the attempt under the weather conditions of the day, was a moot one. His fellow pilots argued endlessly on both sides. Harry Harper, a leading aviation editor, was convinced that Walter Raymond Hinchliffe stood supreme among the airmen flying in Britain. His smooth, masterly flying, Harper thought, put him in a class by himself.

Squadron Leader Johnston, the officer who was being groomed to navigate the airship R-101 on its epoch-making voyage to India, joined with Brancker and others in trying to figure out many of the mysteries behind the tragedy. Because of Johnston's closeness to Hinchliffe, he pondered the facts in the case long after it had begun to fade from the news.

He understood why Hinchliffe had not carried a wireless radio. Every inch of space was needed for petrol, which Hinchliffe once said was his best mascot. Johnston tried to figure out any possible lack of judgment in beginning the flight in the first place. Opinion finally boiled down to a string of logical assumptions: Cranwell was the only aerodrome in England with a runway long enough to get the *Endeavor* into the air. The Air Ministry had repeated its warn-ing that he had to leave by the end of the week, because it simply couldn't handle a longer waiting period. Lord Inchcape was bound to sweep down on his daughter Elsie within a day or so. These pressures made further waiting almost impossible. And when the news reached Hinchliffe that the German pilots Koehl and Baron von Huenefeld were about to take off to America from Berlin in their Junkers monoplane, Hinchliffe apparently lost his patience. It was now or never—and he chose now.

The consensus was that Hinchliffe must have run into severe trouble when he hit the northerly winds that swept down on him at 600 to 800 miles west of the Scilly Islands. Ships in the area were reporting heavy snow squalls, while a sealing fleet off Newfoundland found the weather extremely stormy. Hinchliffe's heavily weighted Stinson could have been smothered in ice and become uncontrollable unless he could get out of the storm.

The Azores would be the nearest land—some 800 or 900 miles to the south. Only a man of Hinchliffe's acknowledged ability could even dream of doing that. It would be a navigational miracle, Johnston thought. By midnight or later, Hinchliffe would be roughly halfway between Ireland and Nova Scotia, over 1,000 miles from either, at the point of no return, with strong winds pushing him south. By crabbing against the wind, he could try to stay on his course, at the cost of a slower forward speed. With heavy icing, his progress would be almost hopeless. After midnight, his fatigue would be great, and he probably would want to stay at the wheel in the face of such buffeting. Elsie Mackay's slight frame would be hard put to handle such a load.

When the talk in the London clubs and the offices at Bedford-Cardington wasn't about the rash of trans-Atlantic attempts, it invariably turned back to the R-101. It was on Squadron Leader Johnston's mind most of the time, because his career and those of his fellow airship crewmates hung on its success.

Brancker and his staff officer Major Villiers felt that way too, even though they were juggling the entire civil air program at the same time. The R-101 crew had been hand-picked, and Major Villiers continued to spend hours compiling information from them to include in the Air Pilot, the Air Ministry's *Annual Report*, and the official handouts to the press. Major Villiers liked the officers of the R-101, spent hours in their company at Bedford-Cardington and enjoyed the camaraderie there.

There was the tall, slim Flight Lieutenant Irwin, a former Olympic athlete and long-time Royal Navy airship captain. They called him Shorty at times. He would command the ship when it was ready. There was Major Scott, his rotund, cherubic face belying his skill in commanding the R-34 both ways across the Atlantic just as the Twenties was ready to dawn. As the director of the overall airship development, he was not only on top of every factor in the construction of the ship, but would play a strong supervisory role when the R-101 slipped its moorings for the trip to India. Scott was a favorite of Villiers. "Scotty," as Villiers called him, would painstakingly explain the technical side of the picture, because Villiers was admittedly weak in this area.

There was also Wing Commander Colmore, who was so quiet and tactful you could hardly tell he was in overall command of the project. There was the first officer, Atherstone, analytical and critical at times, but still suffused with the collective passion of the rest of the team. And of course, Johnston, the navigator, who had become a legendary figure for his capacity to get a craft to its target, blindfolded.

Major Villiers, as a staff outsider to this central operating nucleus of the team, was impressed with the religious intensity these men brought to their preparations. There was a focus of feeling here that threw them into the project like self-imposed slavery. They all shared the joy of flying, and a common goal: To India, in five or six days, at the speed of a mile a minute! Think of it! With up to 100 passengers. Incredible! No other enterprise in the field of aviation could compare with this one, they were thinking.

What worried First Officer Atherstone, however, was the mad rush to get the R-101 out of its hangar and into the air as soon as possible. Political pressure was understandable in the face of the impending competition from Germany and the United States. But Atherstone confided to Villiers that the competition was not a healthy thing. The R-101 design was new; it didn't follow the conventional structure that had been successful with the German zeppelins. The British engineers threw away the book, and redesigned from scratch, depending on new aerodynamic calculations and wind tunnel tests that were theoretically elegant but still an unknown quantity.

Atherstone worried, but he didn't say much about it. If his fellow crew members had similar concerns, they also held them close to their chests. Navigator Johnston, being such a close friend of the missing Hinchliffe, felt there was a lot to be learned from his tragic experience. No one could have been better equipped or qualified for the trans-Atlantic attempt than Hinchliffe. But he had

failed—no one knew exactly where. Their job was to go beyond
Hinchliffe in caution and preparation. Johnston was confident they
could do it, but he still had nagging thoughts about it.

Back in the séance room at the London Spiritualist Alliance,
both Emilie Hinchliffe and Mrs. Earl waited for the first words of
Uvani to come through the lips of Eileen Garrett. Then Eileen
leaned in the direction of Emilie, and spoke:

"You are a newcomer," the voice of Uvani said. "You have not
been here before. There are two or three people around you. One
of them is a lady, around sixty-two or sixty-five. A small figure.
She is Elise or Elizabeth."

Emilie began her shorthand notes. Yes, her grandmother was
named Elizabeth. She had died in her mid-sixties, a very slight
woman.

"You know nothing about the psychic, but you are strongly im-
pressionable," the voice continued. "Your mother has been very
troubled and depressed about you. Around you has been gloom,
doubt and restlessness."

There was no question about this. Emilie knew that it showed on
her face and bearing much too clearly. She waited for more information to come.

"Then here comes someone dear to you. A very young man. He
went out suddenly. He was very vivacious and full of life. You
must have sensed his presence. He passed on due to strong congestion to the heart and lungs, but he was in the state of unconscious-
ness."

Emilie wrote swiftly in her professional shorthand. It helped to
keep her emotions under control. The congestion—could it be
drowning? She would hold back any immediate judgment. She had
to be sure.

"Now," said Uvani's voice through Eileen, "he shows me portraits. He mentions the name Joan, little Joan. He was full of
strength, full of speed. Perhaps cars or planes. He passed after
having flown in an airplane. He says it was no one's fault. He was
thirty-three."

Yes, Emilie was thinking. It was all true, or very close to truth.
Raymond called their four-year-old "Little Joan." The age was
correct. But still, this was information that could possibly have

been acquired through normal channels. She would have to wait longer. She must not jump to conclusions.

"He is giving to me a feeling of being very fond of you," Uvani's voice continued. "He had a great breeziness and lightness and was a great favorite of everyone. A fine mechanic, and very good at everything to do with cars, speed and engineering. The end was a quick one. He suffers with the eyes. He keeps on rubbing over one eye, and is laughing. What has happened to one eye?"

Emilie was not sure she should answer or not, but she did. "He used to wear an eyeshade," she said.

Uvani's voice continued: "He must be your husband. He keeps pointing to a ring on a finger. Was he married twice, or have you two wedding rings?"

The latter was correct, although Emilie wore only one at a time. Specific information was mounting, but it would be far too early to allow herself to be convinced. She continued with her shorthand, making sure she got the phrasing exactly as it came out.

"He talks of a little baby. The baby is not alone. He mentions the name Joan again. In his possession he had a portrait of Joan when he crashed. He asks have you the watch he gave you with his name on it? He wants you to wear it. He says: Don't worry about *his* watch. He has it with him, the one with the inscription on it, that was given him as a presentation. Have you got the ring or bangle with you he gave you as an engagement present?"

The tempo of the information was increasing. Emilie had a little trouble keeping her rusty shorthand up with it. But the details, trivial as they seemed to be, were all true. Raymond had given her a watch just a short time before, as well as a bangle for their engagement. He had a snapshot of Joan with him on the flight. Emilie had noticed his own watch, with a broken wrist strap, just before he left. She had wondered if he had taken it with him. No one other than she knew about this, there was no question in her mind about that. But her doubts held.

Uvani's voice was continuing: "He mentions the names Hermann and Wilhelm. He has seen them both here. . . ."

This was strikingly precise. Hermann Hess, a close friend of Hinchliffe's, was killed in a crash in Holland in 1925. Wilhelm Hepner was killed in another flying accident in 1926.

What did all this mean, Emilie was thinking. Did we *actually* see our friends and relatives when we died? Were we physically recognizable in whatever strange state we entered if life continued on? How could this possibly be true? What kind of body was a recognizable body in this new state of affairs called "the other side." It all seemed as if it were out of a Greek myth. She couldn't picture this, and was disturbed by the thought. She was faced, however, with the reality that the voice of Uvani had clearly presented two names that could not be coincidences, and that would be highly unlikely for a stranger to know. She waited now with intensified interest for what would come next.

"He seems so anxious," Uvani's voice was continuing. "He started in the morning. He was very excited. At two o'clock was the last sight of land. Then eight hours of steady flying. He decided to sacrifice something. Don't know what he means. Left strut breaks. He hovered near water. At three A.M. abandoned hope. Plug oiled. Terror never. But anguish. Knew every half hour it might be the end. Had to change course. I did go south, tell my wife, I went deliberately, deliberately south. I told her I would go north. I never lost my course. I knew exactly where I was, but went deliberately south hoping to find land. . . ."

The words were coming out thick and fast, staccato. Not only that, they seemed to be shifting back and forth between Uvani and a voice that spoke as if it were Emilie's husband. She tried to remain collected, forcing herself to concentrate on her shorthand book. The words and phrases were jumping around, but making sense in spite of it.

The voice coming through Eileen Garrett continued. It still alternated unpredictably between what seemed to be the narrator and the pilot himself:

"He came into Death quick, few miles from land. Approximately one or two," the voice tone that characterized Uvani indicated. "He consulted his compass after the strut broke, hoping to reach land in the shortest possible way, or easiest way. But his companion was terrified, out of all limits. At 3 A.M. he gave up hope completely. He had a last drink out of his flask. He says his wife knows the flask he means. The one he took with him. Then the machine was water-logged."

The sentences were still varying in time sequence but they kept on, like an excited witness at a disaster. "He tells his companion that *he* is the pilot. He carries all his maps and charts. He remembered he was finished from one until three o'clock."

But the information continued to pour out. Now the words seemed to come as if they were direct from Hinchliffe. Emilie was almost in a state of shock, but forced herself to keep up with her shorthand.

"Have you seen Brancker? Brancker told you not to hope any more. I curse myself I did not listen to Brancker. I went against all observations. Everyone said the weather was bad. You knew I wanted to do it. I was coming to the end of my flying. I could not have flown very much longer. You knew I had to do it. I could only have gone on two or three years, my eyesight was my life. I was drowned twenty minutes after leaving the wreck. I knew there was an island group near. It seemed. easier to go south to reach land. But you know it was my intention to go north. I had prepared for weeks and weeks."

The tone of the voice called Uvani now returned. As before, the words spoke occasionally of Emilie as a third person.

"He often talked to his wife about his enterprise. He did it to provide for her. He also felt he was losing his nerve. Now or never was the moment. He took his courage in both hands." Then, at a less frantic pace, it continued. "You have been worried about finances. You have been waiting, waiting, waiting. But you will hear good news soon."

The words stopped flowing a moment, then continued: "I cannot say his name. I see signatures all around. Hins . . . Hins . . . Hinch . . . I will spell it: EFFILHCNIH. I see it as in a mirror."

All through the message, Emilie felt that Raymond was attempting to reassure her that it was actually he who was giving the information, trying desperately to bring up the smallest kind of detail that would identify him. The name Wilhelm was spoken again, this time stating that he flew to Brussels. Yes, Emilie recalled, Wilhelm Hepner was killed flying from Paris to Brussels. The large letter "M" was mentioned. Hinchliffe often called his wife "Milly." Brancker was mentioned again: "Have you seen Brancker? Thank him for helping you."

This, of course, was verifiable. Sir Sefton was trying to help and was a great comfort to Emilie. Then suddenly the voice of Uvani increased in pitch and tempo:

"Oh, God. Oh, God. It was awful. From one until three o'clock. He had forgotten everything but his wife and children. As he grows stronger, he will communicate better. His last superhuman effort was to swim to land."

There was another pause. After a moment, Uvani's voice spoke, as if passing on a message from the airman: "Tell them there is no Death, but everlasting life. Life here is but a journey and a change to different conditions. We go on from unconscious perfection to conscious perfection."

The trance session was over. Mrs. Earl and Emilie were silent. Very slowly, Eileen Garrett opened her eyes. Emilie Hinchliffe was emotionally exhausted. She closed her notebook. She found it difficult to find words. She rose, thanked Eileen warmly, but without identifying herself. She joined Mrs. Earl and they left the room.

Eileen Garrett had never pursued mediumship, as she explained to Hewat McKenzie; mediumship had pursued her. This voice that came through her, which called itself Uvani, was alien to her basic sense of logic. Each time she experimented in these sessions—and she considered them a necessary step in discovering her own identity—she became more convinced that the answer to the mystery lay in the physical sciences. Her mind was already made up that the next step was to get the cooperation of medical men, psychiatrists, physicists, chemists, biologists and representatives of any other discipline. For her own sanity, she had to eventually persuade these groups to get at the bottom of this. She had nothing against Spiritualism, but was sure the answer couldn't be found there, because it was religious in nature. Religion depended on faith; she wanted facts.

Even in the trance, she herself could hear Uvani's voice at times, at other times not at all. She could tune in and out of it, but it was there. It was, in fact, an intruder. When she would read the transcripts that were made of what the alien voice said, she was utterly amazed. Where did these details, these trivia, these bits of devastatingly accurate information come from? How could she know the names of friends and relatives of people she never knew in the slightest? How could she see events unknown to her that had happened, or even were to happen? How could she reveal technical information on subjects she knew nothing about? How could she so persistently give clearcut evidence of the survival of the human individual after death?

One theory she was probing in her self-examination was that a "superconscious" existed, similar to the one postulated by Jung, with his *collective unconscious*, and Emerson, with his *over-soul*. In this superconscious or super–memory bank was everything that ever was or ever would be, like the primeval atom that Eddington and Hubble have credited for the "Big Bang" as the start of the universe.

Through some undiscovered force or interaction, some psychics perhaps were able to tune into this superconscious, she theorized. If they did, they perhaps could find any detail—even including personal trivia. If matter was really energy locked in prison, some force still unknown might trigger a reaction—the splitting of a mental atom—between a medium and the person who came to the session. The wizardry of the computer was unthought of then, in 1928, but the retrieval of cosmically stored information by the psychic might eventually prove to be at least equally miraculous, if not more so.

Eileen chafed at the reluctance of both science and the conventional church to study and examine these clearly documented phenomena. The church was embracing miracles that had happened some 2,000 years ago. But now there were others happening in modern times, right in front of its eyes. Science on the whole was reluctant to take a good look, because it didn't appear to fit into its concepts. Science had pushed religion to one side. There was a wide gap between the two. Somehow, Eileen was thinking, there had to be a way to bridge these gaps. She felt strongly that most of the psychic power in the world was being wasted, because the current culture did not know how to make use of it. The problem seemed to boil down to everyone's fear of having his belief system challenged.

When Emilie Hinchliffe left the London Spiritualist Alliance the day of her first experience with Uvani, her belief system was chal-

lenged more drastically than it ever had been in her life. In her
mind were several very clear questions. Where did this Uvani
come from? How did he or Eileen Garrett know so many details
about her husband's personal affairs? How did this ridiculous voice
know about her husband's friends who were killed and *where* one
of them was killed? How did the voice know about the picture of
Little Joan he carried with him, the two watches, the ring, the bangle and all the other details? None of these particulars had been in
the press. Not even Emilie's closest friends knew about them.

In her methodical Dutch mind, she probed for other possibilities.
There could be a leak about her identity, of course. But even if
there had been, it would have taken days or weeks or months to
track down many of these details, if at all. Such an action would
have to be based on the assumption that Mrs. Earl, Conan Doyle
and Eileen Garrett had gotten together in an elaborate conspiracy
to play a macabre practical joke on a bereaved widow. This
thought was as unbelievable as the story that came through in the
session.

Because the shock to her belief system was so great, she could
not reach a point of total acceptance. It was all too unreal, too utterly incredible. She had lost some of her skepticism. She no longer
condemned the whole idea of communication with the dead as being grotesque and impossible, which had been her basic stance on
the matter up to this time.

Over a cup of tea following the Uvani session, Mrs. Earl suggested that Conan Doyle would probably be interested in hearing
the results. They phoned from the tearoom, and Doyle was delighted to hear the session had been so successful. He invited them to
drop by.

Doyle greeted both his visitors cordially when they arrived. He
told them what had just happened on the phone. He went on to encourage Emilie to explore further through Eileen Garrett. He was
sure that she would not only find comfort and assurance from further sessions, but that she might find the same kind of spiritual
faith he had found.

She was impressed with Conan Doyle's warmth and sincerity, as
nearly everyone who met him was. His kindliness was obvious and
unaffected. She would think over what he had to say. And she
would go home, transcribe verbatim every word she had recorded

of the session, then analyze it with all the Sherlock Holmes acumen she could muster. She would also immediately arrange for
another session with Eileen Garrett to try to trace further the fate
of her husband. She would try to find if there was any remote way
she could be fully convinced that he lived after death.

The exhilaration of meeting Sir Arthur and the excitement of her
session with Eileen were quickly tempered when she arrived home
to her two small children. There was still no word whatever from
Lord Inchcape. She had now written several times. Sir Sefton
Brancker, too, had nothing really concrete to report. He had, however, gotten word that Lord Beaverbrook was keeping a close eye
on the situation. Lord Inchcape was a hard man to stir. But if nothing in the way of positive action came, Inchcape might respond to
more news coverage of Emilie Hinchliffe's plight. This, Brancker
thought, would be the best weapon in reserve.

Emilie dreaded the idea of news exposure, but her financial situation was getting more desperate every day. Previous attempts by
reporters to get a statement had led her merely to say that she
could not comment on the subject of the insurance that had ostensibly been arranged by Lord Inchcape's daughter. The *Evening
Standard* had come out with one cryptic statement: "It is learned
from other sources that everything possible is being done on behalf
of Mrs. Hinchliffe." Whether this represented the behind-the-
scenes efforts of Lord Beaverbrook's or the Northcliffe newspapers' was not clear. The fact was that it was well known that Elsie
Mckay's estate was of staggering proportions. When Inchcape
made his final decision as to its disposition, the financial fate of
Emilie Hinchliffe would be locked and set, for better or for worse.

Meanwhile, Emilie did everything she could to fight off her grief.
She tried to throw herself into her painting, which she had neglect-
ed. Both she and her husband loved painting; they had done it
together. Now she fell back on it, doing the two children in oil. It
helped, but of course it could not relieve the sorrow she was facing. Now, with her full notes on the Eileen Garrett session, she
would have another outlet for her energies.

So instead of continuing to brood, Emilie transcribed. Her skills
from her work at KLM came back better than she thought. But in
the Dutch airline offices, she had never worked on material like
this, so personal, alarming, tragic and unbelievable. The details

were so concrete, so vivid, so evidential. Even if Eileen Garrett and the voice of Uvani were simply master dramatists, they couldn't manufacture these facts, nor could they have gathered them without a pathological desire to wound or hurt. When she reached the part telling of those awful hours from one to three in the morning, when her husband knew that it was hopeless, she could hardly type. She forced herself to. She could not look back. She had to get at the bottom of this mystery.

In spite of the poignancy and the terror the first session evoked, Emilie looked forward to her next meeting with Mrs. Garrett. She was determined to keep her feet on the ground and not go overboard. There was a lot at stake here, including her sanity. On May 24, she arrived at the London Spiritualist Alliance, with renewed trepidation and a guarded expectancy. She would maintain her benevolent skepticism at any cost.

As an added precaution, Emilie had asked Mercy Phillimore, the secretary at the Alliance, to sit with Mrs. Garrett until the medium went into a trance. This might help, Emilie hoped, to continue to screen her identity. The appointment had of course been made anonymously, according to the customary practice at the Alliance.

Shortly after Emilie's arrival, Miss Phillimore came out of the séance room to say that Mrs. Garrett was now in a trance condition, and Emilie could go in. By the time the voice known as Uvani began speaking, she was already concentrating fully on her shorthand, keeping herself alert for every possible verifiable clue from which she could rationally judge the outcome.

The voice of Uvani came again, sonorous and masculine. In spite of being prepared for it, Emilie was again startled.

"You have been here before," the session began, "and very recently. There is a gentleman who seems very close to you. He is in great trouble. He is young, bright. He has a delightful personality, and gives me an impression of strength in a protective way, and gives me the feeling of great cheerfulness. He has been getting in touch with you. He is very tall, slight and I think that he has light brown hair, blue eyes, straight nose. He is rather a strong man. He has been in the Army, held a commission in the Army. I think he still holds it."

This was all correct, Emilie noted, as she began her shorthand notes. He had been commissioned in the Army before his group be-

came part of the newly-formed RAF, in which he still held a commission. But Emilie was waiting now for those sharp, telling details, details that could leave no alternative for her but to accept the
reality of this.

"He was killed very quickly," the voice continued. "He wants
to speak with you privately. He says he is your husband. He is anxious to speak to you of financial matters."

This could be the key, Emilie was thinking. Both she and
Hinchliffe were very reserved in discussing their finances, even
with other members of the family. There would be little or no
chance of leakages here. But the subject did not come up immediately.

"He did go on a southerly course. He did go south toward a
group of islands. He tells again and again that the aeroplane could
not live in the gale and that he was buffeted terribly about. He was
taken out of his course. He believes now that he was between 500
and 600 miles out of the direction he had meant to maintain. But
there must have been some island. . . ."

"Have you seen his mother? She still believes he is alive. But he
says, literally, it is like this. He saw no ship. But he says he was
blown clean out of his course, because the winds and storms were
terrible. When he started the weather was comparatively calm over
the Irish coast. Visibility bad, sea calm, fog. And it was later on
about 300 or 400 miles out he met the storms."

Emilie noted all this carefully. She was planning to make a complete study and review, not only of the weather conditions, but the
possible courses her husband might have taken. There were clues
here that she could not afford to miss. If she could confirm this
material, it would strengthen her belief. She would go to the Air
Ministry, the Meteorologic Service, the RAF—anywhere she could
accurately follow up the information. She had always been a thorough woman; it was part of her Dutch tradition. Then frustration
came again. The subject suddenly shifted:

"He refers to you as Emilie and Milly. He says when he made
the large 'M,' it was for Milly, as he called you." Emilie found herself slightly impatient with this type of clue for identification, even
though it was exactly true. She wanted more remote names, dates,
figures that she could trace and confirm. She listened carefully for
what was to follow:

"He knows you have told Joan that he has gone on a journey, and that she asked when he was coming back."

This was in sharp focus. Their four-year-old had asked that question just the previous evening.

"He does thank you for keeping it from her. Later. Betty is careful. She is trustworthy and is careful with both children. Give a kiss to little Joan. How is the baby girl? He has seen the paintings of Joan and the baby, but it was since he had left."

The sessions were becoming a constant series of electrical shocks. The portraits of the children—and Betty. Betty was the name of the woman who helped with the children. Was there any way Eileen Garrett could possibly know about this? Yes, Emilie thought, but only if she had intentionally tried to deceive her. Emilie found this hard to believe. What she was gathering was a long line of cumulative evidence now, bits and pieces that would fit together into a mosaic, which she was hoping would add up to incontrovertible evidence that she was actually in touch with her husband. She forced herself to withhold judgment, as the session went on. Again, the subject matter shifted:

"He tells now it was his great intention to keep north, to steer a northerly course. He had hoped to go on to Labrador. And he says this was his intention in case of trouble. However, the more he tried to go north, the more he was buffeted and it was impossible to live in it. He was never sure about his plugs. And in the end, before he started, he changed the plugs."

Emilie made a star beside this in her shorthand book. It was something she didn't know, although he had discussed that possibility with her. She did not know if he had gone through with the change. She would check Gordon Sinclair as soon as she returned home. This was the sort of thing she needed, material she knew nothing about, but which could be clearly verified later. It would also help to rule out the possibility that Eileen Garrett was picking up her thoughts telepathically. Such a process could not be ruled out. The fact about the spark plugs was trivial; the implication—if it checked out—would be of striking importance The session went on, and Emilie went back to her stenographer's notebook.

"He was nervy about the plugs, and that he wanted to change the make of plugs. He was a little shaky over the plugs because he had not tried these on a long-distance flight. He says one was not sparking, and that cost him. Because there is no hope as soon as anything like this begins. There was much backfiring, and this really started the trouble with Elsie. Do you remember, he says, the conversation we had to change the make of plugs?''

Emilie found herself nodding, as if her husband were in the room with her. Then another quick change in subject. Emilie was getting used to these abrupt shifts now.

"The name of the island is Maro—Cauro—or Caro—no, *Carvo*."

This would be another fact Emilie would have to look up. Was this part of the Azores?

"He seems to be referring to it, something to do with that, all the time. He cannot say exactly how far in the southerly direction, because his compass went wrong. It happened before."

There was a pause, another shift of gears, then:

"You will change your house, not during the summer yet, but later on."

This was an open question. Emilie had not decided what she was going to do. But then the information she had been wondering about since her first contact with Mrs. Earl came up:

"He makes reference to Edridges. It was the only way at the time that he could draw attention to it. He gave the name of 'Drummonds' because it was easier. He could not give 'Edriges.' He hopes the baby is well."

The constant shifting again from personal to impersonal, from subjective to objective reference to both Emilie and himself continued to make the shorthand difficult, although Emilie was sure she could sort it out after she transcribed it. But here seemed to be the answer to the Drummonds mystery—a key point of possible confirmation. Now, a change back to the flight again:

"He is going to get in touch with you and will try to make some plan of his route, so that you may be able to mark the spot where he came down. He is trying to make a plan or impress a plan where he came down in the Atlantic, and the hour he altered his course. And this could be proved by the charts which indicated the storms."

Emilie resolved again to visit the Meteorologic Service office as soon as possible. She listened further with anticipation:

"He flew in a west-northwest direction. He means he flew west and a little north, at the rate of 80 or 90 miles an hour. He flew this speed from two P.M. until ten P.M., so it seems he was flying easily in the west-northwest direction for practically eight hours, so that he made about 700 miles. Then he went straight north, flew high, visibility very bad. During those eight hours he flew on. Spirits were high, the clouds were dense. At 10 P.M., he seems to have altered his course to a little more north, and he thinks he must have reached something like 100 miles an hour in these two hours from ten to twelve. In these two hours, he covered therefore another 200 miles. Or nearly. So that he feels he had gone 900 miles roughly speaking before he encountered bad weather.'

Who was this personality who was speaking so clearly on technical matters? What purpose would Eileen Garrett have in boning up on aeronautics or navigation in such a precise area of the Hinchliffe trans-Atlantic attempt? Even Emilie was not familiar with these details on a speculative basis. There was more to come:

"This could be proved from the time he left land, as he knows they have the weather conditions in the Atlantic. He blames himself for shifting in position, because he went right into the force of the storm. Also sleet, rain, wind. Then they flew lower. At twelve o'clock, he deliberately altered course, and lost all he had gained in getting north. It is evident that from twelve o'clock on, he flies steadily south, and goes south until three o'clock. He felt the more he got south, the more he would be able to get out of the storm. You know he was not sighted by a ship. He was hoping to come down near the course of a liner. But he had gone too much out of the course of the liners, and he cannot tell how far south because his compass went wrong. He only knows 'south' to get out of the gale. He cannot be sure of his course. He knew of the islands. The name of the island is something like Carvo."

There was a lot of checking on all this for Emilie to carry out. But again an interruption of the stream of thought came through:

"He did not leave his watch at the hotel as you thought he did, but has it with him. He means the watch with the presentation," the voice called Uvani said. Then suddenly it turned back to the flight again. "He thinks later on, currents may reveal wreckage, but he got free of it. Elsie tried to take the controls. He would not allow her, although she could. But any change would not have been good, and he did not trust her flying."

Then, almost in answer to what she was hoping for, the message turned to personal data that she hoped she could clearly identify:

"He knows you sorted out the papers in his desk and drawers. The studs are in a little box in the cupboard. He saw you tidy his papers. The monetary conditions will be all right. Carry on with the house and the car. He remembers the dining room, the garden and the garage on the side of the house, and the house next door. He used to whistle from the garage to you in the bedroom. The bedroom looks out on the garden. He asks about the bookcase, the occasional little table, his portraits in flying clothes and the one in Army uniform. There is also the wireless and he often sees you sitting by the wireless. There are many things which he brought you from different places. In the hall, his cap and coats are still there. You have left them as they were. He used to work in the garden on Sundays and with Joan, talking to Joan in the garden while she helped him. He is devoted to her. He refers to the dog. He is fond of him. He often sees him running around the house. . . ."

All these poignant details were devastatingly accurate. She felt strange, as if Raymond were hovering over her, here and around the house. She did not feel at all morbid. She felt reassured. But one major point would have to be checked: the place where her husband's studs were located.

She had been looking for them just recently, since they were of some value. She couldn't find them at that time. She had promised herself to do it later. If she found them where he had indicated, it would prove to be the most accurate test so far. She scribbled a large mark in the margin of her notes concerning the studs. She noted that the mention of the dog was another telling point of possible identification, but the dog had not been named.

Nearly an hour had passed. Emilie sat and waited for any further information that might come from the sleeping Eileen Garrett. Then her voice, as Uvani, spoke again. The subject was still the last hours of that tragic flight.

"The name of the islands is the Azores. He was making for these islands. He wants you to remember that the financial matters will be all right. He knows you will get the money. He speaks out again about the gales and the winds. Air Ministry has the reports. . . ."

Emilie waited, pencil poised, as the words came to a stop. Eileen Garrett was breathing slowly and deeply in her chair, as if she were asleep. Softly, Emilie gathered together her shorthand book and handbag, and went out to tell Miss Phillimore that the session was over.

When Emilie arrived back at her home, she went immediately to the cupboard Raymond had described, if indeed it was her husband who had spoken. She was almost afraid to open the drawer. She had glanced at it quickly on her previous search, and had not seen the studs. This time, she noticed a little box in the drawer. She opened it. Inside the box were the studs, just where she had been told they would be.

Later she talked with Gordon Sinclair. With some hesitation, she brought up the question of the spark plugs. Had Raymond substituted a different type at the last minute?

The answer was yes—and Gordon Sinclair had been the only one present when Hinchliffe had done it. Then together they took out the atlas. They traced the route and the timing that had been spelled out in the session. The story made sense to Sinclair, as an experienced flyer.

Next they checked the islands of the Azores. There were nine main islands. The farthest to the northwest was the island of Corvo. The voice of Uvani had made one mistake. He had mispronounced it "Carvo."

CHAPTER V

The effect on Gordon Sinclair was marked His skepticism suffered a heavy blow. As for Emilie Hinchliffe, she was on the brink. She revealed that with one more push, she might go over to a belief she never thought she would hold—the belief in an articulate, conscious, palpable life-after-death. While she sought those telling trifles through her sessions with Eileen Garrett, it was not a trifling situation. Walter Raymond Hinchliffe, her own husband, now dead, was talking to her as if he were alive. He was apparently talking without the use of his physical brain or body.

She wondered about the trivia, the trifles that came through the purported voice of Uvani. She wondered why Raymond dwelled on them at such length. Then she thought: There is no other way he could convince me of his identity. Deep, profound thoughts could come from any philosopher who cared to pose as her husband. Her search now was as much for the discovery of a cosmic truth as it was to try to discover why Raymond Hinchliffe wanted so desperately to come back, to communicate, to get some kind of message across.

All through the weeks after the first session with Eileen Garrett, she followed up with Mrs. Earl as well as with Eileen. The messages Mrs. Earl received through the slow and awkward Ouija board continued to be brief, but they were telling. As the month of

June arrived, a message was spelled out purporting to be from Mrs. Earl's son: PLEASE DO BELIEVE MOTHER THAT HINCHLIFFE IS OVER HERE.

Then the indicator moved again: HINCHLIFFE—PLEASE BELIEVE WHAT I SAY IT IS TRUE. MY PLANS WILL STRENGTHEN THE CAUSE AND MY ENERGIES WILL BENEFIT AVIATION THANK YOU FOR ALL YOU HAVE DONE YOU HAVE MY GREAT GRATITUDE. MY BODY HAS WASHED NEAR JAMAICA. Other sessions with the clumsy board followed. Emilie helped Mrs. Earl to record the letters. She did not want to miss a clue. Apparently, one strong motivation for Raymond was his desire to help aviation. All the air pioneers of the day seemed to have this obsessional passion for their work. The fragmented messages through Mrs. Earl continued. As with the trance sessions, they would shift subject matter suddenly and unpredictably:

HINCHLIFFE, the letters spelled out again, as if to identify the sender, IN THE END THERE WILL BE SOME KIND OF SETTLEMENT.

This was another strong motivation, Emilie was thinking. Raymond, always precise about business affairs, seemed to be markedly distressed about the sloppy way the insurance had been mishandled. But how could he, even after death, feel and sense the anguish of her insecurity? The message continued with another change of subject matter:

THE CURRENTS ARE TERRIBLE WE CAME DOWN WITHIN SIGHT OF ROCK SHE IS MANY FATHOMS IN THE PLANE ON THE BED OF THE SEA PINNED DOWN NOTHING MUCH LEFT WILL TRY THE NEXT TIME TO GIVE COURSE LONGITUDE LATITUDE Then, another shift of subject matter: HAD SMALL SCAR ON THROAT SUFFERED FROM THROAT MOTHER WILL TELL YOU THIS BLUE LINE ON STOMACH LOOKS LIKE AN OPERATION CAN'T TELL

This seemed to be more of Raymond's attempt to identify himself, perhaps to make sure that Emilie would believe that such intimate details could never come from a stranger. Her husband had had constant trouble with his throat; he had even had his tonsils removed in recent years. Then the message continued:

A RING A JOKE ABOUT A RING AND A MOLAR

Emilie was startled. This was ridiculous. Neither Ouija board nor Mrs. Earl could know about this in any possible way. When

Raymond had been in medical school, he had taken some courses in dentistry. He had fashioned a ring out of the gold he had used in a practice false tooth. Later he gave it to Emilie as a joke. Here it was now, coming back through some kind of communication that could never be fathomed.

On June 9, 1928, Emilie had another session with Eileen Garrett. It began as usual. Uvani's voice said that her husband was in the room, although Emilie could not see him or sense him. According to the voice of Uvani, there was also her father, who had died three years before, and another flyer—Wilhelm, who had died five years before.

A common phenomenon reported in sessions of this sort was that mediums often "saw" the discarnate subjects they purportedly were in communication with, standing in the room, almost as if they were physically there. This was subjective. There was no way of proving this. But it was common. Another phenomenon was that mediums would report more than one person responding in an attempt to communicate. But Emilie Hinchliffe was still trying to convince herself of the validity of any communication at all.

"Here is that husband of yours," the voice of Uvani was saying. "He passed out suddenly. He is standing very close to your father. Your father helps him to get nearer. He gives me the impression of more peace, much love, and seems to have a great deal of anxiety. He evidently wants to keep close to you to help you regarding material events. He is very worried for your sake. He made a definite promise to give later on, when he is more peaceable, an indication of his own unlucky flight, with longitude, latitude and distances in connection with his flight."

Emilie was already at work on these. She considered them an important check on the validity of the messages. She was getting the help of the Air Ministry to trace the currents of the Gulf Stream, the exact position, direction and velocity of the North Atlantic storms that night, wind and drift conditions, and other pertinent detail. But now Uvani's voice was turning to other matters:

"His great responsibility is in connection with monetary things. He is desirous and anxious to bring things to a head. He promised you that from the father of the girl there should be some recompensation forthcoming. It seems your husband is worried over

Inchcape's attitude. If he will not listen, here is the way out of it: Your husband refers to someone at the *Daily Express*. He says you know whom he means."

Emilie thought a moment, then said: "Does he mean Sir Arthur Conan Doyle?"

"No, not him. But Arthur Doyle would know. If Inchcape would not agree, write him again or get someone else to approach him. Tell him you are without funds, tell him about the children and also tell him that you are a stranger in this country. Tell him that it is all very well for him to say that I am responsible. But tell him that it takes two to make this arrangement, and that I am not morally responsible for the flight, or the conditions. If it is made known through the press to Elsie's father, I think he will then give some money. Talk this over with the *Express*. They will understand what I mean. The *Daily Express*. The name is Lord Beaverbrook. Please do not worry, even though monetary conditions are low. But you are going to get some money so that you can maintain the house and make it possible to carry on. I have the impression that you are getting the money in *July*. Perfectly certain."

If there were anything to the general theory advanced by researchers in parapsychology, the message would tend to verify it. One theory, according to studies of the British society for Psychical Research, was that apparitions and detailed communications from those who had died were most intense when there was critical unfinished business to attend to, as well as the unfinished work the deceased felt should be done. All this seemed to be behind the Hinchliffe message: his concern for his wife's security, his dedication to the cause of aviation. There was also the frequent reference to others who had died, and meeting up with them on the "other side." This was all theory, but it seemed to be all part of a pattern.

What struck Emilie Hinchliffe most was the naming of a specific time when she would receive the monetary help she most desperately needed. How could the so-called Uvani, Eileen Garrett or her deceased husband Raymond possibly know the future with such confidence and certainty? There was no evidence that Lord Inchcape was giving any consideration at all to her plea for help. Even if he were willing, these things moved slowly. And she was beginning to doubt if he were at all willing. But now the message suddenly shifted to Hinchliffe and his friends, both alive and dead. It brought up the two fliers who had met death in the Atlantic just before his own flight:

"I saw Hamilton. I believe they had a terrible time. There was also Minchin. You remember the tale at the time? Everything was true. They turned back and got as near as in sight of the Irish Coast. Hamilton says they never had a hope, and they caught fire. I saw them. They had struck very bad weather conditions."

The message went on to ask about other airmen they knew: Bill Lawford, Gerrard, Wilcockson, Kauffmann, Grey, Irvin Levine, Captain Morkham, Alan Cobham—the entire list of names being exactly correct. Now Emilie tilted back to belief again. She could barely remember the names of all these friends of her husband's. Some of them she had to check later to see if they were right. They were. For so many precise names to flow through was one of the most stunning events in all the session.

The message continued: "Have you told any of these people and do they believe that we have been speaking? They must not think you are being misled." Then the voice added, as if it were reporting on a convention of airmen, "I have seen two Georges here. One is George Sims, and the other George Powell. After all, it has not been so bad. I have met a lot of the old crowd, and those who were killed in the war. I am getting my memory back, bit by bit."

Memory back? The words suggested a man knocked unconscious, then gradually working his way out of amnesia. Was this the way it actually happened when we died? In a sense, it seemed so prosaic, so ordinary, so normal, yet so strange.

The session went on. Sometimes, when the discussion became vague or generalized, after a few moments a sharp, intimate fact would come out to add more evidence that the entity had to be her husband. And at some point during this long session—Emilie could not be certain exactly when—she moved to a full and unshakable belief that it was true, that we did live after death, and that the evidence she had encountered was incontrovertible. It was as if she had stepped into a new world herself.

It was Uvani's cadences that closed the session: "He will keep near you until you are free of worry. God bless you and your household. Remember there is no Death, but everlasting life."

The closing words were the same as in the other sessions. The difference was that, this time, Emilie believed it.

On the way home to Purley, Emilie pondered more about what had been many other details. The name of a friend who owed them £50, the correct name and the correct amount. The identification scars and marks on his body, completely accurate, were repeated again. A mention of Charles Levine, of Mabel Boll, the diamond queen, of his walking stick made out of the strut of an airplane, of the Sinclairs still living with her, of an Uncle Howard, and others.

But two statements that had come out would need careful checking and observation. An exact date was named when the money would be forthcoming from the reluctant Inchcape. It was to be July 25, or by the end of July, perhaps the last day. Emilie had circled this in her shorthand notebook. And another of equal importance. Uvani's voice had come out during the session to say: "Have you been to see Edridges regarding the ground, the building plot?" The reference was to a plot of land they had bought and had hoped to build on. Emilie was worried about this. She could not find the plot plan, the blueprint that defined the property and its exact borders. She would have to search some more.

Now that her carefully-protected belief system had been radically changed, Emilie tried to decide what she should do about it. She was a woman of action and not of dreams. In the back of her mind was the conviction that she would have to tell others of her experience, to share it with them. But she was not an evangelist. If she shared her experiences, she would have to do it quietly, in her own way, to lead people to her discovery in the same way she had been led.

To do this, she needed to know more about the process. She had to gather more evidence, to keep gathering it. The whole scope of the subject, the enormity of it, was not something that could casually be mentioned and dropped. Her belief had grown with infinite slowness. She knew her own skepticism, and knew that every sensible and intelligent person would have the same distinct reservations she had had.

And there were the nagging questions she still had on her mind. If somebody died, where did he go? If they were to hold on to their own personalities, to think and analyze and have the desire to communicate, they just couldn't be floating around in a vapor. Just where were Raymond and her father when they identified themselves at the start of the sessions? How did they relate to this world? How could they observe things here? Were time and space and matter meaningless? Where was the link between this world and the other?

She went back to thoughts of the trivia, the Sherlock Holmes type of trifles she had been receiving. How would she try to establish her identity to a friend or relative if only her voice communication could be heard? How would she do it if she were on the other end of a long-distance telephone, a telephone with a bad connection and a full distortion of tone? All her normal means of identification would be useless. Her voice, appearance and personal idiosyncrasies would be lacking. Yet these were the things people depended on to make themselves known *as* themselves.

In such a case, she would do the only thing she could do to convince others of her identity. She would recall incidents that she shared with the other person involved. She would assemble as many of them as she could, until the aggregate total of them would be overwhelming. Yes, it would be the private trivialities that she would use. She would, in other words, use exactly what Raymond had used, and what Holmes would look for—the trifles.

She threw herself into getting more material, but not for her ego or for her self-indulgence. She wanted to present her case in court, the court of public opinion. She went to Mrs. Earl again, while waiting for another session with Eileen Garrett. For support and confirmation, she brought one of Raymond's close friends, Captain John Morkham, with her. He was helping her in tracing the maps and charts at the Air Ministry. The messages were faltering, but they came.

COME AND HAVE FAITH BECAUSE I AM HERE AND GLAD TO WELCOME MORKHAM I WANT TO CARRY OUT EXPERIMENTS AND GIVE ADVICE REGARDS A QUITE DIFFERENT EASY SUBJECT SIMPLE LANGUAGE PREPARE THE WAY FOR GREATER KNOWLEDGE WHEN YOU HAVE GOT ALL KNOWLEDGE TO GIVE

The words were coming through with difficulty and were obscure. The next words seemed to explain the situation:

I AM SORRY I AM FILLED WITH EMOTION AT WRITING BEFORE FRIENDS BY DEGREES I SHALL GET MORE USED TO CONDITIONS ALL MY POWER HOLD MIND ON MATTERS MATERIAL INCHCAPE MUST DO AS HE LIKES DO GO AND SEE BRANCKER HE MIGHT HAVE INFLUENCE ELSEWHERE HE COULD RAKE UP

Captain Morkham was impressed, in spite of the faltering words. He would have to maintain his skepticism, of course. He was in the same position Emilie had been in several weeks before. He was further impressed, however, when several technical details came through little Mrs. Earl and her strange board:

I WILL ENDEAVOR TO ADVISE AND IMPRESS ON THE DANGER OF PLUGS THAT ARE NOT PROPERLY CONNECTED STRUTS OUGHT NOT TO BE OF FOREIGN WOOD BUT OF ALUMINIUM

"Does it bend?" Morkham asked, as if he were speaking to his friend Hinchliffe.

NOT IF SPECIALLY PREPARED HAMILTON FOUND THAT HIS MACHINE WAS FAULTY IN BOTH STRUTS "I thought it was fire," Captain Morkham said.

YES BUT THE STRUTS AS ARRANGED AS THEY ARE NOW ARE ALL WRONG IF AIRMEN COULD SEE THE DANGERS THEY NOW RUN AS I SEE THEY WOULD NEVER GO UP Then, as an afterthought, the message added:

LIFE USED TO BE SO JOLLY ON EARTH AT TIMES BUT THIS LIFE IS SO MUCH FREER BE GOOD TO MY WIFE I AM ANXIOUS ABOUT MY DARLING JOAN BABY IS ALL RIGHT

The messages ended with two direct instructions to Emilie. One was to go and see Brancker. The other was a clear direct order:

YOU WILL FIND A PAPER WHICH MAY BE OF USE TO HOUSE AGENTS BEHIND A DRAWER ON THE LEFT OF MY DESK

Emilie went home. She carefully removed the drawer on the left side of her husband's desk. Suddenly, she saw a piece of blue, parchment-like paper squeezed in the back, behind the row of drawers. She removed it. It was the plot plan of the parcel of land they had bought four years earlier—and which she had been searching in vain for over many weeks.

As Emilie continued her probe with increasing zeal, a strange set of circumstances was shaping up involving the flamboyant Belgian financier Alfred Lowenstein, Captain Hincliffe's former friend. "Old Lowenstein," as Hinchliffe used to call him, was continuing his plush, posh and profligate life all during the spring of 1928. In spite of his permanent suite at Claridge's, his scattered mansions elsewhere, and his love of the good life, he still kept himself in top physical shape under a stiff regimen of exercise and riding.

Lowenstein was a complex man. Nobody seemed to know what he was thinking, or what else he wanted beyond his glistening empire. His deals, transactions and business life were hyperthyroid. His social life was glittering. His inner life was guarded by a black curtain. It only became known through the reflection of what he did at the beginning of July 1928, of the horrifying, inexplicable action he took at that time.

Old Lowenstein, also known as "Captain" from his World War days, arrived at Croydon Airport, just south of the city of London, about six in the evening of July 1. In moments, he would be ready to take off in his Fokker Tri-Motor for a return to Brussels. This was routine for him. He seemed cheerful enough as he asked his co-pilot about the weather and cruising altitude. Lowenstein didn't like to fly high even though it was generally safer. On this pleasant summer evening, there was no need to. It looked as if the plane would arrive in Brussels in about two hours, flying at about 4,000 feet.

Apparently pleased, he sauntered into the KLM office for a routine business phone call. Then he climbed in through the rear door of the plane, to prepare for takeoff. For such a lavish private plane, the entrance was a bit awkward. The passengers had to pass by a wash basin and a toilet, which could later be shut off in flight.

This was only a minor inconvenience. The rich, thick carpet in the rest of the plane made up for it, as well as the plush armchairs available to the entourage that always accompanied Lowenstein wherever he went. He lived like a prince, and acted like one. He sat down to join his executive secretary, Hodgson, across a large airborne conference table. Two stenographers and a valet sat aft of them, ready to be of service. Forward on the flight deck were his pilot, Bob Drew, along with Bob Little, the co-pilot. They had already completed their preflight routine.

The takeoff was smooth and uneventful. Soon the Tri-Motor was circling Purley, and heading down toward Sevenoaks and Maidstone, over the rich, rolling fields of Kent, where the vines of hops were burgeoning, the oasthouses sprinkled among them, looking like miniature castles instead of silos to dry the hops. Soon they would be over the Dover Cliffs, heading out over the English Channel.

According to the testimony of the court hearings, Lowenstein looked relaxed. He took off his coat, as well as his tie and collar. He leaned back in his seat. For a few moments, he opened the sliding window next to him, apparently to look down to see if they were crossing over the Channel. It was extremely hard to hear in the cabin, with the noise of the three motors and the flimsy insulation of the day. The conversation was minimal, confined to a few shouting comments here and there. Hodgson wasn't sure, but he thought it seemed that Old Lowenstein appeared to be having a bit of difficulty in breathing. He did suffer from a minor chest ailment, but it never slowed him down.

Not long after the plane had headed out over the Channel, Lowenstein rose from his seat without comment. He made his way back to the washroom and closed the door. Hodgson went to work on his papers. The two stenographers were already transcribing their voluminous shorthand notes accumulated during the day.

By the time they were approaching the French coast, Hodgson began to get a little worried. Lowenstein had not reappeared in the main cabin, and almost fifteen minutes had gone by. He rose and began to question the valet, over the noise of the engines. Baxter, the valet, knocked several times on the door, but there was no response. The two stenographers stopped typing, and Hodgson looked concerned. He knocked again. There was still no response.

With a nod to Baxter, Hodgson grabbed the knob and threw his weight against the door. Both the men leaned forward and looked in, as the two typists stared in disbelief. The washroom was empty. There was no sign of Lowenstein. But the cabin door that led to the outside of the plane was open. It was slapping back and forth against the fuselage.

With coherent conversation over the noise of the engines impossible, Hodgson scribbled some words on a piece of paper. They read: *The Captain's gone.*

Bob Drew, handling the controls, didn't know what to make of the note. He showed it to co-pilot Little, turned over the controls, and went back into the cabin.

"What do you mean, gone?" he yelled to Hodgson.

"He's not here," Hodgson yelled back.

"Not here?"

"He's fallen out," Hodgson shouted.

Within seconds, Bob Drew was back in the pilot's seat. He

nosed the plane down, and began circling over the beaches near Dunkirk. He found a broad, clear wide stretch of smooth beach and landed. As the plane rolled to a stop, he cut the engines. They could now at least talk.

There were all sorts of theories as to what had happened. Was there any motive for murder? Was Captain Lowenstein actually on the plane? Did he fall out acidentally? Did he commit suicide? There were no definite clues to any of these. But tests showed it would be very unlikely for the door to open accidentally. Murder was practically ruled out. Certainly no one on the plane had a motive. It looked mostly like suicide. At least the signs pointed that way.

Without a *corpus delicti*, the headline-hungry public and everyone else would have to wait. But Old Lowerstein would be heard from again—just as in the case of his friend, Captain Hinchliffe.

CHAPTER VI

The search for Old Lowenstein's body seemed fruitless. In the blustery, choppy Channel, Bob Drew and the crew of the Dover harbor tug *Lady Brassey* searched through long daylight hours between Dover and Dunkirk, without success. Tests made on the exterior door of the Fokker Tri-Motor indicated that it was almost impossible for the door to be opened accidentally. The shares of Lowenstein's enterprises became a little jumpy after the tragedy, but soon leveled off and held. A snag developed at the Chepstow race track concerning Lowenstein's thoroughbred Lady Starlight, since the death of an owner would rule a horse out of a race, according to the Rules of Racing. The situation brought up the burning question as to whether Lowenstein was really dead or not.

For Emilie Hinchliffe, there was no such uncertainty about her husband. There was only the continuing uncertainty as to how she was going to support herself and her two young children. New medical bills were emerging. Little Joan had broken her collarbone in a fall from her bed. The injury was not serious, but it added to the stress. Emilie had taken the opportunity to write to Lord Beaverbrook. The reply was sympathetic, but he indicated that there was really nothing he could do further. The meaning of "further" was unclear.

Then, in that first week in July, an announcement came with dramatic suddenness: Lord Inchcape had made his decision about Elsie Mackay's private fortune of £527,000 sterling, roughly $2½ million at that time. The conditions were simple. There was to be an Elsie Mackay Fund set up. It was not to be touched for almost half a century. It was to accumulate interest and dividends till that time. Then it was to be presented to His Majesty's Government for the sole purpose of reducing the national debt. There was no mention whatever of Emilie Hinchliffe, or of the obligation Elsie Mackay had assumed in providing the nonexistent insurance policy. The statement was issued by Lord Inchcape from Glenapp Castle, Ballantrae, Ayrshire.

The Chancellor of the Exchequer at the time was a man named Winston Churchill. He gratefully accepted the Mackay fortune for His Majesty's Government. There was no further comment.

Almost within moments of the announcement, a reporter from the *Daily Express* was on Emilie Hinchliffe's door step. Her mind flashed back to her last session with Eileen Garrett. The message had been clear: Speak out to the press. Now, with the shock of Lord Inchcape's announcement, she had no hesitation. She invited the reporter in. She told of how her husband had not received any of his salary or expenses during the last six weeks before the flight. She spoke of Elsie Mackay's promise to her that the insurance was in good order. She told how she was unsuccessfully looking for a job. She stated that she wanted nothing more than the provisions Elsie Mackay had covered in the business agreement with her husband.

Suddenly, the newspaper empires of both Lord Beaverbrook and the late Lord Northcliffe went into full action. Headlines followed, one after the other:

MRS. HINCHLIFFE NEARLY PENNILESS

MRS. HINCHLIFFE'S DISTRESS OVER CHILDREN'S FUTURE

WIDOW OF CAPT. HINCHLIFFE: COMMONS QUESTION

The House of Commons lost little time in examining the question. The barrage of headlines brought up a sharp point of order: Was Parliament justified in accepting the full sum of the estate until the obligations that Elsie Mackay had accepted for Hinchliffe were met?

But Winston Churchill was firm. He notified Mr. Hore-Belisha, the Liberal leader of the House of Commons, that Parliament had no business poking its nose into the Chancellor of the Exchequer's affairs. Hore-Belisha rose from his seat to say: "Without detracting from the generosity of Lord and Lady Inchcape, is the Chancellor aware that Mrs. Hinchliffe, wife of the pilot, who was left a widow as the result of the accident, says she has certain moral claims against the estate?"

Mr. Churchill replied: "That has nothing to do with the Chancellor of the Exchequer."

In the face of the stormy headlines, there was nothing but silence from Lord Inchcape. Queried by the press at his Ayrshire castle, he simply stated that he had no comment.

In this climate of amplified despair, Emilie went about trying to document the technical details of her husband's flight that she had received in her sessions with Eileen Garrett. It kept her mind away from resentment of Inchcape's action, and the anxiety of waiting to hear about several job applications she had filed.

With the help of Gordon Sinclair and Air Ministry officials, she discovered that the flight plan could, under the circumstances of the night of the flight, result in Hinchliffe almost reaching the Azores, under the cruising speed and weather conditions. She traced the Gulf Stream to see where any bodies or plane wreckage might theoretically have drifted with the currents. There were several possibilities. The Gulf Stream passed just north of the Azores, coming from the west to the east. At the Azores, it split in two parts. One part was called the North Atlantic drift. It swept north, past the west coast of Ireland. The west wind drift went south, past the Canary Islands, and then circled back west across the Atlantic, past Jamaica and on to the Gulf of Mexico. Conceivably, any remains of the crash could have gone either to the Irish coast or to Jamaica. The last message she had received about the whereabouts of her husband's body, mentioning Jamaica, could at least be possible. Her belief that she was in touch with Raymond increased.

After the consultation with the Air Ministry, Emilie went home to the children, her concern for their future growing. She was glad the Sinclairs were staying with her; they helped to keep her in good cheer. But the evenings were long, and she went to bed early. The Sinclairs followed soon after. At some time during the night—she later found it was about four in the morning—she was awakened. There were heavy footsteps moving along the hall outside her bedroom door. The sound was unmistakable. The footfalls then moved down the stairs and faded away. She was startled at first. Then she thought: It was probably Gordon Sinclair. Perhaps he couldn't sleep, and wanted to take a morning walk. She lay back and fell asleep again.

The next morning at breakfast, the Sinclairs asked Emilie if she had gotten up early or had put on heavy boots to walk about the house before daybreak. She asked them the same question. It took some time before they could convince each other that no one had been out of bed in the early morning hours. Emilie warned herself that she must not let this kind of thing get out of line. She had to be careful of her imagination. In these times, it could be too easily triggered, and she knew it. The possibility of ghost footsteps was not even mentioned.

Emilie went again for another session with Eileen Garrett in the middle of July. There was still no job in sight, and her anxieties continued to grow. She warned herself that she must not become dependent on these apparent communications. She found herself wondering whether there would be any possible information on the eventual outcome of the financial problem. But if she received an indication in such a strange manner, could she possibly count on it?

The sessions were almost settling into a routine now. Uvani's apparent voice would make several clearly evidential remarks, as if to reassure Emilie that her husband was the actual person speaking through the voice. Then the communication would shift back and forth with Uvani as a go-between, or Uvani repeating the direct words of Hinchliffe. Emilie would transcribe, as always, being careful not to miss a word. On this July morning, the voice came out as usual:

"Your husband wants to talk to you. He has been impressing you to come here. He asks: How is baby, how is Pammy? He saw the photograph you took of her recently."

This was the kind of point that had slowly built up Emilie's assurance that the communication was valid. She had recently taken a photograph. It had been one that she was fond of. No one else knew it.

"Your husband is standing very close to you," the voice went on. "He says he still feels that he must keep close to you, till everything is settled. He gives you very much love. He tells me to tell you not to lose heart, not to give up hope. At the very last moment when everything seems lost, help will come.''

Even if she was coming to believe in the validity of the messages, what assurance was there that this wasn't the urgent wishful thinking of Raymond to encourage her in her financial crisis? But the subject matter characteristically changed again:

"He has talked to Elsie. She is disgusted. They are talking about the insurance. . . .'

Talking? Was there such a thing as talking on this nebulous "other side"? This was what was so hard to believe. The concept kept bothering her. The continuation of life on such an ordinary, mundane basis. But the communication went on:

"He felt it was in order because he knew that such a policy can be taken out. He would never have made the journey if he had known that she had left this in the air. They discussed it twenty-four hours before starting from the runway at Cranwell. She assured him that all was in order. He was also to get the sum of £5,000 sterling for the flight, and she had promised him much work to be done in international flying. He was going to undertake three other flights. He never had a doubt that all would be well. He says that if she had kept her head, we would have made the journey. It was too much for me, he says. I could have made land if she had remained more stable.''

Then, turning to the question that was boiling in Emilie's mind, the voice called Uvani quoted Hinchliffe: "I cannot understand Lord Inchcape giving her money away. He is going to continue his attitude for a long time. In the end, public opinion will be too much. I have great hope for some fund to be released through the *Daily Express*. Lord Beaverbrook might contribute to this. I do not think that Inchcape will give under his own name, but anonymously. Do you remember July 25?''

Emilie now responded to these direct questions without hesitation. "Yes," she said. "It was the date you gave me last time."

Uvani's voice responded, "He promises that it is still coming. But it may run to the last day in July. But it will be in July. Beaverbrook's persuasiveness is coming to some good. Maybe in the end, Inchcape will give it, but not directly.''

Emilie couldn't stop her doubts returning. Inchcape had shown every sign of being adamant. Winston Churchill had shown no inclination to let Parliament even consider the question of her receiving any of the estate. The end of July was only some two weeks off. As if to reassure her, the message continued with Uvani's comments: "The money will come right at the end of the month. Just to show you there is a method in his madness, he gives you the names 'Walter George Raymond.' He says it is not so silly. Beaverbrook's persuasiveness is coming to some good."

But with Inchcape's decision already made so firmly, it was hard not to be disheartened. Still, she continued to listen:

"There is also another paper, the *Daily Mail*, which is very sound. I feel that the Northcliffe press is also watching on your behalf. Someone there is interested, not in Spiritualism, but that does not matter."

The tone of the message became more relaxed: "I have been more settled with my fate lately, but I am unhappy for you. I shall be with you until I see that your future is assured. Thank Brancker for his kindness. Nothing will be done through the Civilian Flying organization, even though Brancker represents them. He is very kind himself. He has our interests at heart. All I want to do is assist you, and get you right. Kiss Pam and Joan for me."

Her husband was saying things like this constantly in the messages. They almost brought her to the verge of tears.

"I am still about the house," the message went on. "I nearly touched the red traveling clock by your bed the other night, but was afraid of frightening you. But I am going to show you that I *am* a reality. Do not get too interested, however, in this psychic subject and all the dabbling. I object to it. It is all right that we can talk, but don't get carried away. I am always in the house. I can hear you all talk about me in the evening. I do not want to be overcurious, but I can hear you all. My thoughts are all of you and the children. I'm glad Joan is better and eating well." Uvani seemed to offer a comment at this point: "He is devoted to the children."

Emilie interspersed a question. "Can he actually *see* us?"

"He is actually in the house," the voice of Uvani answered. "He sees Betty taking them out, and sees Pam in her pram. He heard you say Pam was restless, and that she had trouble with her teeth. He can see and hear all that is going on."

These questions had been building up in Emilie's mind. She still had trouble conceiving this. Her thoughts immediately went back to the strange sound of footsteps in the early morning hours. She asked Uvani, whom she was now beginning to take for granted as a real entity: "Was he in the house one morning early, walking on the landing and down the stairs?" she asked.

"Yes," came the reply. "It was four o'clock one morning. He wanted to give an implication he was starting on an early morning flight as he used to do in the summer. He was trying to imply this. Don't have too much to do with this subject of the psychic. He just wants to help you while there is need. Keep your case in front for the next two or three weeks. Publicity did come, and will come again."

Then there was a pause, and the words came again in measured tones: "Another casualty is coming along that will startle people more than they have ever been startled."

Emilie's thoughts immediately went to the recent tragedy that had overtaken Captain Lowenstein. But the next words seemed to rule that out: "Old Lowenstein is not over here at all. I have not seen him, and have not heard of anyone who has."

Again, this crazy word-picture of a life-after-life on a scale so similar to the world itself. Emilie would have to make it a point to try to clarify this, to learn what possible sort of existence could go on after the body was dead, when all that remained was the mind and consciousness. And what was this new warning? It sounded ominous. She waited for more information. But now the session seemed to be coming to an end, without any explanation of the new casualty, without any further information on the mysterious death of Old Lowenstein. She listened again, as the closing words were spoken:

"If anything unexpected happens or you get into any dilemma, come to me and let me talk to you. I will help until everything will be cleared up. . . ."

The session ended. There was much learned and much else suggested that could or would be learned. She was almost frightened by the prediction that help would absolutely come by the end of July. It was stated as if it were a commitment. If it failed to materialize, she would not only be in a desperate state financially; much of her faith in what she was beginning to believe in so completely, could be measurably reduced.

* * *

If there was any reaction from Lord Inchcape to the flood of news articles about Emilie Hinchliffe's plight, he gave no public sign. Neither the Beaverbrook nor the Northcliffe papers let up in their barrage. As if to remind Lord Inchcape that others were concerned, Lady Houston, the widow of a rival millionaire shipowner, sent Emilie a check for £100 sterling, if only as a token. Emilie was moved, but it did not solve her problem of survival. Parliament's hands were tied in the face of the action of the Chancellor of the Exchequer, and it clearly appeared that the enormous fortune of Elsie Mackay would rest in the vaults of her executors until 1977, when it would turn out to have grown to nearly £4 million sterling, or roughly $7½ million dollars. Neither Her Majesty's treasury nor Emilie Hinchliffe could share in the award in 1928, and under the stated conditions Emilie could not share in it ever.

It wasn't long before more news came of Old Lowenstein. On July 15, a British trawler was making its way through the angry chop of the English Channel, when a crewman spotted something bobbing up and down in the waves, off the starboard bow. The trawler was approximately in mid-channel. The body was that of Captain Lowenstein. It was naked and unrecognizable.

But a wrist watch found on it was unquestionably that of the millionaire, and a peculiar-shaped denture confirmed the identification. There was evidence that the body hit the water with tremendous impact, causing his death either by the fall or by drowning. The case was classified as accidental death or possible suicide, and was closed.

Until the last day of July, Emilie never gave up hope that a miracle would save her from bankruptcy. As the end of the month approached, the chances grew slimmer with each day. There was further bad news.

Lt. Colonel C. L. Malone, a member of Parliament, asked Lord Thomson to see if Hinchliffe's widow wouldn't be eligible for a service pension or other Air Ministry award. Malone pointed out that the widow and her two children were in very poor circumstances and urgently needed help. Lord Thomson replied that as a civilian flyer, Hinchliffe was not eligible for either pension or award, and Sir Samuel Hoare, the famous Conservative British statesman, sealed off the possibility by pointing out that Hinchliffe was not an officer in the RAF reserve, and the Air Ministry therefore could do nothing.

Emilie had accepted her provisional belief in the possible reality of life after death, and possible communication with her husband, in what she called her probationary period. She was hoping that a full belief in this reality might fill the religious vacuum she had experienced since childhood. In her own mind, she did not stipulate the optimistic prediction for the end of July as a condition of her belief or disbelief. She was becoming resigned to accepting the prediction if it failed to be fulfilled, as a possible false note that might creep into an otherwise rich bank of verifiable data that had now mounted to extraordinary proportions.

But on the evening of July 31, the words kept running through her head from her previous session with Eileen Garrett: *It may run to the last day in July, but it will be in July.*

As she finished dinner that evening, she was thinking that there were so few other mistakes in all the long hours she had heard the apparent voice of Uvani speaking through the channel of Eileen Garrett. She determined that she would not, however, allow her disappointment in the failure of the prediction to shake her basic faith that she was in touch with Raymond. She put the children to bed, kissed them good night—two times each, in memory of Raymond. Then she came downstairs to listen to a BBC program on the wireless radio.

At 8:30 P.M., the telephone rang.

Sir Sefton Brancker was continuing his hectic schedule without letup, all through the summer months. In addition to stomping the country to see that every village and hamlet had its own aerodrome, he would be having lunch with the Italian General Italo Balbo at Claridge's, driving to an air display at Hendon with the Sultan of Muscat and other distinguished visitors, dashing to Berlin for an air show, sitting down to lunch in Brussels and dinner in Cologne, flying an old Handley Page W-8 to various continental points, speaking at the Hyde Park Hotel to the Society of Motor Manufacturers, and still wilting his collars on the dance floor, with occasional time out to chew up a monocle or tell a joke.

Foremost on Brancker's mind was the establishment of sensible air routes from England to India, to Africa, to Australia—to every part of the Empire. He flew the plane himself. His landings were not always graceful. They often called him Bad Bump Brancker, and it was not without reason.

In spite of all this, he was keeping his eye on Lord Inchcape. He couldn't believe that gentleman could be so obdurate, so insensible to public opinion in giving away his daughter's entire fortune totally to a faceless government that could do nothing with the money until 1977. Hinchliffe was a hero to Brancker, as to many other airmen. Brancker knew nothing about the long messages that Emilie Hinchliffe was apparently receiving from her husband, but he did know that he would continue to put pressure on Beaverbrook and the Northcliffe papers, and that somehow Lord Inchcape would have to bend under the pressure.

But he was surprised as anyone in session at the House of Commons on the last day in July, when Winston Churchill suddenly made a totally unexpected announcement. The session had been routine. There was plenty going on in the world to catch the attention of the M.P.'s. Stalin was laying down one of his series of Five-Year Plans. The Kellogg-Briand Peace Pact was being framed, which would condemn war as an instrument of international policy. The German dirigible *Graf Zeppelin* now had clearly won the race against the R-100 and the R-101. It was getting ready to fly around the world with twenty passengers and a crew of thirty-eight. It was a bit of a sting to England's pride, because neither of its airships was remotely ready to fly.

When Winston Churchill stood up to make his announcement, the yawning stopped before his first sentence had been completed:

"Lord Inchcape," he announced in his eloquent tones, "being desirous that the Elsie Mackay Fund of £500,000 sterling, given by him and Lady Inchcape and their family to the nation, should not be the occasion or object of any complaint by other sufferers from the disaster in which his daughter lost her life, has placed at the disposal of the Chancellor of the Exchequer a further sum of £10,000 sterling from his own property to be applied for the purpose of meeting any complaint in such manner as the Chancellor of the Exchequer in his absolute discretion may think fit. The Chancellor of the Exchequer has handed the sum of £10,000 sterling to the Public

Trustee for administration accordingly.'' The reluctant grant obviously was for the benefit of Emilie Hinchliffe.

Sir Sefton Brancker felt particularly good about all this. He was glad that he had nagged Beaverbrook and kept after him like a terrier. There were plenty of other problems around, especially the R-101 and its snail-like progress toward completion. Brancker was a little embarrassed by some of the airship's press notices, which had promised so much in the face of so little progress. Not that he wasn't in love with the damned ship; everybody who worked on it was. It was just that when one problem was licked, another seemed to appear.

There were those giant gas bags that lifted the ship and kept it in the air. They were to be fitted as cells into the girder structure, like a series of huge bass drums on end. But the bags were sloppy. They weren't rigid, even though the structure of the hull was. They were flabby, clumsy sacks standing as high as a ten-story building, most of them. They were made of gold-beater s skin, a fine membrane on the outer part of the intestine of an ox, of all things. They had all—Germans, Americans, and British—tried to find a substitute, but nothing worked better.

The R-101, however, was trying a new design. The bags were clumsy to make and expensive. The material had to be soaked in warm water, the fat removed, and the surface scraped with a blunt knife, then assembled in enormous sheets. The gold-beater's skins looked like thin, transparent parchment. When wet, they formed together in continuous sheets, without glue. A little glycerine helped to keep them pliable. This stuff formed the inside layer of the cotton bags that the sheets were later glued to.

Will Charlton, the chief supply officer at Cardington, kept a sharp eye out on the bags. With hydrogen in them, they kept the ship in the air, like a fantastic toy balloon. But if they leaked, the ship could plummet to earth. Charlton was making sure they were free from defects, as they were boosted up inside the skeleton. Small holes were bound to happen. They weren't too dangerous. But a big rip could be disastrous, causing a sudden deflation. A one-foot hole could cause the loss of nearly 10,000 cubic feet of hydrogen a minute.

Inside the bags, the gas could surge and swirl. Then the bags might chafe against the girders or against each other. To stop this, there was now an elaborate web of wires to hold the bags in place. It was a new system, and Charlton worried about it. The wires girdled the bags not only to hold them in place, but to transmit the lift of the bags to the frame of the ship. The new system was supposed to stop the bags from rubbing against the longitudinal girders and against each other. There were several hundred wires attached to each bag to accomplish the job. They formed a mesh, like a giant spider web to keep the flabby bags under control.

Another novelty, among many on the R-101, was its Diesel engines. They had never been used before, on any airship. They were heavy. They were Beardmore Tornados, the kind being used on the Canadian railways. There were five of them in separate power cars. They would be slung along the bottom of the envelope, looking like toy cars at an amusement park. Power eggs, they called them. Together, they weighed 17 tons, compared to 9 for the engines of the R-100, and 7 for those of the *Graf Zeppelin*, which were ordinary gasoline engines. But the Diesels saved fuel, and they used heavy oil, instead of the more volatile gasoline. They were therefore safer, but Charlton and the rest of the team still worried about them.

The heavy Diesels cut down the useful lift of the ship to about 35 tons. The designers had hoped for 90 tons of useful lift. This is the lift that is left over after the weight of the ship itself is taken care of. Thirty-five tons would hardly amount to a profitable payload. The engines were also slow and underpowered for the size of the ship. Even designer Richmond recognized as much. But they were stuck with them. There had been so much publicity about this great new advance, they couldn't back down. Richmond made one attempt to try to shift to the lighter gasoline engines. He was turned down by the top Air Ministry officials.

These were only a few of the problems Brancker was trying to solve in between his trips seeking new air routes across the world. He knew many of his colleagues thought he was biting off more than he could chew, but he had a dream and he meant to fulfill it. So did the others at Bedford-Cardington. They were all determined to override their mistakes.

*   *   *

When Emilie Hinchliffe picked up the phone at 8:30 that night of July 31, a reporter from the *Daily Express* was on the other end of the line. He read her Winston Churchill's statement to the House of Commons. She was stunned. She simply couldn't believe it. He gave her further news, off the record. Ever since her letter to Lord Beaverbrook, the publisher had intervened personally in her cause. The final push had come from Lord Beaverbrook and Brancker, along with the Northcliffe press.

Again, there was no comment from behind the walls of Glenapp Castle. Lord Inchcape kept his silence. Emilie gave her reaction to the *Daily Express* reporter. Controlling her emotions, she said:

"I think the provision of this fund by Lord Inchcape wonderfully good of him. I have no knowledge of course as to what will be done, but my hopes have been very much raised, and my prospects and those of my little girls seem much brighter I have arranged to consult my solicitor in the morning, after which I shall send in my claim for the money. I am very grateful to Lord Inchcape, since he has apparently given this sum out of his own pocket."

The burden was lifted. She felt no rancor, only relief. But the incredible fact that the fund had come through—at precisely the time the voice of Uvani had predicted—was so stunning that it made Emilie reel.

Now there was no question in her mind about the validity of the messages. She went again for a session with Eileen Garrett the following day. Her confidence returned, and her determination increased to try to persuade others in what she now fully believed: Life is continuous. There is no death. We continue with our own personality, we see, we perceive. We apparently go on with our own development after we pass through the door.

She wanted to press for exactly how and where such an afterlife existed. Her sense of logic demanded that she visualize what form her husband and the apparent friends he was meeting assumed. The very matter-of-factness of the picture he was painting in these sessions actually bothered her. It all seemed too pat. How did communication take place? Where was the geography of this strange country, if it did indeed exist? All logic, all reason of the scientific age was against it. Yet logic and reason told her that the hard facts, the unassailable evidence and details that had emerged, could not have been falsified. The event on the last day in July was the clincher.

At the next session, Uvani's voice came through almost immediately after Eileen had settled into a trance state. With its usual Oriental flourish, Uvani's voice began the session:

"Greetings and peace be upon you and your life and your work and your household," the voice began. "There is only your husband near you. He is delighted. His actual words are: 'Milly, I am so glad to find that I am with you again. I never tire of being near you. I am so very grateful to you for keeping so close. If I had not got through, you would have been unhappy, and I would have been in anguish of mind and body about you and the babies. Does Joan yet know that I am not coming back?' "

"No," Emilie answered. She no longer felt awkward about answering this voice. She was waiting to hear what would be said about the unbelievable happenings of the day before. In her excitement and relief, she had almost forgotten her shorthand book. "Time will make it easier," the voice added. Then:

"The days of waiting have been long, but I knew about the fund," the voice went on. "I said he would not do it publicly. I am rather surprised he did it in the open. He has been battered into it. Public opinion has been against him. Thank all the gods, I knew it would be right. The money must be invested on behalf of you and Joan and Pam."

Emilie was moved. She could sense his deep concern. It was just as he had been in life. "I knew, Milly, the money would be coming. I would not have told you so otherwise. Another move in the right direction was the *Express*. I said, the *Express,* the *Express,* the *Express.*"

Then a comment from Uvani came in, as it usually did, in the strange back-and-forth shifting between subjective and objective: "He is very happy and overjoyed. He says he wishes he had been there last evening, when the news came through."

The session rambled on, spelling out in complex detail the events and routine of Emilie and the children since the previous session. Raymond Hinchliffe's apparent message mentioned Little Joan's broken collarbone. He mentioned Bonzo, the dog, for the first time by name. He brought up several messages for his close friend Captain John Morkham. They were technical. He mentioned problems with the magneto, ignition and plugs. He even mentioned the serial number of an old type of magneto: CV11352. Morkham later confirmed the problems, but not the serial number. Then, in another sudden shift, the message was:

"So they have buried Albert, Old Lowenstein, I mean. But I will never believe it. Now put this to John. He knows what I am talking about: If he fell out of that machine, the door would have crashed to, and left a mark on the machine. There was no perceptible mark on the door. I still believe the fellow is not here. I have not seen him yet. Until I meet him, I won't believe it."

But only a few days before this message came through to Emilie, another study group in a London suburb was conducting experiments in automatic writing. The group was headed by Mrs. E. M. Taylor, who had a reputation for caution and sobriety. Automatic writing could be done in several ways. The most effective came through a person with psychic ability, who simply put a pencil in her hand, and made her mind blank, until the hand would automatically begin writing, sometimes fast and furiously. It was a common phenomenon, and the Society for Psychical Research people had documented hundreds of cases with verifiable information.

Mrs. Taylor's group was startled when one of their gathering found her own hand writing at considerable speed, with an apparent message from Alfred Lowenstein. The first information contained names of the financier's former associates. These were later checked, and found to be accurate. But then a personal message followed:

"No idea of suicide entered my head till I went to inspect the plane before takeoff," the medium's hand wrote. "Later I suddenly felt an irresistible impulse to open the door and end my existence. I fought it, but each time it grew stronger. A fierce longing took possession of me which I could not deny.

"What I went through you will never understand. I longed for death more passionately than a condemned man longs for life. Why, I could not explain. Shall I ever forget that awful plunge into space? Yes, I realized for a moment my mistake, but too late. . . ."

Then one of the study group asked: "What happened then?"

"I do not know," the automatic handwriting continued. "I saw a body floating near me in the water. I recognized my own face staring at me. I shrieked with fear. I thought I was mad, mad, mad. Stop—have you the strength to hear the rest?''

The group confirmed that they did. The writing went on:

"Next, have you the power to imagine my seeing gay scenes of my life pass before my eyes? Memories of many foolish words and wrong deeds flashed into my vision. 'Hell!' I cried. 'Hell, I am in it!' I saw my corpse rotting before my eyes. I was connected with it by a kind of cord that would not break.

"All sorts of explanations came to my mind, but I could only think of madness. Was I really in a body? I seemed to be. Yet there was my body in the sea. What was I? 'God,' I cried. 'God,' I shouted. 'Help me!' ''

The message continued. Lowenstein said his body seemed to return to earth. He saw some of his staff, waiting for news as to whether his body had been found. He screamed at them that he was Lowenstein, that he was with them. They were looking right at him, but they appeared to neither see nor hear him. He found himself in London suddenly, without needing to travel there, just as in a dream. The scene just seemed to merge in with his previous scene.

He was on Brook Street, the message went on, on the way to Claridge's. He walked into the hotel. He saw a pile of letters waiting for him. "I tried to touch them," the words of the automatic writing continued. "My terror increased. My fingers went right through them. 'God,' I cried, 'this is hell indeed.' Loss of life was nothing, but loss of power to make impression on earthly things was unbearable to me. I tried to say a prayer for my misdeeds, but no words sounded. A man entered the hotel, John Rosmarck. As I greeted him, he even raised his hand to mine, as if he felt my presence. Then he shivered and said to the door porter, 'How cold I feel. Any news of Lowenstein yet?' ''

Unlike Emilie Hinchliffe, who was only at the beginning of her exploration into the world of psychic possibilities, Mrs. Taylor's group had been studying the phenomena for several years. What reduced their surprise at this harrowing message was that in the dozens of cases they had explored, the same pattern always seemed to emerge.

There was the flash review of the person's life that swiftly passed before his eyes, like a motion picture montage. There was the experience of not realizing you were dead and of looking down at your own body. There was the experience of trying to talk to people you had just left, and finding that they neither saw nor heard you. There was the special, self-imposed hell that seemed to be reserved mostly for those who had murdered or who had taken their own lives. But this was not an exterior hell, or a "day of judgment." It was literally self-imposed, a self-judgment that stung.

The files of the British Society for Psychical Research were also bulging with cases like this. They were monotonously the same. It would not be until fifty years later that such material would be examined and correlated by serious medical researchers like Drs. Moody and Kubler-Ross. Right at this time, in 1928, Mrs. Taylor's group was fumbling, but they were clinical in their outlook. They noticed there was one usual factor that was missing in the message. Usually, there was a report of a guide or a friend who would often be said to arrive at the side of an earth-bound deceased, to help him adjust to the new conditions, and to help him in his gradual spiritual growth.

Mrs. Taylor's group sensed that there would be more coming from the apparently distraught financier later. They closed the session with plans for attempting to renew the contact at a later date.

Neither Emilie Hinchliffe nor Mrs. Taylor was aware that they were almost simultaneously involved with some kind of word from Old Lowenstein, whose death remained a mystery to the world, in spite of the recent finding of the body in the English Channel. The coincidence of two "spirit messages" being received by two separate mediums was another event common in the records of the British Society for Psychical Research. Studies had been made over the years, with careful attention to how the independent information matched up. In many cases, the results had been startling, with detailed information matching exactly. There were sometimes inconsistencies. No psychic channel was perfect. Interference and static would crop up, just as with a radio set. But in the classic cases of the British Society, the mass of evidence led researchers to concede that the material had to come from the deceased or be the result of some kind of residual telepathy. The possibilities, at least, had been reduced to two.

Because of the elaborate details Emilie Hinchliffe was receiving all through her long sessions with Eileen Garrett, she could not accept the telepathy theory. No residual telepathy could predict a future date, or tell what her children had been up to over several weeks, she felt. Her husband's personality was coming through too clearly, as well as the facts reported, which she could confirm at a later date. As her rather joyful and hopeful session drew to an end on the first day of August, she was alarmed by a sudden sense of urgency the next words took on. They brought up the subject of the struggling airship program:

"I am afraid they are getting things rushed. How can I tell Johnston? You remember the last bad accident." Johnston was the navigator assigned to the R-101.

This must be referring, Emilie thought, to the tragedy of the R-38 airship, which had broken in half over the Humber River, just before being delivered to the U.S. Navy.

"I wish to goodness," the words continued, "it were possible for John Morkham to tell Johnston. I may sound silly, but I am certain, if things go on, there will be a buckling because some of the wires holding the fabric are not strong enough. I cannot help thinking there may be trouble with it. I want them to have another look at the wires, to see that all is in order. Johnston must know. I knew Johnston well. If Morkham could tell them in confidence, and ask them to be more careful. I know what I am talking about."

This was Raymond, Emilie was thinking. Aviation had been his life. It was now apparently his afterlife. The subject apparently dominated his thoughts in both conditions.

She continued her shorthand, as the message went on:

"There is also a new type of engine they are trying out which interests me. It is *not* going to be a success. Things are not right at headquarters. Bear it in mind. A new type of engine. It will not be a success. Tell them to be careful. It is not stabilized as it should be."

On the way back to her home, Emilie thought about these things. She could speak the language of the airmen adequately, but how could she possibly warn Raymond's friend Johnston, the navigator of the R-101, on the basis of an alleged message from her dead husband? It would seem absurd, a travesty. She wouldn't mention it even to Gordon Sinclair or John Morkham. In spite of her new convictions, she was still determined not to let them get out of hand.

She would hold her tongue. The last thing in the world she wanted to be was an alarmist. Her main mission, she felt, was to help as many people as possible share her new belief that we clearly went on after life was over.

She still felt the strong need to press for adequate details on how to visualize exactly what could be expected in this indefinable location her husband seemed to exist in. Like everyone else of the age, she was a child of the new scientific outlook.

A young professor of logic at Oxford University was just beginning to formulate some interesting theories along this line. His name was H. H. Price (not to be confused with Harry Price). This question nagged at him, also. He felt that in order to consider even the remote possibility of an afterlife, you had to form a very clear idea of what it possibly would be like. Naturally, it couldn't be physical, because the body was useless after death. But there had to be some kind of body, or there wouldn't be a "you." We'd at least have to take our memories with us, because there could be no *personal* survival without them. We also couldn't leave our personalities behind, *if* we were to continue to be ourselves. But there just possibly might be a nonmaterial body, like the one we have in dreams; a body that could be recognized and communicated with.

Where was the geography we could put these memories, our personality, and our nonmaterial body? According to Price, we could already observe this geography, this real estate—in our dreams. Here was a place outside of the physical universe, but it could be just as real. It was space, but it wasn't physical space. You couldn't locate it on a map, but anyone who had a vivid dream could tell you that the buildings, the fields, the mountains, the cities viewed in the dream were just as real as when awake. So were the people in the dream, and so was the communication between them—even though at some times in a dream, it seemed to be nonvocal. In fact, Price concluded, we would all think the pseudophysical world of our dreams would be the real world, if we didn't wake up to compare them.

This dream-image type of real estate, Price thought, could account for the reports that came through mediums, when they reported that afterlife beings saw old friends, saw other places, communicated with and talked to others, who appeared just as real as they did on the earth's surface. A number of like-minded people, operating under the laws of psychology instead of the laws of physics, could interact telepathically with each other, and share a common dream-image world, including contact with psychic sensitives still living on earth.

It was this sort of thinking that Emilie Hinchliffe was developing in her own thoughts. A dream-image world could never be overcrowded any more than the world viewed in dreams could. It could shift at will. Raymond could summon up his old friends, as he had said so many times, and he could recognize them just as he would in a dream.

She had been meaning to ask Eileen Garrett if, in some session, her husband could be directed in some psychic way to talk about this broad aspect of the question that was foremost in her mind. She was delighted when she was told that it might be entirely possible to get some details, at least, if Emilie would guide her questions in that direction.

Eileen's time schedule was crowded, and she was not in the best of health. But she assured Emilie that she would arrange for such a session as soon as possible. Emilie looked forward to it because she felt this detailed description was the one thing missing in her comprehension of what had become the most important area in her life.

CHAPTER VII

Conan Doyle followed the Hinchliffe case with interest. He knew that Eileen Garrett had integrity, and he knew that Emilie Hinchliffe was screening the results with a cold, analytical eye in spite of her bereavement. He was gratified that Emilie was a highly skilled shorthand specialist. This was important. With so many nuances in the messages, a clumsy transcription of so much material could distort the evidence that came through. Emilie was not only deeply motivated by the personal impact; she was more qualified than any run-of-the-mill stenographer who might miss the aeronautical jargon that she had lived with over many years.

Doyle was still going through his painful verbal battles with researcher Harry Price. At times, they were bloody. Price continued to regard Doyle as sincere and lovable, but entirely too credulous. Price resented the fact that when he came down hard on a medium he tested—as he did with most—Doyle would write and condemn him for unnecessary roughness. But Price noted that when he found one of the rare mediums he considered valid and unimpeachable, Doyle would finally write him a letter of praise.

By the autumn of 1928, the rift had widened to the point where Doyle, as president of the London Spiritualist Alliance, told Price he and his laboratory were no longer welcome in the upstairs quarters of the Alliance building. "You cannot expect to write false and

129

libelous statements about people, and think they will accept them with patient acquiescence,'' Doyle wrote.

But Price stayed on. In spite of an almost daily exchange of calumny, the battle began to abate. Both became more conciliatory. "I do hope," Doyle finally wrote, "that behind the scenes in spiritualism [Doyle preferred the term 'psychic religion'] you have found some noble and beautiful things—consolation for sad hearts and hope for those who are hopeless. . . . I hope you will not dwell always on what is sordid and negative. It is all very well to 'warn the public,' but if some writer wrote about the Church of Rome from the inside, and had nothing to tell but adulteries and robberies by priests, it would not be excused that it was to warn the public. . . .''

Price *was* rough on mediums. What Doyle failed to appreciate was that those precious few that did stand up under his anvil, bore a seal of approval that few could achieve. Chief among those Price considered effective were Mrs. Osborne Leonard, the Austrian medium named Rudi Schneider; an English girl called Stella C.; and Eileen Garrett.

Doyle recognized there was fraud extant. He divided it into two types: conscious and unconscious. The latter type he felt could be tolerated to some degree if it wasn't repeated, and if verifiable material later was produced. Doyle had no patience with conscious fraud. "We are in the presence of the most odious and blasphemous crime which a human being can commit," he wrote.

Price was simplistic. A medium had to submit to scientific tests if he or she wanted to be accepted by psychic investigators. In the crossfire of the battle, Eileen Garrett continued her own work in the Alliance building, bearing the complete stamp of approval of both Doyle and Price—an extreme rarity.

Doyle's years of study led him to search not only for the evidence of life-after-death, and of communication with those who had died, but for a precise description of life beyond the grave. He started with what he called the basis of the "continuity of personality."

If an afterlife is a continuous process, the personality has to remain and move along with us. He studied testimony on the alleged quality of life-after-death from the files of the British Society of Psychical Research and other lengthy reports from the better mediums. He found that there was a marked agreement in details from widely separated sources. The serious accounts describing this netherland were all essentially similar.

They described a life not at all unlike the one we live in here in the world. He compared case after case related by mediums. So many points coincided that he felt these descriptions had to be accepted on the basis of pure Sherlock Holmes–type reasoning and deduction.

Many thoughtful people accepted the theory that communication could be made with those who had died. But many balked at accepting the vivid descriptions of what life allegedly was like there. Sir Oliver Lodge's son had sent such detailed messages that it hardly seemed he had left this life at all. The situation was almost like a son away at college. The verifiable data Lodge received from his deceased son through mediums could be fully confirmed as to the details of his life while he was alive.

Confidential family material of the most intimate nature came through to the famous scientist, not only from one medium but from several at different times and places. This happened even when Lodge sent a substitute to a session so that his own identity would be screened from the medium. Many would accept this phase of Lodge's study. They balked, however, when the son's messages described his conditions in the afterlife. The description of the place where he ostensibly had gone was so clear and concrete that even those who believed he was communicating could not accept the picture. There was so little difference from the current world.

Conan Doyle's theory was that we could not accept one part of the message without accepting the full one. He felt that there was a vast amount of concurrent evidence that gave an exact picture of the life beyond. Few people had studied the evidence with the thoroughness Doyle brought to the subject. He was convinced that any who did would gradually come to accept the validity as he had. Lodge concurred.

Emilie Hinchliffe finally arranged for a series of sessions on this line exclusively. She would not seek personal details for confirmation. She was already satisfied with those. She wanted to explore this nebulous field of what life was actually like in the world in which her husband now seemed to be living.

Again she was cautious. She even made it a point to practice her shorthand again. Whatever information came through, she wanted it to be accurate. She wanted it to be without distortion on her part. If her husband, Raymond, continued to be as articulate as he had been in his personal messages, he would reflect the thoroughness and attention to detail that had been so characteristic of him when he had been alive.

The session with Eileen Garrett began as usual. The words flowed freely, and with little hesitation:

What I want to tell you is what very few people understand: how it feels to go out of the body; what I personally have been doing ever since the realization of the fact came to me; and finally to acquaint you with the impressions I have gained in the new life here since.

Transition from the physical body to the ethereal body occupies only a matter of moments. There is no pain in the severance of the two, and so alike are they, that it is some while—probably in some cases, days—before this transition from the one state to the other is noticed. In my case, it was noticed quickly, because I had been conscious of facing Death for many hours before actually passing.

As you can imagine yourself, when I found myself high and dry in another country, I began to think. What had happened? Only one of two things could have happened. Either I had been rescued whilst unconscious and taken to a land I knew nothing of—or I had died.

It was the latter. If therefore the waking up in my case was attended with so little change registered in my mind, you will understand what an easy process passing from one life to another is.

Actually, I feel no different. Nothing angelic, nothing ethereal, nothing one would think of as being connected with Heaven or the Hereafter.

My actual experience is that I am as real in the life as I have been to you, and that all growth towards that great happiness and that great Heaven they talk of, must be a slower process than most people believe.

Milly, people will not agree that this is true, but it is my firm belief that I am right. The soul or ego is such a delicate structure, that no quick change can take place without shocking that soul and, for a moment, putting the whole thing into a disorganized state.

If you ask me where I am, what I am, and what I see, I have to tell you that in the first instance, I found myself in a grey, damp, and

most disagreeable country that looked to me barren, almost like the
wastes of Belgium I used to fly over. Imagine such a country, with
here and there groups of three or four badly grown, distorted trees
visible under a grey fog, and I think you will get an idea as to what I
awoke to.

You should know why I should want to get out of such a state—
one in which many people dwell for years. . . .

I cannot understand why humans say that after Death all is happiness, all joy, all rest, all cheerfulness, all brightness. Surely they
should be brought to the realization that as they have lived on Earth,
and worked, and done the right thing, so shall their reward be in the
hereafter. For though here physical suffering is not, mental suffering
is much more severe than it can ever be on earth.

People will say: Why? Because here you are more awake, more
alert, more able to perceive things by virtue or possessing a much
freer mind, housed in a much finer body, which does not bind you as
much.

Altogether, you are in a refining process, and not until you have
passed through every scrap of refining process there is in every state
of life here, are you permitted into the brighter state.

This brighter side exists, but at first you are only allowed to see it
for moments. . . .

I passed over holding no thought of the future, like the average
young man of my age. And as on earth, I always wanted to get out of
the mess as soon as possible on finding myself in it, so here did I determine to get out of the dreary, dreary country I found myself in
when I first realized I had passed over. . . .

The session was coming to an end. It was Emilie Hinchliffe's
first probe into what we might face when we were finished with our
present lives. There was no question in her mind that the words
and the phrasing reflected a marked continuity of Raymond's own
peculiarities, tastes and ideas, both in this session and the ones that
were held earlier.

In her mind, she was convinced that her husband's purpose was
to provide her with concise proof of the continuity of life after
death. This in turn would help her in her determination to share her
new convictions with others.

She made another appointment with Eileen Garrett to follow up
on this new exploration. She was confident that her husband would

continue to fill in the vivid picture he was starting to construct. Then, with the help of the Alliance, she set about planning her first lecture.

Psychic study groups in the England of the Twenties were legion, and they were doggedly serious. The better ones kept copious notes and records. Once they believed that they were getting through to an articulate entity, they kept at it. They tried to get as much information as possible. They correlated it with other such experiments, to compare and match up. They also took the theory of "soul rescue" seriously. Over the years, it had been reported through mediums that there was no such thing as eternal punishment. When you died in not-exactly-the-state-of-grace, you had to work like hell and develop spiritually. They were convinced that help could be supplied from this side of the curtain by "soul rescue" sessions, which could lead a "problem deceased" on to his spiritual progress and development.

Groups like Mrs. Taylor's in suburban London worked on the premise that communication with "the other side" proved man's immortality and the existence of a spiritual universe. They also were convinced that this idea destroyed all fear of death, and that there would be eternal progress instead of eternal punishment. But they also felt that the better character you developed here, the better it would be later. In addition, they thought, their ideas swept away the unscientific concept of a personal Devil, and that no one else could suffer vicariously for your sins. You had to work out your own salvation.

There were other beliefs. They seemed to work against the concepts of conventional religions. But many considered that their psychic studies were a jump-off platform to embrace any of the established religions, that their ideas were simply a supplement to the church or temple. They allowed anyone to believe as he pleased, so long as he didn't get hung up on the idea of a vindictive God, a theological heaven or hell, superstition, or religious persecution. Through the complicated communications they recorded so carefully and pored over, they were convinced they were working with facts and corroborative testimony that were objectively valid.

They thought it was a hopeful and helpful outlook. A criminal would sweat like hell from his own self-condemnation, but there would be somebody there to help if he wanted to climb out of his morass, and was willing to work at the problem. People like Alfred Lowenstein would need help, they were convinced. He would need help both from friends in the strange new world and from "soul" rescue groups in this world.

Mrs. Taylor's group was convinced they could help Lowenstein in two ways. The first was by contacting him and getting him to realize that he could lift himself by his bootstraps to a higher level if he really wanted to. The second was by trying to steer more fortunate friends of Lowenstein on the "other side" to reach out and help the man along.

In Emilie Hinchliffe's private session, unknown to Mrs. Taylor's group, Hinchliffe had reported that he hadn't yet encountered his friend Lowenstein, or so the communication through Eileen Garrett had indicated. Without thinking of anybody specific, Mrs. Taylor's study group was continuing to try to get Lowenstein's story, and to push him up the ladder where he could bump into somebody on the "other side" willing to give him a hand.

They worked for many sessions on this idea. According to their apparent communications, they were making progress. If there was any truth to what they were receiving, Lowenstein indicated, through the automatic writing that moved across the paper in such a swift scrawl, that he was progressing. In fact, he had at last run into a friend:

"You will understand my immense pleasure," the scrawling handwriting revealed, "to see a man who held out his hand to me and said he would explain my position. He was my friend, Hinchliffe. He said he had met a similar death by drowning, not by suicide. My heart sank within me when he said I was dead, and not saved, as I thought, by a miracle."

Mrs. Taylor, watching the proceedings with the rest of her group, asked: "Why? What did you think had happened?"

"Mad, I thought, from the fall," the words spelled out.

"But surely," said Mrs. Taylor, "the strangeness of your condition must have made you realize you were dead."

The pencil continued moving in the medium's hand: "No. How could I realize I was dead? All I did seemed to me as a delirium, not death. So I realized now what had truly happened to me. What a shock it was. Life was still before me. No chance of release from what I had hoped would be a long life. You can imagine my feelings when Hinchliffe told me he had spoken to his wife, and she to him. 'How can I do likewise?' I asked him.''

The message continued with the information that Hinchliffe had offered to show Lowenstein how he was able to make contact through a medium. Lowenstein reported that he had watched others talking to the Mrs. Taylor group. He heard the people mention that Mrs. Taylor had provided written messages for the friends and relations who were still living on earth. He said that he was attracted to the Taylor home because light seemed to shine from it.

"The kind of life I led was so material that I was not able to link up with you enough," the words purporting to come from Lowenstein spelled out. "Then I noticed the homes of men and riches and fame, which seemed dark and cold. I asked Hinchliffe the reason, and he said: 'Those men are living in the world only. But when you see a light around people, it means that they come halfway to our side.' ''

To ordinary eyes, the message would read like a fantasy. In Mrs. Taylor's group, they were convinced that this was just another message that matched scores of others they had received directly or studied in the research files of the British Society. It had taken Doyle and Lodge years of study and comparison before they could accept the ideas reflected in this sort of communication. The mechanics were so puzzling. If this world that now housed Hinchliffe and Lowenstein were real, was it like Oxford Professor H. H. Price's dream-image world, where you shifted locations with the speed of thought? Where you met whatever people you wanted to meet instantaneously?

There was no question that this was possible in dreams without taking up any space. This could be verified easily by anyone who wanted to take the trouble to examine and reflect on his own dreams. There was no limitation whatever in a dream. We could construct our own scenery, roads, cars, boats, people, vistas—all faster than the speed of light, and without carpenters, designers, stagehands, or architects. And there was still that vivid reality of the dream, which remained real during its span. It only became less real on waking.

Or could both worlds be something like the way that solipsists looked at existence? Solipsism is the school of philosophy that claims that nothing but the self exists. There were no such things as sky, air, earth, colors, shapes and sounds. They were all inventions of the mind, both here and in any possible hereafter. We projected our own reality, like a 3-D movie or a laser hologram. Descartes had torn the solipsists to pieces. But the theory was still around. Perhaps a modified form of it could explain this picture of life after death.

Whatever the theories, the fact and the reality were that words ostensibly from Old Lowenstein were coming from the hand of one of Mrs. Taylor's most proficient mediums. Whether they came from the conscious, the unconscious, the spirit world, or the imagination was another question. The other fact and reality were that the events recounted by Lowenstein matched in substance scores, if not hundreds, of previous such messages from other mediums over many years.

From that point on, any interested observer would have to draw his own conclusions. If he were like Doyle or Sir Oliver Lodge, he would have to closely study all the evidence before he made up his mind. If he wanted to scoff, he could take one look and throw the whole idea away. The choices were wide and open; the questions, however, remained provocative, and they remained unanswered.

The automatic handwriting that claimed to be coming from Old Lowenstein continued. He seemed to be intent in drawing up a detailed picture of what he was facing. True or false, it was interesting:

"Hinchliffe took me to a medium called Mrs. Garrett," the words from Lowenstein continued. "I watched many spirits around the control [he might have been referring to Uvani]. They were giving their messages to the people who sat with her."

The picture that emerged seemed as if it were like a public phone center in a railway station or an airport. The question would be: was this ridiculous or wasn't it? To the study group, it was not.

"Hinchliffe spoke to his wife," Lowenstein's apparent words continued. "I was amazed to hear her replies. Here at last was a way to live on earth again. Eagerly I asked Hinchliffe to find someone who could hear me. He said he had seen you at work here in your living room. Like a lost dog, I followed him here.

"When I met you in your house"—referring to Mrs. Taylor and her group—"I could not see the walls. You seemed to be in a fog.

You had a light around you. Someone took my hand and walked across to your table. Then I began to realize that you were listening to what a man was telling you.''

There were many people in these times who were impressed by the factual evidence they would receive from a medium. But they were completely puzzled by how and why such a contact could be made from a so-called spirit who was no longer living on earth. They wanted to know what mechanics made it possible even to conceive that these kinds of messages could come across. Lowenstein's purported message continued to explain the apparent process:

"I was told to think first what I wished to say and to speak slowly. My mind was able to listen to your thoughts. You seemed to be sorry for me, so I admitted my crime. That was a relief to me. You made me gasp with astonishment when you said, 'Ask someone to help you.' ''

One of Mrs. Taylor's group, who believed from her background studies that there were usually many on the "other side" who tried to help a recently dead person, asked: "But surely by this time you had come across other people who would help you?"

"I had seen no one but Hinchliffe," came the reply, "and he just tried to make me realize I was dead. You can fancy the mental confusion I had."

The automatic writing stopped for a moment. Then it appeared that Lowenstein was trying to send some messages to friends of his. The attempt was not successful. It was garbled. He later explained that he was forbidden to send messages. "I might have done it if I had not taken my life," the message read. "But I am told that I would only wander about my old habitations and possessions if I linked my vibrations with those still in them."

The session ended. Mrs. Taylor was convinced that the group had helped in their "soul rescue" efforts. They had, she thought, enabled Lowenstein to get far enough out of his initial shock to find a friend, which he hadn't been able to do in the early part of his new life. They had been able, she was sure, to persuade him that he could look up and to make him realize that he could begin to work his way out of his sorry initial condition. To the little study group, these things brought satisfaction.

* * *

Although Emilie Hinchliffe's financial strain was eased on receiving the £10,000 sterling, she did not lose her determination to spread her now firm conviction that people lived after death. She was sure that, knowing this, people might shape their lives more constructively. The Inchcape funds were now legally hers. The settlement by the Public Trustee office was completed. Through the daughter of W. T. Stead, the widely respected psychic researcher who had gone down on the *Titanic*, she prepared for her first lecture. She flatly refused any compensation for it. With the money indirectly arriving from Lord Inchcape, she could now handle her needs, and she planned to take on translating work to supplement them.

On November 22, she arrived at London's Caxton Hall for her first public appearance. She was wearing a trim scarlet suit, with a fur neckpiece, and she looked younger than her twenty-nine years. She was staggered by the hundreds of spectators gathered around the entrance to the hall. They had to be held back by special police. News of the message she was to talk about had traveled fast via Mrs. Stead's lecture bureau.

The small hall seated only four hundred people, and it was packed. Hundreds had to be turned away outside. She gained confidence as she began talking. She gradually revealed the unaccountable evidence she had received through Eileen Garrett about her husband. She went into the details of how she had tracked down the real meaning of the "leeward islands," how she traced the weather and currents of the North Atlantic, and how she continued to probe methodically for any other information that might turn up about her husband's flight. The audience sat in rapt attention, impressed by her sincerity. She didn't mention Elsie Mackay, cryptically explaining that there had been "intervention from an influential source" that blocked her from talking about her. The source was never explained, although almost the entire press and public immediately connected it with Lord Inchcape.

She emphasized several times that she had gone into this strange area as a complete skeptic, but that she no longer could remain that way after the long days and weeks of investigation. When the talk was over, she was relieved. She was also grateful that she had had a chance to try to convince people there was more to the present reality than they suspected. She looked forward to more opportunities to speak. There would be many.

Meanwhile, she was anxious to get back to her sessions with Eileen Garrett. She looked on them now as an advanced course in the subject of what actually happened in an afterlife. Her curiosity had been piqued by her first session of this nature, because it suggested a detailed aspect of the picture that was shaping up in her mind. The words had sounded so much like Raymond. The approach in the descriptions was so much the way he thought. But she had been left hanging, with so many unanswered questions.

She was not disappointed at the next session:

What do we do? [the words apparently coming from her husband began]. We do everything for which we are fitted. There are huge systems of education, huge laboratories and institutions, that deal with all the conditions for which a man has fitted himself while on earth. Here our necessities are met by mental thought, and are organized and focused.

The organized thought starts here, travels around the spiritual states, gathering strength as it does, and eventually finds its final capacity for work through its human receiver.

None of this destroys free will. Rather, it helps you who are still on the earth I have so lately left, to realize your affinity with those who have gone on, to realize their very great humanity and interest in you. Instead of taking anything away from the beauty of the picture, does it not add to it that your day of usefulness is only dawning when you come over here?

I have not found any evil here. I have found many people, I assure you, who are ignorant of every law, but that does not constitute evil. I have nothing to say about the man who is an atheist. So long as he truly believes what he professes, he stands as great a chance as the man who is bound up in his religion. Each one of us has an absolutely straight chance of working out his own salvation.

There are hells and there are heavens just as we have been taught to believe. There are weak people, dissolute people, vicious people, all seeking to still take part in the life they once knew, rather than enter fully into this new life. The man who takes a risk is the fellow you find in the higher states here. Each of these states has to be reached by man's own endeavor.

There are laboratories full of youth, full of life, all working for good, just as there are others whose energies are mistaken ones. Really there are no evil spirits. There are ignorant ones, interfering ones, malicious ones, and blind ones—that is blind to their own faults—and these constitute the so-called evil here, just as they are the pests of your life.

I work all the time mentally and in a sense physically, in the things that interest me. One does work. I revel in it, because here in this state, I find myself free, alert and decisive, my energies no longer curtailed or held down by all the pains, ills and depressions.

What do we work at? We work mentally, and rejoice in so doing—except at making money. Only now one desires to possess the gifts for the soul, and the gift of knowledge, and the gift to enable one to see more clearly, to understand and to realize the greatness of the Universe.

Do we eat and drink? That's another question many people often ask. Certainly not in the way you sit down in your lavish restaurants. Such a pity, because I liked doing it. This ethereal body, so like our earthly body, has still some of the physical structure about it, and it is therefore not perfected yet. It must retain something that is very akin to the physical state. We take food in what would seem to you a compressed or compounded form.

Do we use our senses in the same way? Yes, we do. After a while we begin to drop our earthly need for speech, and begin to use thought transference by sending and projecting our thoughts from mind to mind.

Such a lot of nonsense is being told. I assure you this is all the truth. It may upset some people, for few have the courage to tell the truth of their experiences.

There were other thoughts that came as fast as Emilie could copy them in her shorthand book. Raymond was still trying to get through warnings and suggestions to his earthly fellow airmen, but he seemed frustrated about having to go through the clumsy channel of a medium. He still kept wanting to talk to his navigator friend Johnston about the problems with the R-101. Aside from Emilie and the children, Raymond seemed to be obsessed with the progress in the infant aviation industry, as if he were still alive.

As for what to believe about these strange transmissions concerning a future life, Emilie finally took the same route that Conan Doyle had. She felt she *had* to accept the massive evidence apparently produced by her husband in the earlier sessions. If this information were true, she now saw no reason not to accept the later messages. Regardless of what others thought about it, her conversion from total skepticism to acceptance was complete. With the Stead bureau, she set about planning to give further lectures without compensation, but with unrestrained enthusiasm. Many people felt the same way she did. Many more did not. Her job, she felt, was to change that.

The painstaking and sometimes exhausting sort of session Eileen Garrett was doing with Emilie Hinchliffe, she was doing two or three times a day for others. The results were almost consistently as confirmable and as detailed. Verification of the messages was nearly always possible.

But as a channel for this nebulous character Uvani, she still did not understand how her mind found the images she or "Uvani" talked about. She could not conceive how her mind received these images, without some kind of *conscious* assistance from the senses. She knew that none of her lengthy communications, as accurate and detailed as they were, could be acceptable to the measuring rod of science. This continued to upset her and strengthened her resolve to someday bring all this into the realm of science. It would be the only way to free herself of a burden.

She was interested in the Hinchliffe case because Emilie was as absorbed in the how and why of this process as she was. Going over the lengthy transcripts of the past sessions with Emilie, Eileen wondered at times if they could be sure that Hinchliffe was the actual source of the elaborate details. Emilie was now certain, because she could relate firsthand to the personal, intimate family details that had been revealed. Eileen was no longer amazed at Uvani's capacities. She needed to know—and she wasn't sure she could know.

Meanwhile, both Conan Doyle and Emilie Hinchliffe continued to try to get across the message that the continuity of life went on, and that it could be clearly documented if anyone really wanted to study the evidence. As the year 1929 began, Doyle was packing them in to enormous crowded auditoriums in England and over the world, while Emilie was gaining confidence in herself as a lecturer.

It was during these days in the winter of 1929 that Emilie received an unexpected letter from the Air Ministry:

AIR MINISTRY
Gwydyr House
Whitehall
London SW 1

March 1, 1929

Dear Mrs. Hinchliffe:

I am sorry to trouble you with past history, but I think you should know that the Air Ministry received a report in December last, to the effect that part of an undercarriage of an aeroplane was washed ashore in County Donegal bearing the following numbers and description:

76168547 Goodrich Silvertown Cord
Airplane 150/508. Manufactured by
the Goodrich Company, Akron, Ohio,
U.S.A.

As a result of subsequent enquiry through the American Embassy, a letter was received from the Goodrich Rubber Co.. to the effect that the undercarriage in question was part of the aircraft used by the Hon. Elsie Mackay and Captain Hinchliffe on their Atlantic flight of last year. A copy of the letter in question is enclosed for your information.

Yours very sincerely,
C. B. C.

The letter from the Goodrich company merely pointed out that beyond any doubt the tire came from the Stinson Detroiter used by Captain Hinchliffe. The final evidence of Raymond's death was in. The fragment of wreckage, including the tire, had washed up on one of the two places that Emilie's careful computing had predicted.

Now a determined researcher in the psychic field, Emilie continued to probe in experimental sessions with Eileen Garrett, gaining surprisingly accurate aeronautical ideas from Captain Hinchliffe to pass along to his friends.

* * *

If anyone needed help, it was Hinchliffe's old friends working on the R-101. Both this ship and the R-100 were now about two years behind schedule. The taxpayers' bill was climbing to more than 2 million sterling. Meanwhile, the Germans were running rings around the British. The *Graf Zeppelin* was getting ready for a round-the-world flight, before either of the two British dirigibles were even out of their hangars.

Much depended on what paper you read. One daily would be headlining that the R-101 was underpowered, overweighted, too slow, and able to carry only half of the passengers the specifications called for. Another would describe the ship as a "wonder in steel and silver." Everybody who was inclined toward this state of mind raved about that ballroom. One reporter got carried away, merely after peeking into the R-101 shed at Cardington:

> Its ribs and sinews are fashioned of duraluminum and steel girders, its flesh is pithwood from America, its skin stretched parchment that is well-nigh unbreakable. Phantom grey in the dusk, it will be shining silver in sunshine. A cigar, a supple silver cigar that will be a sign and a portent! It will move with the speed of a racing car!
>
> To a child, it might best be described as an enormous shiny whale being fitted out and taught to swim in the air.
>
> When the magic word is given, the Martian doors at the end of the shed are to slide back. The great air-going liner will slip out, linger for a moment, quivering, then launch herself ghostlike into her chosen element, a gift of the gods that is yet the handiwork of man.
>
> The ship will not only realize the aerial fantasies of Jules Verne, but will treat time and space with a new and airy contempt, and journey in the spirit of an Alexander.

Colmore, Atherstone, Irwin, Scott, Johnston, and the rest of the R-101 crew could not exactly join in the ecstasy of the reporter. Pressure was mounting to get on with the job. The progress of the *Graf Zeppelin* was a sting. The critics of the R-101 program were now screaming that the ship was obsolete before launching. Lord Thomson, from his cabinet-post ivory tower, was letting it get bruited about that he might well fly to India in December on the R-101.

December? In mid-summer of 1929, the construction crew was having trouble getting the ship to float in proper balance inside the hangar. Her gas bags were just now being filled with hydrogen. The gassing-up process was taking over five weeks, at the rate of a million feet a week. At the same time, the bags were being tested for leakage. The hydrogen had a tendency to percolate through the somewhat porous gold-beater's skin, allowing air to slip in. No one could tell yet how the gas bag wiring system would hold up, whether the clumsy bags would be chafed by the girders or against each other. Only actual flight tests could check that.

The engines were still giving trouble. It now looked as if there would be only four engines for forward flight, with the fifth engine in reserve for reversing. As a result, the four operating engines would be hauling an extra two tons of useless load. The five engine pods were now five tons over the original estimated weight. In spite of all this, an announcement by the Air Ministry in mid-August revealed that the entire city of London would be treated to the spectacle of the two largest airships in the world sailing over London the following month, escorted by a squadron of military planes as a guard of honor.

One Sunday morning late in September 1929 the silence of the countryside around Cardington was shattered by the noise of the R-101's giant Diesels as they ran through a warm-up test inside the hangar. The noise was so great that throttles could only be opened on one engine at a time. The ship was now floating in its shed, with heavy ballast holding it down from scraping against the ceiling. The mooring mast stood outside, waiting and empty. The electrical galley was completed. There was a larder laid in. For Colmore and a select crew, a few meals had even been served. The passengers' staterooms were finished. The beds had actually been made up, though there were just half the number originally planned. A uniformed steward was setting the tables for fifty places in handsome sterling. Excitement was growing. You could feel it among the 400-man construction crew, as well as among the officers who were champing to get the ship in the air.

Any approved visitor entering the ship was supplied a pair of light tennis shoes to prevent damage or sparks. To Chief Steward Albert Salvidge, the job was a cinch. He had served on the R-34 and had just completed 107 Atlantic crossings on the great steamship *Majestic*. There would be six stewards under him when the ship took to the air. The crowning glory was the central lounge, with cushioned wicker chairs and numerous writing tables against the canvas walls. The stark metal columns were framed off by balsa wood boxing, like a Hollywood set. The R-101 was—or would be—the only real way to travel.

It was at the end of September that Emilie Hinchliffe was concluding another session with Eileen Garrett, recording it carefully in her shorthand book, as usual. Very suddenly, the message of Hinchliffe coming through the voice of Uvani changed its normal tone to one that resembled Hinchliffe's.

> I want to say something about the new airship. You know some of the people who have to do with it, but you will not like to broach the subject.
>
> They will start without thinking of disaster, but the vessel will not stand the strain. It will come down on one side first.
>
> I do not want them to have the same fate that I had, as Johnston [the R-101 navigator] was a good friend of mine. I have tried to impress them myself, but it is inconceivable how dense these people are.
>
> If the flight is put off, it will be all right. I wish to goodness it were possible for you to tell Johnston in confidence, and ask him to be careful. I know what I am talking about.

Hinchliffe had sent a milder warning some months before. This was more intense, more serious, more specific, and more direct. His appeal was directed at his close friend Squadron Leader Johnston, and his concern was centered on him perhaps because of their close relationship.

Emilie had to make a decision. She had come to believe these communications from her husband. But how many other people did? She was a realist. She knew that she was considered by some friends to be merely a distraught widow who had gone around the bend to some degree. She knew that if she voiced this warning, she could sound like a damn fool to Johnston, in spite of his being such a close friend of her husband.

She talked it over with Eileen Garrett, who leaned toward the idea of taking the chance and talking to Johnston. But Eileen felt the choice had to be Emilie's own. Eileen knew that in spite of the many accurate facts coming through in a session, there could be many faulty transmissions of information, either through misinterpretation, or the intrusion of her own conscious mind into the message. Single facts, taken alone, could not be counted on, she believed. It was mainly the full sense of the message, the cumulative evidence, that counted.

At one time, Eileen had reviewed Emilie's verbatim transcripts. She noted that the voice of Uvani had indicated that he was confused by the technical language Hinchliffe was passing along to his wife. "You must remember," the transcript read, "that I am Uvani, and only an ancient Arab. I have much trouble with this aviation talk."

The medium's mind, some psychic research theories went, was like a wax recording disc, and sometimes a faulty one at that. Sometimes it recorded beautifully. Other times it missed, badly. The only way to test the accuracy of a message was to follow Emilie's methods: careful attention to detail in both shorthand and transcription, followed by careful scrutiny of the clearcut evidential data that could be confirmed.

The extreme difficulty of the sender-receiver relationship had once been recorded in a purported message from the famous psychic researcher who had died, F. W. H. Myers. His message from the "other side" read:

"The nearest simile I can find to express the difficulties of sending a message, is that I appear to be standing behind a sheet of frosted glass, which blurs the sight and deadens the sound, dictating feebly to a reluctant and somewhat obtuse secretary. A feeling of terrible impotence burdens me. I am so powerless to tell what means so much."

Paul Beard wrote in his book *Survival of Death*: "The impression is given that the speed of thought increases greatly after death, and often cannot be slowed down enough to be caught by the medium even when she is at her most receptive. . . . Every medium's mind, apart from the inevitable slowness and dullness of reception complained of by 'communicators,' has as well its own particular personal incapacities, insensitivities, incomprehensions, and emotional blockages. . . ."

In the dilemma Emilie was facing, all these things had to be weighed. She didn't want to cry "fire" in a crowded theatre. Her lengthy transcripts were carefully marked with her marginal notations. Over ninety percent of "Uvani's" factual data had proven correct. In her mind, the ten percent of incorrect statements would in no way cancel out the large bulk of verifiable evidence. But it did warn against counting on any single statement.

Now a crisis point had been reached. The technical information Hinchliffe was apparently trying to get across might be garbled or partially garbled. But the sense of the message was unmistakable to her: Hinchliffe was desperate to warn his friend Johnston and the rest of the R-101 crew.

Emilie brought the subject up to Gordon Sinclair, to Captain Morkham, to other friends of her husband. Opinion was divided. They pointed out that Johnston was skeptical, a super-realist. He would be hard to convince. The information, even if it had come from Hinch, was vague. Morkham by now was convinced that the posthumous communications with Hinchliffe were possible, if not probable. He had screened Emilie's transcripts minutely. He had noted the overwhelming percentage of accurate and evidential information, compared to the minuscule parts that were faulty. But he felt that Emilie should at least try to get more material through before she seriously considered bringing the warning directly to Johnston.

Emilie agreed. She set up more sessions with Eileen Garrett. Morkham agreed to join with her at them. They didn't have to wait long before more alarming material came through.

One day during this period, Eileen Garrett was walking her dog near the Serpentine, in Hyde Park. She looked up. There was another silver airship in the sky, graceful and beautiful.

Once again, she saw smoke belching out of the huge envelope. She was filled with a great sense of dread. The ship nosed down, then disappeared behind some buildings. Yet the only airships that actually could be in the English skies at the time were the R-101 or the R-100, and they were still safe in their hangars, struggling to emerge from their cocoons.

CHAPTER VIII

All week long they had been arriving, by omnibus, by car, by bicycle. They came from Nottingham, Leeds, Newcastle, Cardiff, Swansea, Wolverhampton, London. The cynosure of all eyes was the Royal Airship Works at Cardington, where the R-101 was still floating in her shed, waiting for the early October winds to die down enough for her to slide out of her hangar without her eggshell frame being crushed against the sides. There were official estimates of a million people swarming into the Bedford area, jamming the hotels, the bed-and-breakfast pubs, the roominghouses, for a radius of 40 miles.

From the first days of October, thousands of frustrated spectators had come out each day to the windy meadows near the Royal Works at dawn. They carried sandwiches and scones and biscuits and thermos jugs of tea. They shivered in the darkness before the first light showed. Day after day they left the airfield disappointed. But the R-101 could not come out of its shell. The winds were too strong. The Air Ministry could not take a chance. Even a 10-mile-an-hour gust could send the delicate envelope against the door frame. Everyone was jittery. Colmore, Irwin, Scott, Atherstone, Johnston—these formed the nucleus at which the buck stopped, the responsibilities lay, where the glory—if any—would be reflected. The pressure now came from the reporters hovering about, and

149

the swarms of spectators jamming the roads and boundary fences of the airship station. The officers worked under floodlights night and day, checking details, screening the meteorological maps, plotting the course for the maiden flight, scheduled for the first possible moment the damn wind would let up enough for the ship to get out of the hangar.

They were as ready as they ever would be. The Certificate of Airworthiness had been issued. Every predawn morning, four hundred men were standing by, with a hundred of these rounded up in the streets of Bedford from the ranks of the unemployed. They were hauled unceremoniously to the hangar by bus, by "musterers" who herded them daily.

There was only a 15-foot clearance on each side of the hangar, and 25 feet at the top for the hull to clear. A double white line was painted down the center of the hangar floor. If the airship swayed beyond those markers, there could be disaster. The ship was to be walked out by four "walking parties," forward, aft, center, and under the control car to stop it from bumping anywhere. The men would hold on to crude handling bars suspended from the ship. Six other parties would be stationed on each side, holding the enormous hull by guy ropes, as it strained upward like a toy balloon at the circus. Outside, another crew would be pulling the nose cable in a tug-of-war, coaxing it through the entrance gap after the heavy sliding doors had been pulled back. A spare crew would walk under the ship, to troubleshoot any emergency. The vertical fin was only inches off the ground. Disaster could come there in a flash. The ship was as fragile as a Japanese lantern.

Getting past that open doorway would be the moment of truth. Then there would be a slow, half-mile walk across the field to the lattice-iron tower, waiting to lock into the nose coupling of the ship. There the floating palace would swing, 200 feet above the ground. This is what the crowds were waiting for. This is what they failed to see during thirteen long days of labor pains.

In the first faint light of October 13, it happened. Major Scott, in an old white pullover, tennis shoes and grey flannels, directed the operation. He had a tooth missing, and it accented the strain in his face. At 5:49 A.M., the ship slid out, a few feet at a time. The crowd rimming the field roared with approval. Cars stopped along the nearest road, and a traffic jam formed that stretched 4.5 miles. The people seemed spellbound, hypnotized.

It took only four minutes to walk the ship out of the womb. As the light breeze hit the envelope, a ton of dust was whipped off the top surface. It had settled there over the months—though only a thousandth of an inch thick.

The procession moved slowly across the field in careful rhythm, like a wedding procession of dwarves in lockstep. Then the ship lifted itself toward the tower, as the lines were played out. The tail had to be watched; it was light. They anchored four heavy iron lawn rollers to it, each weighing a ton. The cable from the tower was connected and allowed to play out. The craft hung 100 feet above it, rolling slowly and silently. Then a ton of water ballast gushed from her nose, and she was permitted to rise. She went up to 500 feet and hung level, behaving as she should behave. The mooring cable was hauled in slowly. The nose dipped, drew close, and was locked into the tower arm. Another cheer went up.

On the ground, the police were powerless. The road from Cardington to Bedford was a solid parking lot. Signs announcing "Petrol sold out" were everywhere. For two hours, the jam did not move. The R-101 was ready for her maiden flight, perhaps the following day.

Some weeks before the R-101 left its hangar, at a new session with Eileen Garrett, more disturbing news was coming to Emilie Hinchliffe from the voice of Uvani. Their meeting took place during those days when the public was waiting for the R-101 to slide out of the hangar, before the rousing cheers went up as she locked into her tower.

"I do not think these dirigibles are able to face climatic conditions," Uvani was speaking, purportedly on behalf of Hinchliffe. "They have not the right wind resistance. They are fairly all right until they get to a certain altitude. There is sympathy with the hydrogen which weakens the tissues where the air combustion gas is kept. You get all sorts of locking at a certain altitude, you cannot get over it. These dirigibles cannot cut through the air, and gas envelopes attract currents. R-101's maiden flight may be all right. Nothing may happen for a time. But there certainly is a great risk."

Her husband seemed excited and anxious to get the information through. Emilie had trouble keeping up with it. She could not get all the words correctly.

The tone of the message was urgent, but the very urgency seemed to make the phrases less intelligible. She took it down as best she could, knowing that there was confusion in the words she wrote. What came out of it was the sharpness of the warning, rather than the accuracy of any technical information.

Gordon Sinclair and John Morkham agreed that there had been better technical detail in the past sessions that Emilie had recorded. Morkham recalled the time that he had accompanied Emilie to a meeting with an officer of the British Society of Psychical Research, which was interested in making a thorough study of the Hinchliffe case.

Like Harry Price, the Society spent as much time in exposing false and misleading mediums as it did experimenting with and probing cases that genuinely reflected psychic phenomena.

Charles Hope, the investigating officer, wrote his report of the meeting with Emilie and Morkham by saying: "What impressed me most at my first meeting with Mrs. Hinchliffe was that a great friend of the late Captain Hinchliffe was present—Captain J. P. Morkham of the Croydon Aerodrome—and he was apparently just as convinced as Mrs. Hinchliffe of the reality of these 'messages,' especially since some of these 'messages' showed a technical knowledge which he knew Mrs. Hinchliffe did not possess and which he could not conceive of the medium possessing."

Morkham was especially demanding in screening the evidential material of the transcripts. In doing so, he had gradually changed from skepticism to almost full acceptance.

What impressed him in this latest warning was the urgency. He considered that this urgency might have garbled part of the message, especially since it was coming through the instrument of a non-technical medium. Morkham and Sinclair finally agreed that Emilie should immediately go to see Johnston.

Emilie thought about it, hesitated and finally decided to see Conan Doyle first. Although he was not now in robust health, he listened carefully as Emilie told him of the messages. He was so impressed when he reviewed the transcript of the session that he lost no time in arranging to go to Cardington with Emilie.

They were able to corner Squadron Leader Johnston during the long waiting period before the R-101 was released from the prison of the Hangar.

Johnston knew Emilie well, for he had been close to Hinchliffe. He had also read Sherlock Holmes, so Doyle was also no stranger to him. He listened sympathetically. He told them he appreciated their coming, but reassured them that everyone was taking every possible precaution to make sure that the ship was free of flaws. He thanked them again, and they left.

The trip had been fruitless. Emilie went back to Eileen Garrett the next day pressing for more detailed information. She would try anything to ward off a possible disaster, even if no one believed her.

A new message came through almost at once: "Johnston will not listen at all," Hinchliffe indicated through Uvani. "But you will find he has gone over these things. From what I know, the whole idea of dirigibles is spending money in vain, for they are not practical. Johnston thinks the airship is all right, but I am very dubious about it. Even if nothing happens on the maiden voyage, she is not going to last."

Emilie checked to make sure he was referring to the R-101. The message confirmed that he was, and that there probably would be no trouble on the upcoming maiden trial. But, the message concluded: "There *will* be an accident. I have seen Leslie Hamilton, and he agrees with me."

Leslie Hamilton was a friend of Hinchliffe's who had been killed in a trans-Atlantic attempt in August 1927. Again, her husband seemed to be referring to those strange encounters in his almost prosaic but different world. With her practical mind, she was still having trouble adjusting to this concept.

She tried to drop the idea of warning Johnston again, but she couldn't resist. She made another trip to Cardington to see him. It happened on the day before the crowds watched the ship squeeze out of its hangar. The results were the same. Johnston gave her a pat on the shoulder, expressed his appreciation, and went back to working on the navigational details for the maiden flight.

He didn't have to wait long. Shortly after Emilie's last visit, the winds had abated, the ship was out of the shed, and a day later the maiden voyage was about to begin.

At lunchtime on that day of the maiden voyage, October 14, 1929, Herbert Haseltine, a well-known sculptor of animals, was enjoying an exquisite partridge at his club. Suddenly one of the members jumped up and ran to the windows. The rest of the diners followed suit. The fitful sun, more often smothered under the clouds than not, suddenly broke through to reveal the shining R-101, silent and majestic, moving lazily over London. The partridge was left half-eaten as the diners gaped at the sight. It was Mr. Haseltine who summed up the spectacle. "By George," he said, "it looks exactly like a trout!"

Thousands and thousands of Londoners rushed to the rooftops and streets as the airship moved across the sky. She was coming in from the northeast, bucking a strong southwest wind, then circling over Westminster and later down the Thames to the Old City. She moved gracefully, but very slowly. The engines were not heard above the city traffic. For half an hour, the London spectators craned their necks, gasping, thrilled and ecstatic.

Looking down from the observation deck of the R-101, fourteen guests and some of the five officers and thirty-three crewmen saw the crowds running out to the commons and parks and squares, swarming like ants. On board, the engines were remarkably quiet. From the airship, the noises of steamships and tug whistles on the Thames, greeting the visit, could be clearly heard. The locomotive whistles joined them. Over Trafalgar Square, they saw a sea of upturned faces.

In the control cabin, Major Scott ordered power changes and test turns, while the ship cruised at some 60 miles an hour, slowed, then speeded up again. "There was never a moment," he said later, "when I felt that the R-101 was not under complete control and behaving admirably. We were particularly impressed when the schools seemed to allow the children to come out and watch us. We could hear them cheering and see them waving their handkerchiefs as we flew by."

They were, of course, watching aviation history. The floating hotel was passing by overhead, igniting a new spirit for the British Empire. The airship age would bring the far-flung Empire close together as a stream of these giant airships would eventually sail back and forth across the air routes that Sir Sefton Brancker had already marked out.

At two in the afternoon, luncheon was served on the flying palace. There would be two sittings. Flight Lieutenart Irwin took over the command, standing by the two helmsmen in the control car. One helm handled the rudder, the other the elevator controls. The tail surfaces alone on these mammoth fins covered a fifth of an acre. Her gas bags carried 5 million cubic feet of highly inflammable hydrogen. She was slightly plumper than previous airships, though her ribs showed through her flimsy fabric skin.

Major Scott, pleased with the way the R-101 was handling on her maiden trip, climbed up from the control car, slung under the belly of the ship, as Irwin came on duty. Scott made his way to the dining room on the second deck. The room was trimmed in white and gold, and the tables were decked with flowers and gleaming glassware and silver. He joined the first-shift diners for a luncheon of soup, roast mutton with onion sauce, brussel sprouts, salad, petits fours, coffee or tea. There was beer served with the meal.

Inside the cavernous shell, riggers, mechanics, fitters and other crewmen roamed the catwalks looking for signs of stress and strain. They climbed the sides between the surging gas bags, watching for chafing, for broken wires, for valve leaks. They wore tennis shoes, flying helmets and white sweaters over their dark brown overalls. Each had been issued a parachute. Each had a hunting knife tied on a string at his waist. If the unthinkable happened, they were to slash their way through the fabric covering and jump.

Some 200 miles and five hours later, the ship approached the tower at Cardington again. At 800 feet, the mooring cable was dropped. The ground crew scrambled for it, attached it to the cable running from the mooring mast. A white flag flashed outside the control cabin, the signal to begin winding in the cable. Slowly, the nose coupling approached, then locked into the tower. The gangway opened and the passengers walked across it to the tower, down the elevator and to the ground. As they did, a huge crowd burst through the police barriers to the base of the tower, where they screamed their praises of Major Scott.

No one said much about it, but during the mooring process, a cable snagged the delicate fabric near the bow of the ship. It ripped a hole, and the torn cover whipped about in the wind. It only took half an hour to repair. But there was another, more disturbing event not advertised at the time. The R-101 had been able to use only three of its five engines during the entire trial run.

When the cheers died down, a lot of questions began to be asked. The ship seemed to fly serenely on that first trip—but could it survive in tropical storms on the long passage to India? What about the clumsy, slow method of launching and tying up to the tower? At the moment, there would be only four places in the entire world with a tower equipped to handle the R-101 design: Montreal, Ismailia, Karachi, and Cardington. What would happen in an emergency over the Sahara, the Atlantic, the Mediterranean, the Indian Ocean? What about using a vessel the size of an ocean liner to carry only fifty people who were outnumbered by the crew, with a pitiful freightload to tag along with them? What about that thin-skinned fabric that had torn so easily?

But air history was being made, and the momentum of the program carried everybody concerned along with it. No one could say for certain what would happen, unless of course those persistent messages that seemed to come from Captain Hinchliffe could be taken seriously.

But very few people knew about them. Very few would take them at all seriously, if they did know. Britain, Germany and the United States were all airship-mad. Heavier-than-air craft could never possibly replace it for linking the countries of the world together, now and in the future.

There was no question that an atmosphere of hope reigned for the most part, justified or not. Over the months that followed, the tests on the R-101 went on. On the first long test flight over the Midlands, where multitudes from Nottingham, Coventry, Rugby and Birmingham could cheer, Lord Thomson proudly announced: "I have moved part of the Air Ministry into the clouds for the day. I propose to do a good morning's work. This long air trip will enable me to tackle it without any fear of being interrupted, for you do not get any callers in the sky." While some members of Parliament were grumbling that the R-101 would merely become a vehicle for Air Ministry joy rides in the sky, Thomson went to work in a special suite fashioned out of two of the staterooms. He didn't seem to remain there, however, sending a lyrical radio message: "No one who has not had this experience can have the least idea of its comfort, smoothness and restfulness." After luncheon, he had coffee and cigarettes in the smoking room lounge, followed by tea later. The prospects for the trip to India never looked better.

Hardly anyone took much notice that on the same sparkling October day when Lord Thomson was shuffling papers and drinking tea on the R-101, an all-steel German Dornier Flying Boat, the DO-X, was getting ready for a trial flight with 150 passengers and a crew of ten. It would be roughly double the number of passengers ever carried by a lighter-than-air ship, or three times the number ever lifted by a heavier-than-air machine. It had twelve engines fixed on top of its wings, and its blunt-nosed metal hull could land and take off from almost any good-sized body of water. It boasted a drawing room and a bar 25 feet long.

The Air Ministry in London would want to keep looking the other way, in the face of this potential challenge. As the R-101 returned to the Cardington tower, its cabin windows were aglow in the early twilight. Approaching the mast, the ship suddenly nosed down under the pressure of a cold layer of air pushing down on the warm air near the ground. Major Scott waited until after the sun had fully disappeared. Two more tries missed. On a third try, the nose cable was connected to the mooring cable. As the ship was drawn down toward the mast, the main haul cable got snarled in a tree, ripping off branches, and tangling with two guy ropes. Two hours later, the lines were finally untangled, and the R-101 locked to the tower.

There were more trials, more delays, more refinements. The ship sailed over Sandringham, passengers and crew waving to the King and the Royal Family. The King raised his hat in return. There was an all-night flight of thirteen hours, with speed trials over the English Channel. Three engines failed, and had to be restarted after repairs. The aluminum pipes of the cooling system had cracked, one by one. They were replaced by rubber hoses in midair. At mooring, another guy wire fouled, the ship surged forward and bruised her nose severely against the tower. Another patchwork job was in order.

There were brighter moments. The R-101 rode out hurricane winds of up to 83 miles an hour at her mooring tower, in a storm in which seven died in Britain, and vicious floods struck Scotland, Wales and Ireland. All night long, the ship swung and rolled at the mast, with pressure on the bow force indicator registering up to twelve tons. Officers and crew stood by on the ship, in case it was ripped away and sent adrift in the gales that had even blown hunting hounds off their feet.

In spite of the sturdy resistance to the storm, the pitch and the roll of the ship was considerable. Hunt, the chief helmsman, was inside the guts of the envelope watching the gas bags. He didn't like what he saw. As he stumbled along the catwalk running the length of the ship, every gas bag from Number 3 to Number 14 was surging from side to side, and from fore to aft. In spite of the wire mesh intended to hold the bags in place, they were rubbing and chafing against the radial struts around the main frames. Bag Number 14 was getting worked over by the top girder of the ship, where several nuts and bolts were projecting.

When he reached Number 8, he was horrified to see that a 9-inch rip was formed by a radial strut, and the bag was becoming flabby, like a toy balloon stuck with a pin. More than half of the hydrogen was gone. On top of that, the safety valves at the base were opening up half an inch on every roll of the ship.

It was easy for Hunt to see what was happening. The huge hull was actually rolling *around* the bags, rubbing them as raw as a blistered foot. Every bag was affected, to a greater or lesser degree. An enormous patchwork job was obviously in order.

In spite of the patchwork, the craft completed over 1,000 miles in the air on a single 30-hour trip on November 18. They ran into fog 750 feet deep on the way home to Cardington, but navigator Johnston brought the ship in directly over the mast.

Before the shouts of congratulation for Johnston had died down, however, it was discovered that one of the wire bridles that carried the lift of the gas bag to the frame of the ship, had snapped in half. The pulleys that controlled the bridle were too small. The prescription for the ailment was larger pulleys all through the ship.

The endurance run, however, was considered successful. It was followed almost immediately by a planned excursion for 72 members of Parliament, who looked forward to the jaunt with mixed emotions. No less than six doctors were included with this distinguished group, just in case a rash of airsickness might develop. Seven MP's declined the trip when they learned of this precaution.

There was nothing to worry about. The ship never left the mast

The R101 Crashes And Is Destroyed: Lord Thomson, Sir Sefton Brancker And 44 Others Burned To Death.

THE TRAGIC AFTERMATH.—Dead bodies shrouded in sheets near the wrecked airship.— *Special "Daily Express" Picture.*

GREAT AIRSHIP STRIKES A HILL AFTER BATTLE WITH A STORM.

SLEEPING PASSENGERS ENVELOPED BY SWIFTLY RUSHING FLAMES.

THE giant airship R101, which left Cardington at 7 p.m. on Saturday for India, crashed on a hill near Beauvais, France, at 2.5 a.m. yesterday, and 46 of those on board—including Lord Thomson, Minister for Air, and Air Vice-Marshal Sir Sefton Brancker—were burned to death.

WHAT WAS THE CAUSE?

AIRSHIP IN PERIL THREE MONTHS AGO.

LEAKING GAS BAGS.

"Daily Express" Air Correspondent.

ONLY EIGHT SAVED: 45 TRAPPED IN AN INFERNO.

SIR SEFTON BRANCKER.

Above, the R101 disaster as reported in English newspapers. Below, two news reports on Captain Hinchliffe's tragic flight.

WHERE IS BLACK AND GOLD 'PLANE GOING?

Peer's Daughter in Trial Flight: A Denial.

R.A.F. OFFICERS IN DARK.

Cranwell Hangar No One May Approach.

CRANWELL AERODROME IS THE SCENE OF A MYSTERIOUS SECRET OF THE AIR.

CAPT. HINCHLIFFE, the famous pilot, has been practising daily in a black-and-gold 'plane in preparation for a record-breaking flight. The Hon. Elsie Mackay, daughter of Lord Inchcape, has been an interested spectator, and has taken part in some of the trial flights.

NO DEFINITE NEWS OF CAPT. HINCHLIFFE.

SECRET HISTORY OF THE FLIGHT.

MISS MACKAY'S RUSE.

Reports reached London last night that an aeroplane, believed to be the one in which Captain Hinchliffe and the Hon. Elsie Mackay set out from Cranwell on Tuesday morning to fly the Atlantic, had been seen over the Newfoundland coast.

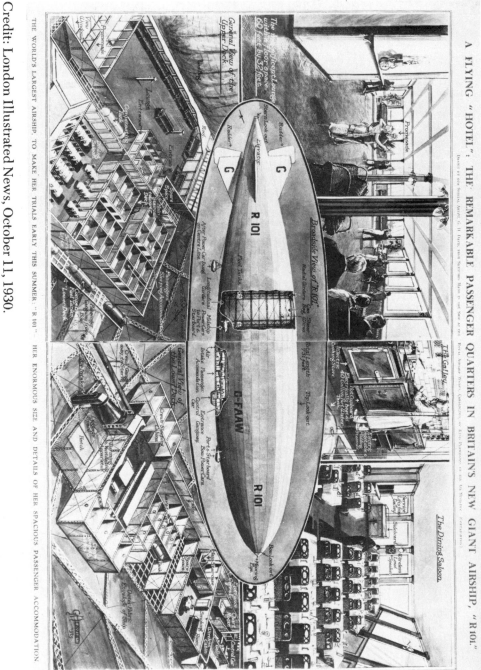

A FLYING "HOTEL": THE REMARKABLE PASSENGER QUARTERS IN BRITAIN'S NEW GIANT AIRSHIP, "R 101."

Credit: London Illustrated News, October 11, 1930.

The lounge of the R-101, where it was thought that passengers could "fox trot their way to India." Credit: Central Press Photos, Ltd.

The R-101 dining room with observation windows on the left. Credit: Central Press Photos, Ltd.

Maiden Voyage, October 15, 1929. Britain's giant airship R-101 was seen by thousands of admiring watchers in London and along her route from Cardington to the Capital and back. A photograph taken from an aircraft, of the airship over the outskirts of London on her return journey. Credit: Popperfoto.

The R-101 at the mooring mast at Cardington. Circa 1929.

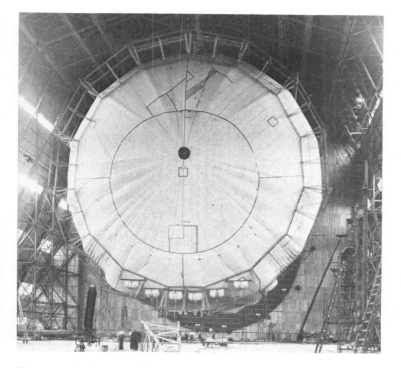

Structural photos of the R-101 used by Major Villiers to check the information he received through the mediumship of Eileen Garrett. Credit: Royal Airship Works Drawing Office.

Members of R-101 flying crew. Atherstone is second from left; Irwin is third from left; Major Scott is fifth from left.

The Airship R-101, the first flight over the town of Bedford. Circa 1929. Credit: Central Press Photos, Ltd.

Eileen Garrett, several years after the communications from Hinchliffe and the R-101 crew were relayed through her. Credit: Angus McBean.

Any communications on the
subject of this letter should be
addressed to :—

THE SECRETARY,
AIR MINISTRY,
GWYDYR HOUSE,
WHITEHALL,
S.W.1

and the following number quoted:—

AIR MINISTRY,
GWYDYR HOUSE,
WHITEHALL,
LONDON, S W.1.

A sample of Major Villiers' rough notes and final transcript of the material received through Eileen Garrett.

End of the dream: the skeleton of the wrecked R-101 after its crash near Beauvais, France. Only this portion of the tail section retained its shape. Credit: Central Press Photos, Ltd.

in the face of threatening weather. There would have been nothing
to view but driving rain. But the guests came aboard anyway, to
have luncheon made in that electric kitchen. Ellen Wilkinson, the
only woman MP among the guests, balked a little at the catwalk
leading from the tower to the belly of the ship.

She didn't like the thinness of the fabric that showed through below the wooden walk. There was nothing between that and the
ground, 200 feet below. It looked as if she could step through it.
The fact was that she could. But once aboard and in the elegant saloon, she felt that she had been projected twenty-five years into the
future. She even dreamed of a trip to New York in thirty-six hours,
that such a flight might even be taken as a matter of course.

In spite of the gale that raged outside, the parliamentarians sat
down in the spacious dining room for a lunch of oxtail soup, roast
chicken with bacon, bread sauce, rice, potatoes, green peas, milk,
rice custard, cheese, fruit and coffee. The great ship swayed and
rolled gently in the 60-mile wind outside, but it stood firm at the
tower to the relief of all.

However, even the brief encounter of that day had its problems.
The elevator of the mooring tower broke down. Half the visitors
had to climb 200 feet down the exposed stairway, soaked to the
skin.

It was that way with the R-101. A taste of honey, with a bee sting
afterward. But the bee stings were beginning to get bigger. Wing
Commander Colmore had sharpened his pencil and was doing
some fast computing. In order to make the passage to India, the
R-101 would have to carry some 25 tons of fuel oil. This would
leave a ridiculous margin for passengers, crew and even baggage.
Something had to be done. They could remove some optional lay-
ers of fat. There was a heavy Servo motor gear that powered the
steering cables, but the job could really be done by hand. There
were those heavy glass windows on the promenade deck. They
could be replaced by celluloid. There were certain tanks that could
be replaced and certainly they could give up a few passenger cabins. They might save about three tons this way. They might loosen
the wiring of the gas bags, so they could fill more space, giving
about three more tons of lift to the ship. There would have to be a
lot of protection from the struts and girders to allow for this, but
the extra lift would be worth it.

There was also another idea: They could cut the hull in half, and add a whole new bay. Another gas bag could go in here, and add about nine more tons of lift. But this would entail a major delay. Static and aerodynamic stresses would have to be computed and double-checked on the drawing boards.

A lot depended on Lord Thomson's passionate desire to arrive in India in such pomp and circumstance. They could do all or some of the above, depending on time pressure. Adding the new midship bay was no small job. It was major surgery. They could probably limp to India with only minor changes, but would have a rough time getting back. The lift of an airship in the heat of a Karachi summer would turn the ship into a lead zeppelin. As the ship lifted in the heat, a disastrous amount of hydrogen would expand and escape through the valves.

Lord Thomson, a man of decisive action even when he was wrong, lost no time in writing a "minute," as the official Air Ministry memos were called:

11 November 1929

I am of the opinion that no good, and quite possibly some harm, might be done by a flight to India in the early months of 1930. The best course would I think be:

(a) To make the various alterations

(b) To insert the extra bay

(c) To make every effort for a flight with 55 tons disposable load to India and back at the end of September 1930.

T.

There was of course the problem of Treasury sanction. The department didn't like cost overruns, especially since the big ships were eating up so much of the taxpayer's money. The glory of the Empire had limits. But approval came through surprisingly fast. With it was the sense of feeling on the part of the Treasury that this had better be the last request. Wing Commander Colmore and his staff were well aware of that. More pounds of pressure were laid on to the success of the mission, to say nothing of an almost impossible time schedule.

There had to be more tests both before and after the new bay was inserted. The ship went back into the shed for the minor alterations first. Each gas bag was taken out of the hull. Every bag except one was found to have holes in it. Number 11 alone had 103. Enlarging the bags for the greater lift, of course, increased the likelihood of chafing. No less than 4,000 pads were manufactured to be wrapped around the joints, the nuts, the bolts, the struts that threatened the delicate gold-beater's skin. The inside of the ship began to look like a kid getting first aid for briar patch wounds, with Band-Aids and surgical tape. No one knew exactly what would be happening beneath the fabric wrapped around the metal joints. The padding would be bound to get wet in flight. Corrosion could set in underneath, and no one would know about it. More than that, the changes in the wiring system allowed the swollen bags to push hard up against the main longitudinal girders, against more nuts and bolts, and the taper pins at the main and intermediate struts at the inner ridge of the girder ends. Those struts again. They were bothersome. So was the installation of 4,000 pieces of fabric padding.

Was it all worth it? What about the possible competition from the heavier-than-air machines? They were getting bigger. And faster. But they still took eight full days to get to India, because they had to land to refuel, and they could not fly at night. The R-101 would do the same trip in 50 hours. No, there wasn't that much competition from airplanes. It still looked as if there never really would be.

By June 23, halfway through the year 1930, the R-101 was hauled out of its shed again. All the changes had been made except adding the new mid-section. She had been in her damp hangar for some six months. She was allowed to lift to her tower, then was locked in tightly with her nose coupling. She swung there, whipped by gusts of heavy rain.

Moments afterward, a sickening, ripping, tearing sound was heard. Nearly 150 feet of the outerfabric, near the top on the starboard side, was slashed off the frame. It flapped in the wind, exposing the naked skeleton of the ship beneath.

With the wind, they could not get the ship back to the shed. All day long, they worked in the drenching rain, desperately trying to patch the tear, 200 feet up. By 5:30 in the evening, they at last succeeded. But the next day, another section ripped, not quite so long, on the top of the ship. It, too, was repaired. Rips in the outer cover would be disastrous in flight. Rain could pour in. Winds could thrash through the ship from stem to stern. Gas bags weren't built to stand that. They could rip wide open. They could lose gas swiftly. The aerodynamics of the entire vessel could be thrown out of control. There was only one answer: An entirely new cover over the whole framework. This time it would not be a pre-doped, pre-coated, fabric, as the original skin had been. The experiment had just not worked.

Before this could be done, however, there was the RAF Air Pageant, scheduled the next day at the Hendon aerodrome. The honor of the airship service was at stake. Quickly, reinforcing tapes were wrapped around the entire girdle of the ship, like huge trunk straps.

On the morning of June 28, the R-101 was limping to Hendon, still proud in spite of her wounds. She soared over the crowds, vying for attention against the sensational acrobatics of the RAF fixed-wing squadrons. The airship came off second best. The crowd of 150,000—including the Sultan of Jahore and the King of Spain—kept their eyes glued on 200 RAF daredevil fighter pilots, as they cavorted in the air.

Over the field, something was happening to the R-101. No one seemed to notice it. She was doing her own acrobatics—but they were totally unintentional. Without warning, she dove to within 500 feet of the ground from her holding altitude of 1,200. Height Coxswain Mush Oughton spun the elevator wheel, and forced the nose up. She rose on the other side of the aerodrome, just in time. As she did, a bridle holding a gas bag snapped inside by frame number 8, near the passenger quarters. The enormous hull jerked violently. They felt it all the way up in the control car. To Captain George Meager, in command that day, the ship seemed too heavy.

They got the craft up to 1,200 feet again. But again it dove. And again Oughton spun the wheel frantically to raise the nose. The ship turned and headed toward Cardington, toward home base. Captain Meager was convinced they were losing large amounts of gas. The situation was serious. Then the ship dove a third time. Meager reached for the ballast release. He dumped a ton of water. The ship was still heavy. He recalled that several days before they had had to dump two tons of fuel oil on the English countryside. A farmer later sued and collected.

They made it back to Cardington. When they examined the gas bags after the Air Pageant, they found more than 50 holes in them.

They were lucky that hydrogen rose. Unlike gasoline fumes, hydrogen would not settle at the bottom of the hull. It would escape through vents at the top. The valves as well as the bags were coming in for attention. If the ship rolled as little as 4 degrees, the loss of gas could be dangerous.

Colmore was in a crunch, and he was worried. The "Permit to Fly" for the ship would expire on July 19, and Inspector McWade, of the Aeronautical Inspection Division at Cardington, was seriously concerned with the use of fabric padding to protect the bags from chafing. In a report to the Air Ministry, he flatly stated that he could not recommend the extension of the permit.

It was no secret that Colmore and designer Richmond had little love lost between them. Any protest Colmore had made on the design was usually overridden by Richmond, who kept a tight rein on design problems. Along with Colmore's difficulties, Irwin, Johnston and Scott had strained relations with Richmond. They felt he was autocratic and dictatorial. He would never listen to their protests. They insisted on more tests than Richmond felt was necessary. They were usually overruled.

All of them were under not only time pressure, but the Treasury's insistence that the flight to India must be made in order to justify the enormous expenditures on the ship. Test flights would not satisfy the taxpayers that their money was being well-spent.

The recently reconditioned gas bags were beginning to be in as bad a shape as they had been before. It looked as if the clumsy fabric balloons would have to be removed from the skeleton again, a job as intricate as removing the stomach and viscera of a whale. There would be serious problems with the Treasury this time, for more funds would certainly be needed.

Wing Commander Colmore was forced to join designer Richmond to persuade the Air Ministry that the padding to prevent chafing would work. To redesign the hull structure would be out of the question, and out of the Treasury's capacity to handle. The R-101 went back into the shed. They got ready to saw the lady in half, to expose her mid-section girders, and insert a whole new section to bring her length up from 732 feet to 777 feet. The job would take well into autumn. There would be little time for testing before the flight to India.

Meanwhile, the R-100 sister ship, unsung and unpraised, was going through her own endurance tests, and she was doing well. She was getting ready for the acid test, a 24-hour final flight before she set forth across the Atlantic to Montreal. If she failed in this, the R-101 was to hold up on repairs to act as a standby. Such a delay might threaten the proposed trip to India.

Lord Thomson was touchy about this. He whipped off a fast, rather arrogant memo on July 14:

> So long as the R-101 is ready to go to India by the last week in September, this further delay in getting her altered may pass.
>
> I must insist on the programme for the Indian flight being adhered to, as I have made my plans accordingly.

Colmore was on the spot. Thomson would only approve the delay in reshaping the R-101 if it didn't delay the journey to India. The R-100 was obviously the poor stepsister in Thomson's mind. If anything was going to be postponed, it would have to be the Montreal trip. Even if the operation on the R-101 were done immediately, there would be no margin for error. But the incision was made, the mid-section parted. Caught between Lord Thomson's insistence, the locked Treasury door, and the need for making his ship airworthy, Colmore could only pray and urge his men to superhuman efforts. Under the conditions, they would need them.

Through the spring of 1930, Conan Doyle was forced to take things easy. He had had a serious attack of angina some months before, and he had no choice but to stay quietly at home at Windlesham, in the town of Crowborough, near Tunbridge Wells. He loved it there, and he loved the garden. He also was sure he was getting his strength back. He could not sit still; he hated that. Each day he would go to his study and write and keep up his voluminous correspondence.

The startling details of Emilie Hinchliffe's case were carefully filed in his mind. It was a classic. He was glad that he had been a small part of it. It added heavy evidence to his unshatterable belief: We do not die; we continue on. He had reached the conclusion not by blind faith, but by Sherlock Holmesian logic and analysis. If his body was weak, his thoughts were sharp. If only people would take the time, the patience to dig into the material he had assembled, there could be no question in their minds. He wished he could continue his tours over the world, to talk and implore.

But he couldn't. He had to take oxygen at times. The need became more frequent. On the early morning of July 7, 1930, he pleaded with Lady Doyle and his three children to help him out of bed so he could sit and watch the sun come up. He had trouble speaking now; his heart had been battered too long.

The family sensed that he was weakening fast. They sat around his chair. The end did not take long. Within minutes, the man who had created Sherlock Holmes was dead. He died convinced that he was moving on to a greater adventure than he ever could invent in the pages of a book. And like Captain Hinchliffe, Old Lowenstein and the others, he would not stay silent long.

While the R-101 lay at Cardington, the crew of its sister ship, the R-100, was bristling with action. Nevil Shute—he rarely used his real last name, Norway—was torn between writing a new novel and throwing himself fully into the adventure of facing the Atlantic ocean on the ship he helped design and build. The publicity and attention the R-101 rival was getting rankled within him. He had been concerned when he learned that the R-101 had only 35 tons of useful load, compared to the R-100's 54. He knew that an airship was safe only in proportion to its useful lift, and in proportion to the weights that it could jettison in an emergency. He also was convinced that the R-101 was considerably underpowered. Even though the R-100's Rolls Royce Condor engines were secondhand hand-me-downs, they were light and powerful gasoline engines, compared to the heavier Diesels.

When Shute first saw the R-101, he found himself forced to admire the workmanship, but found the craft unbelievably complicated in design. When the trial runs came for the more simplistic R-100, Shute noted the long faces on the visitors from the Cardington base. Unlike their R-101 ship, the engines and the gas bags of the R-100 gave no trouble at all.

As if to prove it, the R-100 left England on July 29, 1930, under Major Scott's command—he was working with both ships and was the most experienced pilot. It reached Montreal with very few mishaps. One of them was a ripped cover. The fabric tore on the tail surface. They were lucky to repair it in mid-air. They received a wild welcome in Canada, and returned to England twelve days later with practically no one to greet them.

Since only one design of airship would be selected for future production, the men of the R-101 were understandably upset by the R-100's triumphant round trip. Their ship was still sitting in the shed, sliced in two like a loaf of bread, under a horrendous work schedule that would permit no mistakes to be made. To say they were being rushed was an understatement.

They had to make India on schedule or become discredited and lose their jobs. The R-100's trans-Atlantic success was the worst thing that could have happened to Wing Commander Colmore and his men. Designer Richmond, struggling to keep up with the changes the new bay demanded, remarked to a friend: "I suppose I ought to feel a great satisfaction, but somehow I feel too tired."

Major Booth and Nevil Shute paid a visit to Cardington after their successful Atlantic crossing, aware that they weren't exactly welcomed by the R-101 officers. Waiting in one of the offices, Major Booth happened to notice a couple of square yards of the fabric used on the R-101 outer cover. Shute picked it up in his hands, turning it over as he examined it. Suddenly, his hand went right through it.

"In parts," he said later, "it was friable, like scorched brown paper. If you crumpled it in your hands, it broke up in flakes. I stared at it in horror, thinking of what happened to our tail surface near Montreal."

Booth and Shute learned that the new outer cover for the R-101 had been doped in place over the ship's surface. For adhesive, they had used a rubber solution in certain areas which had reacted chemically with the dope, and produced this incredible effect.

"What do you think of all that?" Booth asked.

Shute asked: "Do you think they've removed it all?"

"I don't know," Booth replied. "They *tell* me they have."

* * *

Emilie Hinchliffe, saddened by the death of Conan Doyle, and frustrated by her two fruitless trips to warn navigator Johnston, turned her attention to her children and occasional lectures on her experience. She never publicly mentioned the dire predictions she had received about the R-101. She still would take no compensation for her lectures. The reluctantly-given Inchcape money was carefully guarded for her children's future.

She concentrated on writing a short book about her experiences with the messages from her husband, but found herself hemmed in by pressure from family and friends against revealing the personal and intimate details of both the financial struggle and the R-101 involvement. In spite of these restrictions, she felt that she could reveal enough to convince many of the reality in her mind, that we continue to live after death.

As the time for the historical journey to India for the R-101 drew near, Emilie received even more warnings through Eileen Garrett and the voice purporting to be that of her husband. One message said: "If I, not heavily loaded and with cubic inches to spare, could not stand up against what I met, what could they expect, knowing that the weather had broken and that there were gales ahead."

Emilie knew it was useless to go back to Johnston again. She was forced to give up in despair and prayed that the warnings had somehow come through directly to Johnston or others on the R-101 staff.

Eileen Garrett, when told after the trance sessions what the messages read, was equally disturbed. They linked up so clearly with her three visions of the smouldering airships over London. She had never told anyone else about these, considering them to be "hallucinatory weaknesses." She still could not understand how her mind found these images, then showed them dramatically on its own subjective screen, nor could she understand how one mind receives the images of another without conscious assistance from the normal senses.

"To prove the existence of spirit intellectually," she wrote later, "has been left to religion, and to sentiment, but neither clearly defines a way to an afterlife acceptable to the measuring rule of science. I live in a world filled with phenomena of a transcendental nature, which does not seem to allow itself to be put aside, but acts continually as a guiding force. I have left these phenomena open to speculation, but I suspect that this field, which is surely discredited by those who do not experience its nature, belongs to the inner workings of what we call mind, as yet to be explored.''

With her analytical mind, Eileen supposed that her three "hallucinatory weaknesses" of the burning airships had to be nothing more than residual unconscious memories of the zeppelin raids she witnessed in terror during the First World War in London. She could accept that. It gave her a rational explanation for three irrational events that were frankly terrifying.

But in the sessions with Emilie Hinchliffe, a disturbing new element had been introduced. At the same time, it brought her a measure of relief. The messages purporting to be from Captain Raymond Hinchliffe seemed to confirm in detail Eileen's "hallucinatory weaknesses." That in turn horrified her with the thought that an accident was about to happen, and she was powerless to do anything about it. This mechanism of mediumship was constantly rocking her stability. She could only analyze it by thinking that some rhythmical periodicity forced apparitions to reveal themselves, along with a persistent imagery that gave her an awareness of psychic events that would take place.

None of her self-analysis brought her any comfort for the events that seemed to be shaping up. As she told Emilie Hinchliffe, a "psychic impregnation of certainty" took hold of her. She *knew* now that the R-101 would meet with disaster. But how could she explain it logically? The more people questioned her on any of the things she revealed, the less she could explain them. Because of the certainty of impending disaster that had now grown in her mind, she felt she should at least try to warn someone, even though Emilie had told her of her own failure with Squadron Leader Johnston.

By coincidence, an opportunity came up in mid-September. It was just a week or so before the R-101 was scheduled to leave for India. She attended a dinner party where her close friend Auriol Lee was also a guest. Auriol was a prominent actress and producer of plays in both New York and London. She was also the long-time friend of Sir Sefton Brancker. He, too, was a guest at the party. Eileen talked to Auriol Lee. It was the first time Eileen revealed her concern to an outsider. Perhaps indirectly, Auriol could quietly warn Sir Sefton, who was scheduled to fly to India on the airship as part of his official duties. She didn't want to broach such a delicate subject directly to Brancker, knowing how impossible it was to justify her concern objectively. She was torn. Not to say anything about it seemed to be as wrong as bringing the warning out in the open.

Auriol didn't hesitate. She went and brought Sir Sefton over to Eileen. In a quiet corner of the room, Eileen told him of her three previsions, and of Captain Hinchliffe's apparent warnings of impending disaster. She did it reluctantly, but she felt she had to.

Sir Sefton adjusted his monocle and laughed nervously. "Have you any idea which ship will suffer?" he asked.

"The R-101," Eileen replied firmly.

"That's the one scheduled to fly to India," he said. "I'm leaving on it soon. I hope you are just daydreaming about what has already been. I'm committed to fly, with Lord Thomson and others."

"I wish I could say something different," Eileen said. "Isn't there any way it can be postponed?"

"We are committed," Brancker said.

They talked further. Were these truly precognitive facts, or were they left-over impressions of something that once had been reality, like the R-38, that had broken up over the Humber?

Eileen, of course, had no answer. She had done what she felt she had to do. She could go no further. She did not like to transfer the burden of these thoughts. But she felt there was no alternative. She would not blame Brancker if he failed to take any action, because she knew what Emilie had experienced in her visit to Cardington. The one thing she did know was that her certainty of disaster was growing, and she felt deeply troubled.

CHAPTER IX

Major Oliver Villiers, commuting back and forth between the Air Ministry and Cardington, noted the strain on Colmore and his fellow officers. He also noted that Brancker was beginning to lose some of his jaunty step. Not since Villiers' World War days had he seen such pressure. He was beginning to think that his duties in the nose of a Vicker Gun Bus were tame compared to the stress placed on the R-101 builders. Villiers' first experience with airships had been in those days. He had been able to spot from the air an important German dirigible base. As a result, British planes knocked out two German zeppelins on the ground and one in the air. Now the machines were being groomed for peace instead of war. But there was little peace evident in the growing internecine struggles between Lord Thomson, the Air Ministry, the designer and the flight officers.

As Senior Assistant Intelligence Officer on the project, Major Villiers was constantly writing reports to keep the Air Ministry and cabinet officials up-to-date and informed on the R-101. For him to interpret the progress at Cardington was almost as complicated as the struggle to get the ship into the air. In his consultations with Colmore, Irwin, Scott and Johnston, Villiers sensed their concern about the airworthiness of the ship, under their surface posture of confidence.

171

Villiers couldn't help siding with them against the arbitrary attitudes of Lord Thomson and designer Richmond. He admired and respected Brancker, his immediate boss. But Brancker seemed to be merely following orders from above, as far as the R-101 was concerned. In recent days, Brancker never even yelled at Villiers to "use his damned intelligence." With all the pressure, Villiers missed his golf and tennis and the rose garden outside his Hertfordshire home. He was devoted to his wife and children, a son and a daughter. His time with them was measurably reduced under the hectic program.

The trip to India, that had become such a must under Lord Thomson's dictum, was also made imperative by the Imperial Conference of dominion prime ministers, to be held in October in London. The prime ministers were being wooed to support the airship program. The best way to do it was to show the value of the airships in clear and unambiguous terms. Lord Thomson made no secret that he wanted to make a grand entrance into the Imperial Conference with the R-101 round-trip under his belt. His arrival by airship in India with the gleam of a future viceroy post in his eye would be the first triumph.

Villiers was racing to finish the special report for the Imperial Conference. In his talks with Colmore at Cardington, he picked up the bad news with the good news. There was a lot of talk of other things that had happened on the trial run to Hendon, structural damage that was not announced. There was also a series of clashes between Colmore and Richmond that were never advertised.

Colmore was still trying to get through to Lord Thomson that it was impossible to give a firm date for the major surgery on the R-101 to be completed. All his memos and reports added up to the same conclusion: "Every effort will be made to complete the ship as quickly as possible, but we have no allowance in our programme to cover unforeseen delays." But on Colmore's desk, Thomson's memo still rested: "I must insist on the programme for the India flight being adhered to, as I have made my plans accordingly."

Colmore was torn. If the ship was not right, they could not leave. If they didn't leave on schedule, there would be no more funds for the airship program. In fact, no one would dare ask for them.

To Villiers, the frenzied program was a continued reflection of the massive conceit of the Secretary of State for the Air. To Colmore, it was the condition under which he had to live and work. In fact, Thomson had followed his curt message up with another: "I should like to be able to count definitely on starting for India during the weekend September 26–28. I ought to be back by October 16."

Colmore kept firing back realistic appraisals, writing up his confidential notes and technical problems in his big loose-leaf ledgers. He also expressed his deep concerns in the notes. He simply could not assure Thomson that he could get what he wanted. He made it plain to Thomson that any departure date would depend on when the work was completed. It wasn't at all certain when they could get a new Tornado engine installed with a new reversing element, when they could get a reversible airscrew suitable for the engine, when they could get good enough weather to slide the newly reconstructed ship out of the hangar, and when they could subject the ship to a full 24-hour test run, before they started out for India. They were working day and night, he told Thomson, but they might not get their new airscrew before September 28, let alone get the ship out of the box for a rigorous test flight.

At a conference on August 29, Lord Thomson told Colmore that he thought that he could arrange for the air business of the Imperial Conference to be put off until October 20. Colmore was now to do everything he could to get the ship ready for an October 4 flight. The R-101 could then arrive in Karachi five days later, turn around and start back on the 13th or 14th. With that schedule Lord Thomson could make his entrance at the Imperial Conference on the 20th.

Colmore, Irwin, Scott and the other staff officers would have preferred a lot longer test run than twenty-four hours. But they were trying to deal with the reality of the situation. They were aware that at times they were suspending their better judgment.

Brancker visited Cardington on September 22 to look over the progress of the ship. He said little about his reaction. He had also written some confidential letters to friends and associates expressing his doubts about the R-101. He questioned whether the ship could actually be ready to adhere to Thomson's optimistic schedule. In fact, he rather hoped it wouldn't. But he was not a man to back down.

A special body called the Air Council actually had final say on whether the R-101 was airworthy or not. Brancker had confidence that they would exercise great caution, in spite of Lord Thomson's enthusiasm to get on with it. The Council's job was to see that the ship would not leave its tower until independent consultants recommended both a Permit to Fly, and a Certificate of Airworthiness, required for all international flying.

A new member had just been appointed, whom Brancker had great respect for. He was Air Vice Marshal Dowding, later Lord Dowding, credited with winning the Battle of Britain in the Second World War as Air Chief Marshal. He had been a pilot and he had vision, which also was to show up in the future when the famous Spitfire and Hurricane fighters came into being under his urging and supervision. Everybody knew "Stuffy" Dowding, as he was irreverently called. Although he was outspoken and often controversial, he was liked and respected.

Dowding came into the Air Council just a few weeks after the decision to make the passage to India had been cast, if not confirmed. He was not an airship man. Because of that, his ultimate decision would have to rest heavily on the shoulders of the experts. The independent expert he would be leaning on most was Professor Leonard Bairstow, who had been granting the temporary Permits to Fly throughout the entire R-101 program.

By September 25, the basic repairs and reconstruction had been completed under exhausting pressure. The airship was gassed up in the hangar on the next day. They checked her lift and trim, and they seemed to be in good shape. On September 27, they were ready to haul her out of her box. There was still little, if any, margin for error. The final trial run with her entirely new mid-section could reveal any number of problems. Colmore and his officers were chafing to get the ship in the air to find out.

But the weather would not cooperate. Four more days went by. In the meanwhile, they had almost forgotten the critical Permit to Fly, to say nothing of the Certificate of Airworthiness, which could not be issued until after the scheduled 24-hour trial flight.

With the ship ready to come out of the hangar the minute the wind died down, Professor Bairstow was hastily contacted by phone. He protested that he had not had time to review the limited information on the remodeling job supplied him by the Royal Airship Works. But he realized the urgency of the situation. Somewhat reluctantly, he gave a verbal Permit to Fly over the telephone. He immediately followed the sanction up with a letter. It was hardly enthusiastic. Although he agreed that the insertion of the new mid-section bay complied with the specified requirements, he had other thoughts:

"The difference between the conditions of loading of R-101 now submitted and those of the original design . . surprised us by their magnitude. . . . A good deal of general thinking and comparison on limited information has been required in reaching our conclusion."

He also emphasized that he did not have proper time to prepare a well-considered report. Lord Dowding, new to his job on the Air Council, had little choice but to go along with the permit. He would be present himself on the final test run and would make his ultimate decision after that. Meanwhile, he talked to Colmore, who had been nervously watching the time slip by as the R-101 was trapped in her shed by gusty winds.

Studying the time schedule, Colmore now found himself forced to reducing the test flight to possibly less than twenty-four hours, if there was any chance at all of making Lord Thomson's demand for the earliest possible starting date.

"Why is it necessary to cut down the duration of the test flight?" Air Vice Marshal Dowding asked Colmore, as the official records later showed.

"So that we may have a chance, if all goes well, of leaving on Friday evening."

"That's October 3rd?" Dowding asked.

"Yes, sir," Colmore replied. "We can then have all Thursday to work on the ship, as well as Friday."

Dowding knew that Colmore was a thorough and exacting man. He agreed to go along with the idea. Dowding did not know, however, the doubts Colmore had in his own mind nor the effect of Lord Thomson's constant prodding.

Irwin, who was to command the flight, and Atherstone, who was to be his First Officer, were not at all happy about any cut in the trial flight time. Before the frenzy of the India flight deadline had been imposed, Irwin had already laid out his ideas for proper testing. He wanted day and night flights under good weather conditions, followed by twenty-four hours of bad weather testing, along with forty-eight more hours in bad weather "to windward of base," including six full hours at full speed in bumpy conditions. He wanted the ship back in the shed for a final look-over. This is what Irwin wanted. This is what Irwin knew he couldn't possibly get.

He and Atherstone had a chat with Major Booth, whose experience they valued.

"How is the program shaping up?" Booth asked Irwin.

"I've been hoping to get thirty-six to forty-eight hours in bad weather," Irwin said. "But we're unable to get the ship out of the hangar."

For the most part, the doubts and fears of the officers were unspoken. They had to be. The choice was either quitting or going ahead, even under the almost intolerable conditions. There was little question that they were slaves to the project, that their lives and honor were at stake, and that they had common responsibility for each other. They were actually being drawn together by a common enemy: Lord Thomson's obsessional insistence on leaving in time for him to get back to the Imperial Conference.

At 6:30 in the morning of October 1, the airship was tugged gingerly out of its shed by 350 men. Two hundred others failed to arrive in time. She was the biggest giant in the air. Her new midsection reduced her plumpness, extended her into a more graceful silhouette. At 4:30 P.M., Lord Dowding joined the usual complement of officers, anxious to see firsthand how the ship operated.

The weather was perfect. Doubts gave way to confidence. Provisioning of the trip for India had already been under way during the days the ship was stalled in its hangar. No detail had been overlooked. Large quantities of compressed cheese had been prepared. A cheese blender worked aboard the ship, carefully blending twenty different varieties chosen for flavor, texture, body and color. He had to taste as much as two pounds of cheese a day from the various samples, and complained that he wasn't able to fancy his dinner on those days.

In the lounge, lush carpets of staggering value were laid down to prepare for greeting the High Commissioner for Egypt when the ship was safely moored at the Ismailia mast. They added weight.

Navigator Johnston had already laid out the possible routes to India, depending on the weather. They would probably cross the coast of England over Hastings or Deal, carefully avoid the Alps and Massif Central in France, sail over the Mediterranean past Malta and on to Egypt for the first stop en route to Karachi. It was a tough haul for an experimental airship in any condition.

In the perfect weather of the test flight, the ship sailed well. Even Irwin and Atherstone were impressed. Lord Dowding, aware of his lack of airship knowledge compared to his vast experience in heavier-than-air planes, observed carefully the crew and performance. He leaned on them to answer his technical inquiries. As he later demonstrated as head of the fighter command that won the Battle of Britain, Lord Dowding was a stickler for technical performance and a realist when it came to anything to do with aviation. He had been a fearless pilot, but had a rare understanding of the limitations of air power. But he felt frustrated on the trial flight of the R-101, having been thrust into the mysteries of the airship without having the proper time for study and preparation. There was no question that he had to rely on the expertise of the designer and officers.

The test under perfect weather conditions went well. One engine, however, did go out of action. There was a broken oil cooler in the starboard forward engine. They kept the ship going all night, however, flying off the east coast of England, and came back north of Yarmouth in the morning, heading straight for Cardington.

The burst oil cooler was minor; it could be easily repaired. But it prevented a very important maneuver: the full-speed engine test. What's more, the failing engine shortened the test to sixteen hours, a far cry from Irwin's wish for twenty-four plus another forty-eight for bad weather tests. Nor could the ship be put back in the shed for a minute examination. The India fever seemed to have taken over even the doubting staff officers.

Squadron Leader Booth, of the somewhat resentful R-100 staff, observed the goings-on at Cardington from a distance. He found himself convinced that the impending Imperial Conference was definitely causing the R-101 officers to become biased in favoring the India trip at the expense of further tests. He was also convinced that Irwin, now to be captain of the historic flight, had not changed his mind about the lack of an extensive testing program.

On the evening of the completion of the truncated test flight, October 2, Wing Commander Colmore went to London for a meeting with Lord Thomson. The atmosphere was strained. Colmore conceded that the test had been satisfactory, and that the oil cooler could be easily repaired.

"In that case, we could probably start tomorrow evening?" the impatient Lord Thomson asked, as the official records show.

"I'm afraid this wouldn't leave time for the crew to get a rest, sir," Colmore replied. "It's a very long journey."

"I see," said Thomson. "We could start Saturday morning, then?"

"If we started in the morning," Colmore replied, "that would bring us into Ismailia at the wrong time of day. It would be important not to arrive there until dusk. There are a lot of technical and meteorological reasons for this. If you like, we could try for Saturday evening. That's October 4th."

"Well," said Lord Thomson, "you must not allow my natural impatience or anxiety to start to influence you in any way. You must use your considered judgment."

"We could leave Saturday at five or six o'clock," Colmore said.

"No rush on my account," Thomson replied. He didn't sound as if he meant it.

Lord Dowding, also at the meeting, broke in to say that he noted that no full power tests had been conducted. Perhaps they could conduct one over England, near the mast, near home, at the start of the trip? It would not be an ideal situation. It would put an extra strain on the ship, and would use up a considerable amount of valuable fuel. The question was left up in the air. The meeting ended with Lord Thomson's comment: "Well, that is all settled. I can make certain of being back on the 20th."

For a contingency, however, plans were made to fly the Secretary of State for Air back to London by airplane if there was trouble getting the R-101 off the Karachi mast.

At noon on Friday, Colmore made his final decision. The ship would definitely leave the Cardington mast between 6 and 8 P.M. the following evening. Even some of Lieutenant Commander Atherstone's doubts were cooled. "Everybody is rather keyed up now," he wrote in his secret diary, "as we all feel that the future of airships very largely depends on what sort of show we put up. There are very many unknown factors, and I feel that that thing called 'luck' will figure rather conspicuously in our flight. Let's hope for good luck, and do our best."

* * *

For three months previous to the R-101's final tests, Harry Price had been intrigued by the number of reports he was getting from mediums claiming to be receiving messages from the late Sir Arthur Conan Doyle. Lady Doyle, who was a psychic sensitive herself, claimed to be in constant touch with her deceased husband. Other reports from mediums came from as far away as Wilkes-Barre, Pennsylvania; Lyons, France; Paris, Vancouver, New York, Belgium and Italy.

Harry Price looked at these with a rather jaundiced eye. He was at a saturation point with claims from phony mediums, and he was damned if he would put up with even those who were sincerely misled into thinking they were getting messages from somewhere other than their imaginations. He respected Lady Doyle, but couldn't help feeling that in her bereavement she was engaging in wishful thinking. He would have to see a lot more evidence than he had received to remotely believe that Conan Doyle was communicating with anyone after his death.

On October 2, 1930, the day that the R-101 returned from her abbreviated test flight, an Australian journalist named Ian Coster, now working in England, phoned Price at his laboratory in South Kensington. Coster was an able editor and reporter, who wrote on assignment for magazines like *Cosmopolitan, Colliers* and the British large-circulation magazine *Nash's*.

He had heard of Harry Price's uncompromising exposés of fraudulent mediums and of his conjurer's ability to duplicate any trick a phony psychic tried to get away with. He also knew that Price was aware of legitimate psychics, who willingly allowed themselves to be tested under Price's rigorous discipline.

Coster was assigned a crazy idea by *Nash's* editors: to write a feature on the remote possibility of contacting Conan Doyle through the best available medium, three months after his demise. That date would be October 7, 1930.

Price reported that when he answered the phone Coster said, "Do you think we could get in touch with Sir Arthur Conan Doyle as a feature for this magazine?"

Price thought for a moment, then said, "Well, we could give it a try. If I can get the right medium."

"Could we do it on the 7th?" Coster asked. "That's three

months to the day after his death. It's also just five days from now.''

Price assured Coster he would get back to him if it was possible. Then Price thought about who might be best for the job. It would have to be a medium he had great confidence in, because he didn't want to waste time. It would be interesting to see what might come out of a possible contact with his old friendly enemy Doyle, for whom he had great respect in many areas.

His thoughts naturally turned to Eileen Garrett. She was a rare talent, and she was not a Spiritualist. Since he was rather down on what he considered the gullibility of many Spiritualists, Eileen might fill the bill nicely. He had heard about her brilliant success with Emilie Hinchliffe, and was aware of many other cases where verifiable information had checked out well.

Price had never sat directly with her as a medium, having only conducted other experiments with her. He could arrange to throw several unexpected tests at her that would indicate to him whether he was getting valid material. Also he knew that Eileen and Sir Arthur had been friends, and this closeness might help. Most of all, Eileen liked to experiment out of her own sense of deep curiosity about what made her tick. She was as hard-boiled about herself as he was about his tests and cross-checking. It might make an interesting exploration.

Eileen was delighted to try an experiment, she told Price when he called her. She knew Price for his intelligent, uncompromising research, and joined with him in thinking that the Spiritualists often got out of hand, even though there were many sincere and competent mediums among their ranks. Price was careful not to give her any clue as to whom Coster wanted to reach, or who Coster was. The time was set for three in the afternoon of October 7.

Price called Coster back to confirm the time. Coster, who knew little or nothing about the whole psychic process, wasn't quite sure what he was getting into. He was anything but a Spiritualist, and he wouldn't believe in ghosts until he saw one in front of his eyes. He wasn't at all sure what he felt about an afterlife. He tried to keep an open mind, although he was sure that the only chances for immortality in man lay in his work and in his reputation. He frankly admitted he was a doubting Thomas. He would approach the experiment very gingerly. Meanwhile, there were other stories to do, and a lot to get done before the session was held, five days away.

When the morning of October 4 arrived, the tension around the Royal Airship Works at Cardington was almost unbearable. Provisions were being whisked up the elevator of the mooring mast, rigging crews were scurrying up and down the steps, frenzied last-minute checks were being made of the ship's envelope, the gas bags, the padding that was sprinkled all through the interior of the hull like cotton blossoms. The passenger and crew list were completed and carefully checked along with the weight each was permitted to carry. Everything taken aboard had to be weighed. The amount of available lift was critical. The baggage of the ordinary crewman was cut to the bone. They were allowed ten pounds each, and parachutes, once planned, had to be sacrificed to lighten the load. For the distinguished passengers, the allowance was 30 pounds, but this turned cut to be flexible. They were simply requested to keep their belongings to a minimum.

The passenger list was impressive, but mixed:

Brig. General The Rt. Hon. Lord Thomson, P.C., C.B.E., D.S.O. (His Majesty's Secretary of State for Air)

Sir W. Sefton Brancker, K.C.B., A.F.C. (Director of Civil Aviation)

Major P. Bishop, O.B.E. (Chief Inspector, A.I.D.)

Squadron Leader W. Palstra (Representing Australian Government)

Squadron Leader O'Neill (Deputy Director of Civil Aviation, India. Representing Indian Government)

Mr. James Buck (Valet to Secretary of State for Air)

In addition to the officers directly under the command of Flight Lieutenant Irwin, captain of the ship for the India trip, Wing Commander Colmore, Major Scott and designer Richmond would theoretically have no command positions. They would represent the Royal Airship Works as senior directors of the project. Captain Irwin would command the five officers responsible for running the ship, which included Navigator Johnston and the half-reluctant Atherstone. There would be five coxswains aboard to handle the rudder and elevator controls, along with nine riggers, eighteen engineers, four wireless operators, three stewards and a galley boy. The entire list would total fifty-four passengers, officers and crew.

The critical point on everyone's mind was weather. At 9:30 that morning, Captain Irwin, Major Scott, and the ship's special meteorologist named Giblett, all met in the Forecast room at the Meteorological Office at Cardington. The weather didn't look too bad. There was a shallow depression near Tynemouth in England moving northeast, and another front moving eastward over Europe. It even looked as if the weather would improve, with perhaps just broken clouds by evening.

But by 3:00 in the afternoon, the situation had deteriorated. A trough of low pressure off western Ireland was spreading rapidly. Rain would come in from the west, probably reaching Cardington by evening. Clouds would drop down to about 1,000 feet, visibility might range from 2 to 6 miles, and in northern France there would be rain and winds up to 20 to 30 miles an hour from the southwest. It was not an ideal picture. Neither was it a hopeless one. No great increase in the velocity of the winds was expected, which was encouraging. Scott and Irwin thought they could handle it, and went ahead with preparing the ship. The barometer, however, was falling.

In spite of the pending adventure, Sir Sefton Brancker had scheduled one of his usual hectic days. He was to visit the busy aeroport in Lympne, down in the Kentish hunting countryside near the channel. Then he was to fly to Norwich, up in Norfolk, inland from Great Yarmouth on the eastern coast. After that he would make his way to Cardington in time for the historic flight. He would have little time to chew monocles or wilt collars on this day.

He could not be flown directly to Cardington, because no planes were permitted to land or fly within three miles of the R-101 when she was at her mast. He could, however, fly to Henlow, barely 20 miles south of Cardington, where Major Villiers volunteered to pick him up. What's more, Villiers could bring Sir Sefton's books and topee—the sun helmet associated with mad dogs and Englishmen in the blistering heat of India. Brancker's main luggage had already left his club in Mayfair, to be pre-boarded before he arrived.

His plans arranged, a well-known woman pilot named Winifred Spooner flew him from Croydon down to Lympne, where he had a consultation scheduled with Lieutenant Commander Deacon, the aerodrome officer in charge.

The first thing that struck Deacon was that "Brancks" was not his old vivacious self. The change was marked. Brancker was nervous, fidgety. He fingered several objects on Deacon's desk. He paced incessantly. He couldn't seem to stick to the subject. Deacon was worried, but he said nothing. There was really no appropriate comment he could make.

Brancker finished his business in spite of his unusual siege of nervousness, mounted the waiting plane on the Lympne runway, and flew to Norwich for his lunch and speech at the Norwich Aero Club. He jumped into his plane again. By 3:30 in the afternoon, he was greeting Villiers on the RAF airfield at Henlow. They walked back to the car where Villiers' wife, Aleen, was waiting. Villiers had been able to get her a permit to see the airship off.

The drive from Henlow took about forty-five minutes. Villiers, who had almost total recall, would never forget that conversation, and recorded it in his private notes:

"I don't mind telling you," Brancker said, "that two days ago, I had a deuce of a row with Thomson. During the past month, I have had several talks with Scott and Colmore. They've become more and more uneasy at the prospect of this journey to India. In their opinion, the ship is not really airworthy."

Villiers was not surprised. He had gathered as much from his own talks with the crew. But he was surprised that Brancker had confronted Thomson directly about it.

"Both were somewhat reticent as to details of the condition of the ship," Brancker continued, "but I knew them well enough to realize they were thoroughly perturbed."

Villiers, who had been growing uneasy all through the past weeks, agreed with him.

"After careful thought," Brancker told Villiers, "I made up my mind to have a talk with Thomson. I didn't mince matters, and I put my cards on the table. He flatly refused to believe what I told

him, although I was well aware that he was not ignorant of the
views held. He turned to me and said the ship must go on, as he
was pledged for the sake of the forthcoming Imperial Conference.
I protested that this was no valid argument. If the ship was not fit to
go, he ought to face the facts. At this he lost his temper and flung at
me: 'All right, if you are afraid to go—don't! There are many others who would jump at the chance!' I was furious at this treatment,
and I immediately left the room.''

It looked as if rain would arrive any moment when Major Villiers
threaded his car past the crowds toward the Cardington tower, to
the waiting ship gently swaying 200 feet above them. Villiers, who
at infrequent intervals had psychic flashes of his own, could not get
rid of an uncomfortable feeling that had gripped him all through the
drive from Henlow. Brancker's vivid description of his confrontation with Lord Thomson was stinging. The words kept going
through his mind. He was sure, though, that if the condition of the
ship were in the least doubtful, Colmore and Irwin would bluntly
refuse to leave the tower.

Darkness came early, with a thick, leaden layer of clouds. They
were scudding and low, and the wind was gusty. Sir Sefton re-
gained his high spirits as soon as he got out of Villiers' car. Grip-
ping his sun helmet and armful of books, he wove through the
wives and families of the officers at the base of the tower, grinning
and affable. The officers were all in their new Air Ministry uni-
forms, dark blue and trim. Their peaked hats bore the gold insignia
''R-101.'' There was a forced gaiety everywhere, like that of a garden party, or a day at the steeplechase. Brancker even took Auriol
Lee aboard for a last-minute look.

The last provisioning was being completed. Every ounce of it
was watched and weighed. For the first four days of the trip, there
was 837 pounds of rations, and 500 gallons of drinking and bathing
water. More would be collected from the rain that would fall on the
broad, whale-back envelope of the ship. There was a cheery note
to the provisioning: a bright, silver-painted nine-gallon cask of beer
was put aboard. It was decorated with the crossed flags of Britain
and India.

Alfred Cook, one of the engineers, was in the hull of the ship,
walking along the keel catwalk. He was a little nervous, a little anxious about the forthcoming trip. He encountered G. W. Hunt, the

chief coxswain, making a final inspection of the interior. Hunt also looked anxious. He was looking up at the gas bags, as big as swollen circus tents above him.

"I don't know, Alfred," he said. "Look at my gas bags. They're gradually going out. If we don't start soon, we're going to have to start gassing all over again. Two of the bags have already deflated about three percent. We'd better get started soon."

At the base of the mooring mast, Villiers was unable to say goodbye to his departing friends personally. They were preoccupied with last-minute duties. Major Scott was standing at the base of the tower. He looked as if he were trying to look unconcerned. Villiers saw Leech, the chief engineer at the Royal Airship works, say goodbye to his wife. Smiling, but with tears, she handed him a sprig of white heather.

As the darkness increased, the tower lit up, festooned in lights, creating a carnival spirit among the wives and relatives next to the mast. Searchlights played and bounced off the low clouds. The officers on the ground prepared to go on board.

Aleen Villiers, watching the scene with her husband, took special notice of Colmore, Scott and Irwin, as Villiers recalled in his notes.

"They look so terribly serious," she said. "I've never seen them quite that way before."

"I guess it's natural," the Major answered. "Their responsibility is so great."

"Irwin, especially," said Aleen. "There's a look of tragedy on his face."

"They'll be fine," Villiers reassured his wife.

They watched for Brancker, who had promised to come back down from the ship to say goodbye. He was nowhere to be seen. All afternoon, Johnston had been consulting with the meteorologists, watching the weather, planning his alternate routes in line with what he might expect. Ismailia was 2,390 miles away. He would like to go down the Rhone Valley, but there were the deadly mistral winds and the constant threat of thunderstorms there. Two alternate routes, still keeping a safe distance from the mountains, would add anywhere from 100 to 400 extra miles. Johnston wanted to avoid rain, but the reports made it evident that he couldn't. The thin skin of the enormous envelope would take on extra weight from the lightest rain, and weight was the most critical factor of the trip, especially at the start, when the fuel load was so heavy.

Lord Thomson was driven up in a car from the Bedford railway station shortly before six. He was the last of the passengers to arrive. He wore a broad smile. His baggage was unloaded from the car. There were many pieces of luggage in the limousine. But more than that, there were several cases of champagne, and a heavy roll of plush red carpeting. Both were last-minute thoughts for the occasion of the greeting of the distinguished Egyptian officials when they came aboard for lunch at the Ismailia mast. Thomson went quickly to the elevator door, stopping only to answer a reporter who asked: "Will you make the entire return journey?"

"Why not?" Lord Thomson answered with a smile. "I am under orders to be back in London by October 20th, and I don't expect I shall have to change my plans. Unless something happens, I shall go out and come back on the old bus."

He stepped into the elevator. His baggage followed. The weighing scales had already been removed from the entrance to the gangway. The luggage, the rug and the cases of champagne were hurriedly stored aboard the ship. There was little time now for checking weight and balance. The time for departure had almost arrived.

From the base of the mast, the crowd looked up. They were shivering and cold now. Some became a little dizzy watching the great ship sway and roll above them. They could see the lights in the power cars. Above the gondolas, the lights in the dining saloon and the lounge glowed cheerily. Lord Thomson and Sir Sefton were seen, standing together in silhouette, looking down at the crowds.

Just before the engines were started, a rather frantic messenger dashed up to the tower, and into the elevator. For some inexplicable reason, someone had forgotten the Certificate of Airworthiness. It was delivered directly to Captain Irwin.

A silence fell among the crowd below, as the forward starboard engine began to wind up. But it failed to start. Engine room telegraph bells could be heard ringing, as the recalcitrant engine turned over and over, without ignition. Suddenly the crowd gasped. A shower of sparks flew out of the exhaust. The engine was sputtering and coughing. It finally began to run smoothly.

One by one, the other engines were fired up, until all five of the propellers were turning. There were more engine room telegraph bells. The hull shook with the engine vibration. The locking cone in the nose seemed to want to hold the ship to the mast. But at 7:34 P.M. she slipped from her bondage.

She failed to rise as smartly as she had in the past. Her nose dipped. Suddenly, from the forward section near the nose, an enormous waterfall gushed, cascading to the ground by the tower, four tons of it. It was nearly half the ballast carried aboard the ship. But the nose finally did rise. The ship leveled. The engines were gunned. The crew could be seen signaling goodbye with their electric torches. The wet and shivering crowd cheered. The ship moved slowly around Cardington in a wide circle. All that could really be seen now were the red and green navigation lights, and the warm glow from the lounge and dining room. Then the bow of the ship turned and pointed in the direction of London. The historic passage to India had begun.

Emilie Hinchliffe was far from the Cardington base. She felt no less tense than the wives and families who watched the R-101 fade into the distance and disappear. She was visiting Mrs. Earl, full of misgivings about her futile attempts to warn Johnston. Although neither of the women really wanted to, they attempted one more communication with Hinchliffe, perhaps in the hope of learning of a brighter outlook than the last somber series of messages.

There was no consolation. The message from Captain Hinchliffe was brief: STORMS RISING. NOTHING BUT A MIRACLE CAN SAVE THEM.

CHAPTER X

The concern for their friends on the R-101 didn't fade when Major Villiers and Aleen arrived back at their Hertfordshire home. Aleen tried hard to shake off her feeling of depression. She was unsuccessful. Villiers was still troubled about why "Brancks," as he called him, had never come back down to say goodbye. He tried to concentrate on completing his report for the Imperial Conference, "An Approach to Civil Aviation." He had a hard time doing it. He was thinking of the R-101 leaving the mast. Why had they had to drop so much ballast? It could obviously mean only one thing—the whole ship was heavy, especially at the bow. He had watched the R-101 leave the tower many times before. They never had had to sacrifice such a large amount of the precious ballast.

The technical section of the report he was working on was too difficult to handle that evening. There were too many disturbing feelings both Aleen and he were experiencing. Villiers was not a technical man. He preferred the subject matter of policy and planning, which he had no trouble in grasping. He finally gave up, and he and Aleen went to bed early.

Both were staunch members of the Church of England, and both of them prayed for a safe voyage for the ship. Villiers' grandfather had been the Bishop of Carlyle. His wife's father had held the same post. Religion was a natural and integral part of their lives, and they carried it into their everyday living. Villiers was convinced that he would never have gotten through the First World War without it, so many times did he come close to death. They both believed in the utter reality of the spirit. They saw no conflict between the ideas of the Christian Spiritualists and the conventional theology of the church.

Villiers' own psychic experiences were few. He would on occasion get an overwhelming sense of the presence of a loved one who had died, and sometimes feel they were in communication with him. Although his rational mind could not explain such incidences, he accepted them as part of a greater picture beyond the senses. He never believed in going to a medium, although he had on one occasion. The experience indicated to him that there had to be some validity in the psychic. His father had "come through." He was described in detail by the medium, along with a number of verifiable facts. His father had also identified himself by describing the crooked finger he had had since birth. In Villiers' mind, there was no possible way for the medium to know this or any other of the multiple, intimate facts revealed about his father, long since dead at the time of the session. But he felt uneasy about the experience, almost as if he were intruding. He never went back.

For the most part, Villiers was a realist and a man of action. At the age of forty-four, he played golf and tennis vigorously, and never lost his interest in cricket. He lived a disciplined life, a hangover from his long and active years in the military. His performance in the service, which had won him his D.S.O., the Croix de Guerre and the Legion of Honor, provided enough discipline to last him a lifetime.

Aleen and the Major drifted off into an uneasy sleep. Around midnight, Aleen woke him up. She was terrified. She had had one of the most vivid dreams she had ever experienced. She saw the R-101 clearly, moving across the sky. Then without warning, it went crashing to the ground.

They both attributed the nightmare to their deep anxiety, and finally dozed off again to sleep.

As the R-101 headed toward its first checkpoint over London, a lavish dinner was being prepared on board. There was an ample supply of champagne. The rains had come now, with gusty winds and a vengeance. They had gone barely 35 miles, over the village of Hitchin, when the vessel began pitching and rolling heavily. It seemed to have trouble gaining altitude, and it kept dipping unpredictably. In the smoking room, sitting on the wicker lounge, Squadron Leader Rope took notice of it. He was the technical assistant to Richmond, the designer. Beside him was Henry Leech, the foreman engineer from the base at Cardington.

"I never knew her to roll so much," Rope said to Leech. "She feels more like a seagoing ship than an aircraft."

Rope didn't seem too worried about it. It was the first time that the R-101 had been flying in any kind of substantial rough weather, and perhaps it was to be expected. In the control car, the concern centered on the dropping of all that water ballast so early in the trip. Four tons, out of nine-and-a-half, had had to be sacrificed, all of it from the bow tanks. The only emergency ballast left in the forward part of the ship was half a ton. It could not be dumped automatically in an emergency. A man would have to be sent scurrying up forward to release it by hand, to lighten the load and try to get the ship level. With the changes in pressure on the gas bags at different altitudes, this could be critical.

They were still over Hitchin, when Arthur Bell, the gondola engineer in the aft-engine power egg, reported that his engine had suddenly stopped. W. R. Gent, the supervising engineer for the flight, scampered down the precarious ladder to the gondola, and joined Bell.

"It's the main oil pressure, sir," Bell told him.

Henry Leech joined them in moments. Jammed into the narrow cabin, the three began working. The rain was heavy, beating on the window. The ship was still pitching and rolling heavily. It was hard to keep their balance.

Down below the ship, in Hitchin, the countryside was drenched in rain, and the trees and bushes were bending in the wind. Shane Leslie, a well-known author of the twenties, and his wife were having dinner at West End Farm, their Hertfordshire cottage. Suddenly, they heard their two servants scream. They rushed out to the garden terrace. Over a field of mushrooms, they saw the red and green running lights of the R-101. The giant hull was barely visible in the lowering clouds and rain. But it was there, and it seemed to be aiming straight for their cottage.

It was low, so low that Mrs. Leslie felt that it couldn't possibly miss scraping their roof. She thought: "This is the end of our cottage." The Leslies and the servants scattered. They were absolutely certain the ship was coming down on them. They watched, their field and garden faintly illuminated by the lights of the saloon cabins. Their farm was on a hill, a sudden rise of about 600 feet above sea level. The ship seemed to barely clear the trees along their driveway. She was dipping, then rising, as if she was straining to get higher. They went back in the house and checked the clock in their living room. It was 8:15 in the evening.

The huge skin of the vessel, the envelope, was now sodden with water, adding weight to the ship, making it harder to control. As the engineers worked on the aft engine, the wireless room sent a message back to the Cardington base:

OVER LONDON. ALL WELL. MODERATE RAIN. BASE OF LOW CLOUDS 1500 FEET. WIND 240 DEGREES. 25 M. P. H. COURSE NOW SET FOR PARIS. INTEND TO PROCEED VIA PARIS, TOURS, TOULOUSE AND NARBONNE.

There was no mention of the broken-down engine, nor of the inordinate pitching and rolling. No change in altitude was noted. All seemed well, according to the message at least.

Shortly after eight o'clock, the Meteorological Office at Cardington had wirelessed a message to the R-101. It was not good news:

NEXT TWELVE HOURS FLIGHT SE ENGLAND, CHANNEL, NORTHERN FRANCE, WIND AT 2000 FEET FROM ABOUT 240 DEGREES 40 TO 50 MILES AN HOUR. CLOUDY LOCAL RAIN.

This was serious. The early forecasts had predicted winds in the neighborhood of 20 to 30 miles an hour. To face a possible 50-mile-an-hour wind would put the heavily loaded R-101 to a flying test she had never experienced, over a terrain where cross-currents and vertical drafts would be sure to occur. No other British airship had met such a velocity over land before.

Below, in London, the spectators gathered, in spite of the chilling rain and the wind. The ship seemed unusually low. Her nose was well down, her tail up. The crowds could even see people in the cabins, in spite of the clouds and darkness.

Major Scott was immediately presented with the storm warning, while the ship was still over London. It was hard to tell where the responsibility for decisions actually lay. The passengers and officers aboard were top-heavy with rank and brass. Irwin was technically in charge of the flight, but Major Scott had many more hours of command experience. Colmore was the overall boss of the project, but not the flight. Lord Thomson and Sir Sefton could, if they wanted to, probably overrule everyone with their authoritative weight.

In this case, it was Scott who probably made the decision not to turn back. He was a resolute and fearless commander, too much so, some of his fellow officers thought. He had headed the R-100 into the teeth of a storm on the Montreal flight, and some of the crew thought they were lucky to survive. The fact was that the R-101 now kept going, heading toward France, toward the center of a rising storm.

With four of the five engines still operating well, the R-101 crossed over the lights of Hastings, site of the historic battle, and out over the darkness of the Channel. It was shortly after 9:30. The alternate routing over Deal, toward Dunkirk, had not been chosen this time. The rain was increasing, as well as the wind. There was no question that its velocity had been underestimated. Over the Channel, the concern would not be too great. It was when they reached the rolling terrain of France that concern would grow. The turbulence and the gusts would be bound to increase.

But the message from the ship was not discouraging:

AT 2135 GMT CROSSING COAST IN VICINITY OF HASTINGS. IT IS RAINING HARD AND THERE IS A STRONG SOUTHWESTERLY WIND. ENGINES RUNNING WELL AT CRUISING SPEED, GIVING 54.2 KNOTS. CLOUD BASE IS AT 1500 FEET. . . . SHIP IS BEHAVING WELL GENERALLY AND WE HAVE ALREADY BEGUN TO RECOVER WATER BALLAST.

The rain water was doing its part of the job, flowing in through the openings at the top of the envelope to replenish part of the ballast lost at the start. There was no mention of the non-operational aft engine, nor of concern for the storms ahead.

Over the Channel, the three cramped engineers were still working furiously on the recalcitrant aft engine. They were not making any obvious headway, and the ship was dragging several tons of

useless weight because of it. Leech paused in his work long enough
to glance out the window, and was rather startled at the low altitude of the ship. He could clearly see the whitecaps through the
darkness. He estimated that the ship was only 700 or 800 feet
above them. Engineer Cook, in the port midship engine, could also
distinctly see the choppy white waves. He looked out several
times. The ship would dip and get lower, then rise again. It was
common for an airship to plunge up and down in squally weather.
He found it hard to believe the control car was allowing the ship to
dip so low.

Electrician Disley joined the wireless operator for a moment, in
the wireless room immediately adjoining the control cabin. It was
around ten o'clock now, and the ship was still over the sloppy waters of the Channel. Nearby, Navigator Johnston was dropping cal-
cium flares to check the drift. As they landed in the water, he could
check the crabbing movement of the ship, as the wind pushed it out
of its course.

Looking into the control car, Disley was surprised to see First
Officer Atherstone suddenly grab the elevator wheel from the
height coxswain. The altimeter, if it was correct, showed that they
had dipped to 900 feet. But there was always a problem with the
barometric altimeter. A reading could sometimes indicate an altitude considerably higher than the ship actually was. Atherstone
spun the wheel at the port side of the control car hard. Then he
handed the wheel back to the coxswain.

"Do not let her go below 1,000 feet," he warned.

It was an unusual procedure. Atherstone must have been seriously concerned to take the wheel himself.

No word was heard back in Cardington from the R-101 until
11:36 P.M., when a new wireless message arrived:

CROSSING FRENCH COAST AT POINTE DE ST. QUENTIN. WIND 245
TRUE 35 MPH.

Back at Cardington, there was surprise. The Channel crossing
had taken roughly two hours. The distance from Hastings to the
French port was approximately 60 miles. The previous wireless reports from the R-101 didn't add up. She should have traveled considerably farther if the earlier reports had been correct. It was confusing.

The watch had changed at eleven o'clock. The fresh crew would stay on duty until 2 A.M., when the alternate shift would come on. By eleven, the stubborn aft engine was fixed. It would help increase power against the increasing winds. By midnight, the ship settled down to the routine details of the flight. At eighteen minutes after midnight, another wireless message was sent to Cardington. The ship would soon be out of range, and would depend on Croydon, Le Bourget in Paris, and Valenciennes for its cross-bearings and communication.

The midnight message read:

2400 GMT 15 MILES SW OF ABBEVILLE. AVERAGE SPEED 33 KNOTS. WIND 35 MPH. ALTIMETER HEIGHT 1500 FEET. WEATHER INTERMITTENT RAIN. CLOUD NIMBUS AT 500 FEET.

After the official information had been dispatched, a more relaxed report came over, heartening the observers at Cardington:

AFTER AN EXCELLENT SUPPER OUR DISTINGUISHED PASSENGERS SMOKED A FINAL CIGAR, AND HAVING SIGHTED THE FRENCH COAST HAVE NOW GONE TO BED TO REST AFTER THE EXCITEMENT OF THEIR LEAVE-TAKING. ALL ESSENTIAL SERVICES ARE FUNCTIONING SATISFACTORILY. THE CREW HAVE SETTLED DOWN TO A WATCH-KEEPING ROUTINE.

It was a comfortable picture now. The lights in the lavishly decorated saloon were turned low. The equally opulent smoking room was dimmed, but was available to anyone who was restless or who wanted to find a fellow insomniac in the early morning hours to share a nightcap or the excitement of traveling in the clouds in such luxury. The passengers, with perhaps a touch too much of champagne, enough anyway to relax in the comfortable bunks in their staterooms. The officer of the watch in the darkened control cabin, monitoring the altimeter, the compass, the pitch and roll indicators, the engine room telegraph pedestals standing by if needed. The engineers in their egg-shaped gondolas, shaken by noise and vibration, but watching with satisfaction the performance of their engines. The riggers on watch on the keel catwalk, more than the length of two football fields, roaming it in silence as the engines purred smoothly beneath the ship.

There would be those annoying and sometimes frightening pitches, yaws and dips. There would also be the likelihood of the storms getting worse, of the gas bags surging and swaying against the struts and girders, of the thin and questionable skin of the en-

velope that had never faced a 50-mile wind beating against it under
cruising power. These were imponderables. They clouded the comfortable portrait of a luxury liner of the air moving like a magic carpet over the villages of France.

At 1:18 A.M., the airship sent a radio message to Croydon:
"Thanks for valuable assistance. Will not require you further tonight." Croydon was not dismissed so easily: "Am remaining on
watch," they wirelessed back.

The R-101 passed over the Poix aerodrome, about 30 miles from
the French coast, on the way to Paris, at around one in the morning. The wind was fiercer now, and the rains lashed at it with greater fury. M. Maillet, manager of the Poix airfield, heard the engines
and peered through the thick rain and mist to look for it. Finally he
saw something—a strip of white lights in a row. He could barely
make out the hull of the ship. She was moving slowly, along the
railway line.

She appeared to be struggling hard against the wind. He was convinced she was low, very low, too low. The ship could not be at
more than 300 feet, maybe less. As a veteran observer of aircraft,
he did not like what he saw. He gauged by her direction that she
was heading toward Beauvais, the next town to the south, on the
Paris route. He felt troubled. She was less than half her length
from the ground.

At Le Bourget, the historic field where Lindbergh had landed the
Spirit of St. Louis, the wireless operator was keeping close touch
with the R-101. The signal was loud and clear. Leech and Gent, the
two senior engineers, had made their way to the smoking room to
relax after the tension in getting the aft engine going again. It
wasn't long before Captain Irwin joined them. He was pleased with
their repair job, and told them so. After a short respite, he left.
Tired, Gent said that he was going to head for his stateroom, while
Leech decided to take another look at all the engines.

It was a long tour of duty. He had to scramble from transverse
frame #4, all the way back to #11. He would have to walk in the
swinging, pitching ship nearly 400 feet each way, climb down the
ladders to the engines, and climb up again into the hull after each
engine inspection. He did it. It took the better part of an hour, but
all was well with the engines, and he was relieved. He went back to
the smoking room, too tense to sleep. It was empty. He poured a

drink, and sprawled out on the settee to have another cigarette. Sleep was hard to come by.

In the control car, there seemed to be trouble with the altimeter. Some of the crew felt they were always nearer the ground than the altimeter showed. Ever since the Channel, in fact.

Shortly after quarter of two, the wireless man at Le Bourget joined up with a station at Valenciennes, and sent the R-101 a clear position fix. They figured the ship to be one kilometer from Beauvais, give or take a fraction. The operator in the wireless room of the R-101 sent back a simple, cheery message: "Thank you. Good night."

They were over Beauvais when the watch was changed at 2 A.M. The change was made calmly enough. Nobody seemed concerned. Engine man Binks made his way along the keel catwalk. He had had a hard time waking up after a restless sleep, and had stopped and poured himself a mug of hot chocolate, as a wake-me-up. He moved through the transverse frames from #8 to #11, and climbed down into the aft-engine car about three or four minutes late. He was relieving his friend Bell, who greeted him in mock anger for being late.

The two chatted a minute, over the roar of the engine, about its performance. There had been no trouble since the oil pressure failed back over Hitchin, some six hours before.

Engineer Alfred Cook climbed down the ladder to the midship engine on the port side to take over from engineer Blake promptly on schedule. Blake was tired. After a quick exchange of greetings, he went up the ladder and headed for his crew quarters.

In the same manner, engineer Savory took over the starboard midship engine from his crew-mate Hastings. He checked over the operation of the engine, which seemed in good order.

Electrician Disley was sound asleep in his bunk, near the main electrical switchboard. He was lying with his head toward the bow of the ship, and he suddenly found himself sliding backwards on his bunk. Then he felt the ship come out of the dive, and was considerably relieved. It had been a steep one.

Leech was still alone in the smoking room at this time, at about five after two. He was about to have another sip of his drink, when he found himself sliding down the settee, toward the forward bulkhead, and came to a stop against it. At the same moment, a siphon and several highball glasses on a table near him slid to the floor. Then the table itself skidded down the floor toward the bulkhead. He leaned over, picked the unbroken glassware up and put it back on the table.

In the village of Beauvais, Louis Petit and his wife were getting ready to go to bed. They ran a general store in the town, and had just finished up a rather busy Saturday night. The hour was later than usual for them. As M. Petit began to undress, he heard a noise that sounded like thunder. He quickly ran out on the street. He looked up. He saw what he described as a lit-up village in disguise. It was low, very low. It looked as if it might impale itself on the church steeple.

He knew that the "Zepp," as he called it, was due to pass over the town, but he immediately realized that the ship was in trouble. The hull was moving broadside, not forward. It was sliding sideways, out of control. It was being whipped by the wind and the rain. His wife was now beside him, and they looked on in horror. Then the lights suddenly disappeared in the sky. Seconds later, they were on again. Then off. Then on and off.

Each time they did this, the ship seemed to be getting lower. Monsieur and Madame Petit stood transfixed, hardly daring to think about what was going to happen next.

George Darling, a British racehorse owner visiting his friend Marcel Debeaupuis near Beauvais in the village of Allone, had gone to bed. But he had not yet gone to sleep. He heard the motors of the R-101 coming nearer. He looked out of the window. Through the rain the ship could be seen low above the rolling hills near Beauvais. There was a howling gale outside now, and he wondered how any aircraft could survive. The strip of lights along the hull blinked off and on. Then he saw the ship plunging up and down like a dolphin. There was no question in his mind that it was in trouble.

He called to Debeaupuis, who had also been roused from sleep. They watched together, both in suspense and uncertainty.

It was nearly five minutes after two. On board the R-101, there was no sign of any restless passengers wandering through the passageways. In the passenger cabins, Lord Thomson, Sir Sefton and the other visitors were sleeping soundly. In the pantry, someone in the crew was having a snack of tinned corned beef and some cold peas. He was surrounded by tins of biscuits and sardines.

Over Beauvais, the ship seemed to circle, like a dog looking for a comfortable place to lie down. It seemed to be skimming dangerously low, over both fields and houses. By now, it seemed that half the town, in various stages of undress, had come out to the streets. Some felt that it actually had brushed against the spire of the cathedral and the side of a factory building nearby. It looked like a drunken, reeling monster with its crabwise motion.

Out on the soaked, undulating fields and orchards near Beauvais, Alfred Roubaille was breaking the local laws by setting snares for rabbits. He was working along a wooded area, near a hummock of land. It was called Therain Wood. It was a lonely spot, nearer Allone then Beauvais. He wasn't altogether comfortable about his illegal hunting, but there was Sunday dinner to think about, and times were not that good for him and his family.

Roubaille heard the sound of the engines too, over the rush of the wind near Therain Wood. He looked up from his snares and saw it. It was brightly illuminated. It was moving very slowly, but it was coming directly toward him. He had trouble believing what he was seeing. The great hull of the ship seemed to be sinking in front of him. It was still moving forward, but its nose was pointed down. He was frozen in horror.

Binks was still chatting with Bell in the after-engine car. They were talking of oil pressure, engine cooling and the rpm's of the Diesel. There seemed to be no problem any more. Quite suddenly, they felt the nose of the ship sink down. The dive must have lasted nearly half a minute. Then the craft leveled off again. In moments, there was another dive. As it happened, the engine room telegraph rang, and the indicator moved to SLOW. Bell grabbed the throttle, and pulled it back.

Alfred Cook, in the port midship engine cab had barely time to get adjusted to the noise of the motor before he noticed the ship diving, and the engine telegraph ringing to SLOW. He immediately cut the throttle back, but as he did, the ship went into another, steeper dive. He looked out the gondola window. The ground was coming up to meet him.

Savory, in his engine cabin on the starboard midship car, felt only one dive. But it was a steep one. He was standing with his back to the starting engine looking aft. Suddenly, he was thrown back against it. He had no idea what was going on.

Right after Henry Leech had picked up the siphon and the high-ball glasses in the smoking room, he felt the nose of the ship take another dive. It didn't seem to him to be as sharp as the first. Then he heard the engine room telegraph ring. All along he had felt that the ship had been pitching dangerously. He still suspected that something was wrong with the altimeter. He was glad his wife had given him that sprig of white heather. He needed it for luck. But he still had confidence in the ship, in spite of the pitching that had bothered him over the past half hour.

Electrician Disley's crew quarters were above and slightly astern of the control car, almost amidship. He had no way of seeing outside, but he could sense that the R-101 was struggling against the storm. He was not too disturbed. He, too, heard the engine room telegraph ring out, and he knew that the sudden change in the engines would have a strong effect on the generators. If a wire broke, there was the danger of fire. The switchboard was close to his left hand. He instinctively reached for it. There were two main switches. He grabbed one of them and tripped it.

Up in the control car, the height coxswain was spinning the wheel to a full "up" position. They were dumping ballast now—including precious fuel oil. Rigger Church was ordered up to the forepeak to dump the manual ballast tanks there. The ship was badly out of trim, and the forward tanks could not be released from the control car. As he was approaching the tanks, he clearly heard the crack of fractured girder or strut. He had never heard anything like it before.

From his position at the edge of the woodland, at the foot of the gentle hill, poacher Alfred Rabouille was still staring upward, as if hypnotized. The gargantuan airship was coming almost directly at him. She was getting closer, closer to the earth. Her nose suddenly dipped again.

On the ship, electrician Disley saw Chief Coxswain Hunt flash by, going aft, along the passage way. He called out one simple sentence: "We're down, lads!"

Roubaille saw it happen, not more than a hundred yards away. The forward part of the ship crunched into the top of the hummock. There was a tremendous explosion. Roubaille was knocked off his feet. He picked himself up. There were two more explosions. Then the whole ship seemed to burst into flames. The mid-ship section collapsed, telescoped like an accordion, as if the ship had broken her back.

He heard people in the ship. They were screaming for help. A blast of heat struck him, burned his eyes. The whole sky lit up. He was seized with uncontrollable terror. He could not look at nor listen to the scene he saw. All reason left him. He completely lost his head. He ran as hard as he could to get away from the nightmare.

Binks and Bell, in the after-engine gondola, felt their car strike the ground, then skid along it as the bottom caved in. An explosion followed, and they were surrounded by fire. Soon the eggshell cabin was engulfed by the flame around it. They grabbed greasy engine-wiping rags, held them over their heads and around their faces to insulate themselves from the heat. They were certain they were goners.

Suddenly a cascade of water came down on their gondola from the burning hull above. Ballast, it would have to be. It splashed through on them, making a pocket clear of flames. They soaked their clothes in it, smashed their way out of the car somehow, found themselves among the bushes on the ground.

All that Savory could remember was that he heard the sound of things breaking, and a rumbling and crashing noise that was terrifying. His engine was still running at cruising speed; he had received no signal to reduce it. There was a vivid flash bolt ing in through the open door of his engine car. It blinded him, dazed him, scorched his face. He remembers little after that—except that a local villager grabbed him, led him away from the burning wreckage.

Electrician Disley never got to pull that second switch. It is doubtful if it would have helped prevent the huge fire and explosion of the hydrogen. A hot cylinder of a ruptured engine pushed up against the hull would co it. Or a spark from a backfire. Or a piston shot into the side. Or any of the electrical wires. The explosion, given the conditions of the crash, was not only probable; it was certain.

The whole ship was impossible for Disley to describe. It was roaring like a furnace. He felt himself drop down to the base of the envelope. There was just the thin fabric to hold him. He kicked and punched at it. It broke, and he dropped to the ground. He looked up to see if he could help anyone else. It was hopeless. The entire length of the hull was now burning. A villager found him, wandering near the wreck.

Engineer Cook succeeded in stopping his engine, just before he felt the crash. He looked out of his gondola window, and saw the main body of the ship strike the ground. It seemed to slide along, and then come to an abrupt stop. The explosion took place almost immediately. He found himself caught in the canvas of the envelope. He clawed at it with teeth and nails, broke out of it at last, fell to the wet grass below.

In the forepeak of the bow section, rigger Church never reached the release valve on the ballast tank. Oddly enough, the crash wasn't too severe, even in his forward position. But he found himself tangled in blazing canvas and twisted duraluminum girders. He fought his way out with his blistered hands, dazed and scorched. He heard a voice yelling from a gondola. He staggered away from the wreckage, then collapsed into the arms of a rescuer.

In the smoking room, Leech felt the ship crunch into the hill. The shock was surprisingly mild. Suddenly, there was darkness. Then, there was the brilliant flash of a flame. The entire ceiling telescoped down on the top of the settee. It left only four feet of height in the room. He crawled toward a partition in the wall, ripped it away with his hands.

George Darling and his friend Debeaupuis were in their car almost at the moment the ship crashed. They threw on boots and coats over their pajamas, gunned the car over the short distance to the hill. They jumped out, raced across a beetroot field toward the burning ship. The flames were lighting up the sky for miles around, coming mostly from the bow and mid-section of the ship.

They found Bell and Binks near the tail section. Leech joined them in moments. Except for some surface burns, they seemed to be all right. They were even calm. But Leech was insistent. He wanted to go back in to save his burning pals. Along the sides of the ship, they could see some of them, clawing at the windows, screaming, fighting to get out, until the victims fell back into the cabin helplessly.

Darling and Leech somehow got into the tail section. They made their way forward. They saw some bodies piled up. The heat was that of a furnace. They were forced back.

Another Englishman, James Bunting, was driving back to the Dover ferry. It was a miserable night to drive. Between Allone and Beauvais, the rain let up a moment, and he got out to wipe off his windshield. He heard a noise that sounded as if a large Diesel lorry were coming down the road toward him. Instead, it was the R-101. It looked like a floating railway carriage to him.

Then he heard the explosion. The flames were orange and blue, like a gas fire, he noted. He ran across the field with some other motorists who had stopped behind him. A quarter of a mile from the ship, it became unbelievably hot. He could hear screaming from the distance. Then a crewman staggered toward him. His clothes were on fire. Bunting grabbed him, rolled him in the grass.

Across the field, the framework of the airship was illuminated by the flames. It looked like a grasshopper in silhouette. The gendarmes and the 51st French Infantry began arriving, in lorries, ambulances and horse-drawn carts. The cavalry arrived, too, carrying bedsheets hastily mustered from the households of Beauvais. They would be urgently needed to wrap the corpses in.

News of the crash reached London and Cardington piecemeal. Sometime around four in the morning, someone in the Air Ministry was awakened by a call from Leech. He was not badly injured. He said they had crashed on top of a hill at a few minutes after two in the morning, that the ship had burst into flames, that only six of the crew and none of the officers or passengers had been saved. He didn't know the names of the other survivors, but knew that Binks and Savory were injured.

News from the wire services was scattered. Just before five in the morning, Reuters reported: AN EXPLOSION OCCURRED ABOARD THE R-101 AT TWO-THIRTY THIS MORNING WHILE SHE WAS A FEW MILES FROM BEAUVAIS.

By five-thirty, a Reuters dispatch from Paris read: ALARM HAS BEEN CAUSED HERE BY AN UNCONFIRMED REPORT THAT THE AIRSHIP HAS BLOWN UP.

The final brief dispatch was at least clear: R-101 HAS EXPLODED IN FLAMES ONLY SIX SAVED.

Whitehall and Downing Street officials were awakened in their homes in the small hours of the morning. They made their way into London from country homes. Prime Minister Ramsay MacDonald went first to the Air Ministry, where he was briefed, then on to his office at 10 Downing Street.

The news traveled fast, once the tragedy was confirmed. Milkmen, delivering in the dark hours of the morning, woke their customers to tell them. In Cardington, there was total shock and despair. The prime population of the community had been wiped out.

When first light came, the rain and the wind had not let up. In the grey light, the twisted metal still sizzled and sputtered in the smoking ruins. Police and soldiers formed a cordon around the wreckage and stretchers were laid out beside the orchard. On them were laid the sheet-covered bodies. None were recognizable. They were literally roasted, their hands clenched, some with their arms raised as if to protect themselves against the fire. There were watches and rings on some. Nearly all of the watches were stopped at 2:05.

To some, the wreckage from a distance looked like a half-built railway station. To others, the smouldering skeleton looked like a beached whale. Strips of fabric still fluttered in the wind. The flat surface of the elevators at the tail still held their canvas. The tail towered over 60 feet above the ground, and there was an RAF flag still intact, luffing in the breeze. A British officer eventually claimed it.

The control car was jammed up into the hull, a hopeless tangle trapping the bodies of the officers of the watch.

Leech, Disley, Binks, Bell, Savory and Cook were the only survivors, except for Rigger Church and a rigger named Radcliffe, each of whom died shortly afterward. The rescuers tried to keep what possessions there were, close to the unrecognizable bodies they seemed to come from. There were some photos that miraculously escaped, a compass, sets of keys, a leather belt with a white buckle, scissors, cigarettes and occasionally a ring on a blackened finger.

When the coffins arrived, each was numbered, and each had a box attached with the same number, so that the belongings could be checked by bereaved relatives, and they would not have to look inside the coffins to see the disfigured remains of their loved ones. The official count of the dead came to 48, after the two who were fatally injured died. The actual number could only be clearly determined by counting the number of skulls. All would be buried in unmarked coffins in a common grave. There were so few who could be identified, even with the help of the possessions found on some. Among the belongings raked out of the ruins, however, was one that could be unmistakably identified. It was a rimless monocle.

No command officer of the ship survived the holocaust. The control car was almost unrecognizable. What went on in those last minutes in that car seemed as if it would be buried forever in the minds of those handling the ship in those short but critical moments of crisis. Only Irwin, Scott, Atherstone, Colmore, or Johnston could provide even a clue to the total background and picture of what brought the tragedy about. And they were dead. As the legend went, dead men could tell no tales. Or could they?

CHAPTER XI

All of Britain was in mourning. Other parts of the world were, too. The *New York Times* gave the story the bulk of the front page. The Pope sent condolences. Paris lowered all its flags to half-mast. The little village of Allone stripped its gardens. Not a flower was left. The villagers smothered the coffins with them as they were placed on gun carriages and carried to the railway station in Beauvais. King Victor Emmanuel of Italy telegraphed condolences to King George, and Adolf Hitler did the same for the National Socialist Party of Germany.

The burning question in everyone's mind was: Why? What went wrong? How could this atrocity be permitted to happen? What was the exact cause? What went on in those last moments, or immediately before, to wipe out nearly all of England's airship experts and airmen?

Sir Dennistoun Burney, designer of the rival ship R-100, would make no illuminating comment, except to say: "I am following every piece of news with the greatest of interest. But until more information to the actual sequence of events is received, *no* person, however great an expert, could hazard an opinion." Other aviation authorities concurred.

The Air Ministry would issue no information whatever. One of the high officials, who went to Beauvais and returned early, flatly

207

refused to discuss the matter. A Commission of Inquiry was immediately set up to establish hearings, several weeks away. Reuters reported on Tuesday, October 7, two days after the crash: "The evidence which is now being collected by the Commission will be placed before the Court of Inquiry, and no announcement will be made until the collection of evidence is complete." *The Times* of London added: "Until the reports of the experts are made, there can be no satisfactory account."

By Tuesday, it became obvious that the Bristish public and press would continue to remain in the dark about the exact cause of the crash and for a long time to come. There were bound to be weeks of testimony at the hearings, and certainly more weeks before an official statement would be issued.

Emilie Hinchliffe, with fresh sorrow, could do nothing now beyond her determination to try to convince others of the reality of the world she was convinced her husband was now part of. Through Mrs. Earl, a further message came through from Captain Hinchliffe, the day after the disaster: "I am in the state of despair. I hoped that the crash would be averted, and even at the last moment we were working in some way to warn those in command of the ship. I know that death is not the end, but I hold life on earth as important to progress as life here, and willful disregard of warnings is suicide. I mean to work harder than ever. I trust with God's help, to be able to bring such evidence that even the Press will sit up and take notice I must make them realize the dangers of these monster dirigibles."

The biggest obstacle in getting across any warning such as Hinchliffe's would be the capacity of officials or the man on the street to believe it. There was, in fact, every reason not to. False messages could come through just as easily as those that might be accurate. How could they be sorted out? What about mere coincidences in such information? Even if the messages were true, what about distortion in the transmission of the evidence, interference of the conscious mind of the medium, inability of the transcriber to record the words accurately and a dozen other mitigating factors? How about the distortion of technical information coming through amateurs or laymen?

Harry Price wasn't at all sure what might come out of the experiment he had set up for Ian Coster on the afternoon of October 7.

He was thinking of the experiment to reach Conan Doyle, not of the R-101. He made sure that Ethel Beenham, his long-time secretary for his laboratory, was on hand, because he could count on her to take accurate verbatim notes with her expert Pitman shorthand. Coster was a veteran journalist. He was both an editor and writer for his magazine. He would not be satisfied with anything but the best along that line. If Conan Doyle did by any chance come across with a message through Eileen Garrett, Price would like to catch every nuance. Since he and Doyle had parted half friends and half enemies, it would be interesting to see how any communication would treat that situation.

At the laboratory, Price and Ethel Beenham waited for Eileen Garrett and Ian Coster to appear. It was nearly three in the afternoon, Tuesday, October 7. Eileen arrived first, and the three of them chatted informally for a few minutes, waiting for Coster to arrive. Nothing was said to Eileen about the purpose of the session, and Coster was not identified by name. She didn't know he was a journalist or was connected with any magazine.

This, of course, was customary procedure to prevent any informational leaks that could affect the session. Eileen talked about her plans to leave for America in several weeks, where the American Society for Psychical Research had arranged for a series of tests that would include both Johns Hopkins University and Duke.

Her determination had grown to get strict scientific appraisals of her clairvoyant capacities. Price encouraged this. It was the only route to follow. There was too much vague and insubstantiated opinion floating around on the subject. It was not an emotional issue. It was a scientific one, and he was damned if he understood why better scientists didn't come down off their high horses and look into it. It was the most magnificent question anyone could examine: Did we survive death? What was wrong with looking at it, clinically and unemotionally?

Coster arrived promptly at three. He liked Price for his clinical attitude, his brittle, abrupt approach to the subject. The only thing Coster knew about Eileen Garrett was what Price had told him: She was objective and had an impeccable reputation. He had no idea what would come out of this crazy idea, but it was exciting and interesting to try. He was sure that the readers of *Nash's* and *Cosmopolitan* would agree. Doyle made good copy. Sherlock

Holmes would never die, and was the widest-read fictional character in modern history.

The serious business began. Eileen sat in an armchair. The other three sat at a table facing her. It almost looked like an inquisition, but of course it was nothing like that. Eileen would simply put her self into a trance, as she did so often. Coster and Price planned to listen attentively, as Ethel Beenham recorded. She was used to this sort of thing, and rarely missed a phrase.

They settled down into quiet. When Coster made the original appointment, Price had explained to him about the mysterious voice of Uvani, and how the voice sometimes shifted to whatever other purported entity might come through directly. He also told Coster how the voices might shift back and forth between Uvani and, say, Doyle—if Doyle did appear to manifest himself. Coster was skeptical, but ready for anything.

Eileen began breathing deeply. Her eyes closed. She yawned. She slipped farther down in her chair. Her breathing became steadier and deeper. Her face appeared drawn.

At five minutes after three, the voice of Uvani came through. He announced himself:

"It is Uvani. I give you greetings, friends. Peace be with you and in your life and in your household."

Coster was glad that he had been warned about this voice. It was a little eerie to him, a little unreal. He listened as the voice of Uvani announced to Price that a German friend of his, Dr. Albert Freiherr von Schrenck-Notzing, wanted to greet him. The doctor was a noted physicist who had died a year earlier. Coster was disappointed. It looked as if Conan Doyle was not interested in the session.

The doctor spoke a few sentences, but they brought no specific information that Price could check out, and he too became a little impatient. It was interesting only because Price regarded the scientist highly, and did not know how Eileen Garrett would know of him or his complicated name, which was pronounced correctly.

Then very suddenly, Eileen became very agitated. Tears rolled down her cheeks. Her hands clutched and unclutched. Uvani's voice became broken and hurried. The sentences became almost disjointed. Ethel Beenham increased the speed of her Pitman to catch up with the words.

"I see for the moment I-R-V-I-N-G or I-R-W-I-N. He says he must do something about it . . . apologizes for coming . . . for interfering . . . speaks of Dora, Dorothy, Gladys . . . for heaven's sake, give this to them . . . the whole bulk of the dirigible was entirely and absolutely too much for her engine capacity. Engines too heavy. It was this that made me on five occasions have to scuttle back to safety."

The words were moving so fast that Ethel Beenham could barely keep up with them, in spite of her expertise. She knew there would be gaps, and that she was going to make some mistakes. But she kept her pencil flying.

"Useful lift too small," the voice purporting to be that of Captain Irwin went on. "Gross lift computed badly—inform control panel. And this idea of new elevators totally mad. Elevator jammed. Oil pipe plugged. This exorbitant scheme of carbon and hydrogen is entirely and absolutely wrong. To begin with, the demand would be greater than the supply. . . . "

The faster the words went, the more determined Ethel Beenham was to follow them. But it was getting technical. What was all this business about carbon and hydrogen? She didn't know. None of them sitting there knew. She put it down in her book, anyway.

"Also let me say this," the words continued. 'I have experimented with less hydrogen in my own dirigible with the result that we are not able to reach 1,000 meters. With the new carbon hydrogen, you will be able to get no altitude worth speaking about. With hydrogen, one is able to do that quite easily. Greater lifting than helium. Explosion caused by friction in electric storm. Flying too low altitude and could never rise. Disposable lift could not be utilized. Load too great for long flight. Same with S.L.8. Tell Eckener."

The swift and urgent words, phrased in technical terms, still meant little to those in the room. But the urgency, the desperate intensity was undeniable. Coster was torn. He wanted a Sir Arthur Conan Doyle communication for his story. How could this material be used, however dramatic, with the Court of Inquiry coming up, and the families of the men of the R-101 in torment, anger and despair? But along with the others in the room, he was riveted to the voice. No one knew what "S.L. 8" meant; no one knew of anybody named "Eckener." They were all amateurs in the aviation business. But the next words were obvious to anyone, technical or not:

"Cruising speed bad, and ship badly swinging. Severe tension on fabric, which is chafing. Starboard strakes started. Engines wrong—too heavy—cannot rise.''

The word ''strakes'' was unusual, Price was thinking. He would have to check this after the session.

''Never reached cruising altitude,'' the abrupt, jerky phrases of the voice apparently Irwin's went on. ''Same in trials. Too short trials. No one knew the ship properly. Airscrews too small. Fuel injection bad and air pump failed. Cooling system bad. Bore capacity bad. Next time with cylinders but bore of engine 1,100 cc's, but that bore is not enough to raise too heavy load and support weight. It had been known to me on many occasions that the bore capacity was entirely inadequate to the volume of the structure. This I had placed again and again before engineer, without being able to enlarge capacity of Diesel twin valve. Had this been interchangeable with larger capacity, we might have made it. . . . ''

Ethel Beenham was getting particularly fouled up in this section. She knew she was missing words, and not getting exactly the unfamiliar mechanical terms that were spewing forth.

Price was aware that even the best stenographer couldn't get everything down with such unfamiliar terminology at a speed like this. But he was impressed with a very important factor in trying to evaluate what was coming out: Eileen Garrett could not possibly be making this up out of whole cloth. No layman could. Even an expert would have trouble doing this at such speed. The jerky pace of the words went on:

''But the structure no good. That actually is the case, not gas did not allow mixture to get to engine—backfired. Fuel injection bad.''

Price thought of a comment here, and he put it in: ''Crude oil is not inflammable.'' He meant to say ''explosive.'' It was too late to change.

Irwin's purported voice answered back quickly. ''This *is* inflammable. Also to begin with, there was not sufficient feed. Leakage. Pressure and heat produced explosion.''

Price figured that the voice was referring to the explosion and heat inside the cylinders here, since Irwin had already commented on the explosion of the ship being caused by friction in an electric storm. The message continued, somewhat repetitively:

''Five occasions I have had to scuttle back—three times before starting. Not satisfied with feed. Already a meeting, but feel desirous to put off and set our course and overhaul completely against this.''

More problem with the shorthand here, more confusion. But the gist of the message would have meaning, Miss Beenham was sure.

''Weather bad for long flight,'' the voice went on. ''Fabric all water-logged and ship's nose down. Impossible to rise. Cannot trim. You will understand that I *had* to tell you. There were five occasions I have had distinct trouble. New type of feed entirely and absolutely wrong. Two hours tried to rise, but elevator jammed. Almost scraped the roofs at Achy. Kept to railway ''

Price made a note for himself on this sentence. He had never heard of Achy, but here was something that could be clearly proved wrong or right. This was the kind of evidence he looked for. The other material, too, would be very important. That needed expertise. He would surely get it later. But everything that he could check himself, he wanted to follow. He listened further:

''At inquiry to be held later, it will be found that the superstructure of the envelope contained no resilience, and had far too much weight in envelope. This was not until March of this year, when no security was made by adding of super-steel structure. I knew then that this was not a dream, but a nightmare. The added middle section was entirely wrong. It made strong but took resilience away and entirely impossible. Too heavy and too much over-weighted for the capacity of the engines.''

Miss Beenham knew she was still missing a lot of phrases. The ''ands'' might be confused with the ''ors.'' Many of the words were unknown to her. She didn't even know if it was making any sense at all. She marveled that anyone could talk at this speed, in or out of trance. But she gathered, along with the others, the sense of importance.

Price and Coster were spellbound. There was one clear thought in Price's mind, as he wrote later: No one could *invent* a story at this speed. No one could fabricate such a stream of technical terms—if they even remotely checked out with the expert help he hoped to get afterward. This would be the major key he would seek. The voice continued:

There was a pause at last. Miss Beenham breathed easier. Eileen's voice shifted gears. Uvani was speaking again:

''He does not come to you. Seems to be holding out something to us. He says: 'Bore, capacity, feed and gas. We could never rise.' "

Eileen fell into another silence, longer this time. It lasted for a full minute or more.

Coster had not forgotten about his assignment to try to get Conan Doyle. But he was stunned by the impact of the alleged Captain Irwin message. He found himself trying to explain it. It was incredible. Along with Price, he was convinced that Eileen Garrett was not consciously cheating. He was also convinced that she, as a layman, was totally incapable of framing that stream of information. He scanned his mind for other explanations. Was it a welling up of her unconscious? Was there telepathy involved? Was it an earthbound mind of someone who had died? But how could it be telepathy, unless it was a complex, extended form passing through multiple minds? Highly unlikely. No one in the room knew anything about all these details. Even the experts were refusing to guess what had happened aboard the R-101 in the last moments before the crash. At the time of the session, none of the reports of the survivors were detailed.

The big problem for Coster was, it was a news break that couldn't be used. Even if it could be taken as factual, who would believe it? It would be better to do the reflective piece on Conan Doyle. And although he didn't expect it, after the traumatic message from Irwin had exploded on the session, he was surprised when Eileen Garrett began stirring again from her lengthy pause. The "Irwin" entity seemed to be gone. It was now about quarter of four. The first part of the session had lasted some forty-five minutes. Certainly, Coster was thinking, Eileen must be exhausted.

But instead, the voice of Uvani was heard again. Instead of the rapid, bouncing, brittle phrases of Irwin, it spoke in a slight Arabic accent:

"There's an elderly person here," it said, "saying there is no reason in the world he should attend you, but he has here an SOS sent out five days ago. He is tall, heavy, has difficulty in walking, is amusing, and at times very difficult. He will talk a lot, but on the other hand can remain silent. Jolly. Great of heart. Deep blue eyes. A drooping mustache, strong chin, dominating, courageous, stubborn, heart of a child."

If this were Conan Doyle beginning to come through, Price got the dig. Those days of in-fighting with Doyle while he was alive would probably not be easily forgotten. Now the voice of Uvani shifted to more British cadences.

"Here I am," the new voice said. "Arthur Conan Doyle. Now—how am I going to prove it to you?"

Coster was pleased. Price recalled their many disagreements about the reality or nonreality of the spirit, and the ways to go about trying to explore such phenomena.

"I myself did not recognize the difficulty there would be," the purported voice of Doyle said, "in getting through this wall or density that stands between us. I am within a slower system but outside your sympathetic system. . . . " Then, after a few more comments, the voice said, apparently to Price: "It was your fault that we disagreed."

"We were working with the same object in view," Price said, "but in different ways. I am trying to arrive at the truth."

The voice purportedly Doyle's was not altogether angelic, if this were coming from the spirit world: "I always had my eye on you, and you used to watch me like a cat watching a bird in a cage."

But immediately, things became more conciliatory. Price and the voice began discussing their general theories, while Coster sat by, still somewhat stunned by the Irwin proceedings that had just been completed. Price then introduced him, almost as if it were an introduction at a cocktail party. Coster even wondered if he shouldn't stand up and take a bow. "Might I ask which of the characters you created you like best?" he asked.

"Now you touch me on a weak point," the apparent voice of Doyle replied. "I enjoyed writing most *Rodney Stone.* It expressed a side of me which was always very much in evidence, and as I grew ill, and unable to cope with the realities of life, I could always look back on the formation of that character and feel a thrill. I feel a great love for my Napoleonic stories, for Brigadier Gerard, the favorite of Napoleon." Nothing was said about Holmes, Coster noted.

The message went on to tell Coster more about the feelings for the Doyle characters. Then the subject shifted to Doyle's reflections on his present condition:

"I think that as a matter of fact," the answer began, to a question Price asked, "when I say I am living in a world considerably like the one I have left, people will be surprised. I find myself doing many of the things which I did there. I find I am living in a world as dark as that which I have left, more's the pity. It is a country where pain is forever ended; where emotion is born a thousand times stronger; where inspirations reach me easier. I find myself in a bodily state. It is a combination of both heaven and hell. Believe me, it is only the beginning. I understand that it tends to confirm the theory of reincarnation and the soul goes through many phases. It is really the soul of me in bodily form. The scientist will disagree with me, but I am still 'material,' and so long as I am material, I feel myself the man I was on earth. . . . "

When Price asked about testing mediums for communications, his prime interest, of course, the answer was: "I see this more clearly now than I did when I was working from your side. Remember now, I am seeing from two sides, and have no doubt about this statement: No message, but it is changed a little by something which is contaminating the human machine. But within each medium there is the pure gold, and it is that we want to look for. . . . I hope everybody will understand that we are now good friends."

The flow of words stopped. Eileen Garrett remained very still for a minute. Then she gradually began to wake up, as if she had been in a somewhat fitful sleep. Although she yawned and stretched, she said she didn't feel at all tired.

But Ethel Beenham did. The spasmodic phrases of Irwin had almost left her with writer's cramp. She had been going at it practically nonstop for two hours. She told Price that she immediately had to transcribe the Irwin portion of the seance, while it was fresh in her mind. She couldn't imagine what it all meant, or whether it made any sense at all. The style of the Irwin entity's speech was something she had never run into before.

Coster left to get on with his other work. He had to interview Edgar Wallace, the mystery writer, on how to deal with gunmen, of all things. He would have a hard time keeping his mind on the interview after what had happened that afternoon. He reasoned that Eileen Garrett might have dredged up the Conan Doyle material from her unconscious memory banks. He wasn't certain, of course. Even that portion was extremely convincing. He planned to keep in close touch with Price about getting expert opinion on the transcripts. He still remained skeptical, but he had become a very benevolent skeptic. He didn't quite know how to handle this for *Nash's* and *Cosmopolitan.*

In all his experience of exposing fake mediums and testing good ones, Price was stumped. He almost became paranoid: Could there be espionage here? Only scanty details of the R–101 technical problems had appeared in the press. He could have no considered opinion about those that were revealed in the session, but he was damned well going to find out. Eileen had spoken fluently of engines, gross lift, air crews, bore capacity, and in almost desperate haste. There was never any groping or hesitation for phrases that Price himself couldn't replicate in a million years—and he was technically minded.

Eileen had no recollection of what had come out during the trance. When she was told, it only increased her bewilderment. She was glad she had arranged the scientific tests in America coming up soon. Maybe she could learn something in those. She knew nothing about bore capacities, or strakes, or gross lift or air screws. She always thought they were called propellers. The whole situation was incredible to her as the Hinchliffe sittings had been—to say nothing of scores of others that had been equally inexplicable.

While Ethel Beenham sat down and began to try to untangle her shorthand, Price did some preliminary digging. He looked up the word "strakes," a word he had never heard of before. It was a nautical term. It was a single continuous line of planking or metal plating extending on a vessel's hull from stem to stern. It came from a Middle English term, meaning "to stretch." This could add up, but he would need to have it checked out further. Many of the airship men were former naval officers. They brought along a lot of nautical terms with them to the airship work. Either it could apply to the metal girders that ran from stem to stern on the ship, or to the canvas covering that was stretched over them.

Then Price went to the British Museum Library, and began searching among the reference books for a town in nothern France named "Achy." First he searched the newspapers from the tragic announcement of the crash to the current dailies October 7, just two days after the disaster. There was no mention of "Achy." The ship had gone down near Beauvais. That, and the town of Allone, were the only local towns mentioned. "We almost scraped the roofs at Achy. . . ." The phrase stood out in his mind. He took out the Michelin Guide, a thoroughly detailed reference book for nearly every country in Europe. There was no mention. He went through large atlas after atlas, maps, charts and Baedecker's Guide, a guide as detailed and complete as Michelin's. There was still no such town as Achy.

It wasn't until the next morning that he located a large-scale railroad map, and a military map of the area around Beauvais. There he found it. It wasn't really a full-scale town. But it was clearly there. It was a railroad stop, just 12½ miles north of Beauvais on the railroad line. It was near the village of Poix, which he had never heard of either. It was on the direct course of the R–101.

Now Price had something to go on. In addition, his instincts told him he had run across one of the most provocative cases yet encountered that showed strong evidence that there was life-after-death. He was already forming his plan for further probing into the mystery, as he made his way back to the National Laboratory to see what progress Ethel Beenham had made in deciphering her shorthand notes.

While Price was planning his careful strategy to try to verify the complicated details of the "Irwin" message, gravediggers were preparing to dig the common grave in Cardington, near the hangar where the R–101 had once proudly floated. The coffins would be placed side by side. The officers and crew, along with the distinguished passengers, would then be united once again, this time forever. The grave would be thirty feet square, its sides lined with freshly cut grass, covered with wildflowers cut by children from the neighboring hedgerows. Meanwhile, the bodies were lying in state in Westminster Hall, ready to receive the thousands of Britons who would march by in silence and solemnity.

The people in Cardington and Bedford were bitter. They had stood by during the hurried alteration of the big ship, and as they had, their forebodings had grown. They had watched in fear as the R–101 left its tower. Even the man in the street noticed its nose-down position, its straining to try to gain altitude. They had read in the press of Lord Thomson's casual boast: "I have promised the Prime Minister to be back on the 20th." They burned with resentment at this. Yet there was nothing that could be done or said that could change things.

Those who were left among the construction officers and crew found the gaunt, cavernous, empty hangar almost impossible to bear. All the noise and bustle, the floodlights, the sound of the engine tests, the workers hovering around the ship were gone. Only a sepulchral silence remained.

In the Bedford-Cardington area, some families and friends, who had lost their comrades and fathers, turned to a Spiritualist center in Bedford for some kind of comfort in their despair. They had done this before, during the terrible days of the First World War, when the casualty lists had stretched to unbearable lengths.

A widely known and reputable medium named Bertha Hirst was invited a few days after the tragedy to speak at a meeting in Bedford. She had had a strange experience on her own, a few days before coming to Bedford for her talk. She had been alone in her room. Quite suddenly, she told her friends, she had seen, clairvoyantly, not physically, a man in her room. He was wearing a dress suit, as if he was going to a formal dinner party. She was startled when she heard the man say: "I am Johnston, of the R-101." Then he mentioned three names: Violet . . . Pip . . . Hinchliffe.

She did not know anyone named Johnston, and had never heard of anyone connected with a "Violet" or "Pip." She only vaguely knew of the Hinchliffe story.

After her lecture in Bedford, Mrs. Hirst was invited to the home of some friends. She consented to hold a seance for them. Among the guests was Will Charlton, the chief supply officer of the R-101, who had lived through all the months and years of the painful construction work on the ship He had come to the seance reluctantly, with his wife and the newly widowed Mrs. Johnston. Neither she nor Mrs. Hirst had ever seen or known about each other.

Charlton, the supply officer, had never been to a seance before. He was a little uneasy. The seance began. Mrs. Hirst went into a self-induced trance. Within moments, it was apparent to Charlton that some of his friends who had perished in the disaster were trying to get through to him. Especially "Johnny"—the name he always used for his friend Johnston, the R-101 navigator. As a novice to any kind of psychic experience, he couldn't believe what he was hearing. Mrs. Hirst's description of Johnston was perfect. The trance voice was saying that he should ask two women there in the group to come to the medium for a private reading after the séance.

There was enough technical detail for him to believe that Johnston might possibly be coming through the medium.

After Mrs. Hirst had finished, Charlton went up to her and told her how startled he was that his friend Johnston from the R–101 had seemed to come through. Mrs. Hirst then told him about the visionary experience she had a few days before. He knew immediately that "Pip" was a friend of his and the Johnstons, who invariably dressed for dinner. "Violet" was the name of the wife of another member of the crew. Hinchliffe was an old friend of all.

Charlton could not help being impressed. But he had many things on his mind. He promised himself that one day he might make a serious study of what this psychic field was all about. In the meantime, he turned back to the dismal job of winding up the affairs at the empty R–101 hangar.

Mrs. Johnston was so amazed that she arranged for a private session with Mrs. Hirst. The meeting brought so many verifiable details that the wife of the navigator shifted from skepticism to a tentative acceptance. The clincher for Mrs. Johnston occurred when Mrs. Hirst identified her husband at the beginning of the session. "I see him very clearly now," the medium said. "Your husband is holding a white rose." At the last moment before Johnston left on the doomed airship, he had picked a white rose and given it to his wife.

Harry Price knew nothing about this sequence of events at Bedford, but for some time he had been puzzled by the way various mediums reported similar messages coming from the same person, not knowing that they were being received by other mediums. Often a complex linkage or interlocking of this type of phenomenon had taken place.

There was no real answer to the puzzle. It had happened, for instance, with Hinchliffe and Lowenstein. It had happened also in the linkage between Mrs. Earl and Eileen Garrett on the original Hinchliffe sequence. It was happening now, unknown to Price, with Mrs. Hirst receiving apparent communication from the R–101 officers and his own session with Coster and Eileen Garrett. Complicated studies of this sort of thing had been made by both the British and American Societies of Psychical Research, under controlled conditions. The phenomenon added strength to the validity of possible communication with the dead—but the interlocking process itself still remained a mystery.

At this moment, Harry Price was having real problems in trying
to locate an airship expert to review and appraise the painstaking
transcript of the "Irwin" communication that Ethel Beenham had
so carefully reconstructed from her Pitman shorthand. She was
amazed at what had come over, but had no idea about the technical
accuracy of the data or the fidelity of her final transcript.

She and Price pored over it, word by word. They recognized that
the process from start to finish could go through several sources of
distortion which would have to be carefully weighed in any final
appraisal. First there was the problem several communications had
mentioned: It was apparently very difficult for someone on the
"other side" to get through a medium. When they allegedly did,
the medium offered a very imperfect instrument for transmitting
the data. After that came the imperfect process of shorthand and
transcription, with no guarantee that all the phrases and nuances
had been recorded. This was before the days of tape recorders,
when there was plenty of room for human error.

The problem in obtaining an airship expert lay partly with the attitude of the Air Ministry, which had clamped an informal lid of
secrecy on official discussion of the disaster, before the Court of
Inquiry would be held. There was also the reticence of any expert
to be willing to examine such an ephemeral process as a seance.
There was a third factor, in that the tragedy was so fresh in the
minds of fellow airmen that it was painful to reconstruct the details. In addition, there was a lot of touchy material in the transcript, material that would point the finger of blame at high officials
who either encouraged or permitted the ship to leave without the
proper testing that Irwin, when he was alive, so earnestly wanted
to carry out.

Price was convinced that nothing should be published publicly
about the "Irwin" message at this stage, before the hearings were
held. Coster agreed with him on this. They would, however, go
ahead with the story of the Conan Doyle portion, with the possibility of using the R–101 material after the hearings had been held and
announced. Although the results of the hearing would not be announced for weeks or months, it would also be very interesting to
note how much of the technical material matched the findings of
the Court.

* * *

Major Villiers was almost totally distraught at the loss of his
friends aboard the R–101, especially Sir Sefton Brancker, to whom
he had been devoted. With his photographic mind, Villiers recalled
every word that Brancker had told him on the drive to Cardington.
This capacity for total recall was both an asset and a liability. At
present, it was definitely the latter. Brancker's confrontation with
Thomson before the journey must have been painful enough. The
pain of Brancker's loss to both the Major and his wife was deep
and unrelenting. They stood together at the memorial services for
the R–101 dead at St. Paul's, their memory of the last farewell to
Brancker and the others fresh in their minds. The services were being broadcast throughout the world. The Prince of Wales was
there, the Duke of York, the cabinet ministers—and the dominion
statesmen who had gathered for the Imperial Conference that Lord
Thomson would never return to. Over 5,000 people were jammed
into the historic cathedral.

Aleen took her husband's arm, and asked:

"Do you notice Lord Thomson's staff assistant over there?"

The Major nodded that he did.

"What awful sorrow on his face!" Aleen said. "Did he love
Lord Thomson?"

"Yes," said Major Villiers. "There are many who loved him, in
spite of his faults."

That was the way it was with Lord Thomson. People seemed to
either love him or hate him. In spite of his ego, he was a dedicated
public servant with a brilliant military record. He soon would share
a common grave with all the others of the ship, where there was no
rank except equality.

The days after the crash at the Air Ministry office at Whitehall
were desperately somber. Villiers went about his chores half-heart-
edly, going home to his Hertfordshire home at night, after winding
down the affairs of the R–101 at the office. There was also the preparation of the files that might be requested for the hearings, and he
would see to it that they were in order.

A lot of the material that would be called for would obviously be
among the information he had assembled for the Imperial Conference. Basically, it would be non-technical. There were drawings
showing the girder construction of the airship, photographs of the
ship under construction, and other data that would help a layman

like himself understand the basic principles of dirigible flight. He pulled the material out, ready to deliver it if the Court of Inquiry requested it. He felt strongly that the truth should be brought out, whatever it was, however painful it might be. The hearings would not be a pleasant experience for anyone.

On October 22, an official announcement was made by Lord Amulree, who had succeeded Thomson, setting the commencement of the hearings:

NOW THEREFORE I, the Right Honourable William Warrender Lord Amulree, G.B.E., one of His Majesty's Principal Secretaries of State, in pursuance of the said Regulations and of all other powers enabling me in that behalf. hereby order and direct an investigation of the said accident and the causes and circumstances thereof to be held. AND I appoint the Right Honourable Sir John Allsebrook Simon, one of His Majesty's Counsel, to hold such investigation and to report thereon.

> (Signed)
> AMULREE
> Secretary of State for Air

The hearings were to begin at the venerable Courts of Justice on October 28, twenty-three days after the tragedy.

Major Villiers was glad Sir John Simon had been appointed. He was a brilliant statesman and jurist, having been a solicitor general, Attorney General and Home Secretary in the past. He had a distinguished record as an arbitrator, and Villiers was sure he would dig hard to get to the bottom of things without fear or favor. Villiers had known him slightly during World War days, at the time Villiers was receiving his Distinguished Service Order, the D.S.O. award. Sir John had been attached to the staff of Sir Hugh Trenchard, head of the Royal Flying Corps. He had seen Simon a few times afterward.

One Saturday evening after the R–101 crash, just before the hearings were about to begin, the Villierses were entertaining Major-General Julian Sorsby, a close friend of whom they were very fond. Sorsby was a successful financier, rather interested in exploring what was going on in psychic research. Over a pleasant dinner, Sorsby brought up some unusual case histories he had encountered in his studies, and Major Villiers and Aleen listened with interest as he talked.

Villiers mentioned that on rare occasions he had had these strange experiences where it seemed as if he received almost direct verbal messages from someone close to him who had died. He was interested in why such things happened. They weren't actually vocal or audible, but they were understandable. Sorsby explained what he could, saying that phenomena like these are much more frequent than is commonly believed—although any explanation still went begging.

They finished dinner about eleven, and all except Villiers retired to bed. He was feeling restless and rather stimulated by the talk they had had at dinner. He poured himself a cup of tea, and sat down by the fire, which was still glowing comfortably. He sat there alone for several minutes, sipping his tea and gazing at the coals in the fireplace. The major was in a quiet and meditative mood.

Suddenly, he felt a presence. There was no physical sign whatever. At first, he attributed it to the discussion they had had at the dinner table. But the impression of someone being present persisted. Then he mentally heard Captain Irwin's voice. It was not audible, but it was clearly articulate and present in his mind. It was saying: "For God's sakes, let me talk to you. It's all so ghastly. I must speak to you. I must!"

Villiers was nonplussed. The incidents he had experienced in the past had all proved out in detail. He heard the inaudible voice again. It repeated the same thing. Then it added: "We're all bloody murderers. For God's sake, help me to speak with you."

Villiers did the only thing he could think of. In his thoughts, he mentally said to Irwin that he would do everything in his power to open up some kind of channel of communication. He told him it was a promise. Then the presence of Irwin seemed to fade away, and Villiers felt he was left alone by the fire.

He had a hard time getting to sleep that night. He fully intended to carry his promise out, but he wasn't sure how he should go about it. He knew that he could not rely on his own skimpy "mental" form of conversation. But he had only been to a medium once in his life. He didn't know any reliable one he could turn to.

The next morning, he spoke to Major-General Sorsby at breakfast. He told Sorsby about his friend Irwin's apparent visit and the great distress Irwin seemed to be in. Sorsby was interested. He volunteered immediately that he would arrange, if possible, an appointment with a London medium he felt was the best in England, if not the world. Her name, he told Major Villiers, was Eileen Garrett. He would call her on Monday and see if she might be free.

Villiers had never heard of Eileen Garrett, but he relied on Sorsby's judgment, which Villiers considered extremely reliable. The only problem Sorsby saw was that Mrs. Garrett was due to leave soon for the United States, and he hoped her schedule could be cleared. If he could make the appointment, he told Villiers, he would do it anonymously, and simply by the initial "V." Villiers was relieved about this. He did not want it divulged that he was with the Air Ministry. It was critical that he remain anonymous. For the Senior Intelligence Officer of the Air Ministry to be consulting a medium at this time would not be exactly appropriate.

Late on Monday, Sorsby called back as he had promised. Eileen Garrett was leaving for America soon, but she had arranged a time to meet Villiers at seven o clock on the evening of October 31, only a short time off. Sorsby had strictly kept Villiers' identity confidential, and the reading would be totally "blind," so that any evidential material that came through could be checked for the validity, if any, of the communication.

Villiers was pleased. He had kept his promise to his friend Irwin, and was looking forward to what possibly might come through that would help relieve the terrible distress revealed on Sunday evening. Villiers had no way of knowing that he was about to be led into one of the stormiest controversies in both psychic and aviation history.

CHAPTER XII

Major Villiers was impatient. Now that his appointment with Eileen Garrett was set, he was anxious to get on with it. He looked forward to finding out the information that Captain Irwin seemed so intensely determined to get through to him. The few incidents of this nature that had happened to him in the past had provided clear, verifiable information. Would the same thing happen if he were able to make a clear contact with Irwin? If Major-General Sorsby had not been so impressed with the abilities of Eileen Garrett, he would be more casual about his forthcoming appointment.

With the R-101 hearings scheduled so soon, however, there were other things on his mind. One of them was disturbing. Brancker's confrontation with Lord Thomson, which Villiers had learned of on the way to Cardington the night of the flight, would have a critical bearing on the Court of Inquiry. The battle could affect the eventual conclusions pinpointing responsibility for the disaster. If it were not brought to light, a whitewash could be entirely possible.

The Court of Inquiry opened its long series of sessions on the morning of October 28, 1930, barely three weeks after both the disaster and the Harry Price–Ian Coster seance, which Villiers knew nothing of. The opening of the hearings was a solemn occasion, held in the magnificently turreted Royal Courts of Justice in London. At the front of the hearing room, to one side, was a large mod-

227

el of the R-101, hung on what looked entirely too much like a gallows. The ship's model would be referred to many times in the days to follow. Major Villiers would be there to demonstrate it in various positions and angles, as the handful of surviving witnesses attempted to describe those critical moments of the last flight. Villiers would also be prepared to supply nontechnical background information and illustrations, so that Sir John Simon and his appointed staff could try to follow the explanations of what might or might not have happened during the ill-fated voyage.

Among many others, Villiers felt uneasy as the hearings began. Rumors were everywhere of an Air Ministry cover-up in the making. Simon had called for every scrap of evidence from the Ministry's files, secret or not. The high officials of both the Air Ministry and the Treasury would be responsible for supplying the records. There would be a lot of dirty linen in the files of both departments, Villiers was sure. How much of this would be held back for the sake of a cover-up? Villiers was convinced Simon wanted the truth. He was not at all convinced that Thomson's staff and other officials were going to supply what Simon needed.

There were two key men who could throw a lot of light on the inquiry. They controlled the most critical files. One was the top staff assistant to Lord Thomson, Benjamin Roberts.* The other was in the same position to Colmore, Franklin Noble.* These two men were among the last to leave the ship before it slipped the tower for India. They had had full access to the last-minute conferences that had taken place on the ship. It was known that the crew officers, Lord Thomson, Sir Sefton and designer Richmond met on board in serious discussion as the ship hung at the tower before it broke from the tower. The two staff assistants, Roberts and Noble, would be the only ones alive who could say whether there was any hesitation about the final decision to leave the tower, about the last-minute reports on the condition of the ship and the attitude of the officers and crew.

Villiers wished he had more confidence in these men. They were in a position to help with a whitewash. Villiers worried about them. Noble was ambitious. He was also rather a sychophant, Villiers thought. He was known for taking any step possible to further his

---

* At Major Villiers' request, these names have been changed.

career, whatever the cost. Roberts was completely in Lord Thomson's camp, and not likely to push forward any information that might highlight Thomson's insistence on getting to India and back before the Imperial Conference was over. If the truth were to be found, the evidence would, Villiers felt, not be likely to come from either of these men.

The hearings began sluggishly. A formula was agreed upon for the conduct of the proceedings. The list of witnesses to testify was prepared and announced. There were over forty, and they included everyone from Air Vice Marshal Lord Dowding to poacher Rabouille. Roberts and Noble would be key witnesses because of their knowledge of the affairs of Lord Thomson and Colmore. The testimony of the six survivors, of course, would have an important bearing on the outcome of the hearings. L. F. C. Darby, the assessor and registrar for Sir John Simon, would be in a key position, in that he would have to stay on top of every detail for the court.

Not much was accomplished in the first four days. The decision was made to devote each session to a specific subject: history of the ship, construction, design details, engines, gas bags and that sort of thing, in categorical order. It was tedious and methodical, but it was necessary. While it enabled the court to consider one item at a time, it didn't immediately get into the details of the crash itself. As a result, no overall picture would emerge at once. Villiers learned little that was new as he listened. After the fourth day, Friday, October 31, it appeared that the guts of the hearings would not begin until the following week.

After the last hearing of the week, Villiers went back to his office in the Gwydyr House in Whitehall to get ready for his first session with Eileen Garrett. He prepared himself with a clipboard and pad and several pencils. He did not take shorthand, but he was a fast and accurate note-taker, which, in addition to his capacity for almost total recall, he felt would enable him to precisely record whatever might come up.

He would be keeping an open mind about the whole process of a psychic reading. His one concern was that Mrs. Garrett should not find out that he was connected with the Air Ministry, or in fact know anything about his identity. He had great confidence in Major-General Sorsby, and knew that he had scrupulously protected his identity when the appointment had been set up.

Mrs. Garrett's flat was on Piccadilly, near the Royal Aero Club, so he had no trouble finding it. It was a pleasant walk through St. James's Park, past the Lancaster House and St. James's Palace. He arrived with keen expectations, and rang the bell promptly at seven. He found Eileen Garrett cordial, well-groomed, and intelligent. Her apartment was tasteful and relaxing. He sat opposite her by the fireplace.

Because it had been so long since his first and only visit with a medium, he wasn't quite sure what the procedure would be. Eileen explained to him briefly about the voice of Uvani, and how he seemed to introduce others who might speak directly. Villiers took his clipboard out of his attaché case, and waited as she began breathing deeply. She did so peacefully for a minute or so, her eyes closed, and relaxed in the chair.

Villiers had no idea whether Captain Irwin would come through or not. There was always the chance that he had persuaded himself of the reality and urgency of Irwin's voice that night alone by his Hertfordshire fireplace.

For several minutes there was silence, except for the breathing. Then Uvani's voice came, clear and articulate. But the information was confused. Whatever personalities were communicating were not at all known to Villiers. Although his pencil was poised above the clipboard, there was nothing of interest for him to take down.

The same sort of unknown personalities continued. Almost half an hour had gone by. Villiers became discouraged. He considered the idea of waking up Eileen to tell her that it seemed to be useless.

After a long pause, Uvani's voice said: "I am so distressed that I have not made contact with any person who wishes to be put in touch with you. I fear it is no good my staying any longer."

Villiers was disappointed. But he knew enough to realize that even the best mediums were fallible. Perhaps he could try again. It was now about seven-thirty. There was another pause. Then a very faint voice came from Eileen's vocal cords. The accent of Uvani came in louder immediately after, as if he were paraphrasing what the small voice had said:

"Irwey, Irwey—louder—Irwing, Irwin. Don't go, please. Stay. I must speak."

Villiers was almost startled. He began scribbling his improvised shorthand notes immediately. "I'm glad you have come," he said.

Suddenly, a rapid flow of information began coming through the Uvani voice. Then it changed in tone to that of a voice purporting to be Irwin's. In fact, Villiers noted, the voice that was coming through most of the time was almost the exact cadence and intonation of Irwin's voice: jerky, with sudden shifts in subject matter. When he asked questions the voice would answer, just as if Villiers were conducting a normal conversation. In his excitement, Villiers almost forgot he was talking through a medium.

An entire recounting of the last hours of the R-101 followed, most of it in a voice apparently that of Irwin. Villiers scribbled his notes as fast as he could, counting on his almost total recall to fill in the rest when the session was over. He was aware that there would be plenty of room for error in the detailed information, and cursed the fact that he had not mastered shorthand. But the wonder of it was that a fairly consistent, rapid and unhesitating flow was coming through this woman in a logical way that made sense.

The end of the session came nearly an hour after it had begun. The voice that seemed to be Irwin's said: "No more now. You must come soon, as Scottie and Johnston say they must each come and give you their own story. It helps them. Please come soon, and thank you for your thoughts. Come soon, come soon. . . ."

The voice of Uvani, or Eileen Garrett, or Captain Irwin, depending on what anyone could believe about this incredible session, faded out gently. Eileen gradually opened her eyes. She did not seem to know what had gone on. Villiers restrained himself from telling her. Aside from his concern about revealing his identity and his connection with the Air Ministry, he did not want to plant any conscious ideas in her mind before the next session. He did, however, impress on her that the information he had received was of critical importance.

Eileen said she was hazily aware that the information concerned the R-101, and Villiers confirmed that much. Although she was getting ready for her trip to America, she agreed to see him several more times, starting two evenings later.

Because of the pressures of his work at the Air Ministry, Major Villiers could not get time to expand his notes until the following noon. When he sat down in his office to do so, he was thankful for the total recall that had stood him in such good stead during his wartime intelligence work. The session had been in give-and-take dialogue, which was difficult. But he found he could fill in the gaps almost verbatim, taking care not to extrapolate beyond what he heard in the session.

When he had finished extending his notes, he felt he had come as close as possible to the original material, although he was sure he had confused some of the more technical detail. As he sat back to go over his transcript, he was as amazed as he had been at the time of the sitting:

UVANI (*Part Irwin*):
Irwey, Irwey—louder—Irwing, Irwin. Don't go, please. Stay. I must speak.

VILLIERS:
Don't worry, old boy. I'm glad you have come.

UVANI:
I see a slim fellow resting with his arm across your shoulder, and his head resting against you, rather exhausted.

IRWIN:
We feel like damned murderers. It's awful, old man. Awful. We ought to have said no.

VILLIERS:
Don't view the matter in this light, old boy. All that matters is this: You and the others had no choice to make when you are faced with a choice again such as this. Remember results don't matter. Just do what is right, that's all. Keep your mind on this point. Who are the "we" you mentioned?

> *(Villiers recalls he felt at this point that if this were Irwin, he needed comfort and consolation. He further recalls using his typical RAF phrases throughout, such as "old boy," and others.)*

IRWIN:
Johnnie, Scottie and I.

> *(This would have to mean navigator Johnston and Major Scott, Villiers reasoned.)*

VILLIERS:
Now try to tell me all that happened on Saturday and Sunday.

> *(At this point, Villiers knew nothing about the Harry Price–Ian Coster material. If so, he noted later that he would have cross-checked at the time.)*

IRWIN: *(Tense and rapid)*
She was too heavy by several tons. Too amateurish in construction. Envelope and girders not of sufficiently sound material.

> *(Villiers was having a hard time keeping up with his notes. Irwin's disconnected speech made it difficult.)*

VILLIERS:
Wait a minute, old boy. Let's start at the beginning.

IRWIN:
Well, during the afternoon before starting, I noticed that the gas indicator was going up and down, which showed there was a leakage or escape which I could not stop or rectify any time around the valves.

VILLIERS:
Try to explain a bit more. I don't quite understand.

IRWIN:
The gold-beater skins are too porous, and not strong enough. And the constant movement of the gas bags, acting like bellows, is constantly causing internal pressure of the gas. Which causes a leakage of the valves. I told the chief engineer of this. I then knew we were almost doomed. Then later on, the meteorological charts came in, and Scottie and Johnnie and I had a consultation. Owing to the trouble of the gas, we knew that our only chance was to leave on the scheduled time. The weather forecast was no good. But we decided that we might cross the Channel and tie up at Le Bourget before the bad weather came.

> *(Villiers noted distress in the voice purporting to be Irwin's.)*

We three were absolutely scared stiff. And Scottie said to us—look here, we are in for it—but for God's sake, let's smile like damned Cheshire cats as we go on board, and leave England with a clean pair of heels.

VILLIERS:
Did Colmore know?

IRWIN:
No. You will understand. We had to make the fatal decision, and we felt it wasn't fair to let him shoulder the decision.

VILLIERS:
Couldn't Thomson have helped?

IRWIN:
It's awful. You see I told Thomson when he arrived at Cardington that gas had been escaping. Thomson said: "But this is negligible, and surely for this small matter you don't contemplate postponement. It's impossible. I am pledged to be back for the Imperial Conference. We must leave according to the scheduled time." I disagreed, and consulted Scottie. But we decided to go. You know how late we were in starting. And after crossing the Channel, we three knew all was lost. We were desperate.

VILLIERS:
How exactly did the end come? And what was the cause? All the evidence seems to show that she dived, straightened, and dived again, and crashed.

IRWIN:
Yes, that's so. Now I will tell you the truth. One of the struts in the nose collapsed, and caused a tear in the cover. Now listen very carefully, It is the same strut that caused the trouble before, and they know . . .

(Villiers was certain the reference here was to high officials of the Air Ministry.)

The wind was blowing hard, and it was raining also. Now you see what happened. The rush of wind caused the first dive. And then we straightened out again. And another gust surging through the hole finished us.

VILLIERS:
Yes. That is quite clear. But what caused the explosion? Was it the electrical installation?

IRWIN:
No. Not that. It was the engine.

VILLIERS:
But old boy, how could the engine cause the explosion?

IRWIN:
It was this way. The Diesel engine had been popping or backfiring after crossing the Channel because the oil feed was not right. The oil is too thick a consistency, and had given trouble before. You see the pressure in some of the gas bags was accentuated by the undergirders crumpling up. And since gas had been escaping, the extra pressure pushed the gas out and came out with a rush. And at that moment, the Diesel engine backfired, and ignited the escaping gas. That caused the first explosion, and others followed.

(Reading over his extended notes, Villiers was aware that there must be mistakes in all the detailed information. Distorted or not, it was of absorbing interest.)

VILLIERS:
Before you go, how is dear old Brancks?

IRWIN:
Poor Brancks is often very depressed. He's worried about his wife and about his unfinished work.

(This was a good description, Villiers thought. Brancker was a pathological work horse. The voice that apparently was Irwin's went on.)

There is one thing you must try to help in. Don't let the other ship come out and do long journeys. Over here, we call her the Inventor's Nightmare. She is all wrong in construction.

(The reference was obviously to the sister ship R-100, which had been put in mothballs immediately after the crash. Villiers felt he could press for some clear evidential information here.)

VILLIERS:
Try to explain what really is wrong in the present form of construction.

IRWIN:
The main thing is this. The stress calculations are correct, but the forces she can be subjected to in bad weather and wind currents are too strong for the present system of calculations.

> *(Again Villiers realized there was distortion in putting down his notes. Garbled or not, he felt he had to record everything and assess the results later. In spite of the gaps, the confusion, the contradictions, and the obvious errors that he would make in recording, he could not avoid the conclusion that here was striking evidence of life-after-death, and of the capacity for the two different levels of consciousness to communicate with each other. The voice of Irwin continued.)*

Even supposing we had not lost gas, and had encountered worse weather, I believe her frame would have buckled owing to the pressure on her bulk size, causing her to twist.

> *(Villiers noted at this point that Eileen had made a twisting gesture with her hands, her eyes still closed as she remained in trance.)*

VILLIERS:
If you had suffered no leakage of gas, and had had good weather, do you think she would have accomplished the journey?

IRWIN:
Yes. I think so. But she is no good unless she has the strength to live up to bad weather. Another thing—they are talking of helium. That is no good because in the capacity, you want one and a half times as much. And the present system of bags are not strong enough. More gas, bigger gas bags, more pressure on bags, system hanging bags all wrong, and will be more so if enlarged.

> *(The phrasing here was all Irwin. The words jerked and stopped exactly the way Irwin used to talk. Now the voice of Irwin shift-*

ed abruptly to an observation on the hearings of the Court of Inquiry.)

It's dreadful to hear what they are saying. All bosh, and they know it, and won't speak the truth.

It was at this point that the first session came to an end. Villiers reread his transcript twice. It wasn't perfect, but it was as close as he could come. He was a man who tried to take things as they came. In situations like this, he tried to keep a calm mind. He was interested in analyzing the entire session objectively. There were many questions in his mind. One thing seemed certain if there was validity to the session: there was nothing ethereal about the "other side." There was pure RAF and Royal Navy diction in the speech that you could hear at any Officers' Club across the Empire.

He made arrangements for his secretary to type up his handwritten scrawl in the privacy of her home, away from Air Ministry eyes. He knew she would keep his confidence. If he reached a point in the forthcoming sessions where he felt the messages might help in clarifying the cause of and responsibility for the crash, he would not hesitate to take action. But the material would have to be clearly evidential and verifiable. It was a strange way to check a possible cover-up, but he was determined to get to the bottom of it.

Even more important was the other thought in Major Villiers' mind. It was the question that had been there since the days when he had faced death so many times during the First World War: Is there an afterlife, and can we find ways to demonstrate it if there is?

Villiers knew that there would be a long way to go before he reached a point where such information as this could provide convincing evidence on the question of life-after-death. The first session might have been a freak breakthrough. Would it continue on in the next several sessions? And, most important, would there be hard evidence that could be confirmed, to the extent that it not only indicated the possibility of communicating with those who had died, but would also clarify what happened in those terrifying last moments of the R-101?

There was enough in what he had in his transcript to convince

himself that Eileen Garrett could not consciously have come up
with such detail, even though parts of the technical phrasing were
fuzzy. There was not enough material yet to make a considered
judgment, and Villiers prided himself on not jumping to conclusions.

When the second session with Eileen Garrett began on Sunday
evening, he was not disappointed. After the voice of Uvani gave its
usual greeting, the session began almost immediately with Uvani
announcing that another person wanted to speak with the Major.

"I see near you a man of about fifty or fifty-five," the voice of
Uvani announced. "Jovial expression. Hair growing a little gray by
the ears. He used to have a mustache, which made him look older.
He now passes his hands across his lip, and takes it away."

Villiers was a little confused. He had been expecting someone
like Colmore, who would continue with Irwin's technical dis-
course. Instead, this sounded very much like Brancker. Especially
the gesture that indicated the removal of the mustache. But when
Villiers transcribed the second session, the full picture emerged:

VOICE OF UVANI:
He is smiling hard at you, and says, no, I won't give my name as I
want to be certain you know who it is. Very important. He is now
putting his hand into his waistcoat pocket, and is putting a piece of
round glass into his eye, and says: "Now—use your damned intelligence."

*(Villiers noted later that he felt as if Brancker were in the room
with him. The voice of Uvani then changed to the cadences of
Brancker.)*

BRANCKER:
Little did I think when I saw you last that we'd meet again with
things so upside down. No parties here, nothing in bottles. But spirits
of other kinds, if you know what I mean.

*(This wasn't a good example of Brancker's humor, but it was
characteristic enough. There followed a few inquiries of a private nature that Villiers answered as well as he could. Brancker
then made the strange request to be referred to as "B." Villiers
saw no reason not to comply.)*

VILLIERS:
Let's get down to brass tacks about the affair.

BRANCKER:
Colmore wants to speak to you afterwards.

VILLIERS:
Yes, but B, would you please ask Colmore to let me speak to Scottie
or Johnnie, as I must get certain facts before evidence comes out tomorrow and Tuesday at the inquiry. When did you first know or begin to realize that things on board were not right?

*(Villiers was probing to see if any information that came
through the seance would be verified by any witnesses at the
hearings, or whether he would be receiving information ahead of
the hearings. If so, this would be heavy evidence that he was actually in touch with the crew of the ill-fated airship.)*

BRANCKER:
Well, we all had a conference, because Irwin, Scottie and Johnston
put the case before us.

*(This was interesting to Villiers because none of the survivors
had been privy to any high-level discussions after the gangplank
had been pulled back into the ship.)*

VILLIERS:
I must get this right. Did the conference take place immediately after
she left, or later on?

*(Villiers was referring to the lady visitor who had gone aboard
with Brancker just before the flight. She had left the ship just before it left the tower. He was hoping he could find a living witness who had heard the final discussion.)*

Did the lady who went on board with you hear?

BRANCKER:
Lord, no. She left before that. No, what happened was this. Scott,
Irwin and Johnston came and told T.

VILLIERS:
You mean Thomson?

BRANCKER:
Yes. Of course. They told him of the gas trouble, and Colmore.

> *(Villiers thought this was an obscure reference to what Irwin had pointed out in the last session. It appeared somehow that the key officer group was trying to shelter Colmore from the wrath of Thomson by spreading the protest against leaving among themselves. Brancker's apparent voice continued.)*

They three—Scottie, Irwin and Johnston wanted to postpone the flight. But Thomson said it was impossible, there has been so much talk, and the general British public are all keyed up, we can't not go. They asked me and I felt I couldn't show a faint heart, and alas said yes. We discussed the weather charts, and saw that if we managed to cross the pond and could land somewhere in a foreign country, our honor would be vindicated, and we could then bless the bad weather and say that the weather forced us to make a descent.

VILLIERS:
Did you have any premonition of this?

BRANCKER:
Yes. In a way. That's why I had those two talks with Thomson.

> *(Villiers thought this reference was to the pre-flight confrontations with Thomson that Brancker had told him about in the car on the way to Cardington.)*

I had a couple of stiff ones, you know, before sailing.

VILLIERS:
I thought you only had champagne at dinner.

BRANCKER:
Oh, no. I put a drop in my pocket, and took two good ones. I felt awful. Of course, we never had a run for our money. Thomson really funked the flight, but felt he had to go. He had already said his policy

was India at all costs. And his hand was to the plough, and I felt we all ought to be at the death—no turning back.

(There were many awkward phrases throughout. Villiers still continued his extended notes, recounting them through his capacity for total recall. Then the voice of Uvani interrupted, with its slower and more precise diction.)

UVANI:
Next, I will describe a round, jovial face, big head . . .

VILLIERS:
Yes, Scottie. I knew at once it was you.

(Villiers noted that he was responding still as if his former friends were in the room with him. The momentum of the experience carried him along in this way.)

MAJOR SCOTT:
Villiers, it's all too ghastly for words. It's awful. Think of all the lives, experience, money, material. All thrown away. What for? Nothing.

VILLIERS:
There's a reason, even if we can't see it now.

MAJOR SCOTT:
There may be. But it's absolutely ghastly.

VILLIERS:
Scottie, try and help me to fill in the gaps. When did you begin to be suspicious that the ship was wrong?

MAJOR SCOTT:
After her first flight. She didn't handle too well, and we had trouble.

VILLIERS:
What was the trouble? Irwin mentioned the nose.

MAJOR SCOTT:
Yes. Girder trouble and engine.

VILLIERS:
Now go slowly. I must get this right. Can you describe exactly where? We have the long struts numbered from A to G.

> *(Villiers meant to say "girders," but his notes said "struts," and he recorded this even though it was incorrect. His technical knowledge was admittedly superficial.)*

MAJOR SCOTT:
Not quite. The one at the top is "0." And then A, B, C and so on downwards. Look at your model.

> *(Villiers had almost forgot that he had brought some sketches and photographs. He found a coded diagram from Cardington, and pulled it out. The cross-section girders were numbered from 1 to 15. The 16 girders that ran the length of the ship were lettered on each side, with "0" at the top, as Scott had said.)*

VILLIERS:
Let me see. Number 5 is the bay just behind the starboard engine, and A-B-C, yes. The third. Yes, I have it. Now, go on.

MAJOR SCOTT:
On our second flight after we finished, we found the girder had been strained, not cracked. And this caused trouble to the cover. This is where she went the last time.

VILLIERS:
All right. We will take up that point later on. Now what came next?

MAJOR SCOTT:
The gas valves proved ineffective. You remember the RAF display?

VILLIERS:
At Hendon?

MAJOR SCOTT:
Yes. We only just got back. I was not too keen on that short trip.

VILLIERS:
Did you ever make a report to the Air Ministry?

MAJOR SCOTT:

My dear man, you know all the damned red tape This was purely technical, and when possible we always avoided technical reports. Otherwise, we should never have gotten our work done.

> *(Villiers recorded here a long explanation about the pressure of the gas being too strong for the valves, and that the officers had figured they were losing an unacceptable amount of gas, and they realized things were desperate. Villiers wondered about the fact that no radio message about the possibility of an emergency landing had been sent to Le Bourget.)*

VILLIERS:

But since you had decided to try for Le Bourget, why did you not send out for a landing party?

MAJOR SCOTT:

We could not do so till after crossing the Channel. If the message went too early, we should have blown the gaff and given the game away.

VILLIERS:

Yes, I realize you had to take all precautions to carry out the bluff.

MAJOR SCOTT:

Yes, exactly. Now you realize how desperate we were. Well, you want to know about the rent in the outer cover. The same place. 5-C this time.

VILLIERS:

Do you mean to say it actually broke and a piece of the girder went through the outer cover?

MAJOR SCOTT:

No. Not broke, but cracked badly and split the outer cover.

VILLIERS:

Who told you the news, and where were you?

MAJOR SCOTT:

We. Johnnie, Irwin, and I were together.

VILLIERS:
In the control room?

MAJOR SCOTT:
No. Johnnie's cubbyhole, you know. And the rigger called to us.
And we saw by the instrument board immediately. We all gasped,
and were horrified at the news. We decided—

VILLIERS:
Did she nose-dive then?

MAJOR SCOTT:
No. Not quite. We decided to make a turn and go with the wind as far
as it was possible, and make for Le Bourget, and try at all costs some
kind of landing. You know how we always turn in a big circle because of the strain. So we decided to try.

> *(Villiers constantly had to remind himself that he was not talk-
> ing to Major Scott directly. The illusion created by Eileen Gar-
> rett's authoritative voice and information made it hard for him
> to conceive that all this was coming through in a seance. The
> purported voice of Scott continued.)*

Well, Villiers, now imagine the picture. We have a bad rent in the
cover on the starboard side of 5-C. This brought about an unnatural
pressure and the frame gave a twist which, with the external pressure, forced us into our first dive. The second was even worse. The
pressure on the gas bags was terrific. And the gusts of wind were tremendous. This external pressure, coupled with the fact that the valve
was weak, blew the valve right off, and at the same time, the released
gas was ignited by backfire from the engine.

VILLIERS:
But Scottie, I don't understand this. You said previously the engine
had given oil trouble, and the valve that went was just near the front
starboard engine.

MAJOR SCOTT:
Quite right. But both engines had caused trouble. At least the engines
were quite OK, only the oil feed was wrong. This engine backfired at
the same time, and caused the igniting. It was all simultaneous. John-

nie was killed instantly. I was knocked out and knew no more. But Irwin, poor man, was crushed with tons of metal and had a terrible time.

VILLIERS:
Look here, Scottie. I sounded Noble out. And I asked him on the train last night if he had any trouble with a girder. You know how he puts his lips tight, and he said: Oh, no, no, no. Nothing ever. So I held my tongue and changed the conversation.

MAJOR SCOTT:
Don't breathe a word, Villiers. And don't trust him. I hate to say so, but he knows what took place.

VILLIERS:
Noble knew? How?

MAJOR SCOTT:
He and Roberts were on board when we had the critical talk with Thompson and the others. They heard all. Every word. Now, by God, they are quaking with fright that things might come out.

VILLIERS:
Surely Roberts must speak out.

MAJOR SCOTT:
He can't, poor chap. He would lose his position. And there would be hell to pay.

VILLIERS:
Another thing. The chief engineer said that the engines were OK.

MAJOR SCOTT:
My God, what a damned lie. Both engines had been giving trouble at different times. No. All survivors have had orders to stick to one tale: All is OK.

VILLIERS:
I must get the truth somehow.

MAJOR SCOTT:
Now, Villiers. Listen to me. It will do no good. They can all deny,

and you would be hounded out if they knew at the Air Ministry you had even a suspicion. The truth will come out later, and all of it will come out. In any case, it helps us so much to tell you all that happened. And we appreciate your thoughts.

Eileen Garrett had stirred at this point, and appeared to be ready to come out of her trance. Noting this, Villiers had said: "Well, dear old boy, so long. Tell Johnnie and Colmore I will talk to them very soon."

Again, Villiers went over his transcript. And again he felt he was learning more here than on listening to the testimony at the official hearing. He felt confident that he had captured the gist, if not the letter, of the second session. There was some heavy and some controversial stuff in it. Nearly all of it was getting into touchy ground as far as the Air Ministry and the government were concerned. He had to consider what distortions there were, and he also had to consider both his own credibility and the risk to his career if he took any steps involving the information.

He examined his options. He could believe—or he could not believe. He could believe parts, and not believe other parts. Eileen Garrett herself had warned him that not everything that came through her as a channel could be totally accurate. She wasn't even sure she was getting communications from the deceased. This was why she was planning the series of scientific experiments in America. She was only vaguely conscious of what was going on during a trance. She knew that in most cases those who had come to her were astounded at the accuracy of the information that came through. But she herself could take no credit for it.

One of the options that could be examined was that Eileen Garrett could have memorized every ounce of material available in such a way that she could spout it out without stumbling, in the various cadences of Villiers' friends, providing technical information that even Villiers wasn't sure of. In a sense, this was the only major alternative to believing that he had been communicating with his friends who had died so recently. There was the option of telepathy from the living, but it hardly seemed logical that such a fund of information could come through in this form.

In examining the options, Villiers finally arrived at the conclusion that he was forced to accept the theory that he definitely was in contact with his friends. There was too much detail, too much authenticity of phrase and characterization to ignore.

But what about the vague parts, the fuzzy parts, the possibility of technical information that might not check out as being correct? What about contradictions?

There was a theory that covered this, if it was to be believed, Eileen told him. Those who died were suspected of being confused and startled at finding themselves in an afterlife that many never believed existed. They were suspected of being no more alert than they had been on earth. Their basic characteristics were supposed, according to the theory, to remain until they developed further spiritually. If they were forgetful and absent-minded on earth, they could be the same in an alleged afterlife.

The shock of a sudden death could add to confusion. The strain of trying to communicate through a wall that could divide the geography of the living from that of the dead was thought to put up all kinds of obstacles to sharpness of detail and articulation. Some of the officers of the ship might say one thing one time, and another thing another, as they might have done when they were living. They might be dazed and stunned, be articulate one moment, and disoriented the next. With such barriers in communication, anything could happen.

When Villiers finished reconstructing his notes in detailed dialogue, he turned to making a set of very precise questions for the next session with Eileen, which was scheduled for Wednesday, November 5. When he arrived at the Royal Courts of Justice after his working lunch hour on Monday, he had the uncanny feeling that he knew more about the roots of the crash than the rest of the courtroom.

Harry Price knew nothing whatever about Villiers' probe into the R-101 case. Villiers knew nothing about the Price-Coster affair. They both, however, reacted the same. The evidence fell in two areas, that which supported the possibility of an afterlife, and that which could have an important bearing on the court inquiry. Price, who had never even heard of Villiers, was just as much of a bulldog. While he searched for his airship expert to review the transcript, he sent a copy to the Air Ministry. It brought interesting results.

Shortly after Price's transcript was sent off, two members of Royal Air Force Intelligence arrived at Eileen Garrett's apartment. They, of course, were entirely separate from Villiers' intelligence division, which dealt only with civil aviation. They were very discreet and softspoken, and didn't immediately make clear what the purpose of their visit was. Eileen listened as they talked in vague generalities, her Irish sense of drama piqued by why they might be calling on her. After some time had elapsed, she pressed them for the reason for their visit. They had trouble in getting it out, but they finally said they had gone over the transcript Harry Price had sent them, which had revealed several things that were more or less secret, and were not supposed to be circulated about. They did not specify what the items were. But, embarrassing or not, they were forced to ask if she had been sleeping with any of the officers or designers of the R-101.

Eileen Garrett stood up. With icy annoyance in her voice, she invited them to leave immediately. They didn't press her further. But Eileen was half-pleased. Whatever had come through the voice of Uvani during the séance with Harry Price and Ian Coster must have been of extreme importance to warrant such a call. She was glad she was going to the United States to put herself in the hands of scientists. She had gone as far as she could go in her own self-analysis, and had no answers.

Without knowing it, Price had another thought that was also in the back of Villiers' mind. He wanted to notify Sir John Simon of the séance findings, in case they could be of any help. As a realist, Price realized the difficulty of carrying this out. As far as he knew, it would be a first in the history of jurisprudence to offer, even as just background evidence, a transcribed séance. A statesman like Sir John Simon was a man of formidable stature, who probably wouldn't cotton to anything of this nature.

Yet this particular incident haunted Price more than almost anything else he had encountered in his explorations. It was so important that both he and Coster had refrained from making the séance public in order not to disturb the critical hearings that were being held. But on November 7, one month after he and Coster had sat down with Eileen Garrett, he took the bull by the horns and wrote to Simon:

Sir John Simon, K.C.

President, R-101 Inquiry
Westminster, S.W. 1

Dear Sir John:

It is with considerable diffidence that I approach you concerning
something that is germane to the R-101 inquiry, over which you are
presiding. But I have thought the matter over carefully, and I consider it my duty to acquaint you with the following facts, however bizarre you may regard them, or in fact, they may be.

During an experiment at the National Laboratory of Psychical Research on October 7 with a noted clairvoyant named Mrs. Eileen
Garrett, and while this lady was in deep trance, the alleged entity of
Flight Lieutenant H. C. Irwin, captain of the R-101 "controlled" the
psychic, who became very agitated and gave us a long, detailed, and
technical account of why the airship sank; why it failed to rise; what
was wrong with the design of the ship and the engines; what caused
the explosion, etc.

I must emphasize the fact that the National Laboratory is *not* concerned with Spiritualism, per se: it is a body of investigators interested in scientifically acquiring data by means of which we hope some
day to discover the laws underlying psychic phenomena.

When I remark that I do *not* believe it was the "spirit" of Irwin
who was responsible for the very remarkable information (recorded
stenographically by our secretary) we received, I must also state that
I am convinced that the psychic was not consciously cheating. It is
likewise improbable that one woman in a thousand would be capable
of delivering, as she did, an account of the flight of an airship, at the
same time showing remarkable knowledge of engines, feed, etc.

Where such information comes from is a problem that has baffled
the world for two thousand years.

Should you consider that the protocol of our experiment is worthy
of perusal, I would gladly forward a copy for your inspection.

Yours very truly,

Harry Price
Honorary Director

Price had no sooner sent the letter off, when he had an afterthought. His caution and qualification of the capabilities of Eileen Garrett might possibly tend to make Simon think that the entire session had simply been telepathy, or that the sitting might just have been set up for the purpose of making a sensational R-101 disclosure. He immediately sent a follow-up letter the next day:

Dear Sir John:

Further to my letter of the 7th instant, I find that I omitted to state that the "Irwin" incident was quite spontaneous on the part of the psychic, the experiment being held for quite another purpose.

Its complete spontaneity startled the sitters, who were not aware that the airship disaster occupied their conscious minds. So it is rather doubtful if thought-transference played any part in the result.

Yours very truly,
Harry Price

Price really didn't have much hope that Sir John would respond favorably in reviewing the material, because it was such an unusual request, in the middle of the storm center of the court hearings. He was right. He received a letter from Darby, Sir John's registrar and assessor, indicating that at this stage of the inquiry, Sir John did not want to review the material. Price was not going to drop his investigation there, but he knew that the time was not ripe for a second approach to Simon. He further hoped he would hear from the Air Ministry, to whom he had already sent a transcript.

In the meanwhile, the aftermath of the tragic crash continued. There were pilgrimages every day to the mass burial ground at Cardington, where fresh flowers continued to smother the grave. Two young widows, whose husbands lay in the common grave, came out to the field to add more flowers, then went to the local authorities to see if they could buy grave sites for themselves, as near as possible to where their husbands were buried. Knighthoods were proffered for a dozen French officials and soldiers who had performed rescue services at the site of the crash in Beauvais.

The hearings continued. Sir John Simon was probing at the question of whether the test flights of the R-101 had been adequate.

Squadron Leader Booth testified bluntly that the judgment of the officers must have been biased by the Imperial Conference and the pressure of Lord Thomson to fly to India and back at the right psychological moment. He was sure that Colmore, Scott, Irwin and the rest of the R-101 officers would have insisted on more trials otherwise.

Franklin Noble, Colmore's assistant, called to the stand, indicated that he felt that Colmore was quite confident about the journey. In his recollection, he said, Colmore seemed quite content to leave on Saturday night, as Lord Thomson had requested. Further testimony indicated that back in November 1929 the gas valves were opening dangerously as the ship rolled at its tower mooring. This was found in a rigger's log, but the chief aeronautical inspector at Cardington said that it had never been brought to his attention.

In the courtroom Villiers listened to this in light of what Scottie had ostensibly said about Noble in the last session. There would be a lot more cross-checking to do. He framed more questions to bring to his next session with Eileen Garrett. By now he was confident that he could learn much more of the inside story there than listening to the trial testimony. He might even find traceable evidence that would indicate a cover-up. If he did, he would not hesitate to act, even at the risk of his job.

CHAPTER XIII

As usual, Major Villiers walked through St. James's Park on his way to Eileen Garrett's for his third session, on November 5. Many things were going through his mind. The identity of the different voices of the R-101 crew puzzled him. Each gave the illusion of a clear identity. It was not that the quality of Eileen Garrett's voice changed to a great extent. It was the rhythm, the manners of speech, the expressions, the personalities that seemed to emerge. It was this part of the mystery, along with the massive factual detail, that lent credence to the material. Villiers also had learned from his friend Major-General Sorsby that it was not at all uncommon for a séance to be carried out with give-and-take dialogue. Villiers had been wondering whether such a process were unique or not.

The new session with Eileen Garrett had no sooner begun than Colmore started to speak. At first he asked a few questions about his wife, which Villiers was unable to answer. Then Villiers got down to the basics of his own inquiry.

Colmore told him of the meeting on board before the ship left, and how angered he was because they had held it without his being present. Villiers reassured him that they had done so because they wanted to spread the responsibility in incurring Lord Thomson's wrath. Colmore seemed satisfied.

Then Villiers pressed on, trying to learn the history of the weak girder at the spot 5-C. From Colmore's voice, he learned that the V-shaped end of the girder had apparently widened in flight, and split the outer cover to expose the interior of the ship to untenable strain. After the split had widened, the crash had become inevitable.

At this point, the apparent voice of Colmore told Villiers of an important set of progress books, coded by different subject matter. "The history of this trouble," Colmore's voice recounted, "will be found in the book marked: A-5-7."

Villiers noted this carefully. It would be his first order of business to locate Colmore's progress books, because they had not been offered as evidence at the hearings. Colmore let it be known that he had little or no respect for what was going on at the hearings. "It's all absolutely a waste of money," Villiers' notes recorded him as saying. "And merely a method of the damn government to help whitewash the inquiry. It makes me boil."

At the end of this third session, Villiers felt frustrated. The official inquiry had taken a recess for 23 days, in order to assemble more technical information. He had lined up four more sessions with Eileen Garrett, up to the 28th of November, before the hearings would recommence. He had told no one about the information coming out of the séances, except his wife and his confidential secretary. He knew that some of the things that he had recorded in his notes would be indefensible under harsh, technical scrutiny. Before he could possibly reveal anything he learned, he would have to collect verifiable leads that were without question provided by these unbelievable communications. The words Villiers recorded in his transcripts were not enough without confirmable data.

He knew the danger of attempting to take the information to Sir John Simon, but he brought the matter up at the next session when the voice of Brancker came through again. Brancker seemed to encourage him to do so.

"But how will Simon take it?" Villiers asked. "You see he can't use the evidence in court, even if he does believe it."

"That's all right," the voice of Brancker said. "Don't worry about that. As a matter of fact, I believe Simon and his wife know a good deal more about this psychic thing than most people realize. And my opinion is that you'll find your talk much easier than you think. He is out for the truth. All this will enable him to ask questions with a definite point of view in mind. And when he tumbles on the truth, there will be some shifting of high and mighty ones from their seats.''

It was still difficult for Villiers to conceive all this dialogue coming through the evanescent form of Uvani: the matter-of-fact exchange of ideas and information; the anger, the emotions still residing in his friends whose lives had been so suddenly snuffed out. It seemed almost like a chat at the Royal Aero Club lounge, and in a sense it was comforting. He was hoping he was capturing the same ambiance in his amateur shorthand, which was improving with practice.

The session continued, with Major Scott coming in for a long technical review of where the first fracture began, and how the gas bags were not strong enough to hold the volume of gas in them, and how hard the surging bags rubbed against the wires and girders.

''Remember,'' Villiers' notes read in recording the voice of Scott, ''the gas is not stationary, but keeps moving around and around when set in motion, which happens in flight.''

Further on, Villiers' notes brought more vivid detail from Scott: ''We heard the straining going on, and sent the forward rigger to report. And he came back and said the coupling had slipped. So we called two others, and told them to try to make a new coupling by drilling new holes, and bolt them together. But of course, there was no time. After that, things happened quickly.''

Villiers asked: ''Now a thing that is puzzling the court is: How did Hunt know things were desperate, since he had time to say 'We're down, lads.' Did you tell him?''

The voice of Major Scott continued: ''All hands on duty in the ship knew the rent had been made. And Hunt was actually off duty. But since he knew an hour before that things were desperate, Hunt did what any other man would do. He tried to give the warning to the mens' quarters.''

''At what time did the rent appear?'' Villiers asked.

''I should say ten minutes to two. About ten minutes before the end came.''

''Was the first dive steep?'' Villiers asked.

''No, it was hardly a dive. You see, the rent had become bigger, and the gusts of wind were hitting her hard, making her difficult to keep steady and to steer. And also the fourth and third girders were badly strained. Our only chance was to try a slow turn, and land downwind, which would enable the damaged starboard side to get shelter from the wind and the terrific gusts. We tried to correct the bump downwards, but she would not respond. Then she practically went into a perpendicular nose dive.''

"But the evidence shows that the nose did not strike the ground," Villiers said.

Scott's message continued: "An aeroplane under those conditions would continue her nose dive. But since we had just commenced to try and turn, the gusts of wind blowing through the rent on her starboard put a terrific strain on her port side. And she sort of got a drag on, and heeled to port. Thereby, she finally landed on more or less even keel. The rest you know.''

As Villiers continued his rapid note-taking, he became more convinced that if Eileen Garrett's unconscious mind was creating all this, it would have to be the most grandiose and bottomless Unconscious that Freud had ever conceived in his theories. Even if she were fictionalizing, it showed a grasp of aeronautical theory that couldn't be expressed so fluently and without stumbling or hesitation. He ruled out both of these alternatives and went unashamedly for the premise that he was communicating with his dead friends, without a doubt in his mind.

Major Scott continued with more talk of his version of what had happened. Just north of London, the altimeter failed. Villiers thought he heard Scott mention that some kind of spring had failed, but later realized this was wrong, because a barometric altimeter contained no spring. There were problems indicated north of London, where they couldn't get up more than 900 feet maximum; over the Channel where they must have dropped to 250 or 300 feet.

Then Villiers cut in to ask: "I believe evidence was given that the order was given to shut off all engines. Why did you do this?" Villiers was not sure he was right in this assumption, but it would be a good cross-check on what finally came out in the hearings.

"I will make this clear," was Scott's reply. "We never did shut off *all* the engines. Just as we contemplated turning, the order was given to slow down the forward port and starboard rear engines. This left us with the forward starboard and rear port and rear after-engines running, which was required to carry out the turn. But the turn was really hardly started when the final crash came. Remember it was the heel to port, and the natural drag that put the ship in her final landing angle when she touched the ground. In fact, this practically acted as a brake.

"Now—Colmore has come to help about these damned books you're talking about."

Villiers had been looking for this moment. It was the key to not only confirming the reality of the information, but to bringing material before the court that should not be withheld.

"Hullo, old man," Villiers said. "So glad you have come. I must try and definitely establish where certain documents are, as I want Simon to see them himself." He still had not made his decision about bringing the transcripts to Simon, but he was leaning that way.

This could be critical, because there were loud noises in Parliament about the possibility that Simon was not getting all the material he needed to fully appraise the case. In fact, Lord Aukland in the House of Lords was asking His Majesty's Government for " . . . all papers and correspondence which passed between the Government Departments and the Air Ministry, and office files (whether secret or not) dealing with the construction and policy of the airship R-101 and especially all correspondence which passed between the Treasury and Air Ministry on the subject." Nothing, Lord Auckland felt, should be kept back from the court.

Lord Trenchard, also of the House of Lords. stated that he was perfectly certain that the officers of the Air Ministry had a strong ambition to provide every scrap of paper that might throw light on the disaster. Lord Amulree, now Secretary of State for Air, joined with Trenchard's position. No question of privilege had been raised, he emphasized. Yet both these men had been great admirers of Lord Thomson, who was the focal point of the controversy as to why the R-101 crewmen were sent off to their deaths.

Addressing Colmore, Villiers' notes continued: "Now you told me that I should find the notes on the straining, and work on the Number 5 Girder, under A-5-7?"

"Yes. That's right."

"Well, try and explain how the various books were kept," Villiers said.

Colmore went on to explain his report system. how he numbered the different classifications under fabric, girder, mechanical and other classifications, including main construction and engines.

"I want to try to see that all these books are in court," Villiers said.

"Good God, man," was the response. "Aren't they there? It's absolutely necessary for them to be."

"I don't know, old man," Villiers replied. "But now that I know, I can find out. Did any of the executive staff have your books?"

"Yes. Richmond kept a diary, and I had my books. I have told you about book A."

"No," Villiers replied. "You said A-5-7 was a department book."

"No, no. It's mine."

"Thanks. I see," Villiers said. "Now go very slowly. Where were your books?"

"In my room. You know it quite well." It was a common Air Ministry practice to call the offices "rooms."

"Yes," Villiers said. "But I have forgotten exact details. I know where your room was."

"I had two sets of books. A to L, and Book A, which was divided up into section A to F."

"I don't quite understand," Villiers responded. "Why are two books marked A? So confusing."

"A to L were small, individual books of records of work in the shed before each flight, or rather work done when not in flight. Now book A contained all my records of flights. . . ."

"How shall I know what this book looks like?" Villiers asked.

"It has a brown-backed cover like a ledger. And on the back is marked A—R-101."

The session came to a rather abrupt stop. Villiers at least felt he had some good clues to go on, and left with the feeling of some satisfaction. As usual, he extended his notes, and prepared as close to a verbatim script as he could for transcription by his secretary at her home. So far, no one except she had any idea what he was up to, and he wanted to keep it that way.

On reviewing the transcripts up to date, he was convinced that he had come as close as possible to the words that were spoken at the sessions, including his own, allowing for the distortions from his own consciousness. He carefully tried to eliminate any entries of this sort. He was convinced that with his copious notes he had kept these to a minimum.

But when he thought about it, there was no way to prove the accuracy of his transcription. About the only things he could go on were his record, his reputation and his fast-growing conviction that he was communicating with his dead friends. With the details that had been coming over, he found that he could hardly think otherwise. If he weren't communicating, then there would remain a phenomenon that was equally startling and inexplicable. When you examined everything, it seemed that there was *no* explanation from a materialist-rationalist point of view.

There were three more sittings with Eileen Garrett scheduled. They would end on November 28, five days before the Court of Inquiry would reopen. The final decision to approach Sir John Simon directly would have to be made soon, if at all. The risk was great, and Major Villiers worried about it. In the next two sittings, more details came through. Colmore apparently became very agitated in discovering that his set of diary-ledgers had been removed.

"I don't think they have been used or asked for," Villiers commented after the sitting had gotten under way.

"Good God," was the reply. "But these papers bear out all this story of protest and pressure."

Then Colmore's voice registered concern: "Look here, Villiers," he said. "Scottie is here, and is damned nervous about you. We all feel you are taking a rotten risk. If by any chance the Air Ministry have half an inkling of what you are doing, you will be turfed out neck and crop."

"Thanks," said Villiers. "I quite realize how you feel. But believe me, I am taking all possible precautions, and that is why I will see Sir John alone, and the Air Ministry will have no inkling."

"All right, Villiers. But take every precaution and explain our fears to Sir John."

The rest of the sitting went on with a review of the material that had come out so far in the sessions. Again, the obviously erroneous matter of the altimeter spring came up. Villiers could not understand why the error appeared again, and thought maybe in the haste to get so much information across, they were referring to another instrument, especially when Scottie mentioned it in connection to the amount of gas that was being lost. Whatever it was, Villiers recorded it anyway and would analyze it later.

On the 25th of November, Brancker's apparent voice addressed Villiers after hearing of the plan to approach Sir John Simon. Neither Noble nor Roberts was doing anything to reveal the background of the struggle. Brancker agreed to Villiers' plan to make an appointment with Simon, as long as he took proper safeguards. Unlike Harry Price, who was an outsider, Villiers was confident he could get the ear of Sir John. If he and Price had known about each other's material, perhaps an even stronger case could have been built by a joint effort.

In the session, the voice of Brancker came through to say: "Well, old boy. Very best of luck, and our thanks to you. Thank God it's you and not us. If you convince Simon and help him to put a stop to all the political pressure and from HQ, and can enable him to lay down such regulations as will in future safeguard future lives from being sacrificed, you will have done a big job. What must be prevented is that the technical staff shall have a fair hearing, and not be overridden by the Economy Government and the mighty ones at HQ."

The key point to the next-to-last session lay in the information that appeared to come through regarding First Officer Atherstone, who had died with them in the crash. According to his co-officers, he was not inclined to speak through such a strange communication method as was being conducted, but Colmore seemed to feel that Atherstone had two diaries—one with his optimistic, cheerful accounts of the adventure, and the other with the realistic appraisals of the condition of the ship and its construction.

Villiers was busy during those next three days. In addition to recording his extended notes, he reviewed them and catalogued them. He was now ready for his risky approach to Sir John Simon. His whole career could go tumbling, and Villiers knew it. He sent a message to Sir John via Darby, Simon's chief assistant, who agreed to hand-carry it to Simon. The answer came back promptly: Sir John would not only see him, but would have lunch with him at a private dining room at the Royal Courts of Law. Villiers was pleased—but he also feared for his career. He was grateful to Darby for paving the way. He sat down and dictated an eight-page summary of the information received over the long series of meetings.

At his seventh and final session with Eileen Garrett, Villiers went through another detailed review. The group appeared to be pleased with his luncheon appointment with Sir John, but again warned him to be careful.

But then First Officer Atherstone apparently came through the voice of Uvani: Unlike his fellow officers, he seemed reluctant to talk. Villiers addressed him directly:

"Now, Atherstone, we have never spoken before. But somehow it makes no difference. You know I told Scottie that I had heard on best authority that you had made an entry in a diary, voicing your feelings very clearly. In which diary was it? Had you two?— because the court has seen one diary which is 'beautiful.'"

"I did not have two. Only one."

"You admit you did write some such words. Well, where did you? Don't you see, I must know the truth, as it will be invaluable for Simon to see for himself," Villiers said.

"But I didn't count or cut much ice."

"That's not the point, Atherstone," Villiers said. Villiers was anxious to press here. There had been one optimistic, lyrical phrase from Atherstone's diary read at the trial. If there were other, less savory ones, Villiers wanted to know. He forgot for a moment that he wasn't talking to solid, human beings, and said: "Colmore, do try and explain why I must know."

After a pause, the apparent voice of Atherstone answered. "Well, I kept a pocket diary which I gave to my wife before going on board, with letters inside, as I somehow knew I might not come back."

There was no great flourish as the seventh and last sitting came to an end on October 28. Brancker was apparently the last to talk, with a message of good luck in the interview with Simon. Villiers went back again to review all the long hours of recorded conversations with his late fellow colleagues. He knew nothing about Sir John Simon's attitude toward this sort of thing. But if his luncheon with him led to uncovering some of the material mentioned in these communications, there would be even more powerful evidence for clarification of the mystery of the R-101 and the mystery of our own destiny after death.

Villiers was aware that the obvious mistakes were noticeable. The altimeter "spring." A remark in one of the séances by Johnston that they had crossed over the Channel at Deal, instead of

Hastings. Some conflicting statements made by the officers themselves, and in conflict with some of the testimony at the hearings.
But he still recorded the mistakes faithfully, since they would have
to be considered in a final appraisal of the experience. There would
be no sense in fooling himself.

Darby was already in the private dining room of the Royal
Courts of Justice when Villiers arrived. Sir John arrived half an
hour late, and apologized. Simon was cordial, but Villiers was
nervous. However, after an exchange of pleasantries, he got
straight to the point. Villiers told the whole story of his strange encounters with the officers of the R-101, exactly how they had come
about and the gist of the information that was passed along through
the sessions.

Sir John took it in his stride. He asked Darby to take notes, and
accepted Villiers' written summary. Villiers emphasized that he
was now convinced that important material was missing from the
evidence being presented at the hearings. He pointed out especially
Colmore's confidential diary notebooks, his official correspondence with the Air Member for Supply and Research, missing correspondence from the Treasury, and the portions of Atherstone's diary that contained his doubts and fears of the construction of the
airship. Simon checked Darby to make sure he had written down
these specific points.

Simon told Villiers that he, of course, could not use the information directly, since it did not constitute legal evidence. Villiers realized this, but felt that if it could bring out some of the missing evidence, it would have served its purpose.

Sir John then turned to Villiers, and made a very puzzling statement. He said that if Villiers had the desire to, he could probably
receive a great deal of money by turning over his report and transcripts to the press. Sir John warned against doing anything like
this, with the hearings still underway.

Major Villiers was shocked and angered. His motives had been
directed only at the idea of seeing that all the truth would be
brought out at the hearings.

"Sir John," he said. "Surely you don't think that I should have
come to you in confidence and told you all I have—and then given
it to the press?"

Sir John mentioned that he brought the subject up only as a precaution. Villiers told him that he had no such thoughts in mind, and to reassure Simon, he would make only two copies of his verbatim transcripts, one for himself and one for Sir John.

It was the sequel to the lunch that proved most interesting. Within a day or two afterward, Darby came to see Villiers. Darby had been sent back to Cardington by Simon to recheck every lead that Villiers had provided. Darby had scoured the Cardington offices looking for Colmore's books, diaries and personal papers. Officials there stoutly continued to deny that any such material existed. Villiers found this hard to believe. Colmore had been so precise and articulate in the sessions with Eileen Garrett. The detail regarding the Colmore records and their location was so carefully spelled out that it persuaded Villiers that he was not dealing with a myth. Simon was apparently not taking it lightly, either. He had asked Darby to prepare a memo summarizing the Villiers material. Darby brought it with him with a request from Simon that Villiers sign it. He did so.

For Villiers, the situation boiled down to this: The material he had received in the seances not only had great importance as far as the hearings were concerned. It extended to the larger question of whether man lived after death. He was now sure that he had been in touch with a group of identifiable entities who reached back into the lives they once lived. In addition, they seemed to be able to transmit articulate technical information to him, almost as if they were still living.

What still counted most in confirming the reality of all this were those sharp and incontestable facts that could be verified without question. The Colmore diaries were one fact that could be checked and matched against reality. The Atherstone diary was another. Confirmation of these two specific items would provide strong evidence to bolster the validity of the sessions, not only to Villiers but to others. Because now Major Villiers was prepared to dedicate a large portion of his life to convincing others that there was a rational and realistic way to believe in life-after-death.

CHAPTER XIV

The hearings at the Court of Inquiry came to a close on December 5, 1931, with a whisper rather than a shout. Through the final days, Villiers was struck with many similarities between his Eileen Garrett transcripts and the testimony—as well as many differences. There were contradictions in both. Some witnesses thought the explosion caused by backfiring, others by electrical wiring. Electrician Disley insisted that the wiring was sealed, and an automatic cutoff would have prevented a spark there. There was really no consensus here on the question. The fact was that the ship had blown up. With hydrogen, the explosion could have happened through several different causes at once.

Along with a lot of other close observers of the hearings, Villiers was sure the whole story had not come out. The final conclusions of the court would not be known for several months, when a written report would be issued. To many, a whitewash seemed inevitable. On the last day of the hearings, Villiers noticed that Simon pressed both Noble and Roberts hard on what they knew. Both men appeared to be holding back. None of Colmore's or Atherstone's heavy criticism had ever been mentioned in the testimony, nor their records or diaries.

With the end of the hearings, came the news of the final curtain for the R-101. Its twisted girders were bought by a scrap dealer.

265

They would be melted down and sold for making pots, pans and kettles. It was an ignoble end for what was hoped to be the pride of the Empire.

Harry Price, in spite of his vigorous skepticism, was almost as passionate as Villiers in trying to fathom the mysteries of his and newsman Coster's session with Eileen Garrett. Was it actually Captain Irwin that had come through to them?

At this point, Price and Coster still knew nothing of the Villiers sessions, and Villiers knew nothing about their experience. Neither Price nor Villiers wanted to make public the material at this time. Like Villiers, Price wanted to do a lot more digging into confirming straight, hard facts.

By the middle of December, some two weeks after the the hearings had come to an end, an article by Coster and Price appeared on the newsstands and kiosks in the January issue of both *Nash's* magazine in Britain and *Cosmopolitan* in the United States. The story centered almost completely on the Conan Doyle part of the séance.

There was a small, indirect mention of the R-101 portion. No details at all were revealed. The mention was treated as a brief preamble to the visit of Conan Doyle, who purportedly had come through in the last half of the séance. The newspapers picked up the story quickly, spreading it far beyond the confines of the magazine coverage.

In spite of its brevity, the Irwin part of the article brought immediate attention. The first sign was a letter to Harry Price from C.D. Galpin, an officer of the Air Ministry:

                    AIR MINISTRY
                    Adastral House
                    Kingsway, W.C. 2

                                        18 December, 1930

Dear Mr. Price:

I see in the daily press that at a recent séance Mrs. Garrett came into touch with Flight Lieutenant Irwin, late of the R-101.

Would you be good enough to let me come over to the laboratory and discuss what was obtained on that occasion? You may possibly have some notes—and it might be desirable to pursue this contact further.

You will appreciate that my enquiry is purely personal: officially this department is in no way concerned. . . .

Yours truly,

C.D. Galpin

This was the opening Price had been waiting for. The hearings were now over, and perhaps some of those connected with the Air Ministry and Cardington would be willing to screen the material for the evidential checks that only a professional could provide. Price wanted no amateurs, either in the psychic or aeronautical fields. He wrote Galpin immediately, and invited him to the laboratory.

Shortly afterward, Price received another letter—this time from the Cardington base. It was from Will Charlton, the chief supply officer of the R-101:

Dear Mr. Price:

Mr. A. E. Garrish, the shed manager at the Royal Airship Works, and myself, the Stores Officer, read your article in the January *Nash's* Magazine with profound interest; especially in regard to the alleged communication from Captain Irwin.

Mr. Garrish was responsible for erecting the airship R-101, and was thoroughly conversant with every detail of the ship's structure. He also knew intimately every one of the ship's officers and crew.

As supply officer, I was also familiar with all parts of the ship and its equipment and personnel.

Would it be encroaching too much upon your kindress to ask if we might be given the opportunity of reading in detail all that was purported to have come through Mrs. Garrett from Captain Irwin?

In return, we should be glad to give you our comments on the information which might prove to be of great interest to you in your praiseworthy investigations.

Recently, I was invited to a private séance given by Mrs. B. Hirst at Bedford, and I was amazed to be told that a number of victims of the disaster were very eager to speak to me.

A ship's officer, whose description given to me was perfect, earnestly requested me to persuade two ladies to go to the medium to get in touch with him. He gave the ladies' pet names, which were perfectly correct. I could not help being impressed.

We both should intensely appreciate the favour of perusing your notes of that part of Mrs. Garrett's séance relating to the R-101.

Thanking you in anticipation, I remain, sir,

                              Yours very sincerely,
                              W. Charlton

Price was pleased to have another opportunity for a double-check, directly by Cardington staff officers who apparently knew the R-101 inside and out. He forwarded a copy of Miss Beenham's transcript as soon as she could type one up. "I shall be glad to have a technical report concerning the information contained in the protocol for our records," Price wrote back to Charlton. "I note that you undertake to regard the enclosed as private, and will not publish or allow to be published, the document in question."

It took until February 10, 1931, for Charlton to respond. He had been very busy, and he wanted to thoroughly study the transcript with the shed manager. Price finally received his preliminary reply on the 11th:

Dear Mr. Price:

Please accept my warm thanks for the verbatim notes of the séance when the alleged entity of Flt. Lieut. Irwin manifested, and also my apologies for not acknowledging receipt of this document earlier.

I have been absent at Pulham [where the grounded R-100 was housed] for some days, but hope to return the copy with what I hope you will find an interesting comment upon it by Monday next.

It will interest me to know that Mrs. Garrett, beyond reading of the disaster in general, *had not read* any expert opinions and technical information concerning the ship just prior to the experiment, whereby her subconscious mind could react.

She would hardly have had time to do so.

If Mrs. Garrett was completely ignorant of these technical matters concerning R-101, then the document is an extremely wonderful one.

                              Very truly yours,
                              W. Charlton

For Harry Price, this was interesting news. At least he now had a technical opinion that confirmed his hunch. He would want, however, to dig into this in much more detail before he could be satisfied.

He wrote back to Charlton that he was certain that Mrs. Garrett had not read any expert opinions at the time of the séance, adding: "It must be remembered that the séance was held on the day following the notification in the London dailies and, speaking personally, I saw no real technical accounts of what might have happened at the smash, and I am convinced that the medium had no *conscious* thoughts concerning the disaster. Where the information came from is another matter. I am not a spiritualist, but I am not prepared to state that Mrs. Garrett obtained the information normally. . . . "

By now, Will Charlton was as interested in getting to the bottom of the mystery as Price was. He had discussed and reviewed Price's transcript with the entire executive technical staff at Cardington. Almost without exception, they were amazed and puzzled. They agreed that it was an astounding document. One by one, they pored over the typewritten pages, and made careful annotations. Charlton coordinated them, along with his own. Together, they found over forty references to highly technical and confidential details. There were a dozen or so other inexplicable reference points. Allowing for mistakes in the shorthand and transcribing, they found it even more remarkable. There were impressive details on what actually could have happened on the flight.

They discussed their findings at length. They tried to explain it in terms of ordinary perspective. Jointly, they agreed that to assume this specialized information could come from any of the laymen at the séance would be "grotesquely absurd."

Tied to all this from Charlton's point of view was his unexplainable experience with the medium, Mrs. Hirst. Charlton was a cautious and thorough man, but he could not help noticing the link between his own experience and the protocol he had received from Harry Price. Both of these non-aeronautical women—Eileen Garrett and Bertha Hirst—had separately come through with a flow of information that simply could not be explained through normal channels.

Charlton called Price and told him he would like to come down to

London, without compensation or travel expenses. He also offered to bring slides and a projector (lantern slides, they were called then), showing various stages of construction detail of the R-101.

Charlton realized he had to be very guarded in his official position. He was even worried about some of the comments he was preparing to make to Price, because they were on the edge of confirming secret data. To avoid it, he reluctantly softened some of the annotations, even thought they would add considerably to the strength and validity of the information. There was more than enough, however, to shock the mind of any professional observer.

Charlton was also interested in seeing if Eileen Garrett would be willing to undertake another séance, with him present to ask questions. Eileen had suddenly taken ill on the eve of her departure for America, and unfortunately was now in the hospital. Price assured Charlton that he would try to set up another session as soon as she was physically able.

Meanwhile, Price reassured Charlton that his identity would be kept strictly confidential. In any protocol or minutes regarding the case, he would be referred to only as "Mr. X." Coincidentally, Villiers had used the same designation for himself in his own transcripts, still unaware of what was going on in Harry Price's inquiry.

At the end of March, just before Charlton was due to come down to see Price, the final report of the official Court of Inquiry was issued. It was an anticlimax. It was vague. It pointed the finger of responsibility at no one. It basically announced that the disaster was caused by the loss of gas—with the comment that it was "impossible" to say how the leakage began. It was considered by many to be a whitewash.

Charlton and the Cardington staff went over the official court report carefully, comparing it to the Harry Price material. Essentially, the hearings report noted that a sudden loss of gas in one of the forward gas bags came at a time when the nose was pushed down by a violent gust of wind. Some of the forward fabric of the envelopes must have been ripped open. The gas bags were exposed to the violent storm. One or more of them were rent, spilling the hydrogen. The wind was blowing 40 to 50 miles an hour, and the gusts were fierce. The gas bags were also leaking through many holes, both at the time of the crash, and before. Two of the engines were ordered to SLOW. The ship was definitely "heavy."

In the rolling of the vessel, during weather it had never experienced before, the gas valves released an additional amount of gas. The bags were hard up against the padded projections, and they chafed. If the rip developed forward, it would be likely to have spread. The vessel lost speed, and with it, control. The report, 129 pages long, noted: "It is impossible to avoid the conclusion that the R-101 would not have started for India on the evening of October 4 if it had not been that reasons of public policy were considered as making it highly desirable for her to do so if she could."

Structural damage was not blamed. No living witness had reported anything of it. The dead couldn't speak, unless the two incredible messages separately received by Villiers and Price could be believed. And neither of those was available to the public. In fact, the only real direct data the court could go on was testimony from a handful of men, mostly isolated from each other, and isolated from the control car and the rest of the ship. The testimony had only been able to report scraps and fragments. It was a jigsaw puzzle with most of the pieces missing.

Charlton again screened the official report with a microscopic eye, in preparation for his meeting with Harry Price. He noted that it failed to mention the testimony from Mr. Maillet of the Poix aerodrome, which stated that the ship was only 300 feet above the ground at that point. Poix was only 14 miles north of Achy, where the Price material quoted Irwin as saying that the airship almost scraped the roofs.

The cable that controlled the elevators had been found broken and jammed. The first experts were unable to determine whether this had happened before or after the crash. The court accepted the opinion of a steel industry expert who claimed that it had broken afterward, from heat. This was highly questionable, Charlton felt. Comparing the official report with the Price transcripts, the Cardington technical crew clearly leaned toward the latter.

Later, a prominent naval architect, E. F. Spanner, wrote a two-volume analysis of the official findings, and branded them a complete whitewash. Studying all the testimony not recorded in the official printed report, he pleaded a strong and convincing case for a structural break of the girders in the air causing the fabric to rip, and the ship to crash as a result.

The exact circumstances would really never be known, or as the Simon report put it: "It is no doubt possible to assume certain variations in data . . . how the vessel began to lose gas can never be definitely ascertained." In view of all this vagueness and uncertainty, Harry Price looked forward to Charlton's visit to the National Laboratory on April 14, 1931. Unfortunately, he fell ill and had to call in an aide to handle the job to guarantee the most careful scrutiny possible of Charlton's comparative findings.

She was one of the toughest psychic researchers on the scene, Mrs. K. M. Goldney, later of the British Society for Psychical Research. She had a long track record of exposing fake mediums, and was regarded as constantly being out for blood when it came to any fraud. She was fair-minded, but she was hard to convince. She was no fan of Spiritualists, and she checked out Will Charlton to make sure he was free and clear of any such nonsense, as she regarded the broad idea of Spiritualism.

Charlton had his own reservations, too. He asked to see the original shorthand notes, and grilled Ethel Beenham on her technical problems in taking down the information. Mrs. Goldney, in turn, asked Charlton to fill her in not only on the background of the R-101, but of earlier airships, so that she would have a general knowledge to base her opinion on.

Charlton told Mrs. Goldney about how the ship had got away badly from the tower, when she appeared to sink. He brought up the four to six tons of weight her envelope took on from driving rain. At Cardington, the belief was strong that the weight of the water was just too much for the engines.

Charlton, Ethel Beenham and Mrs. Goldney then sat down for a painstaking session to compare the Cardington staff's notes with the transcript of the Garrett séance. It was a slow, careful, line-by-line process. Charlton's material was placed side by side with each line of the transcript. The deeper they got into the material, the more the group was amazed. Ethel Beenham put her skills to work again, and coordinated the composite picture. When they studied it, there emerged a startling document that seemed almost incredible:

[*Note*: The Irwin statements which appear remarkable have been emphasized by using capital letters; answers to obscure passages are in italics."]

IRWIN COMMENTS	CHARLTON COMMENTS
"The whole bulk of the dirigible was entirely and absolutely too much for her engine capacity."	This statement agrees with popular opinion. (Official opinion?)
"Engines too heavy."	" " " "
"It was this that made me on five occasions have to scuttle back to safety."	says that on several occasions the ship returned to the mooring tower earlier than was scheduled. Further, after returning from Hendon Air Display, she actually had to discharge two tons of fuel oil to keep her afloat until she made home (the farmer on whose ground the oil descended claiming compensation). As recorded above in notes modifications were undertaken with a view to rectifying this heaviness.

IRWIN COMMENTS	CHARLTON COMMENTS
"Useful lift too small."	This is obvious from ballast discharged to enable her to rise.
"Gross lift computed badly— inform control panel."	Yes—or ship would not have been heavy at tower.
"This idea of new elevators totally mad."	Obscure. *If veridical it* would suggest that a new design of elevator had been contemplated, and that Irwin knew of this.
"Elevator jammed."	Thought probable by many informed opinions.

"Oil pipe plugged."   Obscure.

"This exorbitant scheme of   At the time of their R-101 flight,
carbon and hydrogen is entirely   a series of experiments was con-
and absolutely wrong."   templated with the idea of burn-
                                    ing a mixture of hydrogen and oil
                                    fuel (i.e., of carbon and hydro-
                                    carbon). This was to form the ba-
                                    sis of proposed experiments.
                                    The hydrogen would have been
                                    obtained from the gas bags, and
                                    the carbon from the oil fuel of
                                    the ship. For the purpose of this
                                    experiment at Cardington, a spe-
                                    cial gas main had been installed
                                    from the gas plant to the engine
                                    test house, to be utilized there in
                                    conjunction with oil fuel. No ex-
                                    periment had actually taken
                                    place at the time of the flight, but
                                    preparations were in progress.
                                    This would have consisted of a
                                    highly technical and important
                                    experiment—and would be un-
                                    likely to be known outside of
                                    official circles.

"To begin with, the demand for   Refers to previous passage
it would be greater than the   and suggests that there
supply."   would have been no hydrogen
                                    to spare for mixing with the
                                    oil fuel. Very probable.

"Also let me say this: I have   Quite possible.
experimented with less hydrogen
in my own dirigible with the
result that we are not able to
reach 1,000 metres."

"With the new carbon hydrogen   Quite possible.

you will be able to get no
altitude worth speaking about.
With hydrogen one is able to do
that quite easily.''

"Greater lifting than helium.''   This is obscure in this
connection, but the state-
ment is actually correct:
i.e., there is greater lift
with hydrogen than with
helium.

"Explosion caused by friction   *Slightly obscure. But*
in electric storm.''   *the danger from electric*
                                storm is relevant and real.

"Flying too low altitude and   Very probable and borne out
could never rise.''   by evidence at inquiry.

"Disposable lift could not be   All disposable lift—i.e.,
utilized.''   water ballast—had been
                                already utilized at starting.

"Load too great for long flight.''   Very probable.

"Same with S.L. 8—tell Ec-   The S.L. 8 has been verified as
kener.''   the number of a German air-
                                ship—S.L. standing for Shuttle
                                Lanz. This verified only after X.
                                had been through complete rec-
                                ords of German airships (i.e. it
                                was not known off hand.)—but it
                                would be known to Irwin. Dr.
                                Eckener is the constructor of the
                                "Graf Zeppelin.''

"Cruising speed bad and ship   Highly probable. Language
badly swinging.''   technically correct.

"Severe tension on the fabric   Very probable. Terms correct.
which is chafing.''

"Starboard strakes started.''   Very probable. 'Strakes,''

originally a naval expression, subsequently also employed in connection with airships. Strake are longitudinal plates running parallel in successive strata, so to speak, and forming the sides of ship.

"Engines wrong—too heavy —cannot rise."

In accordance with known facts.

"Never reached cruising altitude—same in trials."

In accordance with known facts.

"Too short trials."

Yes, admitted.

"No one knew the ship properly."

This is felt to be so.

"Airscrews too small."

This is believed by many of informed opinion to be correct. The airscrews were, as a matter of fact, substituted for those originally designed for the ship.

"Fuel injection bad and air pump failed."

Sensible, and probable.

"Cooling system bad."

Sensible, and probable.

"Bore capacity bad."

The expression used is correct—but truth of statement cannot be gauged at this stage.

"Next time with cylinders but bore of engine 1,000 cc's, but that bore is not enough to raise too heavy load and support weight."

If cubic *inches* were used instead of expression cubic *centimetres* (i.e., if this sentence ran "Next time, with cylinders and with

	bore of engine 1,100 cubic *inches*, but that—i.e., R 101's—bore not enough," etc.), this would make sense.
"It had been known to me on many occasions that the bore capacity was entirely inadequate to the volume of structure."	This language is technically correct, and *might have been* Irwin's opinion. It is an opinion that could only be expressed by an expert in the subject, and not one that would be on the lips of the "man in the street."
"This I had placed again and again before the engineer—without being able to enlarge capacity of Diesel twin valve."	Obscure.
"Had this been interchangeable with larger capacity, we might have made it."	Obscure.
"But the structure is no good. That actually is the case, not gas did not allow mixture to get to engine."	*Obscure. But speaking very generally and as a whole, it conveys sense.*
"Backfired. Fuel injection bad."	Very possible.
(Mr. Price's remark): "Crude oil is not inflammable."	Backfiring implies inflammability. Mr. Price voiced a popular opinion in saying crude oil is not inflammable. But—
"This is inflammable."	It was inflammable at high temperatures—that is, it *would* be inflammable after compression in the cylinders of R-101, and *could* backfire.
"Also, to begin with, there was not sufficient feed—leakage."	Technically OK.

"Pressure and heat produced explosion."	Pressure and heat would produce explosion.
"Five occasions I have had to scuttle back."	See above.
"Three times before starting not satisfied with feed."	Very likely.
"Already a meeting, but feel desirous to push off and set our course and overhaul completely against this."	Obscure.
"Weather bad for long flight."	Quite true.
"Fabric all waterlogged and ship's nose is down."	True.
"Impossible to rise."	Right.
"Cannot trim."	Right. Trouble with this before. A difficult ship to trim, and this may have been due to deficient engine power.
"New type of feed entirely and absolutely wrong."	The feed from the ship's tanks had been changed from a motor feed to a hand-pump feed. The remark is therefore very possibly relevant.
"Two hours tried to rise but elevator jammed."	Very likely.
"Almost scraped the roofs at Achy."	Achy is not shown on ordinary maps. But it *is* shown on special large-scale ordinance flying maps, such as Irwin was in possession of. Achy is a small village, 12½ miles north of Beauvais, and would be on the

R-101's route. It was stated in evidence by French air officials, (though their evidence was discredited) that at Poix (14 miles north of Achy) the airship was seen to be only 300 feet from the ground.

"Kept to railway."

Correct.

"At inquiry to be held later it will be found that the super-structure of the envelope contained no resilience and had far too much weight."

Correct. It was the most rigid ship that had ever been constructed. The envelope *is* also considered perhaps too much weight.

"This was not so until March of this year when no security was made by adding of super structure."

Obscure. It suggests sense but won't really bear criticism. It is not sheer nonsense.

IRWIN COMMENTS
"I knew then that this was not a dream but a nightmare."

CHARLTON COMMENTS
Obscure. The entity meant perhaps that whereas the trip to India was going to be a "dream," it turned out to be a "nightmare."

"The added middle section was entirely wrong. It made strong, but took resilience away and entirely impossible. Too heavy and too much over-weighted for the capacity of engines."

Very sensible comment. Very probably the case.

"From beginning of trouble, I knew we had not a chance— knew it to be the feed and we could never rise."

Sensible and possible. But impossible to verify.

The completed comparative findings spread out before them

confirmed what they already were thinking: This was a very remarkable document. Eileen Garrett and those who knew her were aware that she had never owned any kind of engine or motor car, and that she knew nothing about aeronautics or engineering. Beyond that, the airship was a very specialized form of craft. It was an esoteric vehicle. Its technical terms were not even part of a normal aviation mechanic's jargon.

Mrs. Goldney noted in her report: How many women taken at random would understand the use of such terms as useful lift, gross lift, elevator (as applied to an airship), hydrocarbon, disposable lift, cruising speed, starboard strakes, cruising altitude, airscrews, fuel injection, trim, or volume of structure? Charlton noted the same questions. Harry Price already had. Very few men would be able to rattle them off at such incomprehensible speed, so that they made sense.

Charlton and his colleagues of Cardington had been strongly impressed with the reference to "S.L. 8." No one on the staff of Cardington could confirm this designation and number until they looked it up in the complete records of German airships. The "S.L." stood for a designer named Shutte Lanz. The designation was for the eighth ship in the series.

To Charlton, the most remarkable reference was to the mixture of hydrogen and oil. This was a hush-hush experiment that only a handful of technicians knew about. It had not even been put into practical use yet.

Charlton had to admit he was stumped. He could not believe what he had found, and he could not disbelieve it. He made his way back to Cardington with a resolution that he would dedicate the next ten years of his life to investigating psychic phenomenon. His whole life and outlook had been changed.

Harry Price and Mrs. Goldney, in the meantime, sat down and began compiling an extensive report for the annals of the National Laboratory. They summarized the entire case, and wrote their cautious conclusion:

"It is not the intention of the compilers of this report to discuss whether the medium was really controlled by the discarnate entity Irwin, or whether the utterances emanated from her subconscious mind or those of the sitters. 'Spirit' or 'trance personality' would be equally interesting explanation—and equally remarkable. There is no real evidence for either hypothesis. But it is not the intention of the writers of this report to discuss hypotheses, but rather to put on record the detailed account of a remarkably interesting and thought-provoking experiment.''

Now that the official hearings at the Royal Courts of Justice were over with, Harry Price had no hesitation in publicly announcing his results. Modesty was not one of his principal attributes.

He invited the press to the monthly meeting of the National Laboratory on May 7, 1931, six months after the official hearings closed. Charlton looked forward to it, even though his official position forced him to remain an anonymous fly-on-the-wall. He was continuing to review the date on the transcripts, tracking down each item separately with the staff at Cardington. One item that intrigued him was a statement by Irwin that the explosion was caused by friction in an electric storm. It didn't ring true because there were no electric storms reported on the weather maps that night. And the probability was that the explosion resulted from several different causes at once. Irwin could have been aware of one or more of them, and might only have mentioned this one in his apparent haste to get the message out.

On the day before Price's meeting, Charlton was chatting with Flight Lieutenant Harrison, a kite balloon officer at Cardington. Harrison told him he had had an unusual experience the previous Friday. He had unintentionally touched the cable holding the balloon, without taking the necessary precaution of standing on a special rubber mat provided for such occasions. It was a calm, clear day, and he felt no need for the insulation the mat provided. There was no sign of an electric storm anywhere. The moment Lieutenant Harrison touched the cable, he received a severe, jolting shock.

Charlton did some more digging. Searching the records, he found a report by Major Scott, which stated that the R-100 had collected a great deal of static electricity when in flight. It was well-known among airship circles that when the cable from the nose of a ship is first dropped, any of the ground crew would receive a severe shock if they touched the wire before it touched the ground. Even though the shock would not kill, Scott had warned the crew never to touch the cable beforehand. This would also be true whether there was an electrical storm in the vicinity or not.

Charlton pictured the R-101 heavily charged with static electricity. She would of course be carrying no trial cable to hit the ground first to safely absorb the static electricity. If the underside of the ship touched the ground directly, suddenly coming into contact with the earth, a spark and the resulting hydrogen explosion would be extremely probable, he reasoned. If true, it would be one more supportive indication of Irwin's observations, although backfiring and other causes must have contributed to the holocaust. The question of static electricity had never even been raised at the official inquiry.

Harry Price and Mrs. Goldney presented the report to a packed meeting that night. Charlton remained anonymous as "Mr. X."

On the next morning, the story appeared rather inconspicuously in the *Morning Post*. Suddenly, it was picked up by the press all over the world. It made many front pages, from Hong Kong to Brisbane. Then just as suddenly, it died down. Without deep study, it was too much for the public to swallow.

Villiers saw it and was stunned. It paralleled his own information so closely. There were contradictions, of course. Especially the apparent communication from Irwin about the cause of the explosion. Beyond that, they were remarkably the same in style, character and information.

The details Villiers had received were more intimate, more politically explosive. He regarded the information as a trust for his friends. He would not consider revealing them publicly for years to come, if at all. He felt they only served two purposes. The first was to see if they could contribute to the facts emerging from the hearings. They apparently had not done that, although they came remarkably close to the same conclusions as those of the official court hearings. Still, in spite of their flaws and contradictions, they might provide that very strong evidence of life-after-death he was seeking. To Major Villiers, this was the most important factor. This he would try to offer to the public when he felt the proper time had come.

His convictions had grown stronger every day that this was palpable and concrete evidence. Now that the Harry Price material independently paralleled his, there was further support. In his position in the Air Ministry, he could do nothing at the moment. After the acrimony, the despair, the grief and the mourning died down, he would make his decision about releasing the material.

Reinforcement of Major Villiers' conviction came quite suddenly with a report from Darby that Sir John Simon had been much more impressed with the transcripts of the Eileen Garrett sessions than he had seemed. Simon had been so impressed, in fact, that he had sent Darby to question Mrs. Colmore directly about the existence of the private diaries that had been clearly revealed in the Villiers séances.

Darby went to see Mrs. Colmore. He told her that the existence of Colmore's personal diaries had been denied by the officials, and were nowhere to be found. Mrs. Colmore was furious. She confirmed the existence of his diaries, which he kept in his office. On occasion, he had brought them home, and dictated the entries to her directly. All of this had been written down. None of it had been presented at the hearings.

Darby checked for more confirmation. He asked her to describe Colmore's office, and where the missing diaries were kept. She did so. Darby checked her description against the Villiers transcripts. It tallied exactly. Yet the records had never been found.

But there was also the Atherstone diary. The voice in the séance, purported to be that of Atherstone, indicated that he had written down some severe and damaging statements about the lack of airworthiness of the R-101. Mrs. Atherstone had nothing to say. She would neither confirm nor deny the existence of the diary.

Villiers was disappointed. If this fact could have been confirmed, along with the Colmore material that already had, it could have been a substantial piece of evidence to support the reality of the séances. Perhaps someday, Villiers thought, this might eventually be confirmed. If it ever were, it would vindicate his faith in the truth of the sessions, and the implications of an immortality the modern world found so hard to accept.

Eileen Garrett was amazed at the fuss the Harry Price article brought with it. But she was recovering from her illness now, and looking forward to her long-delayed trip to America. She was less interested in the R-101 information that had emerged through her, than she was in finding out where it had all come from. So was the American Society for Psychical Research, which was sponsoring her trip. This organization and several leading universities were deeply interested in finding the source of her rare and unusual clairvoyance and precognition.

Almost without being aware of it, she had launched a series of inquiries by others into little-known territory. As the results of her sessions with Emilie Hinchliffe, Harry Price, Ian Coster and Major Villiers gradually became more widely known, more people joined the search for factual confirmation, with a profound effect on their lives. The events that followed sprawled over a long period of years, where interest increased rather than flagged, with the paramount question always in the forefront: Does man's individual consciousness and self-awareness go on after death—in a form not markedly different from our own life here on earth?

CHAPTER XV

Will Charlton's life, for one, became profoundly affected. There was no longer any doubt in his mind about the life-after-death question. He suddenly changed to a convinced Spiritualist. Nearly ten years after his careful review of the R-101 séance transcript, he saw Harry Price again. Charlton told Price that he was now fully convinced that the only possible explanation was that Captain Irwin did communicate after his physical death.

In spite of Price's tendency to remain noncommittal, he replied: "That in my opinion is the perfect answer."

The peppery Mrs. Goldney of the British Society of Psychical Research was another who continued to probe into the famous séance. Twenty years after the event, in 1950, she reviewed the case again in the light of historical perspective, and wrote in the publication *Now*: "The strength of this case lies in the fact that Mr. Charlton expressed his opinion that many of the remarks not only made sense, but good sense; that not only were a large proportion of the items accurate and relevant, but that in one item the information given would be unlikely to be known outside of official circles."

Being thorough and methodical, Mrs. Goldney boiled down the possibilities to three points:

(1) The medium in a trance state had access to subconscious memories.

(2) There was telepathy between the sitters (Harry Price and Ian Coster), or between the medium and other human beings.

(3) There was communication (presumably also telepathic) through the medium from a spirit who had survived death.

As cautious as she was, Mrs. Goldney concluded: "It must be admitted that there are strong arguments in favor of the spirit-communicator hypothesis, and that this theory is by no means ruled out even if we cannot prove it."

But Mrs. Goldney was still not satisfied. She sought out the best authority she could find to review the twenty-year-old case. She found what she was looking for in former Air Chief Marshal Lord Dowding. He had stepped into the Air Council in the last moments before the ill-fated trip of the R-101, when he had little opportunity to check out the airship's problems himself. Since then, he had built up the British fighter squadrons as Commander-in-Chief of the Fighter Command, developing the early use of radar and spawning the famous Spitfires and Hurricanes that had saved Britain from being wiped out by the numerically superior German Luftwaffe. Dowding was credited with winning the Battle of Britain with his skill and daring, prompting Winston Churchill's comment: "Never . . . was so much owed by so many to so few." Some have set Dowding alongside Sir Francis Drake and Admiral Lord Nelson.

Dowding's interest in the psychic began back in those days of the Second World War. In the process of repelling the Nazis, 449 of his fighter pilots were killed. He was deeply bereaved. He tried to personally comfort scores of widows and families who suffered these losses. He turned to the Church of England to find out what he should say to them. One bishop told him to say that Christ died for our sins. To Dowding's pragmatic mind, this was inadequate. Another told him, when asked about life-after-death: "It's impious to ask."

Dowding found these approaches useless. Neither suggested any kind of systematic doctrine of survival after death. To Dowding's mind, which dealt with vigorous action and tragic reality, the church shirked the issue. He had no real axe to grind about the Church of England. He was a loyal member of his local parish. But he ran across a study that had been ordered by the Archbishop of Canterbury on the subject of communication with discarnate spirits, and on the claims of Spiritualists in relation to the Christian faith. Although it was never published, it was said to have found measurable validity in the process of communicating with the dead.

This sent Dowding on a long inquiry of his own into psychic research. Through it, he discovered that he had come across something he could rationally believe in, and that he could present to the families who came to see him. The result was that Lord Dowding, the tough, technical fighter pilot, commander and acknowledged leader of the Battle of Britain, had become a Spiritualist.

To examine the details of the Eileen Garrett séance, Lord Dowding met with Mrs. Goldney at the home of a mutual friend at Northgate Mansions in February of 1950. Lord Dowding went over the séance transcript before looking at Charlton's comments. The report had been broken down into fifty-three separate statements that had purportedly come through from Flight Lieutenant Irwin.

After a careful screening, Dowding disagreed with Charlton in only eight out of the fifty-three points. Dowding had developed several theories about the possible reality of communication with those who had died. He looked on matter as a conglomeration of billions of electric particles in ceaseless and violent agitation. If our vision had been built on the principle of the x-ray, he felt, we would have no trouble seeing through matter. If our bodies were built on the same principle as the x-ray, we would have no trouble passing through matter. Through this parallel, he rationalized that a living individual could at death shift gears and move into another dimension, still retaining his individuality. He felt the mistakes that occurred in a séance were the result of weak and faulty transmission, just as with some radio communications. After going over his own notes and those of Charlton's, he wrote and signed his conclusions for Mrs. Goldney and the Society for Psychical Research:

"This is not a communication I would pick out to convince a skeptic. On the other hand, it is evidential in the sense that it is quite in consonance with the idea of a person who had passed out under extreme stress, and perhaps physical agony, desperately trying to bring through a communication which he believed would be important and helpful to his comrades."

Dowding's statement, cautious as it was, added considerable weight to the case because of his experience and stature as a leading airman.

By far the most unusual latecomer to study the R-101 material was a hard-bitten, tough colleague of Captain Irwin named William H. Wood. As a flight lieutenant and later squadron leader himself, Wood had flown the same airship with Irwin in the First World War in the Aegean Sea arena. Wood claimed to be the only man in England to hold pilot certificates for aircraft, gliders, balloons and airships.

He sometimes had the disposition of a platypus, but also was generous and warm at times. Above all, he was a direct, spanking, forthright and outspoken atheist. He hated the church in any form, as if his fingers had been burned by an altar candle. He was a regular contributor to an atheist-rationalist magazine called the *Freethinker*. In its columns, he let loose a sustained tirade of abuse against the church and God in both prose and poetry.

His diatribes appeared regularly in the *Freethinker*, and they raised a considerable number of eyebrows:

> The clergy see to it that their followers are kept in darkness, blind and ignorant; for the moment the light of reason enters in, the fog and gloom of religion must vanish forever.
> Science has disproved most of the ignorant statements made in the Bible—yet the priests and their dupes prefer to believe Biblical untruth to Scientific Truth. Thus religion thrives on falsehood.

At times, Wood's softer nature would peek through, as if reluctantly:

> I believe in all that is real and good and true in the world. . . . Let us love all men of all colors, races, and creeds. Let us help all those who are afflicted and comfort those in distress. Let us harm no one by thought, word, or deed.

Flight Lieutenant Wood did not discover the Harry Price–Ian Coster story of the R-101 séance until 1948, eighteen years later. He stumbled across the newspaper article that Price had written, including Charlton's technical review. He knew Charlton slightly, and was aware of his technical mind. As a former airship pilot and extremely close friend of Irwin, he was baffled. The phrasing of the séance transcript, the jerkiness of speech was so typical of his old flying partner that he felt as if he were reading a letter from Irwin. In addition, the mass of technical information was to his mind impossible for any layman to produce.

As a thorough man, and because of his closeness to Irwin, he wanted to get to the bottom of the Eileen Garrett story. He tracked down Charlton in Kent, where he learned about Charlton's explorations into the psychic field, and how his mind had been changed by them. There was no doubt, Charlton told him, that no one but an airship expert could have used the highly technical terms, and woven them together in such a manner. Wood went over the entire transcript with Charlton, point by point. The more he studied it the more impressed he was.

As a result, Wood found himself in an intellectual, if not an emotional squeeze. His conviction was that Spiritualism, along with the entire religious scene, was nothing but a money-grabbing racket. But the idea of psychic phenomena being studied scientifically intrigued him.

Wood kept up with his scathing denunciations of the church, and everything to do with the sacrosanct. At the same time, he got in touch with Ian Coster, who had shifted to the staff of the *Daily Express*. Coster confirmed the sequence of events of the Eileen Garrett séance, and admitted his own bafflement. He could find no rational explanation, but there was no question in his mind as to the authenticity.

Finally, in 1949, Flight Lieutenant Wood shook the foundation of the atheist-rationalist world in England by coming out flatly in the pages of the *Freethinker* with the statement that he was fully convinced that his friend Irwin had definitely communicated, after death, through the channel of Eileen Garrett. He pointed out, as a former airship commander himself, the accuracy of the esoteric technical material, along with the style of delivery of his friend Irwin.

"We must not then deny human survival," Wood wrote, "just because it has never been proved. We condemn the Christian for his dogmatism and bigotry, but by disbelieving without inquiry, we are just as narrow and bigoted ourselves. If this case does not prove survival, then nothing ever will. I consider the R-101 case to be cast iron."

Flight Lieutenant Wood might as well have dropped a flaming torch into an R-101 gas bag. Here was one of the leading atheist-rationalist spokesmen of the British Empire, suggesting that there was possibility of life-after-death—to say nothing of communicating with a deceased personality. The readers of the *Freethinker* raised their pens like a battalion of Bengal lancers to write the editor. Wood was the target—a traitor to the cause, an infidel, an utter turncoat. He had committed nothing short of treason.

The controversy raged for nearly a year in the pages of the *Freethinker* and the *Psychic News*, a leading journal covering psychic events and research. Wood stuck to his guns. "It is not atheism that need fear the proof of human survival," he wrote. "Surely, if the end of this life is utter and complete oblivion, then the whole tiresome business of living seems rather a waste of time."

Charlton jumped in to defend Wood by writing an article in *Psychic News*, which stated flatly that he had satisfied himself beyond all shadow of doubt that the séance had been genuine. "As a matter of fact," he wrote, "I could have made the case even more impressive and informative; but in view of the official position held by me at the time, I had to be very guarded in what I revealed. This is really a classical case of something we can't explain."

The turning point came for Wood when the widely known skeptic G. N. Ridley wrote in the *Literary Guide and Rationalist Review*: "Rationalism has nothing to lose by extending the scope of its interests to embrace the study and discussion of the supernormal, provided it remains true to the principle of dispassionate and objective evaluation of evidence."

Coming from this hard-core center of the rationalist camp, the article signaled to Wood that his enemies had surrendered. But in spite of everything, Wood remained a stern and unrelenting atheist—who now fully believed that we live after death. In doing so, he occupied a unique position in the history of atheism.

More than thirty years after the R-101 séances, Eileen Garrett still had not forgotten them. In the 1960's her life was full and active, in spite of flagging health. She had founded the Creative Age Press in New York, along with a literary and public affairs journal known as *Tomorrow*. She managed to lure into her stable some of the major writers of the world, including Aldous Huxley, Robert Graves, Christopher Isherwood, and others from Pearl Buck to John Hersey, Christopher Morley, and Mark Van Doren. At the same time, she had founded the Parapsychology Foundation, which was bringing together scientists from all over the world at major international conferences.

Her perplexity about her strange powers had grown over the years. She submitted to experiments with Dr. J. B. Rhine at Duke University, with the noted Dr. Alexis Carrel, with psychiatrists at Columbia University and Johns Hopkins Medical School. She also returned to Europe to be examined by scientists in Paris and Rome, and by Oxford and Cambridge psychologists, physiologists and medical scientists. She went through blood tests, electroencephalograms, electrocardiograms, personality, Farraday cage, and word association tests, among others.

But the results were inconclusive. Science was not equipped to handle a phenomenon like this; they were as baffled as Eileen herself. Her authenticity was seldom challenged, but the capacity to define and measure the phenomenon was.

Speaking of her apparent capacity for receiving messages from those who had died, she wrote: "It is my opinion that each communication must be sifted for its verities and realities. Communication cannot be an easy process even under the best conditions. A judgment of it values should never be hasty."

Even in the 1960's there were those who continued to sift the R-101 séances for their verities and realities. The process was far from hasty. Over three decades had gone by. There were, of course, two sets of material to examine. The single Harry Price session, where only Captain Irwin had come through, and the unpublished Major Villiers series of sessions, where several members of the R-101 crew had come through. These were independent of each other. They could be examined separately or together. Each contained material that had later been confirmed in the official hearings. Each set of transcripts had its inconsistencies. Viewed as a whole, in the perspective of time, the chain required sensitive and thoughtful analysis.

It seemed almost as if there were some kind of fantasy or even reality to the idea that those who flew above the earth in planes and airships developed perceptions over a period of time that made them more sensitive to thought waves and other dimensions that other men failed to perceive. In what seemed to be a single, long strand, the events involving Hinchliffe, Lowenstein, the R-101 crew, Flight Lieutenant Wood and others turned into stories that challenged conventional thinking, and penetrated into the question of life continuing after death.

Harry Harper, the British aviation reporter collected many aviation stories that begged for explanation. But they were not legends. They were recounted by prominent airmen of the time. Sir Peter Masefield, nephew of the Poet Laureate, former pilot and later chief executive of British European Airways, reported that he was preparing to land at a small airfield in Britain, when an ancient biplane loomed ahead of him, faltered, then crashed close to the field. When he brought his ship down, there was no sign of the ancient plane, nor had any mechanic seen a crash. Sir Peter learned later, however, that years before, such a plane had crashed at the field in identical circumstances.

Air Marshal Sir Victor Goddard, former commander of the Royal New Zealand Air Force, and administrative head of the British Air Forces in Burma and Malaya, had experienced two inexplicable incidents in his flying days, which led him into a deep study of the mysteries beyond the five senses. He was a technical man, the former head of England's prestigious College of Aeronautics. Like Eileen Garrett, he was absorbed with the idea that the psychic would eventually turn out to be related to Einstein's theory of relativity and Max Planck's quantum theory. He reasoned that science was constantly developing and surprising itself. When he had been a boy, they were saying that the atom was absolutely indivisible. Only a madman could challenge this at the time. Later, the fact became a myth. Now, with growing insight, the atom was becoming as mystical as the sayings of the ancient Oriental sages.

The R-101 case interested Sir Victor because, in fact, he himself might have been named captain of it in place of his friend Irwin. In retirement in 1966, he turned his attention again to the case. He contacted Eileen Garrett, and received permission to carefully go over the Major Villiers séance material.

As a former airship commander, he spotted numerous technical errors, but there were also a great many accurate statements. He sensed the ring of truth behind the evidence, however. He had also learned that Sir John Simon had been more deeply impressed with the Villiers transcripts than he admitted at the time of the hearings. He recognized, as others did, that the biggest weakness in the case was Villiers' inability to take verbatim shorthand, as had been possible in the cases of Emilie Hinchliffe and Harry Price. But there was too much of interest here, especially in the confirmed evidence of the Colmore diaries. The Atherstone diaries, mentioned in the transcripts, however, had not been confirmed. This weakened the case, but did not rule it out. Sir Victor realized it would be a mistake to throw the baby out with the bath water.

It was now thirty-six years after the R-101 events. The ranks of those who knew the story behind the scenes were dwindling as 1966 was drawing to a close. In spite of this, Sir Victor wrote Eileen Garrett that he would like to create a full investigation of the evidence through a joint effort of the Royal Aeronautical Society and the Psychical Research Society. It could be, Sir Victor thought, one of the most important inquiries into the burning question of whether life was continuous or not.

But time was running out. The ranks of those privy to R-101 information were few. A friend of Eileen Garrett's named Archie Jarman had been tracking down leads on the story for some time. He was a wealthy and successful businessman with a healthy curiosity about the unknown and occasional time to explore the more interesting cases. He spent months trying to track down the details behind the scenes of the R-101 tragedy and its strange aftermath. He probably came to know more about the subject than any living person. Blocked from getting anything out of the Air Ministry, he came to the conclusion that there had been a massive cover-up to protect Lord Thomson. He appraised both the Harry Price and Major Villiers transcripts, and came to the conclusion that the Harry Price session was almost foolproof and indicated strong evidence of communication with Captain Irwin. He did not, however, have the same opinion of the Villiers transcripts, pointing out that Villiers' lack of ability to take the material down in shorthand was a serious drawback.

When Villiers learned of Jarman's conclusions, he was bitterly disappointed. His conviction had been growing over the long years that the case was one which could come closest to proving the reality of an afterlife. He felt strongly that Jarman had not allowed for the natural mistakes in transcribing the material from his rough notes. He felt that the mistakes should be weighed in the light of the overall impact. He was proud of his ability for total recall, and had even recorded words that he knew were mistakes at the time of the sessions. Why would he invent evidence against himself and let it remain on the record? There were inconsistencies, yes, just as there were in the records of the official hearings. He felt the single most important thing he could do would be to establish the veracity of the material, because if people could believe realistically in life-after-death, the patterns of their lives would drastically improve. Through rational evidence of an afterlife, their belief in God would increase. The two-thousand-year-old teachings of the church would be strengthened and buttressed by the belief.

Villiers had already joined the Church's Fellowship for Psychic and Spiritual Studies in London, along with Sir Victor Goddard and Air Marshal Lord Dowding. Its object was to encourage study of the paranormal and extrasensory perception in their relation to the Christian faith. Its supporters were impressive. They included the Dean of St. Paul's Cathedral, the Bishop of Chichester, the Bishop of Pittsburgh, U. S. A.

Shortly after the Second World War, when he had served as a senior intelligence officer, Villiers had been faced with a serious and tragic problem. He began to lose his sight. In spite of major operations, he very slowly approached total blindness.

Strangely enough, his blindness did not dismay him or make him lose faith in God or what he now regarded as spiritual reality. His sense of taste, smell, touch and hearing sharpened. He found new enjoyment in music. He found he could type by the touch system, answer letters and recall completely everything his wife Aleen read to him. He learned to navigate in his home by precise angles and paces, almost as a ship did in a fog. He had certain navigation points—the mantle, the fireplace, the Queen Anne table, the doorknob leading to the hall, the hatrack, the arbor in the garden. His food was placed on his plate, and designated by compass points: meat to the north, vegetable to the east, potatoes to the west, salad to the south. The scent of flowers increased for him, and he found the time he now had for meditation was rewarding. "I think," he told a friend, "that being blind has become a divine gift."

He had moved in retirement to the Channel coast at Hythe. In spite of his blindness, he founded the local Preservation Society, in a community where one of England's most ancient castles stood. With the aid of Aleen, he compiled the thousand-year history of his parish church. He never lost interest in cricket, and continued as head of the local cricket club. He worked on his memoirs of the First World War, typing them up with his newly learned touch system. He continued to meditate at length each day. "I see so much more clearly now,'' he would say when asked how his blindness affected him.

In 1967, at the age of 81, what still burned most intensely inside of him was the R-101 case as a lesson that would benefit mankind. Because of his position in both military and Air Ministry intelligence, he had refrained for many years to make any of the material public. He had revealed part of it in 1956, when John Leasor, a highly regarded journalist was in the process of writing a book about the crash of the R-101. Leasor learned from Sir Sefton Brancker's son that Major Villiers had in his hands a story that would be of considerable background interest.

Leasor had come down to Hythe to see Villiers. He spent several hours going over the transcripts. It was the first time Leasor had ever seen anything that had come through a medium. He was convinced of Villiers' sincerity and startled by the content of the material.

Villiers still had to think it over as to whether he should release any of the information publicly. He had assured Sir John Simon that he would not release anything until at least after Simon's death. Since Sir John had died, Villiers decided to release some of the material to Leasor, who printed portions of it at the end of his book *The Millionth Chance*.

In a letter to Leasor, Villiers wrote: ''I doubt if anyone can say that there is sufficient evidence assembled to declare that scientific proof has been established beyond all doubt. I do submit, however, that there is ample circumstantial evidence to be able to proclaim that after passing through the portals of death, our individual consciousness, utilizing its spirit or 'etheric' body, continues to live on, and, under certain conditions, makes its presence known to those on earth.''

At that time in the mid-fifties, Villiers did not know that an event would take place in 1967 that would drastically support his own outlook, and that of many others.

Over the years, Major Villiers had concluded that there were several major points that reinforced his belief in the series of long séances he had held with Eileen Garrett back in 1931. These were points that had been confirmed either by the official hearings, or the missing evidence that Sir John Simon's aide had confirmed. There

was the description of the last few minutes of the disaster, which
identified the cause long before the official hearings were published. There was the long period of low-altitude cruising that was
ultimately confirmed by the hearings. There were Colmore's missing records and diaries, confirmed by Darby when he talked to
Mrs. Colmore. There was the way Brancker had identified himself
in a séance, by indicating his monocle and using the phrase: "Use
your damned intelligence." There were all the other minutiae that
for Villiers supported the reality of the communications.

But what happened in 1967 was totally unexpected. Michael
Cox, a British documentary film producer, began a latter-day
investigation of the R-101 disaster. He conducted a series of interviews of the few survivors left, and of the families of the victims
who had died on the R-101's flight to India.

Cox finally tracked down the widow of Lieutenant Commander
Atherstone and called on her for an interview. At the official hearings some thirty- seven years earlier, a bland and uncritical passage
had been read from Atherstone's diary. Mrs. Atherstone had neither confirmed nor denied to Darby that Atherstone had tartly criti-
cized the faults in the structure of the R-101, as Major Villiers had
been told in his last séance.

Now that the aftermath was long past, Mrs. Atherstone dug out
all of her husband's old papers. Atherstone's diary was among
them. In it was a complete record of the R-101's development and
trials.

Leafing through the day-to-day journal, the documentary producer stumbled on a page which read:

"There is a mad rush and panic to complete the ship. . . . It is
grossly unfair to expect the officers to take out a novel vessel of
this size. . . . The airship has no lift worth talking about, and is
obviously tail heavy."

The entry in the diary was dated a full year before the crash.
London's *Sunday Mirror* picked up the story on October 15, 1967,
and commented: "Imagine the national indignation if charges like
these came out after an air tragedy today."

The unexpected disclosure brought great comfort to Major Villiers. It was the factual confirmation he had been looking for all
through the previous four decades. The experience of his communications with his R-101 friends, now reinforced by the belated

news of the Atherstone diary, buttressed his belief in an afterlife, and built for him a foundation which he linked to his own faith in God, that reached its peak when his wife Aleen died. Although she had been his eyes and his support for many years, he did not despair at her passing, because he had full, quiet confidence that he would soon join her, that death, as he had learned from his R-101 friends, was merely going through another door.

But Major Villiers and his story were only part of the greater picture that had begun to be painted on the windy airfield near Grantham, and had continued down through so many years. Captain Hinchliffe had been linked to Old Lowenstein and to the men of the R-101, who had died in their desperate attempt to conquer the air. The airship crew was linked to Harry Price, Coster and Villiers. The picture that emerged showed striking details that defied normal explanation, even if there were those paradoxes and inconsistencies. Somehow, the very mystique of the attempts to make man airborne had brought disparate parts together to suggest the limitations of an earthbound life, whether it was to leave the ground in an aircraft—or to leave the body for another existence, invisible but just as real.

One by one, the principals in this large canvas had played their parts in it, and were variously affected by it. Squadron Leader Rivers Oldmeadow and Colonel Henderson would never forget their encounter with Hinchliffe's apparition, that night aboard their ship off the Canaries, to the end of their days. Emilie Hinchliffe's entire spiritual outlook was changed from total skepticism almost overnight from her purported encounters with her husband. Harry Price became less of a skeptic and more convinced after his experience with Captain Irwin, while Ian Coster shifted to a point of view of reasonable doubt. Flight Lieutenant William Wood made the greatest about-face in the history of atheism–rationalism when he studied the Price-Coster material. Engineer William Charlton could no longer hold on to his skeptical beliefs, and had become both a Spiritualist and an advanced student of parapsychology. Air Marshals Sir Victor Goddard and Lord Dowding, in spite of their technical reservations about the Villiers material, bluntly accepted its essential validity, and its evidence of life-after-death.

Eileen Garrett, the wellspring of it all, continued until her death in 1970 to support with all her resources attempts to fuse the physical sciences with psychic phenomena, which she was forced to accept whether she liked it or not. She did not subscribe to loftiness, even though her comments were often sweeping and comprehensive.

Once she said: "In the ultimate nature of the universe, there are no divisions in time and space." This was a conviction born of her myriad experiences with what was conventionally considered to be the unreal.

In spite of the baffling and perplexing communications that came through her, she never stopped her pragmatic and empirical search for the reality behind the mystery. "There is a positive and practical need," she concluded, "for these communications to be studied and understood. We need to discover the methods by which communication is established between the two states of being. My wish arises out of my sincere desire, as well as my private need, to discover the factual reality of the whole process by which the controls [like Uvani] presumably operate."

She never quite reached that goal, but the chain of circumstances that began in Grantham in 1928 and continued down through the years has created a challenge that is still unanswered.

AFTERWORD

Three months after our first visit to Major Villiers on the Channel coast, Elizabeth and I had dinner in the dining room of the Hotel George in Grantham. The room was freshly, tastefully decorated in Georgian style. The lights were soft and muted. Fresh-cut flowers and a single candle marked the center of the white tablecloth. Neither Isaac Newton nor Charles Dickens could be seen, nor was there a copy of *Nicholas Nickleby* anywhere in evidence. I did have, however, a sharp sense of another dinner in this room, just about half a century before. I could picture Captain Hinchliffe, along with Gordon Sinclair and Elsie Mackay, talking in tense, muffled tones about the weather over the North Atlantic, about their fuel supply, their cruising speed, the condition of their Wright Whirlwind 200 horsepower engine, the stresses and strains on the 32-foot Stinson Detroiter.

This was the locale where the strange story had started. For Elizabeth and me, our dinner was marking the end of our ninety-day research stint, collecting bits and pieces from dozens of sources, trying to assimilate them, shape them in our minds and assess the critical question: Did all this add up to convincing evidence of life-after-death? We knew clearly that evidence was not proof. But was there a suggestion here, an intimation of immortality that would give food for thought? We carried our small Sony TC-55 with us always in case we came up with any brilliant ideas.

299

When Elizabeth took a sip of chilled white wine and spoke, I
switched it on: "I guess, when you look over all we've uncovered,
that you've got to ask—how can you explain it except by believing
that Hinchliffe, Lowenstein, Irwin, Brancker and all the others *did*
communicate? I don't mean accepting all this naively. I mean, are
the alternate explanations as difficult to believe as the theory that
we live after death?"

"You like to come up with tough questions, don't you?" I said.

"That's me," she said, and she was right.

"Well," I said, trying to show wisdom. "the alternatives are interesting."

"Like what?" Elizabeth asked.

"The first possibility is that a dozen or more people got together
to form a gigantic hoax."

"Unlikely," Elizabeth said. "Highly unlikely."

"I think so, too. But it has to be considered."

"It would be entirely too cumbersome and fruitless," she said.
"I think you can assume they were all basically decent and intelligent people. They were all spread apart, mostly. Both in time and
space. They were objective for the most part. Many of them were
very skeptical. They had nothing to gain from self-deception. And
so many different details linked together."

"What about ESP as an explanation?" I asked.

"That's too easy," Elizabeth said.

"Then are we convinced that there was spirit communication?"
I said.

"Why do you have to use the word 'spirit'?" she said.

"What else can you use?"

"There was a professor of philosophy at Brown University
named Ducasse I've been reading," she said. "He says that 'spirit'
is a weasel word."

"What word should be used?"

"He says why not use the word 'mind'? Nobody can argue that
there isn't such a thing as a mind. A mind is a known fact. Spirits
we're not so sure of. There's no question that minds can remember. So everything boils down to the question, can a *mind* exist after death? There is definitely no proof that it can't. Nobody can say
this is impossible."

"But you can't say for sure it's possible, either," I said.

"So then it's a fifty-fifty chance. That's not bad, is it?"

"But what if that 'mind' is just leftover ESP?"

"The stuff that came through for Mrs. Hinchliffe was a lot more than simple ESP. The details were so enormous, they were like fingerprints of Captain Hinchliffe. If it was his posthumous mind that was talking through Eileen Garrett, he was observing current things going on in his house, and future things too. Like the date when Emilie's financial problem would be solved. Eileen Garrett couldn't invent all this pile of detail if she wanted to. To believe that is harder to believe than Hinchliffe himself communicating. The same with Irwin and his technical details."

"You've almost got me believing you," I said.

"I think you already do."

In a way, she was right, or at least it wouldn't take much of a push. Our search had been thorough and painstaking. The first two weeks included long, sustained sessions with Major Villiers. Elizabeth and I took turns reading back to him the massive material in his files, so that he could stop and explain the nuances, and elaborate on them. At times, it was exhausting, but the depth of his belief was persuasive. His recall of his days with the Air Ministry was prodigious. If I made the slightest mistake in reviewing something we had discussed a day or so before, he would correct me sharply, and he was always right.

There was no question of his sincerity. He knew the great weakness of his sessions with Eileen Garrett was that he could not take verbatim notes. Yet he protested constantly that his recall was so strong that his transcripts were essentially correct, even though they were done the day after each session.

We had rented a small oasthouse in the town of Hawkhurst, in Kent, about an hour away from the Major. Oasthouses are structures that look like miniature castle turrets, where the harvests of hops were once spread out to dry over smouldering fires. It had become popular to convert them to charming cottages throughout Kent. We would go over our notes and material each evening by the fire, weighing the details of the story in our minds.

Two or three days a week, we would take the train to London to scour the source material there. On our first trip in, we took a taxi from Charing Cross to Kensington, where the small, trim, white building of the Society of Psychical Research is housed on Adam &

Eve Mews. We were greeted at the door by Eleanor O'Keefe, secretary of the organization. She was bright, cheery and business-like. She led us past the open library doorway and up the narrow staircase where oil portraits of the distinguished former officers were displayed. Prominent was the portrait of the Earl of Balfour, former Prime Minister of England. Through the years since the Society had been founded, there had been many distinguished presidents, from Sir Oliver Lodge and Professor Gilbert Murray, to Henri Bergson and Camille Flammarion.

"We're rich in tradition," Miss O'Keefe said, "but we're also quite lively and up to date. And we're delighted to try to help you in any way possible. The R-101 story is one that really has never been explained. The same with Captain Hinchliffe."

Locked behind glass doors in the office was a collection of rare books on the supernormal, dating back to the 1500's. They reflected deep interest in the subject, which of course went back far beyond the invention of the printing press. The mass of literature, both ancient and recent, was staggering, much of it probing the key, most important question: The survival of consciousness and individual awareness after death.

In the full library on the first floor, the bookshelves surrounded us from floor to ceiling. Some of the new titles traced the groping attempts to join the supernormal with science: *Parapsychology: Its Relation to Physics, Biology, Psychology and Psychiatry; An Investigation of Soviet Psychical Research; Precognition and the Philosophy of Science,* and others.

Elizabeth and I were, of course, interested mainly in the modern approach to the subject. As Elizabeth had said, the only way it could be interpreted for the present day would be the translation of ancient truths into computer language. What was most damaging to the research was not cynical skepticism, but overcredulous and overenthusiastic acceptance of a spook-and-kook nature. This sort of book was conspicuously absent from the library.

We pored through the rich collection of books in the Society library over many days, zeroing in on those books that concentrated on the survival question. The best ones were rational and low-key. Most surprising to me was the constant popping up of the parallel between modern physics and the potential of life being a continuous process after death—based on the premise that physics was finding the material world far more wispy and ephemeral than had previously been imagined.

We came across a statement by Einstein that punctuated this clearly: "It is not a long step from thinking of matter as an electronic ghost to thinking of it as the objectified image of thought." If this is true, as it might possibly be, then the road is wide open for the mind or personality to exist freely after death; it would no longer need the cumbersome structure of matter to inhibit it. Even Max Planck, father of the quantum theory, expressed the opinion that the atom might be a mentally-constructed sort of particle. If so, again, what is left? Matter might be not only frozen energy, but frozen thought. Or, as has been repeated many times in different ways: The Universe is more like a great Thought than a great Machine.

Sir James Jeans extended this, when he said: "To my mind, the laws which nature obeys are less suggestive of those which a machine obeys than of those which a musician obeys. The motions of electrons and atoms do not resemble those of the parts of a locomotive so much as those of dancers in a cotillion."

As we went through volume after volume in the library, one evident fact emerged: If anyone took the time to study the most rational reports on the evidence of life-after-death, it would be difficult not to at least accept it as a distinct possibility. No such chorus of logical minds could be involved in such a gigantic hoax or corporate falsehood. But how many could take the time to do so? Although we spent many days going over selected material, we could barely scratch the surface.

In trying to find the rationale and deep background that underlay the story from Hinchliffe to the R-101, several questions emerged. Elizabeth and I talked about them on the way back to Kent after our first visit to the Society for Psychical Research. I was running through my notes of the day with her. I flipped on the tape recorder again.

"Here's a phrase from Arnold Toynbee that's interesting," I said.

"Which one?" Elizabeth asked.

"I'll read it to you," I said. " 'Science, applied with sensational success to technology, has substituted the physical conquest of human nature for the spiritual conquest of himself as Western man's paramount objective. . . . Confronted by Death without belief, modern man has been clipped of his spiritual wings.' "

"But even Christianity doesn't get into life-after-death very clearly," Elizabeth said. "It really ducks the issue. Makes it impossible to believe. Like a physical resurrection—a body reassembling itself. Nobody's going to buy that nowadays, naturally. So the church weakens its own position—when it doesn't even need to."

"What I've been trying to figure out," I said, "is what does this R-101 story require us to believe *if* we're going to accept it as real evidence? Just assuming it's true for the moment."

"Well," said Elizabeth, "the first thing we would have to accept is that there's a very real place or location in the so-called next world that we continue on in—if we can believe Hinchliffe and Lowenstein. They saw a geography, and they saw and communicated with other people, wherever that geography was. They also could find a communication channel with the living to get messages through to others. Now the question is: Who can buy that all of a sudden?"

"I don't think anybody, including me, can buy that all of a sudden."

"How can they buy it, then?"

"By going through all the evidence, and then looking at the alternatives. The way we're doing."

"Are we convinced?" Elizabeth asked.

"We're leaning in that direction," I said. "When you think of the number of people who are involved with this story, it's impossible to toss it out. You've got everybody from Hinchliffe to Conan Doyle to Harry Price to Major Villiers to Lord Dowding to Sir Victor Goddard to Charlton and Wood and a lot of others. A conspiracy would be ridiculous to imagine."

"That still doesn't answer my question about how anyone could buy all this without some healthy theory behind it."

"All right," I said. "A lot of little theories build up all along the story."

"Like what?"

"A major question that has to be looked at is: Can consciousness and self-awareness continue to exist after the brain is dead? There are several ways that can be answered in the affirmative. Sir Oliver

Lodge said that with the brain gone, you can't say consciousness doesn't exist. The only thing you can say with certainty is that consciousness doesn't give any signals. But that's different from proof that it doesn't exist.''

"Also, Wilder Penfield and Sir John Eccles. Did you read any of the material about them?''

"Didn't get a chance to today," I said.

"They represent two of the top brain researchers in the world. They both agree that the mind is separate from the brain. So there's a good start," Elizabeth said.

"Also, there's this to think about," I said. "When we go to sleep, the retina is useless and dormant. Yet we can see very clearly when we dream.''

"I'll have to think that one over," she said. "But what about this geography question? You have to figure where this elusive geography is. A lot of these descriptions make it sound vividly real.''

"I guess that's where H. H. Price's theory would come in," I said.

"He's the Oxford professor?''

"Yes. He proposes a non-physical image world. Like the geography we see in dreams. Without a retina, by the way. It's just as real, but it doesn't take up any physical space. He claims the next world would not be a change of place, but a change of consciousness. That's quite a bit more logical than pink clouds and harps," I said.

"So there you have it," Elizabeth said.

"Have what?''

"You have a logical way that this story could theoretically be possible. Isn't that what we're looking for?''

"It gets complicated at times," I said.

"Look at it this way," Elizabeth said. "Modern physics has now reached the point where material things might not be material. They might just be thoughts. Modern brain research is showing that the mind is separate from the brain. Professor Price suggests that the mind could exist in an image world, very much like that of our dreams, where you can exist as a very real conscious personality, very much aware of your own individuality, and complete with memories. It's not so ridiculous, after all.''

Elizabeth and I would talk this way often, trying to feel our way

along, trying to justify our growing conviction that it was rational
to accept the theory of life-after-death.

At the University of London Library, H.K. Wesencraft guided
us through the dark stacks to the Harry Price Collection. It was impressive, with over fifteen thousand volumes on both magic and
the supernormal towering about us. Wesencraft was a gentle and
erudite man who meticulously cared for the collection, and who
was still in the process of cataloguing the voluminous correspondence of Harry Price. In spite of several direct bomb hits on the library building during the Second World War, the collection had
survived well.

Harry Price's letters reflected his nervous intensity and his impatience with any sort of fraudulent practices in the psychic field.
The fact that he regarded the R-101 case as a legitimate landmark
among the thousands of cases he had investigated and found wanting, added to its potential authenticity.

As we moved from place to place to gather both background
material and specific facts about the story, it became apparent that
most of the people involved in serious psychical reasearch were
cautious, rational, and not inclined to jump at conclusions. Paul
Beard, head of the College of Psychical Studies on Queensberry
Place, was one of these.

His youthful face was framed with pure white hair, and he spoke
softly and calmly about his long observations in the field at his
office in the college townhouse.

He considered the R-101 case to be interesting because the evidence was spread over a considerable number of people. He acknowledged the problems in probing the case, especially since personal experience had played such a large part in it. "Personal
experience can't help but become part of the research," he said.
"It's hard to keep them separate. The investigator gets pulled into
areas where he has to think in other ways than as a scientist."

He went on to say that personal convictions and scientific evidence don't need to cancel each other out, however. He felt that
the R-101 case was well worth special study, because it challenges
clearly the theory that extended telepathy could have provided all
the technical detail of Eileen Garrett's communications.

Visiting with former Air Marshal Sir Victor and Lady Goddard in their country home in Surrey was a rewarding experience. Lady Goddard was gracious and hospitable, and Sir Victor spoke freely of his conviction that life was continuous. I was particularly interested in his reflections on the story, because he had not only been an airship pilot, but was an airman skilled in the technicalities of all types of flight, to say nothing of his broad knowledge of science.

He was a sensitive man, erect and military, but with a gentleness and profundity that reflected careful thought about his conclusions. He believed strongly in keeping a balance between intuition and intellect. In his day as head of Britain's College of Aeronautics, one of the most technically advanced in the country, he concurrently became part of the Centre for Spiritual and Religious Studies. In this way, he moved on two levels, the material and the spiritual. He was equally brilliant in both.

Sir Victor saw no conflict between the two levels. He believed that to receive awareness of higher truths, Man had to transcend his own space-time consciousness, just as Einstein did in transcending classical physics. Sir Victor liked to point out that Einstein himself had made the simple statement: "God is All," and that Carl Jung, when asked on a BBC program if he believed in the reality of God, quietly answered, "I *know*."

As Chief of Air Staff in New Zealand and as the British Air Force Representative with the Joint Chiefs of Staff in Washington, Sir Victor was a man of action and a man of command stature. He influenced both Elizabeth and me strongly in our appraisal of the R-101 research material.

On our last day of research, we left Grantham on a cold January morning to head back toward London and the United States. The wind, sweeping in from the Lincolnshire fens, was hostile and uninviting. We detoured north past Cranwell, the RAF base where Hinchliffe had made his ill-fated takeoff. From the road, there wasn't much to see except the long, flat runway and a few hangars. Was this bleak and desolate runway the scene of Hinchliffe's last flight on earth—or his first flight into another world we all would know someday? The choice was open, either way. Neither Elizabeth nor I needed to voice ours.

CHAPTER NOTES

Chapter I

All through the story ran the problem of weighing the evidence and assessing the credibility of the sources. To piece together the mosaic that began in Lincolnshire, there were long and detailed accounts in the local Grantham paper, plus massive coverage by the London papers, exploring every detail, intimate and technical, of Captain Hinchliffe. Never at a loss to look for juicy bits of scandal, the more flamboyant London papers looked for intimacies between Captain Hinchliffe and Elsie Mackay. They found none whatever, nor did anyone else. Emilie Hinchliffe revealed in detail her own feelings, anxieties and activities in long press interviews and her own writings and lectures.

The struggle to complete the R-100 and the R-101 was documented in detail by official reports, personal letters and diaries, and wide press coverage from the time the two ships were put on the drawing boards. I assembled over 700 news clips from the newspaper morgues.

Eileen Garrett's meteoric rise was extensively written about by those who studied her and in her own reflections in voluminous letters, notes and writings.

The strange and exotic incident encountered by Squadron Leader Oldmeadow and Colonel Henderson was revealed publicly in a letter to the press over thirty years after the event, in 1961.

What we looked for constantly in putting together this strange collage was material that would link together so many disparate parts. Because the information was scattered in so many places, it was almost startling to find a story like Oldmeadow's buried in a newspaper morgue that was in no way connected with the files and records found in other places.

The story grew in patches. What impressed us was that the documents revealed in so many details that the story unfolded with all the narrative punch of fiction.

309

The letters, the diaries, the extensive accounts in newspapers and books made it possible to reconstruct the events without fictionalizing, by providing bits of dialogue, streams of consciousness and inner thoughts and feelings of the principals involved.

While this adds to readability and suspense, it also presents another problem: Can the reader believe it—especially when Elizabeth and I had trouble believing it ourselves? We can only suggest that even though many of the scenes read like fiction, they are not.

Chapter II

All her own writings and records reveal Eileen Garrett as a complex and dynamic character. All the writings about her, as listed in the bibliography, reveal the same thing. When she entered a room, she was a magnet for all attention. Her intuitive brilliance was reflected by the company she kept. She was said to be a visceral intellectual. She attracted some of the best minds of the time.

In combing a mountain of material about her, the most outstanding feature that set her aside from other psychic sensitives was her intense desire to discover what her strange powers consisted of. She was constantly looking at herself objectively, and a survey of all who knew her showed that her directness and honesty were above reproach.

This was critical to us in our research. The events in the narrative depended on our conviction that she was unimpeachable. This we gradually came to accept, but not without months of study and checking. To have a trance alter ego like the voice of Uvani is not apparently uncommon among psychic sensitives. What set Eileen Garrett aside was her intense desire to subject herself to testing by pure scientists, a process she continued to go through all her life.

The reconstructed details of Emilie Hinchliffe's own notes, writings and lectures are poignant and impressive. They reveal caution, intelligence, and discipline. They also reveal a strong capacity for analysis and reason. In the situation she had to face, these qualities were most important.

The question of the possible validity of apparitions and messages from the Ouija board, Elizabeth and I had dealt with at length in structuring *The Ghost of Flight 401*. We had begun our research then in an attitude of total skepticism, and ended with the conviction that such phenomena could not be summarily ruled out. In the library of the Society for Psychical Research was a survey which showed that twenty percent of the 18,000 respondents to a questionnaire indicated they had experienced an encounter with an apparition. This, plus detailed studies by the painstaking scientist G. N. M. Tyrell in his book *Apparitions*, demonstrated reflective and sober evidence that they were not to be scoffed at.

Our own experience with the Ouija board in experimental sessions for the *401* story had produced clear, verifiable evidence that information unknown to us at the time could at times be produced—although the board is not a toy, and should not be used frivolously. *The Case of Patience Worth*, a study by Dr. Walter Franklin Prince of the stories, poems, and epigrams purporting to come from an entity who died in the seventeenth century, is a classic concerning the board that has yet to be explained.

We continued to approach our research with an open mind, but aware also of the pitfalls such a narrative presents to credibility.

Chapter III

The doubts and uncertainties in Emilie Hinchliffe's mind in consulting with Mrs. Earl and Eileen Garrett are minutely reflected in her lectures and writings. They show a woman torn between wanting to see if it would be possible to communicate with her missing husband, and her strong Dutch resistance to the whole idea. It is this attitude that makes her experience interesting to examine. She was obviously impressed that Sir Arthur Conan Doyle took a personal interest in the case, and it seems that this is the factor that tipped her over to following up the process.

One of the biggest factors that stimulated Elizabeth and me to explore this story was the material in Dr. Raymond Moody's recent book *Life After Life*, and the studies of Dr. Elizabeth Kubler-Ross. Each doctor had separately made studies of patients whose life signals had stopped, and yet who "returned" to life in spite of it. Each was a reputable medical scientist, and each concluded there was strong evidence of life-after-life in the hundreds of cases they documented. These results cry out for further probing into the question, from a sane and logical point of view, removed from the spook-and-kook atmosphere that has turned off public interest in the past.

One of the biggest assets that Emilie Hinchliffe had in probing her own story was her expertise in shorthand which enabled her to get down the material that was to flow from "Uvani's" voice so swiftly. Her experience as an executive secretary for KLM demanded accuracy and knowledge of the aviation industry, which she found invaluable as she began her startling sessions with Eileen Garrett.

Chapter IV

In screening the newspapers of this period, Elizabeth and I found so many details about the R-101 and its problems that it was a question of selecting the most salient points. Air Ministry reports and recollections of still-living members of the Royal Aeronautical Society, in its dignified, elegant quarters near Hyde Park Corner, filled in other details.

The original transcript of Emilie Hinchliffe's first session with Eileen Garrett was very revealing, including her own handwritten questions about the material that came from Uvani's voice. It was apparent from this, and from Emilie's other writings revealing her thoughts and reactions at the time, that she wanted to track down every bit of minutiae she recorded as a test of whether to believe what she was hearing or not. Her resistance to accepting all this was strong. It did not wear down easily. Her interest, for instance, in the course her husband might have taken was a key point, she told friends. If she could trace this, and it was logical, her belief might increase. All through her transcripts were comments like: "Will check this point later," "Later found to be true," "True," "Possibly true, will verify."

She was obviously very methodical and meticulous—a point that helped establish her credibility as Elizabeth and I reviewed the transcripts line by line. What appeared to begin affecting Emilie Hinchliffe most was the accumulation of evidence, fact after fact that no one but she and her children would know. The confirmation of the change of spark plugs, and the logical possibility of Hinchlife heading toward the Azores for safety seemed to have a profound effect on her.

Chapter V

If the reader finds the mosaic in this chapter a little bewildering, it was more so for Elizabeth and me, as we combed through so many ancient files to track down information that linked up with the narrative. The "Old Lowenstein" portion popped up when least expected in two separate newspaper morgues. Other Lowenstein details were revealed in the official hearings of his strange accident. It is so dramatic that it is bound to read like fiction, which it is not.

Emilie Hinchliffe told her friends and the public to whom she lectured that finding the missing real estate paper from the information supplied by Eileen Garrett was of critical importance in nailing down her conviction that she was actually communicating with her husband.

But the out-and-out prediction that she would receive compensation from Lord Inchcape gripped her most. When she received the notice on the exact day that was predicted, she considered it a minor miracle.

Chapter VI

Elizabeth and I arrived in England in the fall of 1977, some fifty years after Hinchliffe's tragic flight. We were surprised to pick up the paper one morning to see a headline reading: £3¾ REMINDER OF AIRWOMAN'S ATLANTIC BID.

The article went on to tell the story of Lord Inchcape's gift to the British government, and how it had grown to 7½ times its original value. In spite of the growth, the article noted that the gift would only amount to a drop in the bucket compared to the National Debt. Nevertheless, it marked the final curtain for the bizarre endowment that had drawn so much attention in 1928.

In evaluating the research material concerning Emilie Hinchliffe and Mrs. Taylor's group involved with the financier Lowenstein, the problem continued about how to present it without its sounding like science fiction. The question of the ghost steps that Emilie and her friends the Sinclairs encountered brought up the question of the validity of apparitions again. It sent us back to studying G. N. M. Tyrell's study and other sources concerning this phenomenon.

There were several interesting things that struck us as parallels. One was that Dr. Elizabeth Kubler-Ross, who is a highly respected neuro-psychiatrist of the current scene, publicly detailed an encounter with an apparition by one of her patients who had died several months prior to her encounter. In a reality-testing action, she stated that she actually was able to get the apparition to write a note signed with the former patient's verifiable signature, as noted in *Newsweek* in the May 1, 1978, issue. In the same article, *Newsweek* reviews the recent Kubler-Ross and Moody findings, with its results almost identically matching the reports of

Mrs. Taylor's group in their experiences with "Old Lowenstein." The leaving of the body and looking down on it. The scenes of an entire lifetime flashing before the eyes. The return to familiar places, but being sensed or recognized by no one there. The futile attempt to touch them.

In our own reality-testing, Elizabeth and I tried to find parallels that might theoretically explain the phenomenon of apparitions. Except in the serious studies, the subject has been constantly ridiculed, perhaps out of fear. Where, we were asking ourselves, was there a technical parallel that could offer some kind of up-to-date theory that could even suggest an idea for further exploration?

Oddly enough, we came across one such possibility at the British Museum of Science. We were passing through the exhibitions, and in one section we noticed a booth at the end of the room with a man sitting in it. He was a well-dressed, professorial type, and we approached him. Then we noticed that he was sitting behind a glass panel in the booth. He was looking out at us, but he was motionless. When we were beside the booth, the man was no less real, but we saw a sign which told us that this full-sized man was the creation of the process known as laser holography, where a hologram creates a picture of almost total three-dimensional reality. This reality was startling and almost shocking. The question this suggested to us was: Could apparitions be created in a similar way, through some as-yet- undiscovered psychic "laser" force?

That, of course, would have to be left up in the air. But we came across another interesting parallel in a study of pigeons, of all things, at Cornell University. The study revealed that pigeons could see things in ultraviolet light that people couldn't. This poses a simple question: Could apparitions be on a wavelength that some people can see and some can't? Admittedly, all Elizabeth and I had were questions. We had no answers.

Of course, the most dramatic impact of the Eileen Garrett sessions upon Emilie Hinchliffe was the phone call in the closing hours of July, indicating that financial relief had just arrived, exactly as predicted. This is the kind of detail that would be likely to bolster anyone's belief in the validity of the communications.

Chapter VII

The Conan Doyle–Harry Price letters, notes and writings revealed a taut struggle between the two men. It centered on Doyle's persuasion that harsh and vigorous testing of a medium could destroy the delicate communication channels. Price, however, felt that if a medium were worth anything, she could overcome the severity of the testing and prove herself. Since Eileen Garrett became one of the few mediums that Price would certify, her work may be given more credibility than others'.

But when the transcripts of Captain Hinchliffe's purported descriptions of the *quality* of life-after-death are analyzed, there is no factual data to check against, as there is when concrete names, dates, places and personal events are described. The scenes are hard to imagine or conceive, since they require a belief in a world much like our present one, yet matter and form would have to be non-material.

Elizabeth and I felt that the only logical way this sort of description of an afterlife could be acceptable would be to consider the theory of a change of consciousness as reflected by Professor H. H. Price (not Harry Price), rather than change of physical locale. His theory of a dream-image world would also apply, where this non-material world could exist in form, color, real estate, and all the other appurtenances of the present life on earth. And again, the current medical studies of Drs. Moody and Kubler-Ross support the possibility of vivid, personal, out-of-body experiences that were no less real to the patient who "came back" to life than his ordinary physical existence. Beyond this, the archives of the Society for Psychical Research are packed with similar descriptions, as well as the writings of Air Chief Marshal Lord Dowding. In other words, there was persuasive evidence to believe that Hinchliffe's descriptions of an afterlife were not so wild as they seemed at first sight. If so, they give food for thought.

Emilie Hinchliffe's lectures were of great value in tracing her feelings and stream-of-consciousness through the various events. By piecing these together with her séance transcripts, it was possible to bring a more three-dimensional picture to the narrative.

Chapter VIII

It was rather a sad moment when we visited the huge, empty hangars at Cardington. The vaulted ceiling, ten stories high, framed an almost empty, dark shell that could contain most of the large ocean liners. A few shabby experimental balloons hung from supports, halfway up. They looked very much like flabby elephants.

The details available from the Air Ministry records concerning the R-101 were so voluminous that it was a question of selecting the most apt for the narrative. Eileen Garrett's elaborately detailed notes and memos of this period (including dialogue) were also voluminous and revealing, enabling a dramatic reconstruction of the R-101 warnings to be recreated. Nevil Shute's intimate recollections in his book *Slide Rule* contributed to the same effect.

All through the research, the problem continued: how to present these events so they didn't seem like fiction to the reader. The old adage that truth is stranger than fiction prevailed. This story certainly was—and still is.

Chapter IX

The research material on the history of the R-101 is so rich that it was a simple matter to reconstruct the thoughts, occasional recorded dialogue, concerns and impressions of all those involved, in addition to confirming them with several officers and airmen still alive. Official records are most complete.

In recording the psychic material, Harry Price's and Eileen Garrett's records are so complete that nothing is lacking to shape a full-rounded picture.

Chapter X

The transcripts of the court hearings revealed intricate and precise details from the testimony of the survivors, as well as the elaborate press coverage.

Chapter XI

The obvious question in any psychic reading is whether or not the medium has gathered information in advance from non-psychic sources. In the case of these lengthy sessions with Eileen Garrett, the enormous amount of technical data and personal detail flowing through the séances makes it highly unlikely that such was the case in either the Hinchliffe or Harry Price sessions.

In the Hinchliffe case, over two dozen accurate names and family facts were rattled off. In the Harry Price case, the technical information came through at such speed that to assume this was memorized is less logical than assuming it wasn't.

Most evidential is the technical information that was only confirmed later, including the verification of the town of Achy, the fact that hydrogen was going to be used as part of the fuel mixture and many other facts that were only revealed in the testimony of the official hearings.

Chapter XII

The biggest problem Major Villiers had was convincing others that his memory and notetaking were adequate for the transcripts he produced. But his contention was that enough confirmable data came through his séances with Eileen Garrett to make this point nonessential. He recognized that his conscious mind could have produced distortions, but for over forty years has clung to the conviction that his total recall capacity and his notes are over ninety percent accurate.

We spent over eighty hours reading his notes, transcripts and diaries back to him, over a four-week period. His memory and recall were amazing. We became convinced that he was sincere, and capable of coming close to his claim. Although there were some inconsistencies and what seemed to be considerable decoration of the speech pattern, the discovery of the Atherstone diary in 1967 was very supportive.

Most important in judging the entire story was the accumulation of interlocking detail. It was all simply too elaborate to be concocted, from the Hinchliffe story on through.

Chapters XIII, XIV, XV

The most interesting effect of both the Price and Villiers séances was the impact they had on technical and aviation experts. Because of their intimacies with the inside information on such a specialized subject as airships, they would be less likely to be taken in by inaccurate information. Instead, men like Will Charlton, William Wood, Air Chief Marshal Lord Dowding and Air Marshal Sir Victor Goddard found persuasive evidence of an afterlife in the material. Most remarkable, of course, was the impact on Wood, who became a believer in spiritual reality and life-after-death, while still remaining an atheist.

ACKNOWLEDGMENTS

No one can write a nonfiction book without inestimable help from many people. Only fiction writers can have the luxury of writing without outside assistance, and even in such cases, much is owed to others.

The people and the facilities listed below went out of their way to be personally helpful to me, and I am abundantly grateful to them:

American Society of Psychical Research
Maurice Barbanell
Norman Barfield
R. F. Barker
Paul Beard
British Museum Library
Ned Chase
Christopher Clarkson
College of Psychic Studies
Bob and Eileen Coly
V.A. Cornish
Ms. Jackie Davis

Lady Dowding
Edridges & Drummonds, Solicitors
The Freethinker
Mrs. Pamela Franklin (née Hinchliffe)
Kenneth Garside
Sir Victor and Lady Goddard
Mrs. K. Goldney
Mrs. Lilian Hicks (nee Charlton)
Mrs. Emilie Hinchliffe
Mrs. Joan Humphreys (nee Hinchliffe)
Archie Jarman
Mrs. Elaine Kaufman
Captain F. Mc Dermott
Brenda Marshall
Sir Peter Masefield
Walter Minton
A. W. L. Naylor
Tony Ortze
Karlis Osis
Parapsychology Foundation
Michael Perry
Eleanor O'Keefe
The RAF base, Cardington
Michael Randolph
Royal Aeronautical Society
Royal Airforce Museum
Mrs. Dorothy Sillito
Richard Simpson
Society for Psychical Research
Mrs. Judith Stripp
Doris Sullivan
University of London Library
Major Oliver G. Villiers
A. H. Wesencraft
Reginald and Inger Wilson
G. R. Wrixon

BIBLIOGRAPHY

Alcock and Brown. *Our Transatlantic Flight*. Kimber, 1969.

Angoff, Alan. *World Beyond the Senses*. Creative Age Press, 1950.

Barbanell, Maurice. *This Is Spiritualism*. Spiritualist Press, 1959.

Baring-Gould, W.S. *The Chronological Holmes*. Privately printed, 1955.

Barley, M.W. *Lincolnshire and the Fens*. Scholar Press, 1972.

Beard, Paul. *Survival of Death: For and Against*. Psychic Press Ltd., 1966.

Bendit, Phoebe D. *Man Incarnate*. Theosophical Publication House, 1957.

Blythe, Ronald. *The Age of Illusion*. Houghton Mifflin, 1964.

Bohm, David. *Quantum Theory*. Prentice Hall, 1951.

Brahma, N. K. *Casuality and Science*. Allen & Unwin, 1939.

Broad, C. D. *Lectures on Psychical Research*. Routledge & Kegan Paul, 1962.

Bray, Hillary. *How It Strikes a Contemporary*. College of Psychic Studies (London), 1972.

Carr, John Dickson. *The Life of Arthur Conan Doyle*. Harper, 1949.

Coster, Ian. *Friends in Aspic*. John Miles, 1939.

———. "Ghost on an Airship." *Leader Magazine,* May 6, 1950.

Dowding, Air Chief Marshal Lord. *Lychgate.* Cheltenham Press, 1944.

———. *Many Mansions.* Cheltenham Press, 1943.

Doyle, Sir Arthur Conan. *The Edge of the Unknown.* G. P. Putnam's, 1930.

———. *The History of Spiritualism.* Cassell & Company, 1926.

———. *Memories and Adventures.* Little, Brown & Co., 1924.

———. *The New Revelation.* George H. Doran, 1918.

———. *Our American Adventure.* Goerge H. Doran, 1923.

———. *Study in Scarlet and The Sign of The Four.* D. Appleton & Company, 1902.

———. *Through The Magic Door.* The McClure Company, 1908.

———. *The Vital Message.* George H. Doran, 1919.

———. *The Wanderings of A Spiritualist.* George H. Doran, 1921.

Ducasse, C. J. *Is Life After Death Possible?* University of California Press, 1948.

———. *Paranormal Phenomena, Science, and Life After Death.* Parapsychology Foundation, 1969.

Eiseley, Loren. *The Immense Journey.* Random House, 1957.

———. *The Invisible Pyramid.* Scribners, 1970.

Ernst, Bernard N. L. and Carrington, Hereward. *Houdini and Conan Doyle.* Albert & Charles Boni, 1932.

Einstein, A., Podolsky, B., and Rosen, N. "Can Quantum Mechanical Descriptions Be Considered Complete?" in *Phys. Rev.,* 47, 777, 1935.

Ellis, F. K. and E. *Atlantic Air Conquest.* Kimber, 1963.

The Freethinker. Articles by Lt. W. H. Wood, 1948–1949.

Garrett, Eileen. *Adventures in the Supernormal.* Creative Age Press, 1949.

Garrett, Eileen. *Awareness.* Helix Press, 1943.

———. *Many Voices.* New York: G. P. Putnam's, 1968.

———. *Precognition of an Airship.* Unpublished, 1960.

———. *The Sense and Nonsense of Prophecy.* Helix Press, 1950.

———. Unpublished papers, memos, letters, 1928–1970.

Goddard, Sir Victor. *Flight Towards Reality.* Turnstone Books, 1975.

Graves, Robert & Alan Hodge. *The Long Week End.* Macmillan, 1941.

Grey, C. G. *A History of The Air Ministry.* Allen and Unwin, 1940.

Hankey, Muriel. *J. Hewat Mc Kenzie: Pioneer of Psychical Research.* Helix Press, 1963.

Hardwick, Michael and Molly. *The Man Who Was Sherlock Holmes.* Doubleday & Company, 1964.

Harrison, Michael. *World of Sherlock Holmes.* E. P. Dutton, 1973.

Heisenberg, W. *The Physical Principles of The Quantum Theory.* University of Chicago Press, 1930.

Henderson, Alexander. *Aldous Huxley.* Harper, 1936.

Higham, Robin. *Britain's Imperial Air Routes, 1918–1939.* Foulis, 1961.

Hinchliffe, Emilie. Lectures and notes, 1928–1930.

———. *The Return of Captain Hinchliffe.* London: Psychic Press, 1930.

H. M. Airship R-101. Notes for the use of the Press regarding the Air Ministry Airship Development Programme and H. M. Airship R-101.

Honorton, Charles. "State of Awarness Factors in PSI Activation." *JASPR,* Vol. 68, 246–256, 1974.

Krippner, S. and Rubin, D. *Galaxies of Life.* Gordon and Breach, 1973.

Lamont, Corliss. *The Illusion of Immortality.* Philosophical Library, 1950.

Leggett, D. M. A. *The Implications of The Paranormal.* Leggett Lecture, University of Surrey, 1977.

Lodge, Sir Oliver. *Ether and Reality.* Hodder & Stoughton, 1925.

———. *Raymond, or Life and Death.* George H. Doran Company, 1916.

Macmillan, Norman. *Sefton Brancker.* Heinemann, 1935.

Martin, Edward S. "Conan Doyle and the Spirit World." *Harper's,* Vol. 161, Oct. 1930, 637–9.

Mc Creery, Charles. *Science, Philosophy, and ESP.* Faber and Faber, 1967.

Memoir of Lord Thomson of Cardington. *Royal Engineers' Journal,* March, 1931.

Moss, Thelma. *Bioenergetics and Radiation Photography.* Prague: Proceedings of the International. Conference in Psychotronics, Prague, 1973.

Munson, Kenneth. *Pictorial History of BOAC and Imperial Airways.* Allan, 1957.

Murphy, Gardner. "Lawfulness Vs. Caprice: Is There a Law of Psychic Phenomena?" *Journal American Society for Psychical Research,* 58, 1964, 238–248.

———. *Three Papers on the Survival Problem.* American Society for Psychical Research, 1945.

Myers, F. W. H. *Human Personality and Its Survival on Bodily Death.* Longmans, Green & Co., 1903.

New York *Times.* October 5, 6, 7, 8, 1930. March 4, 1928.

Norden, Pierre. *Conan Doyle: A Biography.* Holt, Rinehard, & Winston, 1967.

Osis, Karlis. *At The Hour of Death.* Avon Books, 1977.

Ostrander, Sheila and Schroeder, Lynn. *Psychic Discoveries Behind the Iron Curtain.* Abacus, 1973.

Pearson, Hesketh. *Conan Doyle.* Walker & Company, 1961.

Planck, Max. *A Scientific Autobiography.* Williams & Norgate, 1950.

Price, Harry. *Confessions of a Ghost Hunter.* G. P. Putnam's, 1936.

———. *Fifty Years of Psychical Research: A Critical Survey.* Arno Press, 1975.

———. Letters and documents, University of London Library, 1928–1939.

———. "The R-101 Disaster." *Nash's Magazine,* Jan. 1931. *Cosmopolitan* 1931.

———. *Stella C.* Souvenir Press, 1973.

Report of the R-101 Inquiry. His Majesty's Stationery Office, London.

Rhine, J. B. "Research on Spirit Survival Reexamined." *Journal of Parapsychology,* June, 1959.

Rosenberg, Samuel. *Naked is the Best Disguise.* Bobbs-Merrill, 1974.

Russell, Bertrand *Human Knowledge: Its Scope and Limits.* George Allen and Unwin, 1948.

Saltmarsh, H. F. *Evidence of Personal Survival from Cross Correspondence.* G. Bell & Sons, 1938.

Scott, Mary. *Science and Subtle Bodies: Towards a Clarification of Issues.* College of Psychic Studies, 1975.

Schmeidler, Gertrude E. "Looking Ahead: A Method for Research on Survival." *Theta,* Vol. 5, No. 1, 1977, pp. 2–9.

Sculthoro, Frederick C. *Excursions to the Spirit World.* The Greater World Association, 1961.

Shute, Nevil. *Slide Rule.* Heinemann, 1962.

Simon, Viscount. *Retrospect.* Hutchinson, 1952.

Smith, Julian. *Nevil Shute.* Twayne Publishers, 1976.

Soal, S. G. and Bateman, F. *Modern Experiments in Telepathy.* Yale University Press, 1954.

Starrett, Vincent. *The Private Life of Sherlock Holmes.* University of Chicago Press, 1960.

———, editor. *Studies in Sherlock Holmes.* Biblo & Tannen, 1969.

Stevenson, Ian. *The Evidence of Survival from Claimed Memories of Former Reincarnations.* American Society of Psychical Research, 1966.

Spanner, E. F. *About Airships.* E. F. Spanner, 1929.

———. *The Tragedy of R-101.* E. F. Spanner, 1931.

Tabori, Paul. *The Biography of a Ghost Hunter.* Living Books, 1966.

Tart, Charles. *PSI Functioning and Altered States of Consciousness.* Parapsychology International Conference, August, 1977.

Time. Oct. 21, Nov. 4, Nov. 11, 1929. Jan. 1, 1931.

Villiers, Oliver G. Letters, notes, lectures and transcripts, 1931–1978.

Wallace, Graham. *The Flight of Alcock and Brown.* Putnam, 1955.

Watson, Lyall. *Gifts of Unknown Things.* Hodder and Stoughton, 1976.

White, Stewart Edward. *The Betty Book.* Robert Hale, 1945.

Whiteman, J. H. M. *The Mystical Life.* Faber and Faber, 1961.

Woodcock, George. *Dawn and the Darkest Hour: A Study of Aldous Huxley.* Viking, 1972.

EXTENDED NOTES: MAJOR VILLIERS' SESSIONS WITH EILEEN GARRETT

7th April, 1978

DEAR FULLER,

It was with the greatest joy that I received a completely unexpected letter from Mrs. Eileen Coly, President of the Parapsychology Foundation, telling me that you were about to arrive in England and were most anxious to make my acquaintance. My interest was increased when I heard that you were about to write a book concerning the tragic loss of the Government Airship R101 and that the information I had obtained in my seven sittings with the late Eileen Garratt were of vital importance, and that you wanted my permission to make use of them.

Soon after your arrival you came to my house and during the next six weeks we had many talks together. I soon realised that you would not return home until you had obtained every available scrap of information that threw any light on this tragedy.

I was most impressed by the way in which you questioned me about my life, my personal views over a wide range of subjects and, in particular, how long I had made a careful study of what can commonly be called Spiritualism in all its forms. You explained that your reason was to understand my general approach.

You told me you had a photostat copy of the expanded notes of the seven sittings and my explanatory memorandum which enabled us to discuss all this in great detail. I was, therefore, delighted to give you my written consent to make use of these sittings provided that each was re-produced in toto without any alteration whatsoever, to which you readily agreed.*

These sittings had been referred to as "100% Proof." This was not my doing. The late Col. Lester, founder and President of the Churchs Fellowship for Psychic and Spiritual Studies, having heard of these sittings asked if he might see the transcript and select certain extracts for publication. He selected the following: Colmore's two sets of diaries; all his secret correspondence with various Government departments; the way in which I was reminded of a diagrammatical drawing of the airship; and lastly Brancker's method of making himself known. All these were eventually proved to be absolutely true. . . .

I now feel convinced that when Colmore and the others decided it was imperative that the real truth should be made available to us in this world, Brancker must have realised that since I had been forewarned I was a suitable contact and for reasons best known to themselves Irwin was asked to undertake this.

It is not my intention to write a treatise of my own views on survival or for that matter on reincarnation because many great writers have already covered this ground, nor the difference between the earthy body and one's spiritual body, scientifically called the etheric.

Once again let me wish you all success in this vitally important work you have undertaken because I am certain it will bring not only relief but great happiness to those who are so anxious to know the truth of what is commonly called Survival and to realise that there is no such thing as ' Death."

Yours very sincerely,

MAJOR OLIVER G. C. VILLIERS, D.S.O.

52, Brockhill Road,
Saltwood, Hythe.

*Full transcripts follow in appendix.

31.10.30   7 p.m.

M. Garrett

C. Control Spirit.   X. Visitor.   C.I. Irwin talking through Control Spirit.

From 7 to 7.30 many individuals made their presence known to the Control Spirit but nobody that I knew or had any interest in whatsoever.

C.I am so distressed that I have not made contact with any person who wishes to be put in touch with you. I am so distressed and I fear it is no good my staying any longer.

There was a pause and then a faint voice was heard from afar. About 7.30 p.m.

C.I."Irwey, Irwey" louder, "Urwin, Irwin, don't go please, stay I must speak.

X.Don't worry old boy. I am so glad you have come.

C.I see a slim fellow resting with his arm across your shoulder and his head resting against you, rather exhausted.

C.I.Oh dear, we feel like damned murderers, oh its awful, old man, awful. We ought to have said no.

X.Now old boy, don't view the matter in this light. All that matters is this. You and others had a choice to make when you are faced with a choice again such as this remember, *results don't matter*. Just do what is right and that's all. Keep your mind on this point. Who are the "we" you mention?

C.I.Johnnie, Scottie and I.

X.Now try and tell me all that happened on the Saturday and Sunday.

C.I.She was too heavy by several tons, too amateurish in construction, envelope and girders not of sufficiently sound material.

X.Wait a mement, old boy. Lets start at the beginning.

C.I.Well, during the afternoon before starting I noticed that the gas indicator was going up and down which showed there was a leakage or escape which I could not stop or rectify at any time around the valves.

X.Try to explain a bit more, I don't quite understand.

C.I.The gold beater skins (he used the word gas skins) are too porous and not strong enough and the constant movement of the gas bags acting like bellows is constantly causing internal pressure of the gas which causes a leakage at the valves. I told the chief engineer of this.

I then knew we were doomed. Then later on the meteorological charts came in and Scottie and Johnnie and I had a consultation. Owing to the trouble of the gas we knew that our only chance was to leave on scheduled time. The weather forecast was not good, but we decided that we might cross the Channel and tie up at Le Bourget before the bad weather came.

We three were absolutely scared stiff and Scottie said to us: "Now look here, we are in for it, but for God's sake let's smile like damned Cheshire cats as we go on board and leave England with a clean pair of heels."

X.Did Colmore know?

C.I.No, you will understand. We had to make the fatal decision and we felt it was not fair to let him shoulder this decision.

X.Could not Thompson have helped?

C.I.Oh dear. It's awful. You see I told Thompson when he arrived at Cardington that gas had been escaping. Thompson said, "But this is negligible and surely for this small matter you don't contemplate postponement. Its' impossible. I am pledged to be back for the Imperial Conference. We must leave according to scheduled time." I disagreed and consulted Scottie, but we decided to go. You known how late we were starting and after crossing the Channel we three knew all was lost. We were desperate.

X.Well now, how exactly did the end come and what was the cause? All evidence seems to show she dived, straightened and dived again, and crashed.

C.I.Yes, that's so. Now I will tell you the truth. One of the struts in the nose collapsed and caused a tear in the cover. Now listen very carefully. It is the same strut that caused the trouble before and they know. The wind was blowing hard and it was raining also. Now you see what happened. The rush of wind caused the first dive and then we straightened again and another gust surging through the hole finished us.

X.Yes, that is quite clear, but what caused the explosion? Was it the electrical installation that fused?

C.I.No, not that. It was the engine.

X.But old boy, how could an engine cause the explosion?

C.I.It was this way. The diesel engine had been popping or back-firing after crossing the Channel because the oil feed was not right. The oil is of too thick a consistency and has given trouble before. You see the pressure in some of the gas bags was accentuated by the under girders crumpling up and since gas had been escaping the extra pressure pushed the gas out and came out with a rush and at that moment the diesel engine back-fired and ignited the escaping gas. That caused the first explosion and others followed.

X.Before you go, how is dear old Branks?

C.I.Poor Brancker is often very depressed and is worried about his wife and other lady friends and about his unfinished work. You know yourself how some days he was up in the air like a boy and sometimes his temper was short. Soon after we left Cardington he showed how annoyed he was at the delay in starting and did you realise that Brancker was very capable of picking up thoughts? Because soon after leaving *he* realised that Scottie, Johnnie and I were absolutely scared with fright and what was ahead, and he also took fright, we noticed it. It was he that asked for a bottle of bubbly at dinner to pull himself together (and you know how fond he was of his bottle).

There is one thing you must try and help in. Don't let the other come out and do long journeys. Over here we call her the "Inventor's Nightmare," she is all wrong in construction.

X.Try and explain what really is wrong in the present form of construction.

C.I The main thing is this—the stress calculations are correct but the forces she can be subjected to in bad weather and wind currents are too strong for the present system of calculations.

C.I Even supposing we had not lost gas and had encountered worse weather I believe her frame would have buckled owing to the pressure on her bulk size causing her to twist. (Here "C" demonstrated with both hands).

I.If you had suffered no leakage of gas and had had good weather do you think she would have accomplished the journey?

C.I Yes I think so, but she is no good unless she has the strength to live up to bad weather. Another thing, they are talking of Helium. That is no good because in capacity you want 1½ times as much and the present system of gas bags are not strong enough. More gas, bigger gas bags, more pressure on bags, system of hanging gas bags all wrong now and will be more so if enlarged.

Oh dear, its dreadful to hear what they are saying, all bosh, and they know it and won't speak the truth. (i.e. this refers to enquiry). No more now. You must come soon as Scottie and Johnnie say they must each come and give you their own story, it helps them. Please come soon and thank you for your thoughts. Come soon, come soon.

Finished about 8.40 p.m.

2.1130

M. Garrett   C. Control Spirit   B. Branks
S. Scottie   X. Visitor

C.Gave blessing and again expressed regret that last visit was so long before my friend came.

C."I see near you a man of about 50 or 55, jovial expression, hair growing a little grey by the ears. He used to have a moustache which made him look older. He now passes his hand across his lip and takes it away.

(Note. I was still confused as to identity as I was expecting C.)

C.' He is smiling hard at you and said 'No, I won't give my name as I want to be certain you know who it is, very important.' He is now putting hand into his waistcoat pocket and is putting a piece of round glass into his eye and said 'Now, use your intelligence!!!'

X.' Oh Branks old man, of course its you. I am so glad you have come."

B.' Don't use my name, but call me B. its better. Little did I think when I saw you last we should meet again with things so upside down. No parties here, nothing in bottles, but spirits of other kinds, you know what I mean. If only we had realised things as we do now, how different our lives would have been." (Note. Here followed an intimate conversation, and I promised to talk to him again and help when I could, and I promised absolutely to keep silence on all matters connected with his private life).

B.You know I really hated speaking in public but stuck my hands in my pocket and got on with the job.

X.Well done B. Now let's get down to brass tacks about the affair.

B.C. wants to speak to you afterwards.

X.Yes, but B. would you please ask C to let me first speak to Scottie or Johnnie, as I must get certain facts before evidence comes out tomorrow and Tuesday. When did you first know or begin to realise that things on board were not right?

B.Well, we all had a conference because Irwin, Scottie and Johnston put the case before us.

X.But wait a moment. I must get this right. Did the conference take place immediately after she left or later on?

B.Good Lord no. My dear boy, we all knew well before we started.

X.But if that was so, did that lady who went on board with you hear?

B.Oh Lord no. She left before that. No, what happened was this. Scott, Irwin and Johnston came and told T.

X.You mean Thompson.

B.Yes, of course. They told him of the gas trouble and Colmore

X.(That makes Colmore clearer—will explain later on)

B.They three, S.I. and J. wanted to postpone flight, but T said its impossible, there has been so much talk and I have said so much and the G.B.P.

X.General who. I don't follow.

B.General British Public are all keyed up, we can't not go. They asked me and I felt I couldn't show a faint heart, and alas said yes. We discussed the weather charts and saw that if we managed to cross the pond and could land somewhere in a foreign country our honour would be vindicated and we could then bless the bad weather and say weather forced us to make a descent.

X.Did you have any premonition of this?

B.Yes, in a way. Thats why I had those two talks with T and I had a couple of stiff ones (you know) before sailing.

X.I thought you only had champagne at dinner.

B.Oh no I put a drop in my pocket and took two good ones. I felt awful. Of course we never had a run for our money. T. really funked flight but felt he had to go. He had already said his policy was India at all costs and his hand was to the plough and I felt we all ought to be at the death—no turning back. (Note—Then a little more private conversation and I said I would come again. He gave a salute (military) and said, Au revoir dear boy.)

NOTE A. Irvine said Colmore was not consulted. He apparently meant not consulted till all were on board. Irvine, Scottie and Johnnie knew earlier in the afternoon.

C.Next described a round jovial face, big head and I last saw him in blue with peaked cap. "Yes Scottie, old man."

X.I knew old boy at once it was you. I am so glad to see you again.

S.Oh X. (My name was properly pronounced and this is the first time mentioned by anyone.) Oh X. its all too ghastly for words, its awful. Think of all the lives experience, money and material—all thrown away and what for—for nothing.

X.Dear old man, there is a reason, even if we can't see it now.

S.That may be but its absolutely ghastly.

X.Now dear Scottie, try and help me to fill in gaps. When did you begin to be suspicious that the ship was wrong?

S.After her first flight. She didn't handle too well and we had trouble.

X.Oh, that's important, what was the trouble? Irwin mentioned the nose.

S.Yes, girder trouble and engine.

X.Now, go slowly. I must get this right. Can you describe exactly where? Look here Scottie old man, we have the long struts numbered from A to G.

S.Not quite the top one of top is 0, and then A B C and so on downwards. Look at your model.

X.Yes, wait a minute. All right.

S.It was the starboard of 5 C.

X.Half a jiff Scottie, let me see. 5 is the bay just behind the starboard engine and A.B.C., yes the third.

X.Yes, I have it. Now go on.

S.On our second flight after we had finished we found the girder had been strained, not cracked and this caused trouble to the cover. This is where she went last time.

X.All right we will take up that point later on. Now what came next.

S.The gas valves proved ineffective. You remember the R.A.F.

X.At Hendon?

S.Yes, we only just got back. I was not too keen on that short trip.

X.Why did you never make a report to the A.M.

S.My dear man, you know all the damned red tape. This was purely technical and when possible we always avoided technical reports otherwise we should have never got the blooming work done.

X.Look here, can you explain what the gas valve trouble was? I have seen one of the actual valves in court (and I explained what I had gathered).

S.The pressure of gas was too strong and gas was always forcing itself through. This was all wrong. But do you remember a gas valve was blown out and found away from the wreck.

X.Yes I did hear this but how did it get blown off and not consumed in the flames?

S.It all really happened simultaneously. I will go on with the story of events and come on to that point again later

X.All right, I quite agree.

S.Before we left we all had a conference and having calculated the amount of gas we were losing we knew things were desperate.

X.Yes, B. told me all that.

S.Surely X old man you, if faced with the awful position would have done what we did. We had to uphold the honour of our country. What would Germany, U.S.A. and others have said if we had ratted? We *had* to go and take the 1000th chance of making a landing in France. We started off with that idea but being already late were taken off our course and after crossing the water we knew we had very little chance. It was hopeless to consider landing.

X.But since you had decided to try for Le Bourget why did you not send out for a landing party?

S.We could not do so till after crossing the water as if message went too early we should have "blown the gaff" and given the game away.

X.Yes, I do realise you had to take all precautions to carry out the bluff.

S.Yes exactly. Now you realise how desperate we were. Well, you want to know about the rent in the outer cover. The same place 5 C this time.

X.Do you mean to say it actually broke and a piece of the girder went through the outer cover.

S.No not broke, but cracked badly and split the outer cover.

X.Who told you the news and where were you?

S.We, Johnnie, Irwin and I were together.

X.In the control tower?

S.No, Johnnie's cubby hole, you know, and the rigger called to us and we saw by the instrument board immediately. We all gasped and were horrified at the news. We decided . . .

X.Did she nose-dive then?

S.No not quite. We decided to make a turn and go with the wind as far as it was possible and make for Le Bourget and try at all costs some sort of landing. You know how we always turn in a big circle because of the strain. So we decided to try. Well X. now imagine the picture. We have a bad rent in the cover on the starboard side at 5.C. This brought about an unnatural pressure and the frame gave a twist which, with the external pressure, forced us into our first dive. The second was even worse, the pressure on the gas bags here was terrific and the gusts of wind were tremendous. This external pressure, coupled with the fact that the valve was weak, blew the valve right off and at the same time the released gas was ignited by a back fire from the engine.

X.But Scottie, I don't understand this. You said previously the engine had given oil trouble and the valve that went was just near the front starboard engine.

S.Quite right. But both engines had caused trouble. At least the engines were quite O.K. only the oil feed was wrong. This engine back-fired at the same time and caused the ignition. It was all simultaneous. Joannie was killed instantaneously. I was knocked out and knew no more, but Irwin, poor little man, was crushed with tons of metal and had a terrible time.

X.Look here, Scottie. I sounded N you know (yes, I knew) and I asked him in the train last night if she had ever had any trouble with a girder. You know how he puts his lips tight together and said Oh, no, no, no, nothing ever, so I held my tongue and changed the conversation.

S.Don't breathe a word dear X. and don't trust him. I hate to say so but he is yellow all through and he knows what took place.

X.What, N. knew, how?

S.He and R. were on board when we had the critical talk with T. and others. They heard all, every word. Now, by God, they are quaking with fright things may come out.

X.But old man, this is awful. Surely R. must speak.

S.He can't poor chap. he would lose his position and there would be Hell to pay. N. is going to get all he can out of the swag that's left. But he won't get much believe me. But he hopes to.

X.Another thing. The chief engineer said (I will verify this) that the engines were O.K.

S.My God, what a damned lie. Both engines had been giving trouble at different times. No, all survivors have had orders to stick to one tale, all O.K, you see there are questions of pensions and compensations you will understand. (I am not sure I follow as surely only widows etc. will have pensions) (I will find out more later).

X.But I must get the truth known somehow.

S.Now X, listen to me. It will do no good. They can all deny and you would be hounded out if they knew at the A.M. you had even a suspicion. The truth will out later and all will come out. In any case it helps us so much for us to tell you all that happened and we do appreciate your thoughts

X.Well, dear old boy, so long. Tell Johnnie and Colmore I will talk to them very soon.

5.11 30

C. Control   C.C. Colmore   J. Johnnie   X. Visitor

Very soon after the sitting had begun the name of Colmore was very clearly pronounced so that I was able to make contact at once.

Colmore first of all asked me a few questions concerning his wife (but the remarks do not apply to the case under discussion).

X. Now dear Colmore, let me know your version of the conference held on board before she sailed.

C.C. But I wasn't at the meeting. Oh God, that was the most awful blow in the back that I have ever received.

X. But I was told by B. that you were.

C.C. No, I knew of the meeting but was not consulted. Irwin objected to my presence and I thought that was the limit.

X. But my dear C. do you really assert that you of all people were not consulted.

C.C. No old boy, and that's what hurts so terribly. After all it was I who had the final say.

X. Old chap, I am sorry for you, but don't you think it will help you if you realise that in whatever form the cause of their action appeared to you, their real cause was the real and genuine love for you?

C.C. I know, but its because I always felt that they did love me that it all hurts so awfully. But you comfort me in what you say and it has just struck me that I did mention to little Irwin the fact that the parting with my darling had literally torn me in two. (Here followed some private conversation.) Yes I think that since Irwin knew this and how I felt he did not want to allow me to be placed in the position of giving the decision and Scottie and Johnnie realised this and so deliberately left me out. Its true that almost immediately I went on board I was up to my eyes in work, seeing all the latest reports and we ghing up the details. You know there are "umpteen" things to consider.

When I came into the room they were all sitting round the table and there was a horrible pause and I knew they did not want me so I turned on my heel and left, wondering if this is how the journey starts, how the devil will it end—so much for cooperation.

X. Well old chap, do try and realise that love is sometimes strangely disguised—even in all good faith.

C.C. Johnnie is here and wants to know who shall start first. (Note - I had no idea J. was present or had just arrived till C.C. told me.)

X. Well, if you don't mind, I think that C.C. had better give me facts of earlier history so that I can link up the various points in the last act.

C.C. Yes, I think so too, and Johnnie wants to stay also.

X. Yes, of course. Now dear C.C. I want to fix quite clearly the position of the horizontal girder that caused the trouble at the beginning and I have brought a plan of the ship on which I have marked both the longitudinal struts and horizontal girders.

(C.C. clearly explained in detail that the danger point was at 5C.)

C.C. The first flight was more or less O.K. but, during the second, the junction of 5 C was strained.

X. How did you detect this?

C.C. When you are carrying out trials of this kind you walk about while she is in flight and you keep your eyes and ears open and we heard a creaking at this junction and when we came home we saw, after inspection, that this girder (No.5) was strained. Well, you probably remember the ship was put in again for what was called "overhaul" and a new piece was substituted.

This work must have been badly done and the metal used must have had a flaw, at any rate I now consider it was not up to specification.

Now look at your plan. You will see that the longitudinals C and D have to take a much stronger strain than A.B.E.F.G. This is quite obvious and in my opinion these, C and D must be much stronger, provided we can get the necessary lift .

X. How did you try to remedy this weakness?

C.C. Well, you will notice that each section has a V-shape (X. Yes, I see it on the outer frame drawing), well if there is a strain the V has a tendency to get wider, like this ⋎ so we put a binding round but found this did not work, so it was abandoned.

Now then old chap, remember I was not conscious of events when the crash came, but now I know that this 5 C weak spot actually fractured with the result that the V widened and caused the outer cover to split open.

X. Yes, I see, and the gusts of wind blew into this hole or rent caused uncontrollable pressure on the front part of the ship, especially as the wind was, I suppose, about S.W.

C.C. Correct, but more than that. The wind was actually S S W and therefore we caught it badly. Now look at your plan. The force of the wind and gusts blowing through the rent in the outer cover not only threw a colossal strain on No. 5 girder, but the next two, Nos. 4 and 3, and all this part gave in on impact with the ground.

X. Yes, I think that is quite clear. Now I want to tackle the gas bag trouble. One moment —isn't it possible to trace the history of this weak girder? Are there no records at Cardington?

C.C. Oh yes, quite easily. (Here he explained the system of keeping progress books lettered A to L.) Now the history of this trouble will be found in A 5 7.

X. Good, that may help. Now about the gas valve trouble.

C.C. Well, I will try and explain. You know each bag has its two valves?

X. Yes, but why two?

C.C. Because in a sense one would do, but the pressure would be too great, so we have two. Now the inner valve was not strong enough to control this huge bulk of gas and owing to gas escaping it caused an air lock. (Then followed a mass of technical detail which I have not mastered because I do not know the real system of a bag, but will find out in court on Friday.)

X. I then suggested that Johnnie should speak, so I said goodbye to Colmore.

X. Now Johnnie, you tell me your side of the conference.

J. Well, Irwin, Scottie and I knew we must put our cards on the table and realised that if we followed out our usual practice we should have to include old Colmore. If he had been consulted, then he would have insisted on really being the man to make a decision and he might have taken the plunge and said, "No flight under existing conditions." Now old man, think carefully. Supposing he had said "no flight" he would have taken full responsibility, possibly be made a scape-goat—was it fair to put all the burden of a crisis like this on him?

So, rightly or wrongly, we decided to try and force Thompson to give the word to abandon flight. But no, he was adamant and refused to even consider it and said to me, "You must think of a way out, but go we must," and argued all about the vital necessity of demonstrating to Imperial Conference and all the old arguments about public opinion. As a matter of fact when we got everybody together Colmore was not there. He was busy with some last minute details he was superintending. Well, in the middle of it all, in walked Colmore, gave us one look and said, "Blast the whole damn lot of you" and walked out of the room. He unknowingly played into our hands.

X. (Note—Apparently Colmore had come back, perhaps he had never left. At any rate he suddenly chimed in and said, "Did the French give any useful information?")

X. No, honestly I don't think the evidence mattered a row of pins.

C.C. No, exactly. It's all absolutely waste of money and merely a method of the damn government to help whitewash the enquiry. It makes me boil.

(J. then continued)

J. Naturally Colmore did not come back and we eventually started on a force-doomed gamble. The rest I will give you when you come again but do come again.

X. M. has asked me to give you a message and says he loves you just as much if not more.

J. Oh dear, oh dear (and was much distressed.) Oh, I feel so bad about that. I ought to have said goodbye and did not . Tell Val I know now and at the time thought he was influenced by the condition of a lady who had suffered a bad loss. I thought his head was full of nonsense. I did behave badly to Val and you can tell him this and add that just before the end I remembered his talk and that helped to lift me up to meet the end.

(Note—The value of this record I will make clear when I write an introduction to these talks.)

C. Control   B. Brancker   S. Scottie   C.C. Colmore   X. Visitor
Immediately after Control had taken charge we two began to have a conversation, since nobody had made his presence

known. He told me his history and reason for doing this work and how he had watched over his "instrument" (Mrs. G.) since she was a child. Suddenly C. said, "There is a great friend of yours who is dancing about with impatience and keeps on putting a piece of glass in and out of his eye and laughs saying, "For God's sake tell tha fellow to turn the tap off, I want my innings."

X. Hullo, B. old man. Sorry I kept you waiting. (He gave me a rough outline of the special work he wanted me to do for him, but not till a later stage, possibly the New Year.) We then discussed the plan of action concerning *the* question and I said, "Look here B., the more I think of it the more I am convinced I must put all the information into J.S.'s hands.

B. Well done. I could just wring your hand off with admiration and gratitude, if I could. Anyway that's how I think and I have been urging these fellows to make no more blunders but get the truth out at all costs.

X. Well, I feel I must in spite of the warning. But how will S. take it? You see he can't use it in court, even if he does believe it.

B. That's all right, don't worry about that side. As a matter of fact I believe S. and his wife know a good deal more about this sort of thing than most people realise and my opinion is that you will find your talk much easier than you think and he is white all through and out for the truth. No, of course he can't question you but all this will enable him to ask questions with a definite point of view in mind and when he tumbles to the truth there will be some shifting of high and mighty ones from their seats. Now, old chap, I mustn't keep you any longer because Johnnie is impatient to come.

X. All right, but wait a moment old man. Tell me this, who is going to be your successor?

B. We do not know, but you know.

X. Bill Samson.

B. Yes he is in the running, but God help us if he gets it. Between you and me he won't do, he is "outside the pale" you know that.

X. Well, I have always had my views on that gentleman and I absolutely agree. Well who else?

B. I personally and others here interested are backing Sempill.

X. Yes, of course, I know he must be in the running, but the only thing is that he is not altogether persona grata with the Service and has so many irons in the fire, including financial.

B. True my dear boy, but practically all possible candidates are in this position. No, Sempill is the best, he is a gentleman, and I am convinced he is straight and whereas others might want to cling to their connections he will if given the choice be big minded and be generous in the way of cutting his losses. I back him.

(Note) B and I were discussing something else which touched on politics and he laughed and said, "Ho, ho, there will be a good old dust up before that and all politicians will be swimming around, the same old merry game of general election."

X. Now B. do stop laughing, when will the election be?

B. In February. Now I am off. Scottie has come and says he must talk.

X. Good, but Branks I did promise Johnnie.

B. Yes, I know my dear chap, but we have had a conference and Scottie is right as there are certain technical details you must grasp now, to complete the story. Johnnie shall have his turn—one word of advice—You know on general matters we all work with H (Hinchcliffe) but in this case we five have appointed you Captain and are trusting you to see this matter through. Its no good H butting in here, too many cooks—you understand.

X. Yes, "I get you Steve?"

B. Now Scottie is getting ratty but I am staying here as I am learning a lot, my boy.

S. Well, old boy, Johnnie doesn't mind as he is as anxious as we are for you to master these technical details.

X. All right old man, then we will get down to brass tacks. Now I want to check absolutely beyond a doubt the exact place that the girder broke.

S. By the bye, has Burney been in court?

X. Yes, I saw him one day and said "I'm glad you are not in this" and he said "Yes, thank God they are not asking for our files".

S. Ah, I thought so, Johnnie was right. (I did not ask what they meant as I had so much of importance to discuss.) Sorry old chap to interrupt. Johnnie is grinning all over his face. Now let me see it was—

X. Can you *see* my plan?

S. No, I can't yet. Johnnie is getting better at that, but I can see the old ship. Now it is A B C. Yes at C and the girder is 5 and where they intersect 5 C.

X. Good. Now to be sure, lets see if my terms are right. The longitudinals are called struts, the vertical hoops are called girders and the spaces between the girders are called bays.

S. Yes, quite right.

X. Now what are called reefer girders?

S. These are the intermediary ones but there are more of these at the tail and nose.

X Can you indicate their position? Where do they begin to appear, from No. 6 to 2 girder and 10 to 16, or where?

S. Not quite. Take the nose first. Between C and 4.

X Does the 1st girder count at the nose?

S. Yes, but we count 0—16. Now 0—4.

X Very well, 0—4.

S And 12—16. As a matter of fact, the reinforcement of these girders is more important at the nose because of the great pressure that comes when at the mooring mast, especially if there is a pull or strain when the wind force is strong.

S You know how the struts all convene to a point at each end. Well, these reefer girders help blind these converging struts together.

X. Now Scottie, I want to get back to past history. You told me this No. 5 girder had given trouble before. Was it at the identical place?

S. Let me think. No the same girder, but lower down.

X. Well, where exactly did it show symptoms of straining?

S. A B C D E got it? At the intersection of strut E, so you have 5 E.

X. Yes, I have marked that. Well you first tried fibre binding, but that was no good.

S. Yes, but although as you know we did use this blinding for the gas bag trouble.

X. Well, how did you remedy this?

S. We replaced a section of the girder.

X. From A to C?

S. No. Remember the girders are numbered from O–G on both sides. The trouble was on the starboard side. Now remember this. The replacement was made by replacing the section between struts B to E (A B C D E) B to E.

X. Yes, quite clear. But since the trouble was at E would it not have been wiser to have taken the refit lower down to F or possibly G?

S. Any fool would have thought so, but Richmond declared it is sufficient. After all he had his old nose in every screw!

X. All O.K. Scottie. Now when did this strain first become apparent? What date?

S. Well, its rather hard to fix dates here exactly, but it was on the second experimental flight I am sure and I think it was about June. This flight was not satisfactory and we more or less limped home. Gas trouble was also occurring.

X. I suppose the valves began to play up?

S. Yes, but more. Look old chap, its this. The gas bags were not strong enough to hold the volume of gas. In other words were over-inflated, and when the bags were charged each bag touched the other which caused a certain amount of friction and the skins became porous and so we had additional leakage, or evaporation. Remember, the gas is not stationary but keeps moving round and round when set in motion which happens in flight and every time the ship came into a bump condensation was caused (I am not sure if this is clear but it is hard to memorise all technical details when one does not know the theory). Added to this our valves were weak.

X. Now I want to link the story up with details of incidents during flight, but before we do there is one question I want clearly answered. Is there no written record where one can read of all these defects. Are there no books at Cardington?

S. Of course there are, but Colmore knows more about that side.

X. All right old boy. Is Colmore there?

S. No, but Johnnie is.

X. Well, send Johnnie to get a move on, and call Colmore. In the meantime we will discuss the journey incidents.

S. Johnnie has gone to get him and Colmore can explain.

X. Now Scottie, I thought you said that just before the end you decided to turn and make for Le Bourget, but you were North and had not reached Paris.

S. Yes, you're muddled old chap. What I said was, turning to try and land on our way to Le Bourget.

X. Ah, that's better. Well, now then, the girder had broken and the 'V' had so widened that the cover split.

S. Yes, not exactly broken but the junction of the girder and strut are coupled together and this had actually slipped. First of all this part was strained, then slipped and then perforated the cover.

X. How did you actually know? Were you told?

S. We heard the straining going on and sent the forward rigger to report and he came back and said the coupling had slipped, so we called two others and told them to try and make a new coupling by drilling new holes and bolting together, but of course there was no time. After that things happened quickly.

X. Now a thing that is puzzling the court is how did Hunt know things were desperate since he had time to say "we're down lads"? Did you tell him?

S. Well, all hands on duty in the ship knew the rent had been made and Hunt was actually off duty but since he knew an hour before things were desperate Hunt did what any other man would do and tried to give the warning to the men's quarters.

X. About what time did the rent appear?

S. I should say 10 minutes to 2 (1:50 a.m.) about 10 minutes before the end came.

X. Was the first dive steep?

S. No, it was hardly a dive. You see the rent had become bigger and the gusts of wind were hitting her hard, making her difficult to keep steady and to steer and also the 4th and 3rd girders were being badly strained. Our only chance was to try a slow turn and land down wind which would enable the damaged starboard side to get shelter from the wind and terrific gusts. We tried to correct the bump downwards but she would not respond. Then she practically went into a perpendicular nose-dive.

X. But evidence shows her nose did not strike the ground.

S. No old boy, you're wrong. An aeroplane under those conditions would continue her nose dive, but since we had just commenced to try and turn, the gusts of wind blowing through the rent on her starboard put a terrific strain on her port side and she sort of got a drag on and heeled to port; thereby she finally landed on a more or less even keel. The rest you know.

X. How high were you when the damage to the girder was discovered?

S. I don't know. None of us know.

X. But you had your instrument board?

S. Now listen carefully old boy. Over Barnet the automatic spring of the altimeter failed to function and never functioned again.

X. Well, can you give me any approximate heights at different times? Try hard old boy.

S. I feel sure we never got over 900 or 950 feet and when we got over the channel the wind and torrents of rain beat us down to possibly 250 to 300 feet. As we approached the French coast we seemed to catch a current that lifted us a bit but we never got much higher than 900, possibly not that.

X. During that last 30 minutes what height did you estimate?

S. Certainly not more than 900 feet. We never got to a properly satisfactory height.

X. I believe evidence was given that the order was given to shut off all engines. Why did you do this?

S. I will make this clear. We never did shut off all engines. Just as we contemplated turning the order was given to slow down the forward port and starboard rear engines. This left us with the forward starboard and rear port and rear after engines running, which order was required to carry out the turn. But the turn was really hardly started when the final crash came. Remember it was the heel to port and the natural drag that put the ship in her final landing angle when she touched the ground, in fact this practically operated like a brake. Now Colmore has come to help about these damned books you are worrying about.

C. Colmore is here and asks you to start.

X. Hullo old man. So glad you have come as I must try and definitely establish where certain documents are, as I want S. to see them himself. Now you told me that I should find the notes on the straining, and work on the No. 5 girder, under A 5 7?

C.C Yes, that's right.

X. Well, try and explain how the various books were kept.

C.C. Everything was divided up to departmental or sections design. Architectural—

X. For heaven's sake don't go so quick old chap. Remember I have to use a pencil and my hand—I can't go your rate. Now then, Design—architectural—

C.C. Yes, this section (architectural) is divided up into subsections—steel-boltings, soldering. Then continue No. 3 geometrical, 4 fabric, 5 girder, 6 rigger, 7 mechanical, and this last is divided into main construction and engines. All these sections have their own record books.

X. Exactly, and I want to try and see that all these books are in court.

C.C Good God man, aren't they there? Its absolutely necessary for them to be.

X. I don't know old man, they may be, but now I know I can find out. Did any of the executive staff have their books?

C.C. Yes, Richmond kept a diary and I had my books. I have told you about book A.

X. No old man, you said A 5 7 was a department book.

C.C. No, no, it's mine.

X. Oh thanks, I see. Now go on very slowly. Where were your books?

C.C. In my room. You know quite well.

X. Yes, but I have forgotten exact details. I know where your room was.

C.C. Well, you know the safe?

X. Wait a moment. Now let me draw a plan. How here is the door, fireplace on opposite wall.

C.C. The safe was between the right side of the fireplace and the right corner.

X. Yes, I have put that in. The window was on wall left as you go in.

C.C. Yes, and also my writing table and books.

X. Wait old boy. I have marked window. Was writing table facing window?

C.C. No, at right angles and chair facing back wall—yes fireplace wall.

X. Right. Was the book-case mobile?

C.C. Yes, quite close to chair, so that I could lay my hand on a book.

X. Right, here is a picture.

C.C. I had two sets of books, A to L and H. book A which was divided up into section A to F.

X. I don't quite understand. Why two books marked A? So confusing.

C.C. A to L are small individual books of records of work in shed before flight, or rather work done when not in flight. A. B. C. D etc, each book dealing with sections. Now book A contained all my records of flights.

X. Well, how shall I know what this book looks like?

C.C. It has a brown-backed cover like a ledger, and on the back is marked A R-101.

24.11.30

C. C.   Colmore   S. Scottie   X. Visitor

Colmore made his presence known at once and told the Control that he was very worried all the week-end and had been near me Saturday and Sunday.

X. What has been troubling you old man?

C. C. I have been literally flying about the week-end trying to lay my hand on the books you are worrying about.

X. Well, wait a minute. I have come specially to deal with your private books that were kept by you in your office at Cardington. Now let me go over it again. You had small bookshelf by your writing table within arms reach of your chair where you kept your private records.

C. C. Yes old chap, correct. Now these books—

X. Wait a moment old boy. I must follow this through in my own way. There were two sorts of books. The small books were a series of ones marked alphabetically from A to L which dealt with work done on the airship in the shed.

C. C. Yes.

X. Then there was a single bigger book, divided up into sections marked A to F and these were your records of events in flight.

C. C. Yes. In this book were my reocrds of events connected with her flights and divided as follows:

> A. Construction
> C. Gas Bags
> E. Starboard engines
> F. Port engines

and so on.

X. Yes, that's quite clear and easy to follow. Now if I open this book under section A and turn page 57 what shall I see?

C. C. You would find my notes of the 2nd experimental flight in which girder 5 was strained. That's why it is recorded under construction.

X. Can you give me clearer markings of this book?

C. C. It was an ordinary brown Government ledger, like the ones you have in your office, light brown with dark back on which is written XVT R-101. The small books have A. R-101, B. R-101, C. R-101, up to L. I have been to my room at Cardington and everything has been cleared up. Where have all my books gone to?

X. I can only hope that they are in court. If not, they have been hidden away by "Kingsway," but I am taking steps to have the "sleuth hound" put on the track.

C. C. Now, just behind my writing table chair over my left shoulder against back wall was a sort of book case with pigeon hole divisions in which I kept copies and answers to all my correspondence and minutes.

X. How were they marked?

C. C. Each one had D A D stencilled with an office code number. I was very methodical. Now aren't all these papers in court?

X. They may be old boy, I don't think they have ever been used or asked for.

C. C. Good God, but these papers bear out all this story of protest and pressure.

X. Ah, now go slow, you are touching on a vital point. Did you and others at Cardington ever protest in writing that things were all wrong?

C. C. Yes, of course. In May of this year and onwards we wrote minutes to A M S R protesting about the bad condition of the ship.

X. You don't tell me that A M S R turned a deaf ear to your complaints?

C. C. We were overruled by Richmond who repeatedly stated that the ship was absolutely all right technically in construction air resistance, and that our fears were groundless.

X. Now on which file do minutes recording all this belong? Or was it done by private letters?

C. C. It's all on the main policy file, all quite clear. But where is the correspondence of minutes, Scottie and myself, Richmond and ourselves, and the technical staff and "Kingsway"?

X. My dear boy, don't ask me.

C. C. Copies of all these were in the office files in the pigeon holes in my room.

X. Before I forget Reggie (Colmore) was the 2nd experimental flight in June 1929 not this year?

C. C. No, in 1929, I think about June.

X. Thanks old boy. Now one more matter. As far as I know, no mention has been made of Treasury correspondence and surely they came in.

C. C. Of course, they are co-culprits. We always jokingly alluded to the "economist Gov."

X. But surely this damn Government can hardly be called "Economist." What do you mean?

C. C. We had advocated that we should carry out more experimental work before this flight to India, but the Treasury said we couldn't go on spending money like this, unless we did something to justify ourselves. So they and others insisted on this mad flight. We ought to have spent more money before the flight took place. I suppose you know that if this flight had been successful Richmond would have got the KCB?

X. No, I certainly did not know this.

C. C. Well, it was absolutely common knowledge and talk with us. Now don't you see, old Richmond was not going to queer his pitch by going against the Treasury which to all intents and purposes was the government and remember Richmond carried a lot of weight with the Economical Gov.

X. Well old boy, I am doing my best to have all this rotten game exposed.

C. C. Look here V. Scottie is here and is damned nervous about you. We all feel you are taking a rotten risk as if by any chance the Air Ministry have half an inkling of what you are doing you will be turfed out neck and crop.

X. Thanks old chap, I quite realise how you feel, but believe me. I am taking all possible precautions and that is why I see Sir John alone and the Air Ministry will have *no* inkling.

C. C. All right old X. but take every precaution and explain our fears to Sir John.

X. B. told me I could trust him and he is white and besides Sir J. has met me before. I am not strange to him.

C. C. Look here, I am horrified about all these papers not being produced. What is Nex coing?

X. Well, as far as I can see, damn all, except give such evidence as will enable the court to say, "What a good boy you are"—that's my impression.

Now Colmore, did Richmond realise you and the others did not see eye to eye with him, you, Scottie, little Irving, mistrusted the old ship?

C. C. By Jove yes. Do you realise we only just scraped back from Hendon and the next day we let Richmond have the truth fair and square, and there was a real bust up which we called the "H.Q. Mutiny." Things were so strained that poor old Johnnie was made a go-between, as Scottie, Irwin and myself were hardly on speaking terms with old Richmond.

C. By the bye, you remember when you and I lunched with Branks we taxied back to the A.M. Did you go into his office?

C. C. Yes I did and we had a pow-wow.

X. Did Branks then say he funked the flight? Please tell this old boy.

C. C. Yes, I told him in confidence that we were not happy and he told me he had the wind up, but he realised we had to go and he wasn't going to turn back. That's why he sounded the S.O.S. to try and shake I. off.

X. Yes, of course, I now realise why he sa. the S. of S. a second time although I had my suspicions. Now I want Scottie. I have only a short time more today.

C. C. All right. I am staying on and Scottie is ready.

X. Well Scottie old boy, I want to get clear in my mind the question of the engine orders. Now I want to repeat your engine orders. You told the engineers in the front starboard and port-rear to stop engines.

C. C. No, No, old V. to slow down engines.

X. Sorry old man, my mistake. Now this left the front port and rear starboard and after engines still running.

S Yes, that is correct.

X. And your idea was to turn to the left?

S Old boy you are hopelessly at sea. No, no, when I said turn we meditated a partial turn to get back on to our course after the repairs had been carried out, but of course we never did carry out the repairs and the end came too suddenly. What we decided to do was to slow down and tack first to one side and then to the other so as to ease the resistance at the nose. If we had tried to turn before the damage was repaired we should have put such a strain on the ship that she must have gone.

X. Can Johnnie help in the details of height? I am not sure from my notes if I have got the various heights you estimated last time put down in chronological order.

S. Yes, Johnnie will help next time.

X. Now Scottie, you said you could not estimate heights after Barnet, because the "automatic spring of the altimeter was not working."

S. Yes, the spring kept slipping and making the needle drop just like a loose hand of a watch will do and so we could not keep track of the amount of gas we had.

X. Steady old boy, this is absolute "Greek" to me. What is the connection between the height record and the amount of gas? The automatic spring is not in the damned gas bag.

(S. apparently reared with laughter and said)

S. Oh lor, I might as well try to explain to this old man the difference between a broomstick and a cow and you are nearly as bad, Old V.

X. Well, don't worry now, I don't understand. Now my last question is this. Who was the front rigger who reported that the girder No. 5 was straining? I have brought a paper giving the list of those killed and will read out the names and you say stop.

X. Church.

S. Stop

X. And who were the other two you told off to help Church? I will call down the list. Hastings.

S. Stop. (I then went on.)

X. Houghton.

S. Stop

X. When were Hastings and Oughton on duty?

S. Hastings was on duty but Oughton was not, but we sent for him as he was the best man, and if he superintended the work we should have known it was O.K.

X. Now I must go, but tomorrow I want you and Johnnie and on Thursday and Friday all of you to hear a resume of the story.

S. Don't forget Colmore says that McWade can produce chits of the girder repair work in June 1929.

X. One more question. Why did you take in ballast?

S. What old boy? Take in ballast?

X. Yes, you sent a message, "Making up ballast."

S. Ah, that's quite different. Johnnie will tell you next time about the banks of fog we met off the French coast near Beauvais.

25.11.30

J. Johnnie   B. Brancker   CC. Colmore

Brancker came through first and we again discussed the policy of my meeting S and telling him the truth. He agreed to my plan of procedure, provided I took all pains to safeguard myself. He realised I was out for the truth.

B. Well old boy, very best of luck and our thanks to you. Thank God it's you and not us. If you can convince S. and help him to put a stop to all the political pressure and from H.Q. and can enable him to lay down such regulations as will in future safeguard future lives from being sacrificed you will indeed have done a big job. What must be prevented is that the technical staff shall have a fair hearing and not be overridden by the "economy government" supported by the mighty ones at H.Q.

X. Right Branks. I know, and now trust me and give me all the support you can, and others on the day. Now, where is Johnnie? (B. He is here)

Well Johnnie old boy, we meet at last to talk. (J. then told me of the separation he felt so acutely etc. and how the responsibility of them all for causing this was awful, "but we aren't here tonight to sentimentalise.")

X. Quite right old boy, we must get down to work. Now what happened at *the* conference, who was present? I have been told but just check me.

J. Thompson, Branks, Scottie, Richmond, Irving, Nickie, Reynolds and self. Colmore not, as you know.

X. I did not know that Richmond was there.

J. Of course.

X. What did they all say, in a few words.

J. Well, Scottie, Irving and I told T that engine report was bad, gas bad, weather bad, also slight trouble at head of mooring mast that was incidental. We said it was too risky and T said go we must—dare not face Conference without this being accomplished. Branks said it was risky and did not like it.

X. What did Richmond say?

J. He was furious and said the ship was A I and weather need not count, all bunkum.

X. And Reynolds and Nick?

J. Reynolds said he certainly did think under present circumstances it was a risk. Nick said "he wouldn't mind taking the ship himself" and talked a bit about the honour and glory, so easy to talk when you are not going yourself.

X. Did Colmore say his views or did he never join in?

J. Yes, towards the end after we had talked and talked he said she ought no to go, backed up by us three, but I said go we must. Somebody had a brain wave and suggested leaving, but landing at Le Bourget—the rest you know.

X. All right. That tallies with the others and you still say R and N. heard every word of this?

J. Of course they did, they were on board and took part.

X. Very good. Now to details of the flight. What heights can you record?

J. Only approximate as altimeter was working unsatisfactorily.

X. Yes, Scottie told me that. But give me some idea.

J. Well, over Potters Bar, not more than 700 ft. We managed to go to somewhere about 800 ft. over London and then towards the coast we were back to 700 ft.

X. What route were you taking?

J. Having decided on a possible landing at Le Bourget we steered towards the estuary, in order to hug the coast, for two reasons. First, we thought we had better have more time before crossing the Channel to get more control of the ship and second, unless things were to improve I preferred a possible false landing on shore than in the sea. The ship was behaving, and did all through, like a perfect little "B."

X. Now what height were you over the ship when did you leave the coast?

J. Near Deal and we touched French coast between Dunkirk and Calais but nearer Dunkirk. Over the Channel we came down to about 550 feet, the clouds were very low and driving rain. We did no dare go up through the clouds as we had to conserve our gas. We then got a natural lift over the French coast was just before we got to Amiens or in that vicinity. By that time the gas was revolving round at a terrific rate, really alarming, and the noise was awful. It was pretty bad on the English coast.

X. Now, you explain to me what you expected to do after girder trouble was reported.

J. Well, our idea was to mend the coupling and then since the girder was weakened we knew we could not drive her with her nose to the wind so we hoped that by herring-boning or tacking we should be able to coax her on to Le Bourget.

X. Did you send out a message to Le Bourget?

J. No, we should have done, but of course the end came all to soon. We intended asking for a landing party of from three to four hundred men.

X. You admit then that from the moment she left the mooring mast the behaviour of the ship was d—bad?

J. Yes, we all knew it and having to fly at those various heights was no child's play, believe me. But we had no choice.

X. Then you admit Johnnie old boy, all the W/T messages were more or less bunkum, to put it mildly?

J. Of course X, they were, nearly all.

X. Now, what did you mean by "Making up ballast"?

J. That meant we were changing over ballast.

X. That meant dropping some.

J. Lor no, we didn't drop any because we did not want to go up quickly or to any height because as I pointed out the gas was churning round at a terrific rate. No, we simply changed her ballast from one tank to another to try and trim her to a better line.

X. Now, how were the weather reports before starting and how did they arrive?

J. I received charts at 2 P.M. and 4 P.M. and a 5-30 by W/T and again at about 6 by W/T. The 4 P.M. and 5-30 were not nice. Depression N N E, wind S S W. and I knew when these met we should encounter dirty weather, and so we did. At 5-45 I called, or rather Irving called, for ship's reports. Riggers and out-riggers O.K. Engine was not behaving. We had experienced trouble before. So even at this stage things were not pleasant. Then we started late. If we had started by 7 P.M. I had them meant to hug the coast line, so as to try and get on the outer edge of the depression.

x. Now Scottie, are you still there?

S. Yes old boy, what's troubling you?

X. Just this. Branks mentioned about the 16 hour flight being a farce.

S. Yes, he is right. We had insisted on *at least* a 48 hour flight and even that was short.

X. Did Colmore, backed up by you others, protest in writing?

S. By Jove, yes. A M S R seemed surprised that any trial flight was necessary and suggested two short flights which we pointed out were useless. If only time for a short flight one was sufficient since beyond learning that she could stay the air nothing short of 48 hours would give us the truth we wanted.

X. Was this in writing?

S. Yes.

X. Where?

S. On the main file.

X. Then all Colmore's minutes will be found in his office files?

B. I am a little uneasy about those official files and Treasury ones. I have a feeling they have been "doctored" and certain damning evidence has been taken out. I hope my fears are not true.

X. But B, since all minutes are numbered this would cause a break.

B. True, but I feel correspondence has been tampered with, books kept.

X. Well Scottie, I suppose H.Q. would not agree to a long flight?

S. No, because this would have meant further delay and T. could not have gone and more money would have been spent before the spectacular flight had been done, and remember T wanted to let Dominion Premiers have a short flight, or at any rate visit the ship on her return before the Conference finished and this would have been impossible if we had delayed. The whole thing was rotten.

X. Is Colmore there?

Well Colmore, was the Treasury file of correspondence separate to the main A.M. Policy file?

CC. Yes, quite separate.

X. Can you get hold of Atherstone?

CC. I will try, but it may be a bit difficult. Why?

X I heard that Atherston's last entry in his diary was to the effect that "Well, we have got to go and be sacrificed to appease the d— Air Council." Well, I hear the court have seen this diary, but the last entry is simply that trial flight is O.K. Now how has this story got about? I heard it from a very reliable source and I can't help feeling the last entry was made, but if so, expunged.

CC. I have sent little Irving to try and find him to tell you. Irving says Atherstone won't join our party here, is scared stiff but says he had two diaries. One all nice and official and the other private, which records his true thoughts.

(Note—— believe he agreed that this diary was with his wife.)

X. Thanks old boy, that may help. Now Colmore, here is the list of survivors who ought to know the truth.

CC. Cook, Savoury, Bell and Binks won't know very much, besides being on duty they take most things for granted, but Disley, the W/T operator, he certainly can talk. He knows how the ship behaved and certainly Leech, of course, he knows. Well old boy, we shall keep in touch with you and if you do see S. we shall all be there to help. All best luck dear chap.

X. Oh Johnnie, one thing more. Explain why you hugged the English coast as long as you did.

J. Because old chap, the old ship was going so badly and we wanted to avoid crossing the Channel till things were better. If we had to come down I preferred the land to the sea.

X. Personally I don't see it matters a damn if you crash on land or sea—in any case its all up.

J. Oh no, old boy. I thought it better to navigate them to Heaven dry. They were all quite wet enough with fright!!!

28.11.30
10 a.m.

B. Brancker   CC. Colmore   J. Johnston   A. Atherstone

B. The whole gang are here at your command and Atherstone has been chased around and here *he* is.

CC. B. has told me all the news of your S. O. S.

X. Branks were you in my office when I called for your help?

B. Yes, of course. Your description of Colmore's room was good. You certainly "used your intelligence" in sending out that S.O.S. (Note—He then repeated my description accurately.)

X. Good old man. Now I know I can get you quickly which is very useful.
Now Colmore old chap. Darby says the safe is not there. Can you describe the safe accurately?

CC. Yes, of course. Don't I know my own room?

X. I know of course you do, but I want to have my evidence for S. absolutely pat.

CC. Yes of course, you are right. I see your point. The safe is not the ordinary small safe but a lock-up filing cabinet. You have one, we all do, you know we must keep all secret files and papers locked up.

X. Yes naturally, and in that filing cabinet you kept all your copies of minutes and correspondence?

CC. Exactly and how could Nick lie and say I never had those books or kept copies of minutes—he's mad.

X. What about the old char?

CC. What the devil does she know? Would your old char describe details of your room? We never did trust that fellow—I told you before, but I never thought he would blacken our characters like that. I suppose he thinks "dead men tell no tales." Well that's where he is mistaken and he'll damn well know it one day.

B. I never heard such absolute nonsense. Why Johnnie is saying Colmore was so methodical he probably had the time of his bath painted on the bottom of his bath so as to be on time!!

CC. When that yellow devil left the ship I felt he would tear us to pieces if he could shield himself, provided we didn't come back. Now I know.

X. Well old boy, we must find these books.

CC. But are you sre they aren't in court?

X. That I don't know, but will discuss with S. Now Colmore, Brancks mentioned your last fight to stop date of sailing, was this verbal or in writing and when?

CC. About 10 days before I recorded my views and correspondence is or was, in my filing cabinet between myself and A.M.S.R. and Richmond. Good God, it's awful, if these books and papers have been tampered with.

B. I warned you X. old boy. I had my strong suspicions.

X. Yes I know, but how am I to trace these documents?

B. Well dear boy, don't worry. We are all working hard and will let you know if we get a clue.

X. Before I forget I want Colmore.

CC. Yes, what is it?

X. Darby said the pigeon holes behind your writing table were also removed. I described them to him.

CC. Oh dear, you have put him on a wrong scent. Look here, it's a long board divided up into sections—one on top of the other.

X. Oh lor, I see—of course now I know—what we have on the edge of our writing tables to place daily files on.

CC. Yes exactly, that's what I meant.

X. Then only non-secret papers were there.

CC. Yes naturally, all secret papers were kept under lock and key.

X. Johnnie old boy, are you still there as I want to ask one or two points about the journey.

J. Fire away, and Scottie and Irving are also here.

X. Well, where about did you "make up ballast"?

J. Just after Dunkirk, just after we crossed the French coast we shifted ballast because owing to the gas bumping against the sides of the bags, and some worse than others, it made steering difficult, but we could help to a certain extent by retrimming her ballast.

X. You are certain you didn't throw out ballast?

J. No, no of course not. We had to keep low to keep lift, and that was difficult enough.

X. Could you have crossed the Channel higher?

J. Well we might, but she was fairly steady at that height, so we just allowed her to trundle herself across and concentrated on plans when reaching France. We knew over the sea we should hit notaing, but over land we had to get up somehow and thank God we got that lift when we did. You know we got into fog off the French coast that didn't help matters.

X. O.K. Johnnie, that's clear. Now Branks, I think I had better read out my draft that S's private secretary had done, so listen very carefully and pull me up if it's not right or clear. (Note—I read it out and Johnnie stopped me because I had not brought out clearly the effect of the movement of gas on the handling of the ship. I pointed out I had when describing over France. All was O.K. except the last sentence about her lying on an even keel. I dictated the actual words which can be seen on my draft when handed back to S's secreatary.)

X. Now Atherstone, we have never spoken before, but somehow it makes no difference. You know I told Scottie that I had heard on best authority that you had made an entry in a diary voicing your feelings very clearly. In which diary was it? Had you two, because the court has seen one which is "beautiful?"

A. I did not have two, only one.

X. You admit you did write some such words, well where did you? Don't you see I must know the truth as it will be invaluable for S. to see for himself.

A. But I didn't count or cut much ice.

X. That's not the point Atherstone. Colmore do try and explain why I must know.

A (After a pause.) Well I kept a pocket diary which I gave to my wife before going on board with letters inside, as I somehow knew I might not come back.

X. Thanks very much. Now I don't know your wife, has she a telephone?

A. No.

X. Well Johnnie, has your wife one and does she know Mrs. Atherstone?

J. Yes certainly, they are friends.

X. Then Johnnie, shall I telephone to your wife and go over and tell her how I must have the book and ask her to take me across to Mrs. Atherstone.

J. Yes, by all means, as Mrs. Atherstone is very shy and may have been warned. So you will have to go very slow and watch your step old boy.

X. Well I will discuss this with S.

B. Yes I think I should.

X. Now Brancks, things are going very well and Darby is out to help I am sure. At first I think he was a little uneasy at my demands, but now I am sure he trusts me.

B. Yes things are working well. Who would have believed they would have discussed that Bill. Funny wasn't it?

X. You mean the Medium?

B. Yes, things are working better than we expected.

X. Now, suppose I get S. to agree to my plans.

B. By Jove, that would be splendid and "the Boys" are mad keen for you to try. They won't mince matters.

X. Well Brancks, I must get back to work, and keep in touch with me and I will tell you the time and place of meeting with S.

B. Yes, you bet we'll be there and listen with all ears and help you all we can. The "boys" send their love and will back you to the hilt.

Index